What others are saying abou

"It's one of the very few I looked forward to getting back to when I had to put it down. Nappa offers such a wonderful sense of scene—the death when Clara comes in, the first meeting with Fanny, that fantastic scene with the landlady and canker worms. The author shows a great eye for the particularizing detail."

—**NAEEM MURR**, author of *The Boy, The Genius of the Sea,* and *The Perfect Man.*

"One of the main pleasures I have in these pages is the way Nappa brings the flavor of Longfellow's language into his own prose. The period feels vividly imagined, from the clothes and the furnishings to the way people speak and write to each other in letters… The world of this novel is very compelling and made me care about Longfellow in a way I would not have expected."

—**ZACHARY LAZAR**, author of *Sway* and *I Pity the Poor Immigrant.*

"I really liked it. Henry comes vibrantly to life in these pages, and the way Nappa massages in Longfellow's poetry and writing process is very deft."

—**RICHARD RUSSO**, Pulitzer Prize-winning, best-selling author of *Empire Falls, Nobody's Fool, Bridge of Sighs,* and many others.

"Jon Nappa's *Longfellow* is remarkable. The book does an amazing job of humanizing Henry. It works brilliantly."

—**SHAYE AREHEART**, founder/editor of the Shaye Areheart imprint of Crown Books

Writing with passion, compassion, wit, and erudition, Nappa delivers a compelling story laced with poetry and real insight into Longfellow's life and his art. Best of all, it inspired me to reexamine the poet's work, and with far greater depth and appreciation than before.

—**ROY SEKOFF**, founding editor of The Huffington Post, and creator of HuffPost Live, its award-winning live streaming video network.

What Longfellow Heard

A NOVEL

JON NAPPA

N·I·P·I™

NIPI BOOKS
jonnappaprojects.com

ISBN 978-0-9985450-2-8

Cover design by Arvid Wallen, RAWcreativity

Library of Congress Publisher's Cataloging-in-Publication Data

    Nappa, Jon, 1958- author.
        What Longfellow heard: a novel / Jon Nappa. –First edition.
        pages cm
        Includes bibliographical references.
        ISBN 978-0-9985450-2-8

        1. Longfellow, Henry Wadsworth, 1807-1882–Fiction.
        2. Poets, American–19th century–Biography–Fiction.
        3. Creation (Literary, artistic, etc.)–Fiction.
        4. Biographical fiction.
        5. Historical fiction.
        6. Novels.   I. Title.

    PS3614.A663W43 2017   813'.6
                        QBI17-900031

Printed in Canada.

To my Beatrice—

JULIANNE

My best friend, only lover, constant inspiration, and cherished wife.

ACKNOWLEDGMENTS

Thank you, Jamie Perlman Goetz Schamp, for being my all-time favorite English teacher, and for being the first to encourage me to write.

Thank you to my creative team of Kris Wallen, Arvid Wallen, and Diane Gardner.

Thank you to Rebekah and Luke for investing especially large amounts of time listening to and discussing Longfellow with me. Thank you Jacob and John for your kind support.

Thank you, Shaye Areheart, for your editorial excellence, genuine friendship, and immense contributions to this work.

Thank you to the founder and chair, Fred Lebron, and his entire faculty at the MFA Creative Writing Program at Queens University in Charlotte, N.C.

Thank you, Richard Russo, for your example and our many funny and inspiring conversations during the final months of completing this novel.

Thank you, Chris Finn, for positively affirming that Longfellow indeed became my magnificent obsession.

Thank you, Roy Sekoff, Naeem Murr, and Zachary Lazaar for your belief in the manuscript.

Thank you to Kate Hanson Plass, Museum Technician at the Longfellow House–Washington's Headquarters in Cambridge, Massachusetts, for your helpful assistance with historical accuracy, and to John Babin, Visitor Services Manager at the Wadsworth/Longfellow House in Portland, Maine, for your kind praises and encouraging support.

Thank you, Henry Wadsworth Longfellow, for a life well lived.

Look then into thine heart, and write!
  Yes, into Life's deep stream!
  All forms of sorrow and delight,
  All solemn Voices of the Night,
  That can soothe thee, or affright,—
  Be these henceforth thy theme.

—HENRY WADSWORTH LONGFELLOW

Chapter 1

A POET SEES. HE FEELS something about what he sees and writes it down, a task that grows heavy with time. That's how some describe the muse, but I don't.

Before ever writing a word, while mostly blind, a genuine poet feels. It is his nature to do so. He is stirred, agitated, or amused until at last awakened by what he feels, and only then, if he also listens well, does he see. And what he sees he begins to see everywhere. He sees it in the stars and the flowers, in the seas and the trees and the breeze, in beaming faces and trembling hands, and suddenly, he must behold it as intimately as possible. He craves it, pursues it, endeavors to capture it, and when his pen at last exhausts every single note of it, he feels it no more. He and his inspiration have gone the way of the wind.

They are not vanquished, only changed.

I wish you to no longer esteem me as an eminent man of letters. I am nearly finished in this life and almost done with being a poet. My sheets are full, my pens worn to stumps, and my lamp expiring. I've penned my last lines. Well, most of them.

It is as if I stand beneath an aged oak with trembling leaves feeling like one myself, straining to lift my head high enough to not see but hear. Crisp leaves speak if you listen. Their utterances are equal in strength to bring pleasure and pain, and they do both well.

Their slumbering sounds are like the sounds of a bell after it ceases moving and the clapper is still. A hollow murmur lingers for some moments, but only moments. Sounds of invitation follow, as formal as any written one. They are momentary, fading while in pursuit of your cognitive attendance. But if you contemplate them you may understand that the events they invite you to will not be the same themed galas you've previously attended, though many mistake them to be. No, if you are to make the most of the invitation you must understand there are no birds in last year's nests. You must cease looking for them there, for they will never return. Epiphanies are elsewhere.

If you think this invitation to be for a stroll into the forest primeval you are only half right. I would not call it a stroll, nor is it an invitation to the murmuring pines and hemlocks despite such timbers populating many places. On the contrary, it is into the murmurings themselves that we go, unless you turn away. I ask you to not be afraid, or if necessary, bring your fears with you, but do not turn back. There is something I'm feeling I want you to see. But you will never see it without listening first.

When you were younger such an invitation might have filled your imagination with images akin to fairies or heroes or mountains capped with snow. There are shadows and types of those things along the way, but there are other places within the murmurings where iron pounds the anvil and the heavens are black with sin, where men are shackled and called niggers and learned men craft false charges and women with anguished faces in pretty dresses melt in grisly fires and children ignore your voice and depart from the safety of your shade.

There are times when soft rays of sunshine may warm your face as slender fingers caressing your cheek. Passing rivers may flow with peaceful ease, but remember that no matter how mild the currents appear, they will in due time lead to a crashing place that falls into roar and spray—they always do—as do each of the inviting footpaths spreading in myriad directions eventually lead to vulnerable places of wintry blasts where the rustling leaves fall earthward and decay until only naked branches remain and another language articulates. It is the silent language. In that quiet place, deep feelings become undeniably yours. There you will feel yourself straining to lift your wizened head to where the rustling leaves are no more, to where childish things have at last been put away, and to where you finally feel and hear something you've never felt nor heard before, except in distant ways resembling a musty dream, and then for the first time, not only see it clear, but see it everywhere. And you will keep seeing it, until you and it are exhausted and wearied and changed.

Chapter 2

I WAS SIX YEARS OLD and standing in the shadow of my mother's father, General Peleg Wadsworth. He was a Revolutionary War hero who had led the American forces in Maine before being captured by the British. He escaped through the rafters of his cell, and since then many times recounted his adventures to my siblings and I. He owned at least three houses including Wadsworth Hall in Hiram, but it was the brick house on Congress Street in Portland, the first brick house in the city, where I lived.

The two of us walked toward Munjoy's Hill. It was late afternoon in early September, and the seven-story signal tower and telescope lookout to which we were headed, although straight down the same street, seemed a great distance to my six-year-old strides. We descended one slope and ascended another.

Boom! The topmost branches of coastal pines jettisoned birds. *Boom! Boom!* The ship cannons were distant, beyond the range of the fortified places of Casco Bay. I heard them. Roars of exploding gunpowder continued in waves across the waves, making waves in me. Telltale smoke swirled in far-off ocean breeze though the battling ships remained unseen to unaided eyes.

My grandfather and I approached the tower resembling a lighthouse. In the wide open space sloping down to the sea, were town elders and their offspring peering back and forth between the distant naval action they could not see and Captain Moody, whose reports were relayed by unseen men mounted on each stairway landing and the one man we could see standing outside the entrance to the red brick tower. Moody was on the observation deck at the top with his famed spyglass. My grandfather clutched my hand as we neared the thickest part of the crowd. Familiar faces nodded, even bowed while making way like a splitting sail.

Grandpa wore a tight-fitting Revolutionary War uniform with a puff and ruffle chest. His gnarly walking stick stabbed the grassy hill. His silver shoe buckles glistened, and his powdered club of hair flopped from under his cocked hat. A friend of his snorted a prideful cheer, his own hawking eye searching the distant parts of the sea. "The British dogs are being driven back to sea!"

A wave of jubilation washed over the crowd. Men slapped men on the back, women dabbed tears with hankies, and children wove in and out of the multitude with as much dexterity as the fleeing fish hawks. One man blurted, "Murder the bastards!"

I saw a man swipe his tongue along the wet corner of his mouth. "Back to old mother England where they belong." He pressed his yellow teeth hard along the length of his lip, and cheers erupted from those huddled near.

During my growing-up years this place was mostly filled with different sounds. Sailors and stevedores of every shade of white and brown moved betwixt rushing wagons and swinging wooden cranes with flying bales of freight. Cattle swallowed up great expanses of road while whips cracked the backs of men and the hides of animals. I never liked that and could not understand why my father and grandfather did not stop it although they hated it—they told me so, and often became irritable whenever they saw it. But it would pass as though it was something they were powerless to change. Burly men with rings in their ears gulped great quantities of ale and spoke loud with burps and blasts. They mocked and cursed the men with darker skin. But these were not the sounds of this day.

This day my ears rang with the distant booms of blustering

cannons and the much nearer reverberations of church bells sounding the time. My family and I later discussed this series of events at the dining table. Earlier that week, the fear of a marauding British vessel had swept every merchant ship and fishing boat of crew, and the wharves had become desolate of commerce. None of the tightly moored ships possessed defending guns or military men, except for young navy Captain Burroughs and his crew aboard the fishing boat-turned-brig-of-war, *Enterprise*, which had arrived a few days earlier from Portsmouth, New Hampshire. When Burroughs and his crew, and a local pilot named Drinkwater, rose to defend, there were none in Portland considered braver. I remember one day seeing Burroughs neatly dressed in pants and shirt and buttoned overcoat with captain's cap, but on the day of the conflict nothing but the sound effects of his actions were clear to me.

"All hail Captain Burroughs," a sailor shouted from atop Munjoy's Hill, "Defender of our shores!"

So enamored was I with the imagined theater of a faraway sea fight, that I waved my tin gun in honor of brave Captain Burroughs and sported wildly splayed powder across my chestnut hair in emulation of my grandfather-general.

"I believe Burroughs has driven them away!" my grandfather's friend shouted. He looked down grinning. "Good day, General! The coast is clear. I believe." He assisted my grandfather farther up the hill. I remained a step lower but listened.

"It didn't take much to scare them off, hey?" Grandpa asked, his voice weak and his breathing heavy.

"Burroughs is much the aggressor," his friend said.

"Ha!" Grandpa leaned on his stick. "I can remember when I was twenty, hey?" He laughed so hard his puff-and-ruffles bounced over his chin. He reached forward and tousled my powdered hair.

Captain Moody appeared from the tower, his lips flubbing like a snorting horse. "Coast is clear!"

The crowd cheered several times.

Captain Moody approached us and pointed at the signal flags he had placed atop the tower moments earlier. It was the American ensign flying above the British ensign flying above a black ball. "What say you, young man? Do you know what that means?"

I stretched out my tin gun toward the unseen action so many leagues away and squeezed the toy trigger. "Bang! Bang!" I said.

"Are you certain of the outcome?" Grandpa asked Moody.

"As certain as possible from here. I'm sure the old Brits were just harassing to see what they might find. Burroughs knows what he's doing. He's made this a fine autumn day, wouldn't you say?"

I looked up at the trees and agreed they were beautiful.

It was one or two days later that the same lofty tops of the pines had since become smeared by hovering fog, silent but for murmurs of quaking limbs and trembling needles. The *Enterprise* had returned to anchor in the gray waters of Casco Bay with the British brig, *Boxer*, in tow. They were severely damaged. The dark hulks sat atop the water like gravestones, unwilling to sink but unable to move. The cries of the fish hawks and the jubilant cheers were replaced with somber drums and soft sobs.

Burroughs's men, encompassing two caskets in the center, paddled a barge ashore, their faces like water under gray sky. The usually raucous sailors and heaving, cursing workers along the wharves were not absent from their stations as they had been the day of the apparent victory, but were as silent now as when they were gone, looming like the anchored vessels—afloat but still. Burroughs's men lifted the caskets to the flatbed and the funeral procession plodded through Portland to the cemetery near Munjoy's Hill.

The two young sea captains, Burroughs of the *Enterprise* and Blythe of the *Boxer* no longer squared off in boisterous and patriotic opposition but laid quietly side by side in respective coffins, with no breath left between them.

The community huddled. The collective sighing formed a new kind of fog. Somewhere a dog barked, an oar splashed or fish jumped, and a few people coughed while the preacher cleared his throat and thumbed his small black book, but it all puzzled me. What had been the purpose of the joyous celebrations earlier?

My family stood near me. I wore no powder in my hair despite my grandfather being as martially adorned as before. My right hand was empty of my tin gun though it was tucked into the waist of my creased black pants.

Crack! Crack! Crack!

I jerked.

Crack! Crack! Crack! The minute guns fired their salutes, and I clasped my hands over my ears. Distant cannons had sounded to me like muffled bells without the music, but the rifles pierced my head with a sound that brought pain. My face twisted and my eyes welled. *Crack! Crack! Crack!*

I felt grateful for my grandfather's hand resting on my shoulder, but I felt no comfort. The somber formality of the adults didn't fit with what I was feeling. The foreign commander whom I had previously understood to be wicked looked very much like the good commander whom I had always liked. I felt ashamed for feeling as poorly about the British captain as I did the young American, but I was also confused. The people around us had celebrated the battle as an honorable thing and had expressed hatred of the Brits to the point of calling for death. Yet now they spoke of honor and tragedy as pertaining to both young men who had died with their boots on. The sentiments moved like shifting tides.

I never imagined the captains would be so fair, so fine looking, and so fresh appearing, lying with their eyes closed and uniforms neatly tucked. It seemed a simple thing for them to open their eyes, smile, and march off in their splendid uniforms taunting and touting each other with defiant words and bold challenges, just like I had often done in Deering's Woods with my brothers and friends. After such mock battles, I always returned home, washed up, and sat at the table sharing reports of our exploits, and with both of my eyes still blinking.

Thump!

The preacher was finished before I collected myself enough to dismiss what groaned deep inside. I watched another shovelful of dirt fall atop the caskets. *Thump.*

As the crowd dispersed, my grandfather pressed my shoulder to turn me away and begin the quiet walk home. I yielded to his urging but my heart and head buzzed with a dull sound. I felt nauseous, and my pants felt tight, my stomach feeling pressed. I grabbed the tin gun tucked at my waist and hurled it.

"Henry!" My mother's tone was disapproving.

"It's okay, Zilpah," my father said. "Leave him."

"But Stephen—" my mother started.

I charged ahead. I was about to throw up and didn't want anyone to see. My thoughts became thick and hot, as if written in hot coal inside my brain. I stumbled and fell headlong. I rose to all fours and lost it. The heat burst out of my mouth like liquid fire.

> *"I remember the sea-fight far away,*
> > *How it thundered o'er the tide!*
> *And the dead captains, as they lay*
> *In their graves, o'erlooking the tranquil bay,*
> > *Where they in battle died.*
> > > *And the sound of that mournful song*
> > > *Goes through me with a thrill:*
> > *A boy's will is the wind's will,*
> *And the thoughts of youth are long, long thoughts."*

Over time, I had watched many ships come and go by night and by day. Most of them were not ships of war, and they eventually birthed in me a longing to return with one of them to the far-off places they came from, but not as a soldier on a quest for glory. I had new ideas because I had heard new things. Some of the newest soundings were from stories my mother read aloud, but there were many others I read by myself. The voices of books filled my brain. One of the voices was Washington Irving. One story of an old man who fell asleep for a very long time and another story that had a headless horseman were only parts of *The Sketchbook*, which detailed far-away travels that truly mesmerized me. I ached to travel to Europe as a reader who wanted into the page.

When I reached eighteen years of age I graduated fourth in my Bowdoin College class, fearful my father might have plans for me unbefitting my soul. I demanded he inform me of his intentions. As I feared, he hoped I would enter the legal profession alongside him and my older brother, Stephen V. I recoiled instantly and raised my voice as much as I dared. "You think more partially than justly," I said. "Such a coat does not suit me. I know myself to burn for eminence in literature and will not disguise it in the least. My entire soul burns for it, and my every earthly thought centers on it."

My father saw it differently at first, and convincingly offered no other future but the one he prescribed, so much so that the five-hour stagecoach ride across the thirty miles from Brunswick to Portland on that September day my brother and I graduated couldn't have been more endless. I knew it to be a trip to the gallows of abandoned dreams. My life would be a short, unhappy one.

It was at the family dinner table that very night, my father revealed a most extraordinary opportunity. No doubt, I realize now, he must have managed to secure it for me due to his influence as the son of one of the Bowdoin co-founders and a trustee himself, but he kept such maneuverings hidden from my sight. From that meal forward, throughout all the days of his remaining life, he never swerved from claiming the opportunity was attributable only to my academic performance, even going so far as to say that one of my teacher's, Benjamin Orr, had been supremely impressed with my translations of Horace's Odes from Latin to English, and my handling of the French language. With that as the only explanation he would offer, my father announced in the midst of the main course, for all my family to hear, that I was being offered the new chair of Modern Languages at Bowdoin at only eighteen years of age.

If ever my mouth hung open as wide as Casco Bay, it was then. I could not imagine how I might ever become more surprised than that if it were not for the moment immediately following.

"But first"—my father was barely able to repress his smile—"you must assist your brother and me at my law office until spring when you will depart for Europe. There you will spend one year perfecting your knowledge of French, Spanish, German, and Italian. That is the requirement laid down by the college." As my mother burst into tears my father continued. "It is impossible to give you all the instructions which your youth and inexperience require, but I hope to conjure you to remember the objects of your journey."

Chapter 3

I REMEMBER MEETING Professor George Ticknor, chair of Harvard's modern language department. He was thrilled with the prospect of a young man going to Europe as I was. He gave me several letters of introduction, including one to my favorite author residing in Spain, Washington Irving. He also made great emphasis upon my being certain to study the German language and literature at the University of Gottingen.

By the time I was ready to leave for Europe in May of '26, I had also crafted as much poetry as I could, believing myself to be in possession of as much innate skill and inspiration as would be expected from any bard or skald or troubadour from across the ages. I will spare you from even a single line of those trite songs that I cobbled together in those days despite more than a dozen of them being published during the year before my departure. I will not name the capacious gazette that gave them shelter other than to describe it as a foundling hospital for poor poetry. Truly I tell you, my muse in those days would have been better off in a house of corrections. Nevertheless, at nineteen, to Europe I sailed.

The trip that had been intended for one year lasted three. I traveled and studied in France, Spain, Italy, and Germany. The letters of introduction from my father and his friends permitted me exposure to successful men and women and tutors, including the great Irving. But strange adventures and stranger characters are to be expected when one journeys so far for so long. My encounters were anything but exclusively academic. I could tell you that Paris was gloomy. I might add that its chief composition of yellow stone was streaked and defaced with smoke and dust and crossed by narrow streets full of blackened mud rising up through the cracks and seams, or I might instead choose to speak of elegant Parisian gardens, magnificent boulevards, or simply express my delights with French theater. To my young mind these were the courses of a grand meal made to nourish and improve me, and there was more to come and much more I could tell. I could mention that everyone in Spain wore a cloak whether rich or poor, high or low. With the poorer it often dwindled down to something closer to a blanket, but whether silk or rag each wore his or her covering with a certain grace. Or I might tell you Bayonne is a dirty little city, or I may fondly recall for you the nut-brown Basque girls with their long, flowing braids, perfect teeth, and wide, dark eyes. There was one whose image haunted me for weeks. Of course, I could jump to Germany where I spent the last six months of my trip and boast of how focused my studies of the German tongue became at the University in Gottingen, just as Professor Ticknor had advised, and I could add to that what I learned of Goethe and his works. Then again, there are always the tales I could tell from the eleven months prior when I traveled Florence, Rome, Venice, and Genoa—and other places in Italy—the literature I discovered there, and the beneficial tutoring I received. What my young eyes saw and my journaling, letter-writing pen recorded are free for the taking, and I could recount some or all of them in the space of these pages with the thrill and exuberance I felt during most of the time I was there, but to what end? Did I not say that as heads tilt upwards they ought to strain to listen beyond the leafless limbs for another language altogether?

I shall not open any of those above-mentioned tales but for one, though I must caution you regarding it. What sparkles from afar may not be what gleams when one arrives. For now you must see what you can, but as your feelings awaken over the course of our time together you will no doubt see much more in what I am about to share than what you will likely recognize at first acquaintance.

I was upon a rooftop in Naples overlooking the bay where the broken cone of Vesuvius rose in the distance and a thin cloud of smoke wreathed itself above the summit, fading into the evening sky. Sorrento jutted into the sea not many leagues distant and, beyond that, the Isle of Capri rested quietly atop the waters.

A friend who was four years my junior, George Washington Greene, sat at my side. He was from Rhode Island, and I had recently met him in Marseilles and traveled with him and a few other Americans to Italy, but it was only he and I that April night in 1828, intoxicated with the dreamy business of young men surrounded by history and grandeur.

"As I watch that rising trail of smoke, I think of Pliny the Younger." Greene walked to the edge of the roof, looking invigorated despite all the walking and exploring of museums we had accomplished earlier. The sun still lent an early evening glow from its place below the horizon and the sky glossed bluish-lavender. "I feel I understand something of him despite him being an ancient from the first century."

"You must mean Pliny the Elder," I said with full assurance. I stood beside him. The street below teemed with gesticulating Italians, and their loud voices merged like a buzzing hive.

"No, I don't."

I watched the distant smoke dissipate into the evening atmosphere. "But it was the Elder who died at Vesuvius. He was attempting a ship rescue of friends trapped by the eruption but was overcome by the fumes and died in the effort."

Greene turned and smiled. "*To si sono corrette!*" He spoke perfect Italian and I envied him. He knew much about art and antiquities and was a fine conversationalist whose acquaintance I was fortunate to make. He had come to Europe for his health, but there were other interests we were both discovering. "You are indeed correct," he repeated, "but it was the Younger who memorialized his father in a letter to Tacitus, another one I admire."

"Ah! Tacitus the statesman."

"And historian." Greene took a deep breath. He was apparently relishing some secret notion, but I sensed, like Vesuvius, it might blow forth at any time.

"Be careful," I jested, "lest you inhale the vapors like the Elder."

Greene laughed. "The Elder's son wrote, 'For my part I deem those blessed to whom, by favor of the gods, it has been granted either to do what is worth writing of, or to write what is worth reading. It is more blessed for those upon whom both gifts have been conferred.' The Younger was crediting his father with both deeds. He honored his father well, and he did us all a great service by the letters he left behind so posterity would know he had a father of letters *and* action."

This seemed a humble thing for him to say. I was intrigued. "Then why not more favor the father?"

Greene shrugged and then stared upward as if searching for the first stars of the night. "I am the grandson of a Revolutionary War hero, Major-General Nathanael Greene."

"I know what that is like. My mother's father was one, too. General Peleg Wadsworth of Maine."

Greene looked at me and smiled, his head bobbing. His Vesuvius was about to pour forth, I was sure. "Then we have that in common as well."

"We do seem similar in many ways," I added. I saw the first star of the evening shining in the north; at least it was the first one I noticed.

"I don't fancy myself a war hero or a doer of any great act such as those done by my grandfather." He was becoming as animated as the mingling Italians traversing the street below. "But more like a historian of a kind. Maybe an author, I don't know. But definitely no great doer of deeds."

I liked George Washington Greene. He was bright and inquisitive, respectful and humble. And he spoke wonderful Italian! "I recount something I once read. I forget who said it: 'Supreme Art is to silence the enemy without fighting.' I think becoming a historian is a noble endeavor."

Greene laughed and patted me on the back. "Thanks for the encouragement." He pointed to the Isle of Capri, which was darkening by the moment in its solitary place on the sea. We stood in silent admiration for a few moments. "So what does Henry Longfellow desire?" he asked quietly.

It was a simple question. It could have been answered in a pinch of time, but I welcomed his query as a signal that our evening atop the rooftop would go well into the morning. So, beginning with Dante, and his eternally unfulfilled quest for the beautiful Beatrice, and marveling over some of the verses of the Italian poet's *Divine Comedy*, which remained largely closed to me due to my not yet grasping the breadth of that beautiful language, I proceeded. I spoke of the tomes and tales of authors and poets. I told him everything. Everything that swelled and swam within my young mind about the life and power of words and literature and the fathomless spirit that embodied every scratch or stain or instrument that fashioned them. I don't remember exactly what I said but I'm sure I could say it again. He was provoked to add his own dash of spice about other philosophers and historians. We were dense and specific. I'm certain you think it needful and deserving of space to hear every jot and tittle of what we spoke and of whom we nearly worshipped, but that is not really what mattered most, though both George and I would have then agreed it was as the sky darkened and the stars shone innumerable and the cities of Pompeii and Herculaneum lay not far away, covered by years of hardened lava at the base of an ancient volcano. Yet they were there as certainly as millions of other stars we could not see, in whose unseen beams we lived and breathed.

Chapter 4

FOLLOWING MY EUROPEAN ODYSSEY, Brunswick felt a small, dull town in Maine, and I feared my life was becoming an empty dream with only the grave as a reward. Though my teaching reputation was fine, while I was reciting lessons, Greene was reciting vows. News was that he would soon be walking down the aisle of a Roman cathedral with a voluptuous Italian bride on his arm. Reading the letter over and over made me feel like my youthful aspirations were dragging like a dusty garment across the corridor of time. Then came the evening I attended the First Parish Unitarian Church in Portland. Not since crossing the border from France into Spain to enter the company of those dark-haired lovelies of the Basque region had I seen such an angel.

I had attended Portland Academy with her years before, but her being five years my younger, I had never noticed her. I had never seen her with the vision now mine. While the minister spoke about King David dancing in his naked reverie I could think of nothing other than the blue-eyed, dark-haired beauty seated near the front. While everyone else attended to prayers, I imagined Mary Potter, daughter of a local judge, to be the wife of this local professor and the bearer of his children. I prayed right there and then that all the associated activities toward such ends would soon be afforded us throughout eternity.

At the end of service, I don't know what possessed me, but I swiftly navigated the crowded aisle, endeavoring to come up beside her to chance a conversation but it was her large, stern father I found instead.

"Henry." The judge shook my hand. "Nice to see you. Is your father here today? I haven't spotted him." I took advantage of his momentary search for a sighting of my family to scan the crowd for a sign of his daughter. I knew my family would be upon us soon. "Oh, there's your father!" The judge boomed with that all-encompassing voice he used when calling the courthouse to order.

"Judge Potter," I blurted, "I want to marry your daughter!" For some stupid reason I thought I needed to act quickly. He looked as surprised as I felt.

"Pardon me, Henry?" His tone sounded as though he were about to accuse me of something awful. "Which one?"

"Either one!" I cocked my head in a stupid gesture.

The judge laughed, relieved. "Oh, yes, yes. Thank you, Henry. They are fine ladies, aren't they? Thank you, son, for the compliment." My arriving father patted his shoulder. "Stephen, a blessed morning to you and the family."

I didn't wait to witness the mingling. I couldn't believe what I had said. I hurried for the door.

"I can't believe you said that!" My brother Stephen was beside me, laughing.

"Ssh," I whispered. I felt enormous relief stepping outside.

"I know who you meant!" Stephen elbowed my ribs. He skipped down the steps and hustled away. I wiped my brow and squinted.

"Hello, Henry." Her voice spoke from behind me.

I turned around. "Mary? Oh. I didn't realize you were here. Nice day."

"May I walk with you?"

"Of course." I offered her my arm.

It was a perfect day for three or four steps until I heard voices behind us. I didn't have to turn around to recognize them. My own family and Judge Potter, along with Mary's older sister, Eliza, congregated behind us as we walked home.

Beginnings are not endings. Beginnings are not middles. Beginnings are beginnings. At a time when I had feared falling prey to the drudgeries of life beyond the dreamy borders of youth, Mary came to me as the Moon goddess of the Greco-Roman myth came to Endymion. Like Diana, she came upon me sleeping, thought me handsome and admirable, and awakened me with a kiss. It was effortless, to tell the truth. It was seamless and without a wrinkle, except for the discomfort in wooing her during a short period of time in which I wasn't sure whether Judge Potter would rule in our favor or not. But he did, and with the help from my younger sister, Anne, who acted as a messenger of secret letters in both directions, Mary and I laid bare our hearts to one another in ink, and then finally I inked the request to her father.

Dear Honorable Judge Potter,

I wish to express the grateful acknowledgment I owe you for helping to bring into this world Mary, in whom I find the inestimable virtues of a pure heart and guileless disposition—qualities which not only excite an ardent affection, but which tend to make it as durable as it is ardent.

I think I have formed a just estimate of the excellence of Mary's character. I can say to your ear what I would not often say to hers—that I have never seen a woman in whom every look and word and action seemed to proceed from so gentle and innocent a spirit. Indeed, how much she possesses of all we most admire in the female character!

On this account I esteem myself highly privileged beyond the common lot in seeking your approval of my engaging her

*affection. I hope to merit both by attention and tenderness
to her the hope and promise of a life of happiness in the social
intercourse of your fireside and the domestic quiet of my own.*

Respectfully yours,
Henry W. Longfellow

We married in September of 1831 and landed in a small Brunswick
cottage of our own beneath the shade of elms and honeysuckle. Our
home was comfortable, even if fashioned in a more humble style than
our parents'.

Over the course of our first four years, I fashioned a study in one
corner within sight of nesting birds. I was the professor and Mary
was my wife. She amused me, delighted me, adored me, and had all
of my heart. We bobbed on the surface of life, young enough to feel
as though we would live forever, stationed well enough to feel secure,
and fortunate enough in our features to enjoy all of the delights that
came with matrimony.

I began to organize my notes and thoughts from my European
travels into my own Irving-like sketchbook. I called it *Outre Mer*
and hoped it might become something. In the doing of this, I began
viewing Brunswick as too isolated from the world. I also despised the
wrangling going on at the college. The Overseers were straining under
obsessions with religious leanings and other nonsense and, frankly, I
resented the empty nest in the honeysuckle outside my window while
my home remained occupied in much the same way for half a decade.
Mary was not certain change was the correct prescription, but she
graciously embraced my desire to stretch my wings. She accompanied
me to visit Professor Ticknor in Boston.

"I understand the frustration," the old man began "It is wasteful
not to apply what has been given, and you must remember: to whom
much is given, much is required."

We didn't understand fully all he intended by those remarks

but both Mary and I were emboldened to believe something like destiny awaited us. In our hearts, we were preparing though we did not know for what. In the meantime, *Outre Mer* found an interested local publisher, and at first we thought that might be the doorway to something larger. It proved only a slight bump of excitement, not quite strong enough to boot us from our confines in Brunswick. We felt certain somewhere over the horizon a new day would arrive and we would recognize it when it did.

That day came unexpectedly by way of a letter from the president of Harvard. He offered a conditional invitation to teach at Harvard. I accepted at once. His condition was that I again travel to Europe to gain the proper exposure to foreign language and literature. Over the next few months, I tendered my resignation at Bowdoin, arranged for the required transatlantic trip, secured two female traveling companions for my somewhat nervous but definitely excited wife—they were good friends of hers, of course—and couldn't thank Professor Ticknor enough for what he had helped achieve for me.

There are times when dreams seem very much alive and like divine appointments though they unfold differently than dreamed. From this vantage I see everything clearer now than then, but I must relate it as I saw it. That is why feelings are vital, but not feelings that change direction like wind-tossed buoys dancing atop the undulating surface. I speak of feelings anchored fathoms below that are with us always. We just don't know it until we do. At first telling, you must see it as I saw it, as most of us are prone to see it while we are living it.

Chapter 5

IT ALL BEGAN IN A MOST unusual way with an unexpected question that came to mind, shortly after leaving our American shore in April of 1835.

How does one look after the needs of ladies on a reckless sea?

We were aboard ship, sailing for England. This day my wife and her two traveling companions surrounded me except for the direction I faced, where the roiling Atlantic endlessly fussed. The captain of the packet *Philadelphia*, Elisha Morgan, had assured me that we would reach England in three weeks time, but it was now day twenty-five with no land in sight.

Dizziness caused me to grip the rail as sweat rolled down my temples. The ladies were unusually quiet, yet that was not what caused my discomfort. Mary squeezed my arm, the deck plunged, and my stomach deformed.

"Locating ourselves near the rail is a poor choice," Clara announced, taking defensive steps, like a tipsy ballerina failing to hit her marks. No sooner had she completed her declaration than she fell on her bum and slid away, her layers of clothing scrubbing the wet deck and leaving a wide swath behind her.

"Good lord!" Miss Goddard's alarm momentarily got my attention. She ran after Clara in shoes too slippery for a packet's deck as she attempted to palm her bonnet more securely. Suddenly, she seemed to skate and fall, a maneuver that appeared painful. She tried but was unable to take advantage of a more cushioned landing upon her abundant posterior. It flashed as she slammed forward onto her stomach, her lace-decorated bosom flattened against the deck. With legs bent, feet skyward, and hems gathered at her waist, she slid into the cabin wall. She seemed mostly embarrassed, and I would have found the whole thing amusing if not for my profound nausea.

"Henry!" Mary's hands squeezed mine tighter. "We must do something. This is terrible!"

I knew she was right, but no sooner had I begun to respond than up it came—on the deck, on my shoes, and all over Mary's pretty feet and hose.

"Henry!"

The thought returned. How *does* one look after the needs of ladies on a reckless sea while vomiting the entire contents of a recent meal? "Impossible!" was all I could muster before my gut convulsed again, rivaling the fits of salt spray sweeping the rails.

I watched Clara and Miss Goddard make an admirable show of picking each other up, then falling several times more before reaching the door to the main cabin. A flash of white darted out like a gull over the rail, streamers dancing to the left and right of it, and then swooped into the sea forever lost in foam. Miss Goddard's naked head appeared from the cabin door. "My bonnet! I've lost my bonnet!"

It was all too much for me as my stomach convulsed again.

"My dress!" Mary moaned. There wasn't a trace of resentment in her voice, not a shred of anger in her demeanor, only a vast helplessness.

I wanted to help but my stomach was traitorous.

"Henry."

I looked up. Despite my blurry vision and the wrench in my gut, I found her pout adorable.

"Henry." Her voice was soft.

Sentences tried to line up in my brain, but I could not form one word.

"Henry, this—is a mess," she said, and then began laughing.

———

Later, in the confines of our cabin, I was surprised at how quickly my body recovered. I watched Mary rise from beneath a mountain of blankets to scurry to the dresser for her brush. Her naked flesh, so beautiful and flawless, draped in nothing but her long, dark hair, was as white as cream. Four years of marriage had not diminished my desire for her. I was as attracted to her aboard this rollicking vessel as I was the day I walked her home from church. "Come back to bed; you'll catch cold," I said, hearing the seduction in my voice.

Mary rummaged through piles, looking for the brush while her slender form shivered. She was frail, and her constitution was not as strong as mine, but I still felt my father's concerns were unwarranted. A trip across the sea in the clean salt air would be good for Mary who had never traveled beyond Brunswick or Portland. How could I have left her behind? With her two friends along, she would not only be entertained while I studied, but we were together—and as she rushed back to bed with the brush, I relished the specifics—*with me* in every way.

Mary lifted the covers to climb in and laughed. "You are obviously much better, but I need to brush my hair or it will look like a rat's nest tomorrow."

"Love is awake." I said with a half-smile that I hoped she would find irresistible. I could see her resolve faltering.

"You are a poet."

"Better, you are a flower and I am a bee." I kissed her and pulled her under the covers.

"My petals are closed." She pouted. "But do say more," she murmured, still shivering.

"Come close and I will be your own true sun. Your petals will open for me, I am certain."

Her throaty laughter was a joy to my ears, as were her gasps and moans of pleasure. It was some time before we lay motionless, and I was only moments away from falling asleep when we were interrupted by a knock at the door.

"Pardon me," Clara called excitedly. She rapped again. "Dear Mary, Longfellow! You must come up on deck!"

"A minute! I said as I pulled myself to a sitting position. I cleared my throat. "What is it?"

"A speck on the horizon." Clara's tone pitched high "Land, I'm told! Closer than anyone expected."

London, May 1835

My dear father,

May 14. We reached Portsmouth on Friday eve May 8. The ship hove to about six in the evening, and a little sloop took us on board with our luggage, and carried us within a stone's throw of land, whence we were taken ashore in wherries, at a shilling a head!

May 15. We shall commence our rambles tomorrow. For two days past it has rained so incessantly that the ladies have not been able to go out much.

Most affectionately yours,
Henry W. Longfellow

I sorted through my valise until I found my letterbox. I brought it to the desk and carefully removed a few of the documents. Most, but not all, were letters of introduction I had brought along. When I found the one I was looking for with the Harvard seal, I opened it for the hundredth time:

Dear Sir,

Professor Ticknor has given notice that it is his intention to resign his office of Smith Professor of Modern Languages at Harvard University, as soon as the Corporation shall have fixed upon a successor. After great deliberation my determination is made to nominate you, provided I receive assurance from you of your acceptance.

Should it be your wish, previously to entering upon the duties of the office, to reside in Europe, at your own expense, a year or eighteen months for the purpose of a more perfect attainment of the German, Mr. Ticknor will retain his office till your return.

Very respectfully, I am Yours, etc., etc.,
Josiah Quincy

Great things had come unbidden to me, and I knew I was fortunate. Holding the letter, I saw it as a living and breathing epistle—better still, a *glass* through which I could see the future. As it had done the instant I first read it, the letter quickened my pulse and fired my imagination. We would travel from London to Germany and make stops in Sweden. I would come to know German better and some of the Northern languages as well. Ticknor was fluent in German and Spanish, and very much renowned, but he had no knowledge of Danish or Swedish or Finnish. I could carve a larger territory and expand the reach of the chair I would hold.

When I traveled to Europe the first time, I had learned Spanish, French, and Italian. It was then, too, that I was first exposed to the German. I had been a boy on a quest, a dreamer in a land of magical possibilities. I fell in love with the history that leapt to life around me. It was my first exposure to Europe. I was older now, a veteran of travels at twenty-eight. I would be almost thirty when we returned to America. I could visualize my future as easily as I could see across a cloudless sky. Once this trip was over, Mary and I would rent a home in Cambridge. I would chair the Department of Modern Languages at Harvard—teaching, organizing, and leading bright young men, and in the evenings I would write poetry and prose. Eminence would come, I hoped, not only through scholarship but also through my writing. I was an emissary of sorts. Yes, I, Henry Wadsworth Longfellow, could be a *literary* emissary.

I crossed to the full-length mirror beside the window overlooking Princes Street in London. I tugged on the bottom corners of my waistcoat and pulled my shoulders back. I looked passable for one with less-than-conventional looks, and wouldn't object if my nose were a little less pronounced.

———

For the next two days I wandered through bookshops and engaged breakfasts with literati whom I accessed through those letters of introduction, while the ladies toured and shopped to their hearts' delight. On the third day Mary and I strolled hand in hand and watched the evening settle over the Thames. We stopped and held each other until the sun slipped below the edge of London.

"I am glad Clara and Miss Goddard are here. You were right to have me bring them," Mary said. The softness of her voice was like lapping waves, but her excitement was salt from the sea. I made a mental note to write that in my journal. "Henry? Did you hear me?"

I turned from the water and looked into her eyes. "Yes. I thought the ladies would keep you entertained. I didn't want you to be alone. You deserve to have as much fun as possible on this trip."

"Clara is as curious about things as you are," she said, "and Miss Goddard is a constant delight as she interrogates Clara's every supposition."

"How does Clara feel about it?" I asked, laughing, because I had observed the same behavior.

"It is the spring in her step, I think," she replied. She cupped my hands in hers. "What about you? Are you having freedom enough to haunt every bookseller in England?"

"With you happily occupied, I am content with all my ramblings," I said as I admired the moonlight on her hair. I kissed the top of her head and said, "I thought the dinner with the Carlyle's was very much a highlight. Didn't you?"

Mary looked up, bridge lamps finding her eyes. "Mrs. Carlyle was sweet. I was glad you took me to meet them." She rubbed the flatness below her bosom and turned her head to cover her mouth with her scarf—there was a muffled sound—but she quickly recovered. "She was much brighter than I had expected. A boon for her husband."

I raised her chin with the edge of my hand, concerned. "Was it the cranberry sauce?"

"I think—," She quickly covered her mouth with her glove this time. "I think, yes." Her cheeks puffed, and the muffled sound repeated. "Oh, Henry, I'm sorry. Forgive me. Mr. Carlyle's unpolished ways have nothing on mine."

I laughed and felt her forehead. "You've no fever."

"It may have been the cranberry sauce."

I nodded and led her along the river. "You're right, Carlyle was somewhat clownish in his manners. But don't you think his conversation was glorious?"

"His expressions were beautiful," she said and pointed to the river. "Look!"

I saw a silvery star moving ghost-like above a gliding black hulk. Unseen paddles slapped the water's surface. "It's a signal-lamp on a masthead," I said, excitedly. "Listen. Harp music." A flute joined and then horns. Laughter rose and songs sounded. We eagerly watched the dark shape edged with lights and filled with joyous souls unknown float on until it dissolved into the distance and the night. I slipped my arm around her waist.

Mary pulled away and covered her mouth with her hankie and belched, then moaned. "I beg your pardon, darling."

I touched her waist and pulled her into my arms. "Tomorrow we take the steamer toward Stockholm, so long as your digestion permits it." She pinched me and giggled.

"And who blanketed my shoes and nearly drowned me in unmentionable substances when we last sailed?"

I craned my head and narrowed my eyes. "Funny, I can't recall. But I do remember what we did afterwards." I kissed her smirking mouth and tugged her in the direction of our lodgings. Looking back I noticed distant spars along the far side of the river under the glow of the fogging lamps and stopped. "Those masts look like a winter grove of leafless branches from back home."

"I thought we were heading to our room. Don't divert me with poetry." She swayed, her arm outstretched, still gripping my hand. "You have made me long for bed."

I grinned and pulled her along, all the while thinking I had to find a home for those phrases. *Winter grove. Leafless branches.* Another journal entry until I could find it a better home.

"Henry? Are you writing even as we walk? I am chilly."

I smiled. "No, I was just thinking about how nice it's going to be to make you chillier." I stopped and pulled her into my arms for a long time. A heavy iron bell clanged from St. Paul's cathedral. Another from the south answered next, and then another from a different direction. In a matter of moments, church bells chimed around us, at least thirty or more clanged and banged. Their steeled sounds seemed to seal us in a cocoon of intimacy and we kissed without restraint.

The trip the next day was uneventful though the stops along the way proved most unpopular with us all. We ate bad soups and endured cold, dreary weather. I managed to pick up a bad cough, and Mary continued to have an unsettled stomach. Clara and Miss Goddard remained staunchly healthy, thank God, but began to express a good deal of homesickness. After a long day we were at last on our way by steamer to Gothenburg where we would connect to a vessel that would take us to Stockholm. The ladies could enjoy summer there while I studied the language and literature of the Swedes.

The ship wasn't as comfortable as I had envisioned, but it was getting us to Gothenberg until the storm hit near Kattegat and forced us to shelter near Elsinore. We missed the connection at Gothenberg and were stranded.

"What awful luck" Miss Goddard said, as we disembarked. I couldn't see her face under her umbrella, which dripped heavily in the on-and-off drizzle.

"From one city of the dead to another," Clara complained, holding her shawl above her like an awning.

"Now, it's not *that* bad," I said, "though there's no other connection by water for two weeks." I looked at Mary as we trudged away from the dockyard and expected a comment, but none came. She simply massaged her midsection and walked along, her wide-brimmed bonnet protecting her hair and face from the damp. The wide bands on the sides drooped. I took her hand and helped her step under the overhang of a plank-built tavern with a large, welcoming door.

"May we sit?" Mary looked pained and was pale.

"Of course, darling." I guided her to a bench near a window.

"Come now! May we at least go in?" Miss Goddard asked impatiently.

"Are we certain we want to?" Clara looked concerned as she squinted through the window. She sat beside Mary and wrung out her shawl. "I know I don't want any more fruity wine soup. If I wanted

New England porridge I would have stayed home."

Miss Goddard, her new bonnet tied snugly under her chin, closed her umbrella and tapped it on the planks, as though to get my attention. Droplets sprinkled her skirt. "There may be *something* worthy of sustenance inside." She spoke with a bouncy rhythm as if addressing school children. "How can we know if we don't inquire?"

I thought she had a point, and trying to maintain a courteous demeanor, I said, "Every Swedish stop can't be as dank as the last. Agreed?"

I scanned the moss that invaded the cracks between the uneven bricks of the slick street. Wind rattled shutters and tumbled crates. All of it, under the sporadic, cold rain made the prospect of solving our dilemma gloomier than I would have preferred. I stepped to the door and Mary rose to follow. Miss Goddard smiled and Clara moaned. As I led us inside a boy approached and bent far over until his chest was parallel with the floor. "Sir? Ladies." He maintained this position. "Carl is my name," he said to his shoes.

"You needn't prostrate yourself, my dear," Clara said, turning to Miss Goddard. "An adorable lad, don't you think?"

Miss Goddard tapped the boy's chest with the handle of her sopping umbrella. "May we get something fine to eat in your establishment?" Her tone seemed sincere but I detected a smirk.

The boy returned to his full height and nodded. I noticed the pine sprigs scattered across the wooden floor. *That's* why the place smelled like a forest. It was thick enough in the air that it might very well influence the flavor of the food. I motioned to the boy. "Is there no way to Stockholm but the steamer?"

"There is, if you desire a coach."

"Henry." Mary touched my arm. Beads of perspiration dotted her forehead. I cut off my conversation and escorted her to a table.

"Bring us some tea, please," Clara said as I helped Mary into a chair.

"I hope they have meat," Miss Goddard said eagerly, sitting opposite.

Clara placed her shawl around Mary while I knelt holding her hand. "You're famished. First tea and then some warm food."

"I think that sounds nice." She looked at me sadly as I removed her hat.

"See to it you all get the best food offered here," I said to Clara. "I'm going to learn more about this coach."

"Don't go out in the rain again," Mary said to me, her voice urgent. "Rest."

"We don't want to spend two weeks in this place, now do we? I'll return quickly." As a pleasant-looking young woman brought a steaming teapot to the table I searched out the boy. "You, lad! What of this coach?"

"Come with me," he said, motioning to the front door.

I followed then stopped to spin a large man in an apron to face the table. "Please look after them and serve them whatever they want." I handed him a pound coin and stepped outside.

"It is a Russian carriage," the boy said as we walked around the side of the tavern. "You see?" He pointed to a carriage that appeared heavy and stable, its wheels large and smooth.

"Is it comfortable?" I asked.

"Yes." The boy opened the side doors. "I can drive it for you. You seek Stockholm?"

I peered in. It was large enough for all of us and thickly upholstered in green velvet. "How long would it take?"

"Five or six days. I can take you."

I pulled myself inside and sat down. It smelled faintly of grease, but it was well cushioned if somewhat squeaky. The Swedish countryside by carriage could be adventurous I decided, and clearly superior to remaining two weeks in Gothenberg. "Name a fair price."

———

The carriage was built well but the roads were not. Miss Goddard and her new bonnet struck the roof more than a few times, but I figured if the cabin wall of the *Philadelphia* hadn't made a dint in her headstrong ways, neither could the crushed velvet of a Russian coach. Sliding in mud occasionally turned us sideways, and I feared we might flip over, but we remained upright. Mary uttered no complaints, though I worried about her constantly.

After several days of damp weather, my own cold symptoms worsened and every barking cough raked my chest. Fortunately, none of us wanted for food. Miss Goddard, ever mindful of her station and privileges back home, had been certain to load the carriage with beverages, sausages, chocolates, cheeses, cakes, and breads. These temporary pleasures did a little to offset the discomfort from the incessant rains and harsh winds. The Swedish blasts of late June felt colder than the October gales back home.

When at last we arrived in Stockholm, we managed decent boarding and fair meals. My studies began nicely enough, and the ladies experienced ample samplings of culture and community through attending the opera, social gatherings, and well-attended meals at the hotel table. This continued for two full months of supposed summer, but the weather had improved little. The constant cold and wetness eventually fostered a bored state among the women, hindering their walking travels. The same was not true for me. I was becoming increasingly acquainted with the literature and language of the region and spent much time in bookshops, lecture halls, and one or two smoking rooms. I did not forsake my companions, of course, and certainly not my wife, but I did relegate our in-common social maneuverings to the evening hours.

Mary was without complaint, but she could not completely shake off the feverish ague she was suffering from. Clara was courteous without sacrificing her honestly expressed disappointments, and Miss Goddard was mildly consoled by the existence of at least some of our social exploits. It wasn't until the unexpected letter arrived shortly after our journey to Copenhagen in September, that I discovered in her a more sympathetic strain.

"I was to meet Mary Goddard's brother in Germany, but…." Clara stopped reading aloud. It was the latest thing she had discovered to help the ladies stay occupied—reading letters from home and from the continent that each received. She dipped her chin and lowered the letter into her lap.

"Go on," Miss Goddard ordered, leaning forward, her dress rustling, and sounding to me like wind through autumn leaves. "What does she say next?"

I was ready to be amused, a chilled glass of white wine in one hand, Mary's soft shoulder under my other. This new occupation of ours felt somewhat like shameless gossip, but it was a balm for everyone's homesickness to some extent. I was always game to listen in as long as my studies were completed, as they were this night. I had no idea why Clara was glancing at me with what appeared to be alarm. The letter in her lap was written from her friend who was beginning to tell of a missed encounter with Miss Goddard's brother in Germany. Clara looked to Mary.

"What else?" Mary clasped my hand in excited anticipation.

"Must you exaggerate the drama?" Miss Goddard rolled her eyes. She picked up the velvet pillow from her couch and squashed it onto her lap. "The suspense is accomplished. Continue, Clara."

Clara swallowed as if something were stuck in her throat. She offered the letter to my wife who accepted it and read what had already been recited. "I was to meet Mary Goddard's brother in Germany, but he had to return to Boston. His father—" Mary gasped.

"What?" Miss Goddard flushed as red as her painted lips. "Now I will see it!" She stood and took the letter from Mary's loose hold, and scanned it. After a moment, she struggled to catch her breath and then collapsed in grief.

Clara and Mary embraced her, stroking her back and hair and murmuring to her through their own grief.

"It cannot be," Miss Goddard sobbed.

I retrieved the letter from the carpet. Miss Goddard's father had taken ill quite suddenly and died. As Miss Goddard's grief grew louder and more anguished, I found myself filled with sympathy for her. Much of the trip had been borne under the weight of her sharp comments and self-absorbed petitions, but she had never been completely boorish or impossibly unreasonable. I knelt beside her. With every heave and gasp that shook her, I felt the immensity of her sorrows. *There is a reaper that cuts both flower and grain.* There it was, in the midst of her sorrow a lyric rose unbidden from within me.

Miss Goddard raised her swollen face. "I must go home, Henry. As soon as it can be arranged." Her gaze was hard, sensible, unlike the sobbing woman of a moment ago. At last I understood her facade. How much pain did she carry buried beneath all these previous weeks of arrogant pokes and prods? They now appeared more like walls she erected around her castle than arrows she shot from her towers. My own thoughts snapped me out of the moment. I was amazed, even embarrassed, at what inspired the poet, the writer in me. Here I was feeling an urgent need to write the *castle walls* and *tower arrows* into my journal so as not to forget them, while a friend mourned. I felt guilty for the verses that flooded my brain. I forced myself back into the moment.

With the assistance of a young American diplomat we had met in Stockholm but who had come calling on us in Copenhagen, I arranged for Mary to have an escort as far as England where she could once again cross the Atlantic with Captain Elisha Morgan. Our party was reduced to three and, despite having once hoped we would leave

Copenhagen to winter in Berlin where the finest university in Europe was situated, I chose a different passage in the direction of Heidelberg. Frankly, without the ongoing financial assistance that would have been provided by the Goddards's support had Mary continued with us, the new destination would have to do because it wouldn't cost as much. Besides, and more importantly, there was Mary's condition and another rugged overland route might prove too demanding.

———

We weren't far along our new course when my concerns proved entirely correct. Mary had grown seriously faint. It seemed wise to stop in Amsterdam, call upon a doctor for Mary's sake, and refresh each of us for some number of days.

"It is not the ague," the physician began after the examination.

I had been prepared for the word *ague*, but the doctor's mouth spoke on.

"You are pregnant," he said to my wife.

"I thought as much," Mary said, looking at me.

"With child?" I asked, stupidly.

Mary squeezed my hand. "You didn't suspect? Not once?"

"I—I—"

"Is it certain, doctor?" Mary's tone was calm, as if she were asking if a glass of water were safe to drink.

"Most definitely."

Of course I had wanted to have a child. Eventually.

When we returned to the hotel, my nervousness calmed as I watched Mary tell Clara the news. The women embraced and cried, their joy evident. Was my own odd mix of joy and concern as obvious? I hoped not. I calculated the conception to have likely occurred aboard the *Philadelphia*; however, I did not offer this math to the women who were as ecstatic as schoolgirls. And, upon further reflection, and with my heartbeat slowing, I realized I was happy, too. After all, it was funny and sweet and beautiful—as natural as blossoms in spring.

"We will no longer wonder how to fill our time!" Clara's eyes sparkled.

"I am glad to know there has been some purpose to all of this discomfort!" Mary tried to dry her eyes with her dress sleeve. "Being pregnant is a most uncomfortable state!"

"It is normal to feel terrible. It is the morning sickness," Clara assured her.

"Yes," Mary said with quivering voice. "It has been morning sickness all along!" Her eyes glistened as she looked up to me.

I suddenly realized how greatly relieved she was to know that her health was good. She was pregnant, and not ill. My joy overflowed for the both of us. "Neither will you have to make any excuses for a hearty appetite," I leaned and kissed her.

"I'll permit neither of you," she said as she pointed to Clara and me, "to report about *that*." Happy tears rolled down her cheeks again.

"I will write volumes!" I laughed, handing her my handkerchief.

"You'll not!" Mary alternately laughed and cried, and reminded me of a daisy with dew on its petals. Later, when I wrote that down in my journal, I changed the flower from a daisy to a blue flower. I don't know why. It felt right.

Clara drew a heavy breath and sat up, her face radiant and glistening. "I will join you, Mary. You shall not gorge alone."

"Alas, if that be the commandment, count me in as well," I added, placing a hand on each of their dear heads. "We shall all be fat by the time the holidays arrive!"

In full embrace of the spirit of our miraculous circumstance I hurriedly made arrangements for a celebratory meal that evening, but it was not to be. "Mary is none too well," I explained to Clara as she opened the door to her room after I knocked. I could see in her face the understandable shock over the unsuitability of my wardrobe for a fine dinner. "Her energies are expended. Let us wait until tomorrow. The downstairs supper can suffice until then."

Clara's disappointment was obvious, she was dressed for a bigger evening than the alternative I suggested, but her eyes turned soft. "What can I do for her?"

"It is good of you to offer, Clara, but rest is what's needed, I think, and truth be known, something I desire as well. May I escort you downstairs and see to it that you are in good company, before I retire?"

"No, Henry, I am well able to do so myself, but thank you," she said, petting my arm. "Do tell Mary I am available at her call—and yours."

I kissed her cheek and returned to our room where Mary already snored gently. I couldn't get into my nightshirt quick enough and then slipped under the covers beside my warm and feverish wife. I rolled on my side to face her and placed a hand on her stomach and watched the rising and falling of her bosom. Before our new life in Boston commenced we would have a baby. I imagined our rosy European-born child at her milk-swollen breast. *Stephen. Mary. Annie. Henry.* Names floated before me. My mother would have to understand that we could never choose Zilpah or Peleg. The thought made me smile. A child would bring joy to everyone, and someday I would explain to this little unknown soul how it came to be traveling European roads, lakes, and rivers, while father perfected his study of literature and language. It was peculiar not knowing whether it would be a son or a daughter, but whatever gender the child, I envisioned our baby perched on my lap while I wrote or sitting at the dining table with more sauce on its face than on the plate. Other thoughts came but soon began to lose shape. I don't remember closing my eyes, but I know I had fallen into a deep sleep because it was well into the evening when I heard our child calling my name.

"Henry." I tried to open my eyes, but I couldn't. I heard my name again and decided it must be the child grown—a daughter—for the voice was mature.

"*Henry.*" No, it was Mary's voice. I pictured her as she spoke. "Henry, please wake up." I opened my eyes, fully awake, and moved my fingers to touch her shoulder but found only linen. She was not beside me. "Henry, I am not well." Her voice was soft, sad. This was no dream.

I sat up and somehow bumped her. "Pardon me, darling. What is it?" The room was dark and her outline as equally dark as the vessel we had watched steaming along the Thames back in England. I felt for her and placed my hand on her waist. She sat on the edge of the bed, soaked in perspiration.

"Mary?"

She heaved.

"What? What is it, dear?" I asked frantically, longing for light.

She fell backwards hard enough to rock the bed, pinning my hand. "HENRY!" she yelled, a hopeless sound that made me shiver.

I pulled my hand free and drew close enough to find her face. It was hot and damp. "Mary, tell me what it is? The ague? The baby? What is it?"

She sucked for breath and muttered a long, horrific syllable, and grunted as if pushing a great weight.

"Let me light a candle," I said, jumping from the bed and falling onto my hands and knees. I struck my head on the corner of the nightstand. I clambered up, using the bed for support, and moved across the room in the vicinity of the dresser.

"HENRY!" She grunted several times in succession.

"Mary," I said, completely rattled, desperate. I reached the dark hulk of the dresser and felt for a match and tinder. A candle. Bottles fell over, small cases toppled. Innumerable items moved in and out of my hands but none of them was what I sought. "Damn! Where is the flint? Where are the candles?"

Mary shrieked, "Henry, you have to help me! GOD!"

I ran to the bed again and realized her legs were spread wide and covered in something thick and that it was flowing from her. I reached for her and pressed my mouth to her ear. "Mary, oh God, Mary."

"It's coming, the baby. I can't stop it. Oh God! Henry, it's coming."

I was suddenly paralyzed. I didn't know whether to go for help or hold her. I kissed her face and said, "I'm here, Mary. I'm here. It will be all right."

"OHHHHhhhhh," she screamed. "GOD nooo!"

"Mary!"

I felt her go limp.

"Mary!" I slid my hand down her torso and found a hot, lumpy mass between her legs. "Oh, God. Mary!"

"Henry." She spoke to me as though in a trance.

"Mary!"

"Don't worry," she whispered. "It is over."

"No, don't say that," I sobbed.

"The baby is gone."

"Oh, Mary."

"No, no. Hush love," she said. "Hush. I love you. Stay with me."

I heard footsteps and a knock at the door.

"Henry?" It was Clara's alarmed voice. I ran to the door and Clara stood in nightcap and gown with a candle in her hand. Later I would recall the look of horror on her face for I was covered in Mary's blood, but in that moment I simply said, "Give me your candle!"

She stepped into the room, and the sudden light illuminated a gruesome scene. Blood was everywhere. My own nightshirt, hands, and face were also painted. Mary seemed asleep, and I wanted to wash her.

"God in heaven!" Clara rushed to kneel beside Mary. "Henry, hurry downstairs and wake the clerk to send for a doctor. HENRY!" Clara snapped. "You must get a doctor, now!"

I stared at her. I was in shock.

"Henry! Do you understand me? A doctor! Now!"

I nodded and felt for the door behind me. I stumbled down the hallway and descended the stairs. The clerk had heard the screams and told me he had already sent a boy to fetch the doctor. I returned upstairs, unable to answer his anxious questions, needing to be back with Mary.

"Let me near," I said to Clara. She was stroking Mary's face with a cloth she had moistened in the pitcher of water we had been given to wash with in the morning.

"Henry, there is a cabinet in the hall. Bring me all of the linens you can find."

I turned and did as she requested. The clerk came upon me in the hall followed by a very small and short man with a great mustache and large bag. The clerk pointed me out, and the little man spoke, "Le medicin." I led them to Mary, my arms full of linens.

The Frenchman-doctor assessed the situation quickly and directed the clerk to find more water and bring it to our room. The clerk mentioned a washbasin and cistern downstairs in the kitchen and rushed off. The doctor assured me Mary would recover and be well, and then sent me away.

In the morning, Clara and I sat beside Mary while she slept. Restless and desperately sad, I excused myself to wander the streets. I knew nothing about where I was going or why. I was a man who breathed and walked with purposeful strides to nowhere. When I returned, hours later, I found Clara asleep in a chair beside our bed. Mary was covered in blankets to her chin but stirred when I entered.

"Henry?" I felt relief flood through me. I realized I had been longing to hear her voice.

I knelt beside her. The mattress was softer than I wished and I felt clumsy when I saw her tense with my movements. "I'm sorry, darling. So sorry."

"Hold my hand," she whispered.

I reached under the covers and took her small hand in mine. "I'm sorry," I said again.

"You are here. You are my everything." Her face was peaceful. "That is what matters."

"I am here and you are here, but the child is not and I feel responsible. All of the travel was stressful. I should have seen that."

She moved her hand and cradled my cheek. "It is not your fault. It is God's will."

"I think not."

She touched my lips with her fingertips and I kissed them. "Then you mustn't think at all."

"You are my angel, Mary. My true love."

"And you are mine."

"I am your fool." I kissed her palm. "Forgive me, Mary. Please forgive me."

"Forgive what? Your love? Forgive your heart? Are you the giver and taker of life? Should I hold you accountable for all that happens upon this earth?"

I shook my head and tears filled my eyes. "I should have been more aware. I was too preoccupied to use common sense. We should have stopped traveling. I was thinking only of my own needs."

"Your needs are our needs, Henry. Have I not failed you?" she asked.

"What? Never!"

"I have no child to give you and cannot even tell you whether we've lost a son or a daughter."

"As you said, it is God's will. Together, we will come through this, though I don't know what we do now."

"You are a Harvard professor, and I am your wife." She clasped my hands, and I smiled.

"I cannot study. I can never do what we came here to do," I murmured.

She smiled, too. "Then I will become dumb. For whatever you are, I am."

I loved her in that instant more than I had ever thought I could love anyone. I leaned forward and kissed her lips.

Clara coughed loudly and rose from her chair. I had forgotten entirely that she was there. "It is good to see the two of you smiling," she said. "I will leave you alone." She grazed Mary's shoulder and walked away.

"Thank you, Clara," I said. "I was helpless before you came to us."

She turned at the door and looked directly at me. "I thought you nothing less than a man dearly concerned for his wife. I've read there is such a thing as a paralysis that can grip us when harm befalls those we love most. I witnessed you overcoming that. Everything you did last night was done in the name of love, Henry."

———

The short Frenchman-doctor and the giant of a nurse who periodically came with him were so mismatched in height that I might have been amused if not for the seriousness of my wife's recovery. Alas, Mary was well attended by them and she slowly recovered her strength in the coming days. She was sitting up more, one to two hours at a time, and her color was returning. The American consul in Amsterdam, Van den Broek, and his wife, paid us a visit with a bowl of sago soup, filled with, they claimed, restorative ingredients particular to the region. It did seem to aid Mary's strength and joy. Clara and I took turns reading passages from several books, Clara from books in English and I interpreting from the Dutch books I continued to acquire, the most recent purchases from a local Jewish bookseller. I delayed indefinitely our departure to Rotterdam until I could be certain that Mary was fully recovered. I took advantage of the extended stay to locate books that would be useful to the library at Harvard and made arrangements to ship them home along with our letters, though I was careful about how I addressed our recent complications. I didn't want to raise unnecessary alarm about something which was now mending and thought it better to properly inform all concerned parties only when we were at last recovered so that those who learned of our misfortune would also know that we were very much alive and well and walking hand in hand. It was weeks later, a Thursday in late-October, I remember it well, when the doctor announced Mary as the picture of health and that after fourteen visits, he would not return a fifteenth time. He promptly handed me the bill, which I was most happy to pay. Thus, with our hearts, minds, and bodies restored we traveled on to Rotterdam.

We were dropped a few blocks from our accommodations. We proceeded on foot, following the boys hauling our luggage, crossed a bridge spanning a murky canal, were nearly run over by more than one noisy carriage, passed a market I hoped we would visit afterwards, and finally reached the hotel Des Pays Bas. I was able to secure adjoining rooms overlooking a pleasant backyard with a large parlor to share. I had a hotel employee build us a roaring fire, and I rang for dinner at five. It was then I surprised the ladies with a packet of letters I had retrieved prior to our departure from Copenhagen but had kept hidden until now. My little Mary loved surprises and eagerly broke the seals to find an assortment of goods. To our surprise, Miss Goddard had sent tokens of her affections including a pin for me, and dainty watches for each of the ladies. We were happy to learn that among the other passengers sailing back to America aboard the *Philadelphia* Miss Goddard had discovered a family friend, a certain

Mr. Gocker, who had assisted her every need until she arrived safely home. This provided great relief to the ladies, and Mary looked better than she had in months. She and Clara were both happy to lounge and read their many letters again and again, so I ventured into the lamp-lit streets to inquire about the steamers' upcoming departures and destinations, wanting to properly arrange for the next leg of our trip. I decided that whenever possible, water would be our preferred means of travel, a good boat being less strenuous than most overland carriage rides. The early evening was cool and damp, but with our tiny group revived I felt new life in my steps. So eager was I to inquire and dream and wander about in this newfound state of gratitude and hopeful expectation that I walked about the early evening absent a proper scarf and paid the devil for it the next day.

I awoke to a dead fire and a blasted cold that had returned with a fury. It made me irritable. A giant rake clawed my insides, and my innards felt like tumbling coals. In my feverish state, the guilt of Mary's miscarriage returned. No sooner had she become healthier but I must grow ill and unable to enjoy her company in ways we both desired. I felt like our trip was filled with too many disappointments. This was so unlike my first trip to Europe when I had traveled mostly on my own, meeting contacts in every city and finding other travelers from back home to converse with and share meals, drinks, and smokes. I had enjoyed seemingly endless amounts of times in the universities, libraries, and parlors of learned and published men. I had received tutored instructions to speak in new languages and spent much time reading and translating along the way. This trip was entirely different, because Mary's health had been a near-constant concern. Now, with her mostly recovered, I was suddenly too ill to leave my bed. Convolutions swirled like eddies. I remember reaching for my journal needing to write down that metaphor when I suddenly felt ashamed that my intellectual needs were relentlessly pushing to the fore. Perhaps if I removed the call for study, it might help me prioritize and keep my focus where it should be—the *welfare* of our traveling group. Mine included. I was beginning to wonder if an early return to America was the most sensible idea.

But by the end of the week, not only had I escaped the clutches of a disabling cold without any vestigial symptoms to speak of, but best of all, Mary had rallied to begin enjoying long walks with me in the early evening along the Rhine, as we had enjoyed previously along the Thames. We strolled hand in hand and watched the evening passages float by. I never spoke of our dead child but wondered if it moved in and out of her thoughts as it did mine. I cannot express strongly enough how I wish I had understood at the time that there was more than physical healing required. I was ignorant of the reality that her soul needed tending at that very moment. It's not that I didn't understand the existence of such need; it was that I was deaf in that instant of time. I failed to recognize the moment we were in. Mary was too precious to risk in any way no matter the cost to my studies. Whether poet or college professor, without a life filled with moments like those, what is there worth living for or writing about? If our experiences during that season had done anything they had loudly proclaimed life as precious and unpredictable. Days pass never to return again, and whatever joys might be found are joys worth cherishing, for everything is fleeting, whether sorrow or happiness. When we remember that then we can endure difficulty and appreciate the blessings, but I was dull and I perceived it not. There were plenty of feelings swirling within me, as there must have been inside of her, but if one isn't listening, one doesn't hear. If I'm not hearing, I am not seeing and if not seeing, my ignorance remains despite the possibility that everywhere around me the truth resides.

For the next several weeks we indulged ourselves in the enjoyment of a variety of activities and foods. We dined well, and Mary and Clara particularly enjoyed the sugared tarts, fresh berries, succulent pears, roasted nuts, and plump bonbons. We indulged so generously that

Clara finally found fault only with her clothing, which she thought must be shrinking. We all laughed with her, even while she cut and sewed her adjustments, and I watched my beautiful wife begin to be herself again. The joy that came to me in those days and weeks was both exhilarating and liberating.

I had the fortune of meeting many interesting travelers at the hotel table, but found a most agreeable friend in an English clergyman, the Reverend Dr. Joseph Bosworth, chaplain of the English Church in Rotterdam. He was also an expert lexicographer in the Anglo-Saxon language and in the process of completing a dictionary and invited me to make contributions to it. It was beginning to feel like my first trip to Europe only better. With Mary by my side and Clara happy to be along, we enjoyed a renewed social life, and I had ample time for my studies. I went to work translating the Danish ballad, *King Christian*, and often met with Reverend Bosworth to discuss art and faith and of course, his dictionary.

The evenings also fared well, as Mary and I were able to press close and often. She loved to prance around barefoot in our room since, for the first time since coming to Europe, we had carpeting! Dare I say, she never pranced for long that I did not chase after her and lift her to our bed and into my embrace.

One morning, after such an evening of prolonged intimacy, Mary asked to sleep in, a benefit I was happy to grant. I invited Clara to accompany me on a walk but her tutor was arriving soon. These past weeks she was unusually engaged in her new interest in studying German, and when not doing that was either found to be sewing or, even more surprisingly, trying her hand at sketching trees from a window near the garden. She was not very good at it, I'm afraid, and I tried to comment honestly when asked without dampening her spirits. I am not sure I succeeded but, my, how nicely things had changed. Everyone had assumed a better self. I remember thinking how strangely runs the course of the River of Life. What had been so storm-wracked was now whole, cloudless, and warm. The image in my mind was no doubt inspired by the geography of the nearby delta formed by the Rhine, the Meuse, and the North Sea. I couldn't stop thinking about how a man grasps the waterway on a certain level when viewed wholly as on a map but then quite differently when traveling it league by league.

It was in such a state of mind and with hope so filling our sails that Mary began sleeping in late each day until even Clara was beating her to the breakfast table, if Mary came at all. Yet, upon every inquiry as to the cause, Mary insisted she was only enjoying for once in her life certain *laissez-faire*. Honestly, I missed her company at the morning table but found her so enlivened each afternoon that I could only admire her newfound commitment to a schedule that made her more awake at night than in the early day. Her nights were increasingly active and so, consequently, were mine. We enjoyed long walks beside the river and long kisses in the shadows, but I will not say what more she introduced to me except to say that never could I imagine a husband more pleased with the affection shown him by such a beautiful, adoring wife.

Ignorant as I was, it wasn't until some of her nights became sleepless and accompanied by fever that I again suggested—but failed to insist—we should more thoroughly determine what these changes were about. She did not want to discuss any topics other than to hear me tell of my musings and studies and to teach her the newest Dutch words I had learned. She had me read my translations and gushed praises about how brilliant she thought I was and how fortunate was she to have found me. It went on this way until November, but when the snows began to fall, I finally insisted she reconsider her resistance to my concerns and allow for a doctor to be called. It was strange how at those times of my petitions she made every effort to deflect me with kisses and hugs and sudden interest in topics never before a part of her fascination. But I would not be further frustrated in this area.

My concern for her was too great, and with the help of Reverend Bosworth I found her a doctor to make a general examination.

The doctor said plainly, "Her fever is great. I wonder if it is rheumatism more than anything else."

Thank God! It had been too hard to even suggest to ourselves that anything so debilitating as what had happened before could be happening all over again. With a diagnosis like this, we could take action to ease the symptoms and not fear the worst. The doctor was familiar with a treatment that Clara and I could easily apply. So, each day and night, precisely as he had instructed, we wrapped poor Mary's arms and legs and elbows and knees in brandy-soaked clothes. It was funny to see, and we more than once found something to say about mummification and ghost-like apparitions. But the humor did not last.

It was one week later, after a subsequent visit by the same doctor, that his report took a bad turn. I followed him out of the room. "Can you be more specific?"

The doctor's lips pressed together. He pushed his glasses up his nose. "She may be in jeopardy. Time will tell. But you must not move her."

Jeopardy? She had recovered. All was well. "What are you saying? Is it not rheumatism?"

The doctor shook his head. "I am not certain what it is, but she is failing."

"Failing? In what way? To what extent?"

He had nothing to say that comforted me, and I was at a loss to know how to make sense of this. It did not make sense until Mary, at last, said something to me that crushed my spirit.

"I hope these past few weeks have been to your heart's desire," she said, pale and clammy.

I knelt beside her. She had been told to stay in bed these past two days and had grown only weaker. The sheets clung to her form. She turned and smiled; there was no sweeter woman alive.

"Henry." There was something in her voice I didn't recognize. It was somehow beautiful and alarming. "I reserved my strength for you as well I could manage," she said with perfect peace. "I hope you are pleased."

"What do you mean, Mary? What are you saying?" I brushed the hair from her temples.

"I think the angels are calling me, my love. I pleaded with them for a little more time. I hope you will never forget our walks along the rivers, our nights of happiness."

I heard her words but found them difficult to understand. Had she been managing her hours to simply attend to me, to please me, to love me? I never left her side after that. Several days passed and I did not wash my body or change my clothes. I felt thin and grimy. More than once, Clara stirred me awake after finding me slumped next to Mary on our bed. Eventually, Clara convinced me to take turns with her reading to Mary from scripture. Reverend Bosworth had arranged for an English-speaking nurse to assist, but I never left the room. I soaked Mary's nightclothes in brandy, I helped her sip beef tea, and I spoon-fed soft eggs to her lips. But soon she stopped eating altogether, and often complained of an indelible thirst. I made her drink water and tea with honey; I kissed her lips but she barely responded. Once, she opened her eyes wide and hope sprang in my heart. She looked at me eagerly and I realized she recognized me.

"Henry, read from the prayer book," she said in the faintest of voice.

I read her favorite passage from it:

> *Father! I thank thee! May no thought*
> *E'er deem thy chastisements severe;*
> *But may this heart, by sorrow taught,*
> *Calm each wild wish—each idle fear.*

"Henry," she spoke my name again. Would she rally a second time? Oh God, I prayed for exactly that. "Read from the New Testament," she said, "and slowly, that I might think about it."

I read to her, but she drifted in and out of a kind of delirium and sometimes became incoherent. One evening, I set the prayer book down and reached for the Bible. Before I could open it, my beautiful, wonderful Mary stroked my hand and my heart skipped. She *would* rally again!

"Tell my family and friends I thought of them in my last moments. Tell them I love them."

"What?"

"My poor father will mourn. Please help him bear this." She spoke with her eyes closed. A rattling sounded from her throat.

"Mary!"

She opened her eyes. "Everyone has been so kind to me all of my life, and none more than you, Henry."

"It is because you are a good, gentle woman," I said. I worried that the quivering in my voice might frighten her.

"Do you think God will take me to him?"

"Whenever it is time for that, he undoubtedly will, but not now, my love."

"Do you think I will see my mother?"

"Not now, she is in heaven. You will see your father when we return home. And we are going home soon."

"I think you are mistaken." I could not believe she smiled so large. "I think I will see my mother, first." My throat tightened, and Mary clasped my wrist. "It is hard to leave you."

Everything in me wanted to insist how wrong she was. Tears filled my eyes. I slid my arm under her neck and gently lifted her head and leaned in close, when unexpected words suddenly escaped me. "You have nothing to fear, my darling. You are going to your best friend," I whispered. Someone, God perhaps, had given me those words for her.

"Bless God who makes me suffer so little. I will come see you if I can." She closed her eyes and the rising and lowering of her chest slowed. I lowered her head into the pillow and held her hand. Suddenly, a great breath erupted with a gasp. Her eyes opened wide, and she clenched my hand with great strength.

"Mary! MARY?" I shook her. "Mary?" Her final breath sounded like a slowly emptying bellows, and she went limp in my arms, her eyes staring.

I do not remember how it was that the doctor and the reverend and Clara came to us and how Clara escorted me to her room to lie down while she sat nearby, but that is how I found myself upon waking. Upon hearing again from Clara that Mary had passed, I suddenly burst into bitter tears, wailing in ways I had never done in my life. Clara knelt close and wept beside me. The next day she told me things I could not remember. She told me I had opened the door and called for her urgently. She said I gently closed one of Mary's eyelids and had prompted Clara to do the same to the other. She said I kissed Mary's lips and then stared at her in silence. She described how I slipped the rings from Mary's fingers and placed them in my pocket and walked away like a blind man.

Chapter 6

SILENCE CAN BE COMFORT of a kind, but not when it comes with a chilling recognition. I peered over the length of my resting body to the light coming through the window of my room in Rotterdam. My neck ached. I forced myself to the edge of the mattress. My joints throbbed as I lumbered to my feet and walked to the window.

You grieve. You stop grieving. Then you grieve again.

Blessed are those who mourn.

I used to think the scripture should read, "cursed are those who mourn," but now, of course, it made sense.

They will be comforted.

The one left behind weeps in the wake. Your heart breaks open in ways you never thought possible. Your mind rushes with recognition for every shadow you see, but it is never the one you seek.

The knock I heard next was as loud and unsettling as a pistol shot. "Henry?"

I jerked and bumped my nose on the windowpane.

Another knock. "It's Clara."

It reminded me of the time when Clara had rapped on the cabin door while I had been at sea with Mary. We had just made love. We had laughed and spoken unmentionable things to each other before dozing off. She might have conceived our child then. It was possible.

The sudden desire to be with Mary consumed me. I wanted her

57

in my arms. I wanted to cover her bare shoulders with kisses. I was filled with both desire and guilt.

A third knock. "Henry, are you in there? We must be leaving soon."

I wished I could conjure a comforting silence and make it grow so large that Clara would be gone from my door, but I had no such power. Besides, she was right. Weeks had passed. It was time to go and she needed me to bring trunks downstairs, some of them filled with pretty dresses that would never be worn. I would go down and help load them into the smell and bounce of a carriage to journey along the Rhine in the dead of winter.

"I'll be with you soon, Clara."

I don't know exactly why I did it, but I burned all of our love letters and the portions of her journals filled with dreams and hopes and expressions of our love. I think I saw them as pages for only Mary and me, but she was gone. I wanted no private records to survive if she could not survive with them. The feelings that drove my actions were not from the deep fathoms of my spirit but from the insanity tossed wildly on the crests of the waves. I failed to recognize the better thing to do during a storm was to batten all of the hatches and wait until the skies clear. One can think then. Everything will not be salvaged but at least regret won't be added to the havoc and the harm already accomplished. Unfortunately, when I stood beside my room's fireplace I could think of nothing else except to burn them.

The ensuing trip was uneventful. The attending chaperone I had secured for the sake of Clara's reputation remarked of small things he thought interesting, but Clara and I offered him little in return and even less to each other. She disembarked at Frau Herr's home as we had agreed she would. There she could enjoy further introductions I had arranged and pleasantly await a plan about when and how we might return home, which I was in no hurry to contemplate since I imagined the effort too difficult for my present state. We parted with the formality of a man and woman who have no true ties. We had experienced too much of an unusual intimacy, and it was, at least for now, a nearly unbearable task to look each other in the eye. I traveled to a different part of Heidelberg. I needed to dwell apart from her but wondered if reconnecting with others might help. I knew Greene was traveling in Europe, and I nursed a silent hope that he'd pass through Heidelberg by chance, although I'd done nothing to tell him what had happened or where I was. I decided to write him, having no idea if my letter would reach him.

Heidelberg, Jan 1836

My dear Greene,

Mary died on the twenty-ninth of November at Rotterdam from great debility brought on by miscarriage, which happened in Amsterdam nearly two months before. I little thought that death could be so stripped of all its terrors. She died as calmly and willingly as if she were but going to sleep. Thus——. But I can write no more. The whole scene comes rushing back upon me—and I cannot command my feelings. O, my dear George; what have I not suffered! I am completely crushed to the earth; and I have no friend with me, to cheer and console me. Miss Goddard has returned home on account of her father's death. Miss Crowninshield has come thus far with me, but now resides with a certain German family until such time as she departs this place. Such obligation for her arrangements does properly fall upon me but is beyond my capacity to presently calculate. For my own part, I shall be obliged to remain here in Heidelberg through winter and till the close of the summer, unless some unexpected occurrence enables me to remain longer. Will you and I ever sit together upon the rooftops of Naples again? I wish it so.

Very truly yours,
Henry W. Longfellow

I pictured that long ago evening in Naples with my friend and wanted desperately to return there, to go back in time. It was there that I dreamed of literary fame and a future of significance and a life filled with romantic love. It was not to be, it seemed, for youth and time and love had all fled.

Meanwhile, my room at Frau Himmelhahn's house in Heidelberg was well suited to me. The sparkling windows overlooked the Neckar River on one side while other windows offered a broad view of the rear of the property where a path begged exploration. I had lost joy, not liberty. I grabbed my overcoat and was down the stairs before one arm was in a sleeve.

The steep path was overgrown with leafless shrubs, dusted with snow, and led to the giant ruins of Heidelberg Castle. Despite the January cold, or maybe because of it, the pulse in my neck and the pounding in my chest were pronounced. I was moving. I was alive.

Beyond the ancient ruins, I saw the peaks of the Geissberg and the Kaiserstuhl capped with mist. They brooded over the decayed fortress like parents refusing to accept their dead child.

The friend of your youth is dead.

The past haunts like dead among ruins.

Poetic taunts flooded my mind. They lingered there, wanted or not.

The timid fear before battle.

"CEASE!" I yelled, my shout bouncing off the distant peaks.

The cowardly, during.

Suddenly, I realized this was not an epiphany of new verse. It was the other kind of poetical meter that often swam through my soul, the kind filled with the voices and verses of the many poets I'd devoured. I recognized these taunts. They weren't my progeny. They were someone else's. I had read them somewhere, but where?

The courageous, after.

I remembered a trip to Athens years before, on my first tour of Europe. I had seen the three statues of Minerva. One of them was made of olive wood, the second was bronze, and the third a mix of gold and ivory. These recollections were the fruit of having been so immersed in history and literature at the time. Now, I wondered whether I possessed any sure footing in the land of the living. Were my best thoughts nothing but a wreckage of quotations from those who had come before me? Were my thoughts nothing beyond what echoed from ancient genius? Perhaps I had no claim on anything born from me, perhaps that was why my child was dead.

The olive wood had fallen from heaven and symbolized youth. The bronze commemorated military triumph with sword and shield. The ivory and gold had to do with age and wisdom and maturity. It was all coming back to me. Were these thoughts "the comfort that comes to those who mourn" or were they the further effects of a broken mind? Was I defaulting to the rote because I was devoid of revelation? Lucid thoughts continually rushed through me; I did not control them, I only witnessed their movements.

My hands ached and I unclenched them. I looked over the placid rooftops of Heidelberg to where the Neckar flowed across the valley. As I traced its path westward to where it sprawled wide to enter the Rhine other ideas leaped from the river of my thoughts like so many fish jumping into a boat, ideas untethered to others so far as I could tell. I noticed the narrower parts of the Neckar rushed swifter than the wider open places. My life was in a narrow stretch of stream.

I feel the freshness of the stream,
Crossed by shade and sunny gleam.

Those felt like they might be my own verses. Perhaps there was something within my brain that paddled instead of drifted. I descended the path and returned to the Himmelhahn house with a sliver of hope, a trace of calm and a growing appetite.

The dinner table seated several guests, two of whom seemed peculiar enough to be fascinating, but I was too weary to make conversation although I ate well. I excused myself shortly after and retired before nine.

I would have slept soundly if not for the terror and angst from a fragmented dream. I was floating in water that was deep and cold. The undersea world was checkered with light and dark, sunshine and shadow. Far below, lay mounds of gold and jewels that I knew represented happier days gone by. But the waters were so clear that I reached for the treasure, which appeared obtainable. I clutched and drew up a prize but found it was clumpy and slimy. Seaweed oozed between my fingers and thorns pricked my skin.

Then I saw *Mary.*

At first she appeared to float like an angel in garments of sheer white, but, as I watched, she sank deeper and deeper until she was difficult to see. I tried to hold her in sight, but she was gone.

Awake and sweating, I listened as the bells finished chiming. I had not counted the strikes but the light in the window told me it was not too early to rise. Once bathed and refreshed, I found myself wishing I had other clothing to choose from. I wanted blue or purple gloves but found only gray and drab green and white. I descended the stairs to breakfast barehanded.

"Young Sir!" A gentleman called out to me in German, but with a Russian accent as I was making my way to the dining room. He was fully extended on a sofa, dressed in a soft gray morning gown and purple, velvet slippers. He held a small guitar. I didn't recognize him from the night before. "Tell me what you think," he said, and then moved the pipe he smoked to one corner of his mouth, and began to play and sing:

"The water rushed, the water swelled,

A fisher sat thereby. . ."

He stopped. "Well?"

"Well what, sir?"

"What do you think?"

"Is there more?"

"No."

"I think it short."

The Russian man laughed, set down the instrument, and stood. He was much taller than I had expected. He tapped out his pipe and slid it into the pocket of his gown. "Baron van Ramm at your service." His handshake was powerful.

"Henry Wadsworth Longfellow, sir."

"Yes, yes," he said, crossing to the dining room. "Join me, please. We shall dine and delight this morning while the weather remains mild. Mark my word; it will soon change. A greater snow is on the wing. Trust me."

I made myself comfortable at the table and reached for a basket of warm biscuits with sides of butter and cheese. I placed the red linen napkin on my lap.

The Baron sat across from me and asked, "Have you visited the castle?"

I took a small biscuit and sliced it open. Before I could answer, a pretty young lady arrived and described the morning's offerings while pouring us hot coffee. She was younger than my Mary. The Baron and I made our selections and the woman curtsied and left.

"Margaret is her name," the Baron said, sipping loudly from his cup. "You've explored the ruins, have you?"

"Explore may be too generous a term. Visited, yes." The butter was too soft, so I reached for the cheese.

"Did you see the Frenchman?"

"Frenchman? I'm afraid not. I saw no one."

"You did not enter the halls?" He asked in a tone of wonder. There was something likeable about this man with his bright blue eyes and his gentle tone.

"I did not."

"He's often within those halls sketching; he's been doing so for years."

"Sketching?"

"He draws the ruins, inside and out, and writes wonderfully about them. He claims birds of prey traverse the place by day and screech owls by night. You must buy his book and his sketches if this sort of thing interests you." The Baron's tone was persuasive.

"I'll consider it." I said agreeably and took a large bite of the flaky biscuit and cheese.

"You speak the German tongue well."

I smiled, and he smiled in return. The Baron did *not* speak the language well.

"Let us cross over to your native tongue, shall we?" the Baron said in English. "I am told you are"—he paused as Margaret placed a steaming pile of dumplings and breakfast sausages before him,—"a scholar from America." He lowered his bearded face and breathed deeply. "Ah. I do love the German meats, especially in the morning, late morning though it is."

Margaret disappeared into the kitchen.

"I am joining the Department of Modern Languages at Harvard," I said. "So I am deepening my familiarity with the tongues and tomes of these regions."

"Tongues and tomes?" The Baron appeared amused as he sliced his sausage. "You mean language and literature?"

I felt uncomfortably warm and cleared my throat. "Yes, of course."

Margaret returned and placed an almost identical dish before me. I watched her walk away, until she disappeared through a swinging door, where I caught a glimpse of Frau Himmelhahn. The sausages smelled of spices that I didn't recognize and fresh black pepper. I cut one open and it squirted a thin line of grease onto the tablecloth. I glanced up self-consciously but the Baron appeared none the wiser.

"They're juicy, aren't they?" he suddenly asked, his head bowed over his food. When he looked up, his cheek was packed round and he chewed rapidly.

I couldn't help but grin. "After breakfast I may visit the castle again and look for the Frenchman." The sausage was making me thirsty so I took a big gulp of coffee and gasped from the heat.

"You can warm your bones with such brews." The Baron lifted his cup and lightly blew across the top before noisily sipping. He smacked his lips and set it down. "Go soon or the heavy snow will thwart you."

"Snow?" I found the tender dumpling much more to my liking. They were doughy, but neither too salty nor too hot. "I've wondered about this weather. It is like 'a winter painted green,' to borrow a phrase. A little dusting, of course."

"Oh, you read Richter?"

"I have, and I hope to find more of his works. I so admire his writing that I'd like to carry one of his books around in my pocket, if I could." I blew over the top of my cup as he had done, and then sipped my coffee.

"Which volume would you carry?" The Baron burped without embarrassment.

"*Kampaner-Thal.*"

"Do you think you truly understand him? He writes in a language that is not your own, though your command of it is fairly precise."

I thought about this carefully as I cut a slice of sausage and partially covered it with dumpling. "If you can understand the character of the author then, I believe, you may peer deeply into the meaning of what he writes."

The Baron burped again. "An interesting thought. But how can we understand the character of an author if we have only his written words by which to judge him?" He pushed his plate aside and held his cup of coffee before his face, speaking through the fading steam. "I don't know his character, but I find his work serious and comic at the same time. He leads you up majestic climbs in the company of men of interest, only to have one of them offer up a slice of bologna, somewhere near the top. Such antics become distracting and weaken the point, I think."

"But it is intentional, is it not?"

"Perhaps, perhaps not. Is it intention or mere sloppiness?"

"It is craft." I felt certain. "His thoughts are like a mummy embalmed with spices and wrapped in curious envelopments; but inside lies a king."

The Baron laughed charmingly. "Excellent, my dear American friend. Excellent!" He set his coffee down. "Tell me, have you ever read Herder?"

"Many times." At last, I had found a new friend of letters whose mind was alive with literary thoughts. "You?"

He nodded. "But we digress. Unless we begin our hike up the castle trail while we still can, we will not be going, for by afternoon it may be too late and the ice and snow will bar us from the climb." The Baron stood and reached into his gown pocket and withdrew his pipe and tobacco.

"Your company will be a welcome addition." I said, standing and wiping the corners of my mouth. I straightened my waistcoat. A fresh scent of something like rosewood filled my nostrils.

"You have need of some?" he inquired. "I have two pipes in my possession. We'll smoke and then climb."

"My pleasure, Baron. Thank you." I accepted the second pipe, which was packed with tobacco, and drew too heavily as he lit it. The ensuing coughing and belching of smoke embarrassed me though the Baron seemed to notice none of it. He simply waited for me to recover. He was a gracious man, well-mannered and kind. I truly was in luck.

———

It was early afternoon before we exhausted our opinions of Herder and Richter and reached the trail, but just as the Baron had predicted heavy snows began falling. Despite the change in the weather, we climbed the path to the top, dressed as we were in our heaviest clothes and the extra scarves Frau Himmelhahn had pressed upon us.

We did not speak much during the climb and even less when we reached the top. It was so silent and white that I was certain I could hear the sounds of the flakes falling, the *footsteps of angels.*

Footsteps of angels.

Richter had used this phrase somewhere in his writings—in a passage having something to do with walking over gravesites. My thoughts were alive, but were they mine? Mary had often encouraged me on this point suggesting we were all a product of what influenced us, but I found limited comfort in that.

I noticed the slender branches of one of the smaller Linden trees already bowing under the growing weight of the wet snow that collected at the ends of its forked branches like a frosty orb or a snowy fruit. I toyed with the question of what I might relate to the likeness of this snow-fruit. An unripe fruit could be something like a promise, perhaps, and a frosty one could be the hope of an unborn child. Suddenly, I imagined the globe papered over with frozen scales, burdened with weight and falling to shatter on a rock at the base of the tree. Everywhere was blood. I felt undone. I needed to be back in my room. I needed to be alone. I was still mourning.

"I tell you. . ." The Baron's voice brought me back with a start. "We must explore the halls and inside spaces. Somewhere that Frenchman is present, I assure you. Some say he has not missed a day painting in this place since eighteen hundred and ten." The Baron wrapped a strong arm around my shoulders and, to my relief, pulled me away from the Linden trees. "Let us look into the castle briefly."

It was as though I had blacked out somehow during the vision, and I worked hard to recover. "We shall explore the past together," I said, sounding more tentative than I preferred. Every thought seemed to have two meanings.

"No, no! Ha!" The Baron became animated. "We are not here to look into past glories. Beware the mournful past, my American friend. Let us find the Frenchman and improve the present, dah?"

We entered the castle, and soon found the artist engrossed in his work. We also discovered it was not birds of prey or screech owls that echoed the halls, but the laughter of men like us, behaving foolishly. When we finally returned to the house, I was much revived and very grateful.

That evening the fireplace burned alongside a noisy dinner and the frivolity was well-attended. I raised a glass of wine, and laughed with the men all around me.

Mittermaier, a law professor, was richly laden with liberal views and had a tone that commanded much authority. Professor Schlosser, between his large gulps of Rhine, offered fascinating accounts of German history. The impressive Reichlin-Meldegg was leaving in the morning to continue his lecture circuit on Schiller and Shakespeare and was not in the least hesitant to share his expertise at the table. The Baron, however, was second to none with his fascinating opinions and constant humor.

"Scholars and literary men matter to society," I said as the evening bell struck ten.

"Prost! Prost!" Reichlin-Meldegg's wine escaped the rim of his tipped glass. "That is fine, but *Shakespeare is the world*!"

"But what of the Italians: Michelangelo, Raphael, Dante?" I spoke loudly and clearly, certain they'd agree.

"I see your point," the Baron said. "What would become of Italy without these men to speak of her past?"

I nodded and walked a small circle along his side of the table, and then crossed to the fireplace and faced my companions.

I studied Reichlin-Meldegg's face with its arcing brows and accompanying frown. Across the room, slumping in a leather wingback, Mittermaier blew smoke rings, his arm and leg draped over the side of the chair.

Schlosser stood and waved his cigar frantically, drawing everyone's attention. "What would Germany be without Martin Luther, Goethe, or Schiller?"

"Exactly!" I crowed. "Philosophers, poets, and historians find ways to preserve the past and the truth of the past, so men will not forget." I was excited, but everyone stared at me in silence.

"Blah! Shakespeare said it all," Reichlin-Meldegg exclaimed. "There's no need for anyone else."

The Baron packed his pipe and touched it with a match, speculating between flares. "No time—or people—is wholly barbarous if they have even one—worthy of note." He exhaled a large puff of smoke. "Honorable names have been spoken by each of you."

"Hear! Hear!" Mittermaier crossed to the table, suddenly infused with energy, and poured himself another glass. He laughed and moved about as if ready to add a few observations of his own, but once he had a full glass in hand, he crossed back to his chair and sank into his former posture.

Like a falling circus tent. The inner voice returned.

"Let us consider the scholar who aims too narrowly, like a monk," the Baron said. "For I am no friend of too much seclusion from the world. It can be injurious to the mind." He stopped and raised his pipe in the air and spoke directly to me. "Do you know: *a single conversation with a wise man, is better than ten years study of books?*"

I looked into the flames of the fireplace. "How did the wise man become wise?" I asked quietly, but no one replied. Even the Baron stood in silence, attending only to his pipe. A gentle snoring drew my eye to the passed out Mittermaier slumped in his chair.

Reichlin-Meldegg rose with a wide yawn, thanked us for the amusements of the evening, and disappeared up the stairs. I looked for Schlosser but saw him nowhere. When had he left? I peered at the Baron who was seated again at the table and wondered when it had been cleared of the settings. I could recall no sight of Margaret doing so. I sat down, too, suddenly exhausted. "I think the night is over," I said.

The Baron puffed to relight his pipe, smiled, and spoke, all at the same time. "Are all American professors as young as you?"

I didn't know whether to feel embarrassed or proud. I decided the question did not need an answer, so I waited a moment before excusing myself, and retiring to my room.

In the morning, there was a forge in my head. Frau Himmelhahn brought me a warm seltzer with mint leaves but no comfort came. I slept until early afternoon and felt only slightly improved. I imagined walking downstairs and talking with whoever might join me but quickly found the idea irritating. I needed to be solitary and recover. I could read or write letters. Or sleep more. I stared up at the carved ceiling and traced the circular patterns with my eyes. Motions. Everything seemed to be in motion. If only Mary were here. I felt numb with loss, and I wept until no tears were left.

It was several days before I resumed my walks with the Baron. Our friendship continued to strengthen while other guests came and went, speaking mostly of the weather and the local geography. There were other sojourners but it was the Baron and I who remained constant throughout the winter. I attended lectures at the university, read in bookshops and in my room, and wrote in my journals. I was in motion, but whether or not it had direction or purpose, I wasn't certain. The act of being in motion was all I could muster. It offered at least an illusion of progress being made.

By the time spring arrived, the Baron had departed and I followed the advice I had received in a consoling letter from Professor Ticknor, to "give yourself to constant and interesting intellectual labor; you will find it will go further than any other human means. I pray God support you with all that external consolation is unable to do."

In service to that counsel, I consumed volume after volume of German poetry ranging from the Frankish legends of Saint George to Songs of the Minnesingers and Mastersingers. I delved into *Ship of Fools* and *Reinecke Foxes* and *Death-Dances* and *Lamentations of Dead Souls*, and many others. I even translated *Song of the Silent Land* by Salis. I greatly improved my grasp of the language and the culture, but I did it cautiously, without passion, without hunger.

I stopped thinking obsessively of Mary but a dull pain remained lodged in my chest. When June ended, I departed Heidelberg for the Tyrol, intending to use my last batch of letters of introduction. I had promised Clara I would take her with me, but I could not locate a proper chaperone for the journey so I was forced to break my promise, leaving her at Frau Hepp's house. I admit, I still had some need to delay a more regular reunion with her. The mere idea of resuming a daily traveling schedule with her touched me with the pain of those last days when I was losing Mary. I was still a man who had tragically lost his wife, but I also grasped that it was not everything I was, even if it did feel like that from time to time.

For her part, Clara had many friends I had introduced her to by way of my own associations there, and she was improving with her drawings and her studies of the German language. Still, she was not wholly pleased with my decision to go without her, nor was she especially impressed with my new promise to return to her in the fall for the journey home.

———

By August 1, I was in Interlaken, in the parlor rooms of Christen Hofstetter when something completely unexpected happened. A young lady dressed in black entered the room and nodded to us. She spoke seldom—I was listening—and hardly looked my way, but when she did speak her voice sounded like music. Somehow she reminded me of Raphael's Madonna. After several more encounters with her both in the bright sun and dimming twilight of summer days, I had multiple theories and numerous speculations concerning her. Frances Appleton was her name, but everyone called her Fanny. Something about her quieted my pain.

On the day after an excursion to the foothills of the Grindelwald, the rain kept us indoors in the parlor at Interlaken. After brief niceties with her family and others in the party, I inched closer to Fanny. She was sketching in a large book, completely absorbed.

"There'll be no picnic today, I fear." I knew my observation was obvious, but no other words came.

"It affords more time to draw," she said pleasantly, but without looking up.

"It is a fine pastime," I announced, feeling the color warm my face even as I said this. I watched her pencil glide effortlessly across the page. "You draw well."

She looked up for a moment and smiled slightly before continuing unaffected.

I cleared my throat. "I have never seen a lady's sketchbook before. Your lines are straight." I sat down on the sofa beside her.

She did not appear pleased by my observation.

"When some ladies draw towers they seem more like leaning Towers of Pisa," I explained, attempting a feeble joke. "I tremble for the men under them." I laughed.

She did not. "How absurd," she said. "Straight lines are simple. I have labored for over thirty minutes to make this wheel-house round but round it will never be."

"It may pass for a new invention then," I said, widening my eyes and nodding.

Fanny shifted farther away, making it harder for me to observe her drawing.

I sighed and placed my hands upon my thighs, and leaned forward to rise when suddenly she slammed her book shut and placed it on the sofa between us. I froze in this awkward pose, unsure what was to happen next.

"Are you in pain?" She sounded more annoyed than concerned.

I could think of nothing to say, so I relaxed and pointed to her book. "May I?"

"May you what?"

"Examine your sketchbook?"

She formed an unusual expression. It was alluring to me, but possibly unfriendly. I knew her so little. "Examine?"

"Admire."

She leaned back, but said nothing.

I thought she should be sculpted in precisely that posture. I picked up the book and carefully leafed through it and stopped at one particular drawing. "This must be Murten and the battlefield. Am I right?"

Her eyes glanced at the page and then looked straight into mine. Raphael's perfect Madonna only nodded.

"Did you ever read the ballad of Veit Weber? Apparently, the Burgundians jumped into the lake, and the Swiss Leaguers shot them like ducks in the reeds."

"Is that so?" Her words were no match for the indifference in her tone.

I turned the page. "This must be the head of Homer!"

She glanced again at her handiwork. "Yes, I saw the marble bust in Rome and thought him more God than man."

She was no dull woman. "I have seen that bust. You have done it justice," I said sincerely and smiled, but she did not. "You have a true feeling for art. I believe art is power; that is the original meaning of the word. Did you know that?"

She held my gaze—for an eternity. "I enjoy art and nature," she finally said, softly.

I felt I had made a true connection. I closed the book and turned to her. "I think nature is a revelation of God and art a revelation of man. What do you think?"

"I think you sound like a man who has just returned from Germany. For my part, I cannot endure their harsh language."

My hands began gesticulating. "You would like it better if you knew it better. I can teach you, if you would like."

She simply stared at me, as though not comprehending, as though I had spoken to her in German.

"It isn't harsh," I explained. "It's hearty and comforting, like the sound of happy voices at a fireside. The German men are hale and hearty, and the Fräuleins kind and honest!"

Fanny laughed—or scoffed—I wasn't sure. "I think of men with pipes and beer," she said, "and women with knitting work and much sausage-making to do. No thank you."

I shrugged. "Could that be your English prejudice?"

"And their literature is the same." She ignored me, rose, and walked away.

I started after her, gripping her sketchbook. By the time I was close enough to speak we were in the dining room and I noticed the others watched us enter. I was a widower, by God, and I mustn't forget. "Miss Appleton, you forgot your sketchbook."

She stepped back, took it from me, and curtsied slightly before joining her party gathered at a table near the windows.

In the days ahead, Fanny and I read Coleridge, Uhland, and other ballads. We shared a basket of sweet cherries we bought from a little girl across a meadow. We strolled lakeside at Lucerne while discussing poetry. One afternoon, we rowed across the lake and discussed *The Castle by the Sea*. That evening, studying by the fire, she became my scribe—my amanuensis—while I translated it from the German.

"Well saw I the ancient parents, without the crown of pride," I recited as I translated. "They were moving slow, in weeds of woe, no maiden was by their side! Do you like it?" I asked.

"It's graceful," she said, "and pretty. But Uhland leaves too much to the reader's imagination. His readers must be poets themselves, or they will hardly comprehend him."

"I feel like I comprehended him, although it is difficult for me to explain."

"You shouldn't have to explain it. Some feelings have no language, and besides, are you not a poet? Isn't that what you've told me?"

I am only realizing now that it was her words that first pointed me in a direction to consciously consider silent language. I didn't realize it at the time, nor afterwards, only now in the telling. It's amazing what telling a story, even a familiar one, can do. Things break loose from their anchors and rise to the surface.

Nevertheless, when she spoke those words at the time, I thought of Mary. But as she continued to speak, the resemblance disappeared. She wasn't like Mary, and the realization that I was comparing her to my dead wife troubled me. I pushed back those thoughts and tried to listen.

"Some feelings gleam upon us through the twilight of our fancies, but when we bring them close, and hold them up to the light, they lose their beauty; just as when glow-worms are brought in from the dark, to where the candles burn, and are found to be only worms." She looked at me as if asking a question though she had made only statements. She was no shallow person and her allure stole my focus, so I was embarrassed to admit that I had comprehended nothing she had just said. "Do you feel differently?" she asked.

I had no idea. All I knew was the evening, and the rest of my weeks there, passed in a cloud.

In the fall, a pleading letter arrived from Clara and I knew the departure to America was at hand. My responsibility to her was without question. I made the necessary arrangements and as the fateful day drew closer to head back to Heidelberg to retrieve Clara and then on to Paris for the trip home, Fanny appeared saddened though she never admitted it outright. I had hoped she would see me off in some meaningful way, and it was my sense as late as the very night before that she would do just that, but as the family gathered outside the front entrance in the cold, early morning, while I stood beside the open door of a waiting carriage, Fanny had evidently slept in and missed my leaving entirely. I had hoped, of course, for a different departure but, in the end, what could I truly expect under the circumstances? It was time to return to America and face a life alone.

Chapter 7

Cambridge, Feb. 1, 1837

My dear Greene,

I've been back in America since December last year. At last, two nights ago, as I returned from an evening visit, your letter looked down upon me from the mantle-piece with a most friendly, albeit outlandish aspect, its face being tattooed with post-marks black and red. It seemed to me like a voice of old—like the voice of the Northern God Mimer, with all his wisdom.

Enough of the past, let us turn to the present. I have taken up my abode in Cambridge not far from the college halls. My chambers are very pleasant; with great trees in front, whose branches almost touch my windows: so that I have a nest not unlike the birds; being high up—in the third story. Right under me, in the second, lives and laughs Cornelius Felton, yes, your friend and mine, the professor of Greek History. He is engaged but for now remains a much available friend in the social realms as well as in the halls at Harvard.

My life here is very quiet and agreeable. To Boston I go frequently—and generally on foot. I am now occupied in preparing a course of lectures on German literature, to be delivered next summer. In this course something of the Danish and Swedish (the new feathers in my cap) is to be mingled.

All would be well with me, were it not for the excited state of my nervous system, which grows no quieter, although I have entirely discontinued smoking.

This letter will reach you in Rome, your wife's native city, and the city of your choice. Walk with me again in the spirit through the Forum, and visit La Riccia in the summertime and all the old familiar scenes in and around the Eternal City and remember me and the times you and I had there so long ago. My love to your dear little wife; and write me soon and long, long letters.

Yrs. Truly,
H.W.L.

P.S. I go nowhere near Brunswick or Portland. Unbearable.

I rose from my writing desk, fully dressed for an evening out. I pulled on lavender gloves, grabbed my walking stick, and headed down the stairs. On the second floor I tapped the head of my cane on Felton's door.

"Enter or die!" Felton's voice was musical.

I turned the knob and pushed the door open.

"Ah, Longfellow!" Felton said, breathing heavily as he pushed his short, thick arm into his sleeve. His belly hung over his belt and shook while he laughed. "Will we ever read by candlelight again?"

"I think not." I crossed to the wingback and placed my shiny black boot on the footstool beside it. I polished the toe with my thumb.

"George Hillard and Henry Cleveland, friends of Sumner, will be joining us in the parlors tonight."

"More lawyers, no doubt." I switched position and polished the other toe.

"Yes, but like Sumner, lawyers with a taste for literature." Cornelius hiked his pants, donned his cap, and tipped it higher with his walking stick before crossing to the door. "Do you think Boston is prepared for five of us tonight?"

"Pray no ladies take notice of at least one of us," I said with a wink.

"Hah! I wouldn't notice if they did, so lucky am I!"

I loped down the stairs with Cornelius' heavy steps behind. It was good to be on the stairs heading down because it was clear what needed to be done. You descend and when you reach the foyer you politely greet whomever you might see and then head straight for the outdoors. No close examinations, no penetrating eyes, no lingering stares or uncomfortable shifting under sympathetic countenances. You simply exit, and once out of doors one can easily delay all but the most superficial conversation until such time as a destination is reached. Upon arrival there are new souls to meet and niceties and comments regarding temperature and forecast followed by the customary offering up of hats and canes while nodding and smiling en route to a parlor or drawing room where silent observation accompanied by thoughtful nods and ponderous expressions are not thought strange and certainly not evidence of pain. All personal emotions and pestering thoughts were safely stored within the wine cellar of one's soul and gratefully, no one would dare attempt to dig into it for signs of hurt, no thirst for a '36 Longfellow this night! We would heartily quaff only reds and whites from other dates.

Despite this self-preserving protocol devised for appearing in public as a young widower, it was not wholly devoid of discomforts—an internal shakiness mingled constantly with a steady chill in my bones. I thought no one noticed though I was well aware of the occasional pulse in my temples. Hopefully, others were not.

Getting to this point nightly had proved swift, sure, and bear-

able—thus far. Being settled amidst fellow socializers, it was predict-
able that others more aggressive than I, such as Sumner, God love
him, would move the conversation into literary topics or inquiries
of things European. Such foreplay could be tedious but worth the
safe harbor when finally obtained. It never failed at this stage that I
easily found a suitable measure of buoyancy with the cork vest of my
learning. I could offer up, in short bursts, French, Spanish, German,
Italian, and even Swedish and Danish words, phrases, and literary
samples to the delight of others and to the distraction of all else. So
far no one had dared broach the subject of Mary, and I hoped to God
they never would. Some things were too sacred for public exchange. If
only Mary was as mindful of my preferred decorum and would cease
haunting me each night.

"Henry?"

I felt her touch my shoulder.

"HENRY!"

I jumped. Of course, it was not Mary. It was tall, thin Charles
Sumner. "Longfellow, are you of a mind to agree or not?"

I felt my anchor lines cut. I thought I had been coping, but
found myself adrift in a conversation I had lost track of. "I'm sorry," I
mumbled. "Repeat the thought."

Charles boomed like a cannon. "I was saying that Goethe is not
so much a purveyor of wisdom as a peddler of things sensual. In truth,
he was a heathen!"

I pulled down my waistcoat and prolonged a sip of port. I nodded, trying to drive out the fog. "He was sensual, yes."

"I told you so!" Charles motioned his arm across the semi-circle
of men. "That's why his critics called him the 'Old Humbug!'"

Cornelius slapped my knee. Instinctively, I shifted my crossed
legs while he raised a pointed finger. "Goethe may have been no saint
in his *Roman Elegies* and *Elective Affinities*, but in other places he was
as cold and passionless as marble."

"You think him honorable?" Charles seemed hurt.

"Hardly." Cornelius's eyes danced playfully above his twitching smirk. He was egging Charles on, and I knew it.

"We ought not apply any measure or scale," I said evenly. Charles was a new and pleasant friend. He was bold and forthright with an admirable moral center, but he sometimes saw only opposite sides and nothing in between. I softened my tone as much as I dared, making sure I didn't sound condescending, and faced Cornelius. "Goethe must not be faulted for not being a politician any more than he must not be faulted for not being a missionary. He sought to avoid ditches on both sides. Admittedly, he often ran at least two wheels closer to one side than the other."

Cornelius feigned shock, and Sumner meekly offered, "Personally, I think the artist reveals his character by the subjects he chooses. It is lamentable that Goethe picked so many ragged and rampant souls in his works."

I tapped Sumner's arm and then raised my glass. "I somewhat agree with your premise, Charles. It is better to dwell on the praiseworthy and virtuous, but can we fault one for choosing otherwise? Do not the shadows bring dimensions to the light?"

Charles shrugged.

I loathed robbing the wind from the sails of a friend, so I sipped the very fine port and drew from deeper casks within me. "Take yourself, Charles. Your disposition is very much that of a statesman. Such conviction can produce a noble courage in the hearts of a people. It cannot be underrated."

"Why thank you, Longfellow." Charles' face shone with self-assurance.

I looked at the others and drew an excited breath—I wanted to proclaim how their trades and vocations were the engine and power of America's emergence and influence in literature, art, politics, and the world, but I hesitated because something like fatigue suddenly overwhelmed me. My mind was racing with notions of manhood and poetry, literature and fame, and I wanted to affirm everyone there, but my momentary desire to express myself disappeared as quickly as it had arrived. It suddenly felt disgraceful to the memory of Mary, for me to be the center of attention at this gathering. I leaned back and exhaled. I shifted my legs and, with all eyes on me, I smiled like an imbecile and, for want of a safe harbor, welcomed a former habit recently shunned. "Let us smoke our pipes," was all I could think to say.

From there the conversation bumped along. Wherever it went, I had difficulty focusing. My mind was adrift, snagging on every reef and shallow of grievous remembrance. Eventually, the night ended, and as we walked home the conversation I shared with Felton tilted heavily to one side.

"There's a resonance hovering us as a group, wouldn't you say?" He was in high spirits.

"Resonance?"

"The five of us. You know! Hillard, Cleveland, Sumner, you, me."

"Yes," I tried to follow his point. "I suppose."

"We ought to formalize our little society, don't you think?"

"Formalize?"

"Yes!" His voice filled with merriment. "Give ourselves a name. Burden ourselves with a sense of obligation to get together regularly to drink and discuss, smoke and quip!"

He wasn't wrong. It was an intelligent group with each of us fascinated in our own way with history and literature and making a mark in the world. "It would suit me. Like the one from that British author, Dickens. He had his male characters form a club in that Pickwick book."

"Yes, exactly! We should form a club. Exclusive, of course!"

"How about the Club of Five?" I offered. "It can't get any more exclusive than that."

"I daresay, Longfellow, you are a rapid wit. The Five of Clubs it shall be!"

I liked his version better. "And you are a helpful editor." I smiled, but weariness was gaining fast and I longed for sleep.

Over the remaining distance my jolly friend replayed the evening, often pausing for a sign I was listening. I replied as required, but my inner thoughts were self-obsessed and troubled.

When at last we parted and I eventually entered my bed, I closed my eyes only to open them with an urge to write. It felt needful, not desirable. I tried to resist but it pressed me. I decided it might quiet my mind. Reluctantly, I got up and tried to write. Not a lesson, not a lecture, not a translation, but something personal. To my chagrin, despite the urgings that had dragged me out of bed, I stared at empty pages for what felt like an endless time. I eventually wrote, but nothing emerged that satisfied me. The result of my creative effort was abysmal, and I knew why.

Mary. Ever since she had promised from her deathbed to come back to me, I imagined strange possibilities. When I returned from Europe the fear of apparitions rattled me nightly. I could feel her. I sometimes thought I could smell her. I felt certain that I could hear the trails of her garments whisper across the floor. I was immobilized by these experiences, and, frankly, unnerved.

I couldn't understand why this scared me. Did I not ache for her presence? Guilt seized me. I could not think. I could not write. I heard her trailing garments again, and this time I swear I felt her breath. I shuddered as I called out. "Mary?"

There was no answer. I crossed to the fireplace and added wood. I fixed the screen. I noticed her steamer trunk. I hadn't shipped it to her family and that was something I must do. What was I waiting for? I stood over it, stared at it, and wondered if these hauntings would ever end. I felt ashamed for wanting them to end, but also scared. I knelt and undid the latch. The trunk creaked open. I lowered my open palms as if dipping them into an Elysian pool and closed my eyes. I pressed deep into the garments. I lifted a dress and pressed it to my cheek. I stood and took the garment with me. I spread it out on the half of the bed that I thought she would prefer. It wasn't clear in the flickering firelight but it was either her light blue or her pale gray dress. Both had buttons all the way up the front, as this one did. It didn't matter; she liked them both and was beautiful in either. I spread it out as perfectly as I could and lay down beside it. I rested my face sideways onto a pillow and faced the dress. I crossed an arm over the waist, curled my fingers over the soft brocade, and closed my eyes.

The carriage ride was not your fault.

My eyes opened and I froze.

None of us understood how ill I was.

"Mary?" My voice trembled now.

I listened for more but heard only the crackling fire. I blamed myself for not waiting for the steamer. Why had I insisted on renting the Russian carriage? That's what had killed her—and the baby.

Stop.

I rolled onto my back. The tin ceiling was dappled with fluttering shadows. "Mary, I'm sorry. I'm sorry. Where are you? Are you frightened?"

You are young. You will be fine, Henry.

I rose up. "Mary?"

There was no one there.

I turned back on my side and clutched her dress.

———

The next morning I awoke with a need for fresh air. I dressed and descended the stairs. I decided to skip breakfast, crossed the foyer, and darted outside to disappear down the walk, not wanting to see Felton or anyone. I knew I just wanted to breathe.

It was a beautiful day in May and people were out and flowers were blossoming. I saw blue flowers along the path and wondered what they might say if they had a voice. Would they know secrets? Some flowers appeared vibrant while others looked bowed with grief. Were flowers like hearts?

Maybe I should write about flowers and creation, the stars and the prophets and poets. The nature around me was affecting me, in ways I appreciated. It soothed me somehow. My sorrow was transforming into something like indifference or weariness or surrender. I opened myself to imagine cleansing rains. Is that what a downpour was to a flower? If there were anything virtuous, anything worthy of praise, I wanted to think of it, to know it better. I longed to be full of song—alive and always young, immortal. I didn't want to die. Ever. Mary was dead, but I was not.

I stopped walking and looked around me. I had traveled without any thought of direction or destination. I realized I was on Brattle Street. I knew someone who lived here, an acquaintance. Who was it? McLane? Yes, I think that's right. His house was somewhere nearby. I suddenly wanted to be with someone I knew. I knocked on the door of a large Georgian home that looked familiar.

McLane did not answer the front door, but an older woman in a Revolutionary-era dress and a white turban, did. She looked me over, and none too approvingly judging by the scowl on her wrinkled face. "Yes? What is it? I have no rooms for you."

"Rooms?" I tipped my hat. "No, no. Good day, ma'am. Henry Wadsworth Longfellow calling on Mister McLane."

"Oh." She walked away, leaving the door wide open and retired down the center hall into a room on the left.

I watched her disappear and waited a moment before cautiously stepping inside. "Ma'am?"

"He's in his room. Upstairs," she said unseen.

I slowly approached the archway through which she had passed. She was seated on an ornate sofa surrounded by dainty tables and slim volumes of books stacked two and three high. The fireplace was quiet and the windows were all open. An Elm tree drooped its branches close to one window, and something like three or four canker worms were lowering themselves onto the sill.

She picked up a book from the side table, and I noticed that she owned a copy of *Outre Mer*. It was resting on the same table. I smiled. The small publisher had managed to circulate it to some extent and it always felt pleasant when I discovered it in the possession of someone other than myself. "I see you have a copy of *Outre Mer*."

She looked up, as though startled to see me. "Oh!" She frowned. "Yes. Enjoyable to read. Some sparks in it." She squinted as she peered into the other book in her hands. "I swear the world is dimmer than it used to be." She crossed to the open window where the Elm tree grew and sat on a window seat next to the sill. She faced inward so the sunlight illuminated her pages. "Now that's better."

"Ma'am?" I cleared my throat.

The woman rolled her eyes and peered over the top of her book.

"Whom do I have the pleasure of addressing?" I asked, as I noticed a canker worm dangling several inches above her turban.

"Mrs. Andrew Craigie, if you must persist." She did not lower her book. Her eyes returned to the page. "But you may call me an old widow who lives in a shoe—or Elizabeth."

I smiled. I liked her spirit. "And a nice shoe it is!"

"Without rooms to let, I'll mention again," she barked.

"I understand. It's just that I've never been inside of your home before and I'm not sure which room to find Mr. McLane in."

"Upstairs." The canker worm dropped to the top of her turban and settled there. Another one was lowering toward the same end.

"Ma'am," I wanted to knock them off but moved only one step. "Mrs. Craigie."

She looked up with narrower eyes. "What now?"

"I'm sorry to point this out, but apparently, this is such a nice shoe, that even the canker worms are seeking rooms."

Elizabeth Craigie dismissed my comment with a shrug and returned to her book.

"Ma'am. They have located themselves upon your turban." I pointed with my cane.

Elizabeth Craigie lowered her book, lowered her chin, and raised her eyebrows. "Young man, is it your intention to persist in interrupting my reading?"

I lowered the cane. "The canker worms are traversing your head."

"If this was troubling to me, might I do something about it?"

"Ma'am?"

"Young man. They are our fellow-worms and have every right to live, as do we. Now leave them alone."

I found it difficult to look her in the eye. I was trying hard to keep my mirth in check. My eyes darted around the room but finally landed on the spine of the volume in her hands. "Yes, ma'am, upstairs and to the right. Thank you." I bowed slightly and left the room but not before hearing indistinguishable mumbles behind her raised copy of Voltaire. The lady had interesting taste.

I climbed to the upstairs hallway. There were closed doors on both sides, four doors in total. I walked past the rear stairs and knocked.

There was no answer.

I retraced my path and almost knocked on the southeast door when something like a bird chirped in the room opposite. I leaned nearer the sound. It was a magnificently played flute.

"Bravo! Nicely done!" a voice sounded from within. It was McLane.

The door opened and out he walked dressed in long tails, a top hat and cane, white gloves, and an astonished face that quickly transformed into a wide smile. "Longfellow! What are you doing here?" He vigorously shook my hand. Behind him stood a disinterested tall man with a flute in his mouth.

"I was about the town and happened upon your street." I nodded to the man with the instrument but he did not acknowledge me.

"Good of you to visit. Unfortunately, I'm on my way to call on a certain fashionable lady." The tall man approached, but only to close the door on us. "Why don't you accompany me as far as her house?" McLane asked as he headed toward the front steps. Suddenly he spun around. "Wait, as long as you're here you should see my rooms."

"Thank you. I met—"

"Yes! She's an oddity, hey?" He crossed to his front room and opened the door. "Take a look. I love it, really. Too bad I'm abroad this fall or I'd stay forever."

I followed him inside and liked the room very much. Two tall windows faced the front, and the Charles River was visible over the meadow. Two more windows faced the east side overlooking a vast yard with a broad garden in the rear. I surveyed the paintings adorning the walls, the half-empty bookshelves, and the well-appointed Victorian furniture.

"It is quite the study I enjoy here," McLane said. "Come see." He crossed to one of the two doors on either side of the fireplace on the north side of the room. He opened it and waltzed into the rear room with one arm extended. "A very comfortable bed and fine cherry furniture. George Washington slept here! No pun!"

"President George Washington?"

"General! Craigie House was his headquarters at one point. These two rooms were his."

I saw the rear garden just beyond the eastern windows and the barn through the back windows. I envied the space. "You say you are going abroad?"

"In the fall!" McLane strode over and gently tapped my breast with the head of his cane. "Do I see a calculation underway?"

"Are there many other boarders? Are you required to share meals?"

"Not at all on either account. Habersham—he's the one who was playing the tune—lives in the room across the hall, and he is the only other tenant. There's a farmer and his wife who live below in back, and she'll deliver meals to your room whenever you want for a separate charge."

"That's preferable."

"A little steep on her charges, but then you don't always have to eat, do you?" McLane tapped me again. "I must be off, friend. Walk as far as you can with me." He hurried into the hallway and I followed as he pulled the door shut. "You don't even need to lock anything here. It's all safe."

I followed after him. "McLane?" I whispered.

He stopped on the landing and turned his ear. "Yes?"

"You think she'd consider letting your space to me?"

"Don't see why not. One way to know." He cocked his head toward the front parlor while checking his pocket watch. "Look, I really must hurry, though. Good luck!" McLane leapt the last two steps, flung a departing remark to Mrs. Craigie, and banged the front door shut as he left.

"No slamming doors!" Mrs. Craigie boomed from her reading perch.

I slipped into the doorway, holding my hat at my waist, and cleared my throat.

Her eyes rose from Voltaire. "You again?"

"McLane tells me he will be vacating at the end of summer. I was wondering—"

She lowered the book. The canker worms remained on her turban but in new places and numbering four. "I already told you I have no rooms to let. Besides, I am of a mind to no longer rent to students. With their rapid comings and goings at all hours and the noises they create, it is more than this aged soul can bear."

"I am no student," I said, promptly dropping my cane which made a terrible clatter. Stooping to pick it up, I dropped my hat. I scooped them both up and stood quickly. My face was hot. "Professor Longfellow at your service, ma'am."

She eyed me head to toe. "Professor? Of what?"

"Modern languages at Harvard," I said.

I found it hard not to look at the canker worms. One of them was moving itself close to her ear. "You appear very young to be a professor. And your gloves!"

I glanced at my gloves. I had worn the lavender. "My gloves?"

"A shade too light for a virtuous man." There was no hint of humor in her tone. The canker worm reached her shoulder.

"I assure you, ma'am," I cleared my throat and tried to look her in the eye. "There is a worm on your shoulder."

She glanced down but couldn't see it. Without any alarm, she felt for it and gently curled the worm onto her palm. She examined it, turning it over. "Amazing, aren't they?" She offered a polite smile. "We're all God's creatures." She stood and placed the worm on the sill while the others decorated her turban with small streaks of black. "Are you a virtuous man?"

I nodded rapidly. "I can assure you that there is no danger of my importing any corruption into your home."

Mrs. Craigie crossed near the middle of the room, Voltaire in her hand, and distrust in her eyes. "And how does an old widow come to trust the words of someone she does not know? Will Mister McLane vouch for you? And are you so certain that would impress me?" She set Voltaire on the center table next to my own slim volume.

I smiled. "Whether or not you choose to grant initial favor is a choice you alone must make. But I do submit that you are not so unfamiliar with me as you might think, and my words not entirely without precedent here. Apparently."

"Speak clearly, young man."

"You already mentioned you enjoyed *Outre Mer*."

"And your point?"

"I am the author of that modest volume, ma'am."

For the first time since I met her, she appeared genuinely surprised and then as another first, genuinely delighted. She picked up the book and read my name on the spine. "Longfellow." She lit up like some kind of torch and snapped as loudly. "An author and a professor? That is something of a different kind to consider." She set the book down and approached. "Are you writing anything else?"

"Perhaps I may write from within these very walls, if you would consider it." I found myself bowing again, this time to her obvious pleasure.

She held out her hand. "Help me up the stairs and I'll show you the rooms of my home. My dear departed left me no choice but to rent a room or two to keep it going. George Washington once dwelt here, I'll have you know. Do you know the story?"

I took her hand and helped her, and her passenger worms, to the stairs. "Please tell me."

She told me more history than I was prepared to hear, but it was true that the house had stories to tell. She took me to every room except those rented by McLane and Habersham, explaining each time, "But this room you cannot rent." Finally, after having gone back downstairs and touring the remainder of the large Georgian home, she again requested my assistance upstairs and we entered McLane's rooms. "These two you may have upon his exit and not before."

"Very well," I replied. "I am delighted, and I thank you." We went downstairs and exchanged pleasantries at the door. She followed me to the front porch.

"Consider it done, Mrs. Craigie." I pecked the back of her hand.

"You are a right and proper gentleman, even if your gloves are too light."

I didn't know what to say about this second mention of my gloves. "This fall it shall be only Mr. Habersham and I, old Longfellow, who will be darkening these doors."

"No," she said with a slight bow of her head. A worm fell to the porch. "Habersham goes the way of all piping birds and flees for the ricefields of the South when the cold weather comes. There will be only two of us plus my helpers. You'll meet them when it is time. Good day, Professor Longfellow."

I watched her retire inside and quietly close the door before nudging the worm off the porch with the toe of my boot.

———

With summer's arrival, I began to lecture and found the focus good for my soul. I spoke of Goethe and Richter and cultivated my extemporaneous style by interrupting the readings of the classics with my speculations about poets and artists. All Harvard seniors and some underclass law and divinity students attended. Some thought me flowery and were unafraid to offer honest opinions, as I requested, but most expressed enthusiasm for my colorful style, and particularly appreciated my addressing each of them as Mr. so-and-so and Mr. such-and-such. They assured me that I was much more accessible than other faculty members. But when I read to them in French, German, Danish, or Swedish, and required them to do the same, I heard more groans than praise. I persisted, and translated verse-by-verse, making notes in the margins while I taught. I injected my lectures with stories of my European travels, both the first and second odysseys, and became increasingly popular as an enviable man of the world.

By fall I was fully installed in the gracious rooms at Craigie House, and found my muse to be an artesian well. The haunting memories of losing Mary grew less frequent and of shorter duration while my drafts accumulated. I mostly wrote creatively while sitting before the window facing the winding Charles River, and my poetry blossomed with a rhythm not unlike the pounding of my strengthening heart.

What Longfellow Heard

Brilliant hopes, all woven in gorgeous tissues,
Flaunting gaily in the golden light;
Large desire, with most uncertain issues,
Tender wishes, blossoming at night!

These in flowers and men are more than seeming,
Workings are they of the selfsame powers,
Which the Poet, in no idle dreaming,
Sees in himself and in the flowers.

I knew I was skipping stones across the surface of very deep feelings but beginnings were important. Where it would end was too distant to fret about. What mattered was that it had begun.

Chapter 8

"A HEIGHTENED MIND seeks for a long-sought, unknown somewhat." I paused and let them think about that.

Each and every young man sat blank-faced around the mahogany table in the Harvard room that more resembled a parlor. The usual lecture hall was unavailable and I knew this was where the Harvard Fellows would dine later, but there were many hours between now and then and sufficient time in between to lecture my class. They were as puzzled as I'd hoped.

"I'm speaking of the pursuit of creative discovery or is it creative disorder?" I sank my hands into my vest pockets, my unopened papers neatly stacked before me on the table. "Until discovered, the object of the quest is unknown though the hunger for it is present. And though accidental discoveries do happen, intentional pursuit drives many an artist. It is vague at first. To some types of people affected with such pangs, they are troubled that they are vague and they agonize over where they originated or why they exist at all, but not so with the artist. It is enough that the burden has arrived. It is a lure that compels pursuit. The hunt is on. He doesn't know exactly what it is but trusts he will know it when he finds it. That is, if he is to be an artist with a heightened mind." I let that settle for a moment. "He also must be patient, for it will likely require more time than he first imagined." A bushy-haired, beak-nosed student raised his hand. "Please stand and state your name, sir."

The student looked around nervously and stood. He was of average height and slight of build, but with long arms more fitting to a taller man. His blue eyes grew wide beneath thick brows. The entire effect reminded me of those shoreline rocks that overhang the small caves along the riverbanks. I liked that image. I'd have to remember it. Use it somewhere. "Your surname, please."

"Thoreau, sir. Henry David Thoreau."

"Yes, Mr. Thoreau. What can I do for you?"

"What if you feel certain you know what you're after? Can that not also proceed forth from such a mind?" Thoreau's hands tightened and loosened.

"When I make statements and follow them with a pause"—I motioned the lad to sit—"I do so to invite reflections, not questions. A moment is often the only distance between a question and an idea. That said, yours was an excellent question, Mr. Thoreau."

Thoreau's already noticeable lips formed a troubled pout. His eyes lowered, suggesting an attempt at reflection. "Be quick to listen, slow to speak, gentlemen. Most importantly, between the listening and speaking, you must think."

Thoreau shifted his eyes around the table without turning his head, and I felt a strong desire to soften my rebuke. "You are brave to be the first to risk a question in our assembly and I shall make a positive note of it."

Thoreau blushed slightly and smiled.

"A heightened mind seeks for a long-sought, unknown somewhat." I paused and no one raised a hand. Some appeared distracted by book corners or buttonholes. One apparently found more interest in the journey of a beetle across the carpet, but a few of my students actually appeared to be thinking. Their foreheads were deeply furrowed or their heads cocked or their intense stares aimed firmly at me. "We are professors and students here," I continued, with more eyes returning to me. "We are scholars and literary men." I tapped the table so even the student engrossed with insect life returned his attention to me. "As such, nature has placed within our hearts a love of books and literary pursuits and seclusion. Has it not?"

No one stirred.

"When I ask a question," I smiled broadly, "I'm hoping to see at least one hand raised."

Again, it was Thoreau.

"Yes, Mr. Thoreau?"

"I believe—" the young man began, popping up again from his seat, "that it is nature herself who prompts us so. In the same way she urges the bird to sing or the fox to hunt. But I also think we sometimes have a glimpse of the divine and know quite well what we are searching for."

"Yes, I've known such confidence myself, and I think it good you have it. But here's a fair warning. You may discover it is not so well known to you early on as you might think." His expression told me he doubted my veracity. I tried another approach. "Consider this: if you are disciplined enough to maintain the work required in pursuit of following such impulses you may discover your long pursued somewhat to be *more* and *other* than what you first saw or thought you saw. It is like the difference between a fuzzy shape on the horizon you observe from across an open sea and the actual terrain of a new island once you set foot on it. It will be similar to what you thought you were after—in other words, dry ground, but different ground. It is often more and better and revelatory! And yes, young sir, I do agree that it is part of the very fabric of our divine nature to inspire such quests."

Mr. Thoreau nodded slowly and sat. His stare became distant and peaceful. I felt certain he was visiting some island of his own. Good for him. He was sure to be a satisfying student. Another student, red-haired and massively freckled, blurted, "Maybe it's not so much nature motivating us as it is the long arm of a father with a paddle!"

The class chuckled. I knew patience would be a chief requirement these first classes, but I would have the environment I required. "Let us hope you offer a pun and nothing more. To be here for any reason less than a commitment to shape this world in a form deemed worthy is tragic, to say nothing of foolish." I folded my hands behind my back and walked the perimeter of the table.

"May I take a guess at where you're going, sir?" The redheaded student twisted in his chair. "Might it be duck-duck-goose?" Some chuckled, but only Thoreau appeared frustrated by the quip.

I offered another slight smile but said nothing and continued walking around them. Most of them were around twelve to fifteen years younger than I, and that was a long time. What is patience if it cannot withstand the test of the first few days of lecture?

Fortunately, it took only one complete circle before the young men settled into silence and, hopefully, were at least considering my words. I tried to tighten their focus. "We must consider how the artist feeds the undying lamp of thought. As Mr. Thoreau has wisely pointed out, nature has placed such unction within the hearts of those who come to be known as artists, scholars, and literary men. They are men obsessed. But, and this you must think about carefully, this light of the soul is easily extinguished and thus, the life and craft of the scholar and literary man is wrought with difficulties. Compelled yet resisted. Pulled as well as pushed. Do you think you are man enough to survive it?" I stopped and faced the large window overlooking the campus, my back to the boys. The sky was gray and the campus bathed in a flat light.

"We are all men enough!" the voice of the red-haired student sounded again.

I turned and motioned the youth to stand. "You've yet to properly raise your hand and rise to speak, yet you have spoken enough despite none of us having the advantage of your name. You are. . . ?"

The lad stood. "Joseph David McCurdle, sir."

"Pleased to have you in attendance, Mr. McCurdle." I motioned for him to sit, then returned to stand behind one of the chairs and placed my hands on its upright posts. "Gentlemen, many great men languished in poverty and died with broken hearts despite ingenious achievements. There is much to admire, much to pity, and therefore, much to consider. Do you know of Johnson or Savage who traversed the streets of London with no place to sleep? Have you heard of Otway who starved to death? What do you know of Cowley who howled like a dog to the sound of church music while scurrying up and down the aisles of Chichester Cathedral? Have you considered what was roiling within Goldsmith when he paraded up Fleet Street in a peach-blossom coat and, with one of his heavier volumes, knocked a bookseller flat on top of his skull?" I wanted to leap on the table and twist on my heel. These were gold bars and fistfuls of pearls I offered, and these boys better not be swine. I poked myself in the forehead. "Think men, and inquire of yourselves expecting to find answers, but not too soon! Answers rarely come the moment asked but only eventually, somewhat in step with the half-belief we can muster, or trailing slowly behind in the muddy ruts of the desperation we haul. It's first the blade and then the ear. If you're fortunate maybe you'll one day find corn in that ear." I pushed my waistcoat back with my forearms and sunk my thumbs deep into my side pockets. I aimed my chin high, knowing my nose would otherwise dominate. "Are you doomed to insufferable destinies by the mere fact of your profession? Are you to be forever impoverished and rejected? Shall you each go the way of the bullet to the brain or the descent from the bridge? Will you one day find yourself wandering along the river's edge maddened by your own words?"

The boys were quite astonished if their wide-open countenances were any gauge. Only the one named Thoreau had something re-sembling a smile. Everyone else looked aghast. One actually rubbed his scrappy beard with the side of his fist while frowning and shifting side to side, as though a spring might have worked up through the padded chair to poke his backside. I laughed and leaned forward with both palms against the cool mahogany tabletop.

"During these lectures we will ponder why these calamities befall artists. You may be surprised at what you find. Many of these tragedies sprang from exaggerated ideas of poetry and the poetic character, from a disdain of common sense, from an aloofness with the world, from viewing society as frivolous and wasteful. Art alone was their king." I straightened and slapped my palms together. "Many a monarch of the mind has been dethroned in bitter isolation by too much ideology."

I resumed a trek around the table. "When such is the sole lifestyle of the artist, he has nothing truly to write about but the vanity of his imagination. He is too little informed, or maybe, too exclusively in-formed." Someone covered a yawn. I clapped again. All heads snapped to attention. "This is nature's law!" I spoke as loud I thought possible without risking drawing inquiries from without. "If the mind, which rules the body, ever forgets itself so far as to trample upon its slave, the body is seldom generous enough to forgive the injury; that slave will rise and smite its oppressor!" I stopped, surprised to find my arms extended. I lowered them and returned to my chair as casually as I could while my heart hammered my chest. I sat down, crossed my legs to the side, and turned toward the young men. "To which you reply. . . ?" I asked.

Even Thoreau seemed stumped, although he showed something like admiration while most of the others appeared confused. I thought of reminding them that Socrates claimed confusion always preceded knowledge, but decided against it. I didn't want to give them any-thing else to think about. I really wanted my spoken words to float around in their brains until they became eventual nourishment for their souls. I waited, using the time to better manage my heaving chest. I had almost resumed normal breathing when McCurdle raised his hand.

"Rise and speak, Mr. McCurdle."

A scarf and pocket square would fit him out nicely, I found myself thinking, especially in light of the brightness of his red hair that drew focus too quickly away from the fine cut of his suit. Suddenly, I realized that I had been so involved with my own wandering thoughts that I had failed to hear most of whatever McCurdle was saying.

"—can't all be geniuses, can we? I think some might be more delicately arranged than others, even comfortable and not so compelled. What say you, sir?" McCurdle sat down.

I wasn't entirely sure what he had been addressing, but I decided to take a stab at it. "I suppose that depends on whether you think genius is a place of departure or an earned destination." I let that sink in where it could, although it appeared to be floating atop most of the heads in the room. "I personally believe it may be a destination available to any and all who dare attempt the climb. But do take care to not idealize everything. That is too narrow a road. Even deformity of vice will gleam under those terms! That is often the mistake that works like blight upon an oak and has ruined many a bright mind. So, pick your peaks wisely."

Another boy raised his hand.

I nodded and motioned for him to stand.

"I am Alfred. Alfred Whitestone," his voice quivered as he rose. He was thin and pale. "Shouldn't an artist be free of such trifling notions of whether or not something is virtue or vice? Is it not enough to be found authentic?" The accompanying murmurs suggested others might be wondering the same.

I grinned and stood. "Well done, Mr. Whitestone." I walked to the window and looked outside. It was all so delightful. The boys were contesting, and well they should. I had baited and they had bitten. Perhaps there may be hope for genuine debate and my lectures may yet transform from traditional, one-sided droning into something more useful. I faced the class and pointed over my shoulder with my thumb. "The world loves a spice of wickedness. Impulse will always be attractive, even if it occasionally goes too far." I returned to my spot at the table and glanced down at my notes and considered referring to them, then dismissed the thought. "I condemn them not! But neither do I seek to imitate those ways. Do you?" I scanned their faces. "Your answer may very well reveal what you consider the purpose of art." I took a slow, deep breath and smiled.

"Gentlemen"—I panned the air with an open palm—"more important is what you determine. For me, I think we should pardon men of genius, particularly in their youth when their passions fly high. It is easy to forget the cruelty of falconry when beholding the dauntless skills of the gallant hawk, but no one can deny the brilliance of the act, though it may, in some ways, exact a high price." I walked to the closed double-doors of the parlor and opened them. I cocked my head pointing them to the exit, while speaking in a softer tone. Nobody moved to leave, so I continued. "The world and society may corrupt us—or—you may disdain the world and isolate yourself and still find substantial ideas which others will admire and exalt, however narrow or dark, or false, they may be." I momentarily froze and wondered if I believed my own words. They flowed so easily, yet was I certain of their reliability? Was this an occupational hazard? I did my best to focus. "Who can harshly judge men being fooled by that which seeks relentlessly to fool them?" My own missteps could certainly disqualify me; I knew that. Perhaps charity would serve me well. I looked at my students and their eager faces gave me confidence.

"Or, you may be a lover of humanity and participate in all of its grandeur—its color and scope and scale—while still finding time to be truly virtuous and worthy of praise. Will you know the library *and* the drawing room—the blank page and the ballroom? Or must it be one or the other?" I crossed to the hutch along one side of the wall, hoping to find a pitcher of water and a glass. I would have to arrange for that before the next lecture. I spun around, my waistcoat whipping about my hips. "One path may bring works of salvation, the other, suffering, but who is to say which it is? If you can choose one and be hailed as ingenious, cannot another man choose the opposite and be equally affirmed?" I smiled. No one moved an inch, and not one set of eyes stared anywhere but at me. "All right, gentlemen, you have your contemplation for the week." I flapped my arms. "Come, come, you are excused. Move out."

As the students passed, many shook my hand and most expressed sincere gratitude, especially Thoreau. I called after them as they moved down the hall. "When you return we shall study this question as it pertains to Goethe, Schiller, Shakespeare, Chaucer, Dante, and others. Be on your toes, gentlemen. The world awaits you!" I closed the doors and strutted around, excited that I may have gotten through to them.

It was important to be dramatic, I knew. Seizing wandering minds is like herding wild beasts. You must anticipate when they want to run like thunder and head them off. You need to position yourself to gather as many as you can.

I walked to the window and stared into the courtyard. I watched as a gardener hammered a stake next to a sapling and tied it fast.

Chapter 9

THE NEAR HALF-MILE WALK to Craigie was too short for the mood I was in, so I continued south on Garden Street past Mason and along the edge of Cambridge Common. I crossed the small park to the street leading to Boston Bridge. It would take more than an hour to reach Beacon Hill, but Felton was a good source and he had claimed the Appletons were back. If in fact it turned out they had not yet returned to America, it could be a long walk, but the Boston Common was there and no doubt others to mingle with, and Ticknor resided only a short journey farther up the street.

The trees were not as saturated as some falls I had known, but they were colorful just the same. Stately Elm and Chestnut trees lined my way. Occasional greetings warranted a tip of my hat or a wave of my cane. I felt like I had the strength and energy to walk for days. I'd written a poem I cared about, sensed others coalescing within me, and my lectures were going well. As I trekked, I imagined further applying my pen to the translation of great works from as many layers of European bedrock as there were colors in the boughs around me. I would find good publishers who could give me velum covers, quality typesets, and sturdy paper every one. The images of what these might look like orbited my head like sparrows around a fountain. My thoughts were twinborn, I decided. They came in literal and figurative pairings. This idea made me smile as I turned onto Beacon Street.

I wanted to write songs, and for the first time in many years I began to feel like I might in fact write of love and faith, beauty, and maybe even the history of my country. I would embolden men and comfort ladies; grant hope to children; and pay homage to those old, forgotten, and gone. And I wouldn't forget the church bells. I enjoyed their ancient sounds. There were other themes, of course, like those of Dante's. I passed a side street and looked ahead, and all of my literary thoughts ceased to be important and I stopped in my tracks. The Appleton house was only a few yards ahead.

"Are you all right?" A lady's voice called from behind me.

Startled, I tripped on the toe of my boot, dropped my bundle of books, cracked my cane, and would have fallen if not for the wildly lucky hold I managed upon the iron railing of a Beacon street residence. "What?" I had wrenched my back and stood with it pressed against the wrought iron spears of the fence, each hand tightly gripping a post. My cane and books lay at my feet. I couldn't believe Fanny Appleton stood before me in a dress of muted green velvet, decorated in lace, and comfortably shadowed by her twirling parasol. Her dark locks sprang out from the edges of her loosely worn bonnet, framing her beautiful face. Her perfectly straight teeth formed a full smile, and her dark eyes shone with merriment. Her sister was muffling giggles and had to turn away for a moment.

I forced myself to release the fence and coughed into my glove. "Hello, dear ladies! Pardon me." I stooped to retrieve my things, but a pain traveled diagonally across my back, causing my eyes to water. I grabbed my cane and stood.

"May I help you?" Fanny asked, looking concerned.

"No! NO! You needn't be troubled." I squatted in a fashion less hurtful and fumbled with the books until I was able to rise with an untidy stack under my arm. When I regained some semblance of composure, I said, "How do you do, ladies? It's—" I leaned slightly onto my cane but the cracked end gave way and I fell against Fanny. I quickly righted myself, mumbled an apology, and lifted the cane to display the disfigured end.

"Oh, I'm so sorry about your walking stick," Fanny said. "And it was such a fine one."

"Thank you. Yes, it was." I shrugged. "Oh well." Her skin was perfect. Flawless. My mouth was open but no words came to me. I managed to close it but hated the sigh that escaped.

"What brings you to Beacon Hill?" Mary asked, with a charming smile.

"I—I was lecturing at the—I was strolling to reflect on—I—I often take long walks—often." My mouth felt completely dry. I shook my head like a wet dog. Good God, this was horrid. "Helps me think. Walking." I cleared my throat.

Fanny eyed me head to toe as if estimating the damage, and then smiled warmly. "It is nice to see you again, Professor. We have only just returned from Europe, did you know?"

I shook my head. "Yes." I corrected myself with a frantic nod. "No. I suspected you might be returning soon and hoped you would. What a pleasant surprise—this is."

"Well, success to you and your strolls, Professor Longfellow," Fanny said and walked ahead. "Come along, Mary, we mustn't keep the professor from his reflections."

Mary smiled sweetly and pointed to a house several doors up. "We're only steps away at number thirty-nine. Do come visit us some-day, should your walks return you here."

"Mary?" Fanny called from a few feet away.

I watched Mary hurry to catch Fanny, and the two of them strolled like two countesses down a palace aisle, their large puffy dresses swaying like twin church bells made of cloud. I wanted to rush after them and say that this was as perfect a time as any to visit but could not imagine any way to do it with dignity. Ha! Dignity. What in heaven and earth did I know of that?

I would have watched them until they disappeared through the large front doors of their grand brick home, but I had enough wits left at least to know I shouldn't get caught staring after them. I sighed and tapped the head of my cane against my head, hoping to conjure more sense. I hugged the books that were beginning to slide out of my grip, stepped forward, and set my cane down, forgetting the recent shortcoming.

A falling man in a suit with an armload of books and a broken staff might make a softer or louder sound than one might think but certainly enough of a racket to be dreaded by the man himself.

Lying in a crumpled mess, across the pavement, I didn't even try to look up or move. I only prayed that the ladies had simply entered their house and missed my fall from grace. It was a simple matter and one that I considered a reasonable request deserving of being granted by our Redeemer at least this once.

I struggled to a kneeling position. My back ached worse than ever. I was pretty sure my right trouser leg was sticking to my knee because of blood. I gathered my battered books—I hated it when the pages were bent—and stood with difficulty, but without looking back. I needed to tuck and pull, arrange, and shift but I was willing to neglect all of that in exchange for a fast exit from Beacon Hill.

"Professor Longfellow! Are you all right?" a voice asked.

Oh God. It was Fanny.

"Are you hurt, sir?" her voice was urgent and caring.

I stopped. They had witnessed my circus, but I couldn't be made more pitiful. "Oh, no, no. Just fine." I turned and waved and nodded while surreptitiously pushing my cane under the iron fence with my toe. I would not be betrayed again!

"Do be careful, Professor!" This time it was Mary.

"And don't forget your cane, Professor!" Fanny called. "The Hildegard's will be loathe to find it there."

With as pleasant a countenance as I could manage, I backtracked, opened the gate, recovered the cane, regained the sidewalk, and closed the gate. I lifted my broken cane in a kind of salute, and—*blast-it-all*—limped home.

Chapter 10

"IT'S NOT THE WANT OF QUESTS for reform that befuddles me," Charles Sumner continued, but not about literature, history, or law. He had been bellowing in a most wandering fashion for over an hour and sounded nowhere near finished. "It's more a question of how and why. Consider if you will that there is a certain wisdom and inevitability to class distinctions."

"I object!" Corny shouted as his teeth tore into a lemon pastry. The fare was rich and plentiful at Henry Cleveland's stately home at Pine Bank where this session with the Five of Clubs was happening. His society wife did much to raise the standards of our gathering, and we held no complaints about that.

"Hold your tongue! I'm not finished," Charles insisted. "Consider this: Scripture states we will always have the poor among us, and I understand it remains our duty to not neglect such stark realities. I am not suggesting we do such an injustice. I am merely saying—"

"You are preparing to justify paternalism because you are a certain type of Whig!" Even with cheeks full, Corny's smile was unmistakable.

Charles raised both palms to the man several inches his junior and, with eyes closed, exhaled slowly as if he were counting to ten. "Nevertheless, Cornelius"—his eyes opened—"you can't disagree with the idea of a wise parent who knows better than the child. There are some of us with greater education and experience that are better qualified to manage the public dole. That's all I'm saying. If we do it

109

selflessly, it is, of course, the safest way."

Corny reached for a triple layered tart and licked the cream topping. "Ha! Selflessly! As a professor of ancient history let me tell you there is no such thing as selfless aristocracy!" He wiped the corner of his mouth and adopted his professorial air while rising to his toes for an instant; I'm certain he was quite unaware of this mannerism. "However, I thank you for recognizing my superior education, Charles." He lowered to his usual height and examined the tart, as if considering how best to devour it. "As one of your superior patrons, I move we redirect the economic in the direction of those whose welfare is presently burdened by forces beyond their influence." He plunged the tart into his mouth in a manner beyond the usual social graces.

Charles pointed at the smirking Greek professor while addressing the rest of us gathered around the fire. "Did you ever hear anything more Jacksonian than that? Of what 'plenty' does he refer? These are difficult times. And he numbers himself among the enlightened of New England? Gentlemen, how can you remain silent?"

I'm confident my friendly smile was obvious though George Hillard seemed indifferent as if waiting to hear something he hadn't heard before. Henry Cleveland rolled his eyes at me and then stood up with a smile. "What say we move to critiquing recent articles, hey?" He crossed to the decanter behind the sofa. "Anyone ready for a fill?"

"I am." I patted Charles on his shoulder as I crossed the room. "I thought you said you had no use for politics, Charles."

"I loathe politics and politicians more. I am not intending to sound political—"

"Yet you call me a Jacksonian Democrat!" Felton beat me to the decanter.

"Only after you called me a certain type, as if odd!"

"Well, aren't you?"

"Well, aren't you?"

"I am Whig enough, but more a Greek professor with a taste for something strawberry and a thirst for something dry!" Henry Cleveland filled our glasses. George arrived in time to receive the same.

Charles stood like a lost child in the middle of the room. We raised our glasses to him and waited. He finally surrendered with a weak laugh. He lowered his head and shook it like a dog emerging from a pond. He looked up, his face red but grinning. "I get carried away. You're right." He found his glass, still full since he had spent his time talking, and raised it. "We can at least agree with those who advocate antislavery principles, can we not?"

"We can," I said, knowing full well there remained nuances of dissension in those discourses as well. We tasted our wine and it was quickly evident that we were all glad for a return to activity more social than somber. Not so evident to us at that moment, as it may have been to Charles, was that Boston and New England were birthing a mix of reform-minded men and women. The combination of increasing industrialization and rapid expansion with the current economic slow-down was producing strains throughout all territories. As the five of us crossed to the library in the adjacent room, I thought about none of that, and wondered if we might get to critique a recent article of mine, but Charles wasn't finished.

"I've subscribed to William Garrison's new publication. Have any of you?"

We took our usual seats around the large oak table. I crossed to my bag and pulled out the recent issue of the *North American Review*, as did Felton, Hillard, and Cleveland.

Charles produced a copy of *The Liberator*. "This is a well thought-out response to all those disgusting anti-abolition mobs that have tried to gain a foothold in recent years. There are some considerable persons rising up. Have you heard of Wendell Phillips or—"

"Charles," Hillard said. "I know him and think him a fine man, and I share much of your enthusiasm, only not this night. What say we consider one of Longfellow's recent articles in *The Review*? As a matter of fact, you have one in this issue as well, don't you? A rather scholarly consideration of historical law?"

Charles was a tower of silence. I thought he might be feeling hurt. "Go right ahead, Charles," I offered. "Share what you intended."

"No, no," he said as he sat down. "George is right. Let us move to those things we truly enjoy and cease this other nonsense."

And with that the night moved in accordance with our usual way. We shared and quipped about things literary and philosophical, amusing and inspiring. We praised and critiqued and sought to better each other's prose and ideas, and it was as tastefully satisfying as the expensive port and exotic cigars Cleveland served next.

In between the gabs and the stabs and the pokes and the smokes, I considered my tall acquaintance of this past year, little knowing then what manner of friend Charles Sumner would become.

I had first met him as I did the others, through Cornelius. Henry Cleveland was a proctor at the college, and George Hillard and Sumner were law partners despite Sumner's heart not being in it. He lectured on law whenever the elder Judge Story, who had since become a Supreme Court Justice, was absent. In truth, Charles Sumner usually spoke with much more enthusiasm about history and literature when in social settings. Had I known this night was not an aberration but a show of things to come I would have shuddered.

At twenty-six years old, Charles stood six-foot-two and was crowned with a gaggle of dark hair. He was already prone to passionate diatribes; he truly was an accomplished student of literature, language, and history; but he was socially awkward and unsure of which direction he should aim. He was four years my junior and a graduate of Harvard. He was heavily influenced by his strict father, the sheriff of Suffolk County, who had ingrained his fertile mind with strong sympathies about humanitarian causes including the reformation of prison conditions, assisting fugitive slaves escaping to the north, educational reform, and the desegregation of Boston schools. He stoically embraced those ideals and I could fault him for none of it. He had spoken to me about whether the legal profession was truly his path. He claimed to love literature as much as I, and I thought him quite sincere. He was certainly up to it and was no slouch in bright or witty conversation. But there was much in his life that pushed him into roles assumed for him. Rumor had it that Judge Story, a former Harvard roommate of his father's, had been whispering into Charles' ear about the possibility of the chair of the law school, should Charles continue to tread wisely. Maybe that contributed to the reasoning behind what my tall friend announced at the end of the evening. None of us had seen it coming.

With all of the cigars smoldering and no one desiring another drop of wine, Charles motioned for our collective attention. "No, no!" Corny jokingly pleaded. "We are each becoming abolitionist-friendly, at least this night. I promise. Please, no more harping!"

I was afraid Charles would immediately move to defend his earlier statements but, fortunately, he did not. "No." I remember admiring a deeper part to this man than the blunderbuss. "There is a matter I must inform you about," he said simply. "I am going away."

Charles explained he would be leaving for Europe in two weeks. He would pursue an opportunity similar to the one afforded me, except his would be in service to his legal career. We were all cut to the heart. He was a presence in our small group and his absence would be felt. We were happy for him and wished him well. We begged a delayed departure until after Christmas, but his plans, much like his other convictions, were steadfast. As friends, we insisted he would depart with no short supply of letters of introduction in hand. The group finally disbanded from Cleveland's home, little knowing we would not gather again for over three more years, and under very different circumstances.

Chapter 11

DESPITE THE CONVICTIONS of my European-bound friend, life was not actually black and white, although such perceptions could be understood. The nation was grumbling and stumbling and economically strained. Tensions and complexities were springing up like wildfires on the plains, yet there remained a sense of new beginnings. It was as if we were all children learning how to run after having at last walked independently. Many of us saw the growing pangs as temporary and felt only sporadic conviction about sacrificing our freshly acquired conveniences and comforts to some greater purpose. Though calls for reformation had begun, they remained vague. Learning and acquiring, as well as improving our national identity in every field of endeavor while simultaneously pursuing personal happiness was the prevailing spirit of New England.

Life was full of colors though most of us traveled along one or two shades at a time. That's exactly where I was during that season of early widowhood and burgeoning scholarly achievement, and it was in this current that I arose, clean-shaven and well dressed, standing in the foyer, tipping my hat to Mrs. Craigie.

She was engrossed in her reading and never noticed the bouquet in my hand or the rolled paper tied with purple ribbon jutting from my hip pocket. Undaunted, I stepped into that cold December day in 1837 with a bosom that radiated so much warmth that I was certain if the feeling could be converted to fuel I could heat most of Cambridge. I strode down the front walk and whistled something I had heard at a concert the night before. I felt completely in step with my world. I was current with my obligations at Harvard. The Five of Clubs was on hold. Social activities comprised a sufficient number of days on my calendar, and my muse was alive with promises of more poems to come.

A particular fascination had developed. I had encountered Fanny a few times since the cane fiasco and enjoyed our subsequent social discourses, despite their brevity. However, it was always in a great mixture of company that she appeared, unaware of my intentions, if not aloof. It felt acceptable to me to pick up the tempo a bit, lengthen my strides, so to speak.

With a recently completed poem about autumn tucked into my pocket and my hand holding a small container of paper whites that the florist had forced into bloom, I hoped I had devised something of an infallible strategy. I walked along, breathing deeply and enjoying the encompassing fragrance of the small flowers and recalling the letter I had sent her, an artillery of sorts, to soften things in preparation for whatever fate might allow.

My dear Madonna Francesca,

I send you the volume of German romance containing Jean Paul, which I intended to bring before; but have been occupied and could not get into town. I am almost sorry that your acquaintance with Jean Paul, the magnificent painter of spring and blossoms, should begin in these minor works, where the genius of the poet has not elbow room. However, perhaps you will be encouraged by glimpses here and there of his grand style of art to persevere in reading him, even unto his biggest novel, Titan. I have enclosed others and wish these scraps of antiquated song might please you.

Did you ever read Tennyson's poems? He too is quaint, and at times so wondrously beautiful in his expressions that even the nicest ear can ask no richer melody.

I saw you some nights ago from a distance at the play. I tried but could not reach you. Did not the cold night air chill you as it did many others?

I intend to call on you soon and with it bring a new composition, which, despite it now being winter, has been in construction for many weeks, celebrating as it does the autumn of the year in which you and your family had first returned home.

> *Most sincerely yours,*
> *H. W. Longfellow*

P.S. Do you plan to attend the Emerson lecture coming up at the Masonic Temple?

The walk toward Boston Common and Beacon Street was long enough in warm weather, and though my heart radiated with the warmth of kindling affection, my bones notified me of a colder state, but chilly or not I would prevail. Then again, a circuitous route might afford some elements of incidental conversation with various persons of note which could be entertaining in the retelling, though none would be so entertaining as she. There was no saying whom I might run into and there was no need to hurry.

Fashioning some manner of ritual seemed as pleasurable to me as savoring an appetizer like oysters and cream. If I managed patience, I might possibly enjoy the anticipation of seeing Fanny while not only filling my lungs with the freshness of cool air, but also my head with ideas and my heart with inspiration. By the time I reached her dwelling I might possibly be bursting with news, gossip, and maybe a verse or two of a new poem. The afternoon air glanced my face. I lifted my chin and imagined a playful taunt to the weather.

Hold your tongue and your thunder, control your bladder and your blasts, and let me be a spirit gliding through the cool nip of the hour.

I loved it when my muse was naked of inhibitions and carried no thought about where a verse might one day fit. I was glad, too, for the chill, because without it there would be no occasion for the scarf or the gloves or the topcoat. The coolness granted me an opportunity to add a dash of color to the world. I felt happy. Satisfied.

It may have been that I was more like a caterpillar, cozy and warm in its cocoon, while the nation prepared to explode into storm and tempest. Yet even from the vantage of an aged oak, it is difficult to tell. Is it *permissible* to be in pursuit of love and joy despite torments all around? Is there a balance one may strike, even a need for counterbalance to the ills and sorrows of one's world, or is it denial?

Either way, I was not to be deterred by such questions as I strutted forth that day. I did know I would have new student papers to grade. There would come boomeranging perplexities and doubts concerning my craft and pen, and there would be unpredictable occurrences in the life and health of friends and family and foes. Many real labors and toils remained, and someday, hopefully in the far-off distance, I would be required to surrender the spirit. I was also aware that I was little published but sensed there was happiness nearby. Life did have its delicacies, and though they might be small in size, they were rich. I considered it a strong possibility that I might find Fanny Appleton at home and that she would be delighted to see me.

As I passed Faneuil Hall, I was distracted by loud voices from inside. There was something about the ruckus that drew me close. I cracked one of the large oak doors and looked in. The place was mobbed, and I saw George Hillard at the dais.

Dressed in a fine, dark suit, Hillard appeared aghast, so unlike the last time I had seen him at Cleveland's. He waved both his arms but the crowd was not settling down. Behind him stood Dr. Channing, a clergyman I quite liked and who was an old schoolmate of my father's, and beside him, the honorable Judge Hallett. Each of them waved for the crowd to settle enough to permit a voice. Finally George could be heard.

"You know we were granted this meeting by the mayor and aldermen due to the very large number of names on the petition to do so. Everyone whose name is on that list is here, but there are others of you who it seems have come with no other purpose than to protest. Why would you shout against your own interests? We are here to protect the freedom of the press and of speech, and that is the sole purpose of the resolutions Dr. Channing has uttered. Nothing less. Nothing more!"

"Lovejoy got what he deserved!" someone from the crowd shouted.

"He deserved worse!" shouted another, to the delight of those who echoed in agreement.

I was confused. I knew the name Lovejoy from the papers. He had been a publisher and an anti-slavery advocate who was killed by a mob a few states over. But what did that have to do with this current unrest in Boston? Equally surprising, a group of ten or more ladies stood nearby. That was not a usual sight at a public meeting at Faneuil. I recognized Mrs. Chapman and closer, separated from me by only a few others, Miss Sara Southwick. "Sara!" I shouted.

She turned. "Henry!" She lifted on her toes to better see me. "Can you believe these sentiments?"

"Excuse me. Excuse me please." I pressed to reach her, protected the flowers, and felt to be sure the scroll was safely tucked. "I don't follow. I've just arrived." Her eyes were puffy and her face flushed. I felt embarrassed by the Paper Whites in my hand, but she didn't seem to notice.

"Such ill-concealed impatience! But thank God for Dr. Channing and George Hillard."

"What's all of this about?"

She opened her mouth to reply but a sudden eruption of cheers drowned her out. I saw a man crossing the platform to center stage. It was James Austin, the attorney general of the commonwealth. Hillard and the judge made room.

"I desire to speak, Dr. Channing." Austin spoke loud enough for all to hear.

The crowd shouted its approval. A smiling Dr. Channing patted Austin on the shoulder, shook his hand, and stepped back.

"You know me as an attendant of your church services." Austin continued to speak loud enough for all to hear but directed his words to Dr. Channing. "In that setting, I consider you a most able purveyor of inspiration for the masses with wisdom from the Holy Writ. But on this matter, Dr. Channing, a matter of debate in the public assembly, you are marvelously out of place."

The smile fell from Channing's face.

"A clergyman should wield no gun in his hand, as you are doing now by calling for laws and appeals!"

Sprinkled among the crowd were rowdies who agreed with fists in the air.

Turning to the crowd, Austin stepped away from the lectern. "To regard the Alton, Illinois, shooting and killing of Reverend E.P. Lovejoy as a 'murder by a mob' and then to defend the actions of Lovejoy as one who would 'defend the liberty of the press' is an outrage!"

The angry members of the crowd intensified. "Send the preacher home!" someone cried. "This is no business of the clergy!" shouted another. "Lovejoy was a traitor!" came a voice from the front.

I suddenly recalled the details. Lovejoy and his supporters were overrun by an angry mob in Illinois that killed him and burned the building that housed his printing press to the ground with all of them inside.

A few ladies near me began crying into their hankies, except for

Mrs. Chapman, whose face tightened with defiance. The room was becoming uncomfortably warm, and I glanced at the flowers.

"Yes!" Austin continued. "Lovejoy was a traitor, but worse than that—he was a fool, and he died as the fool dies!" Many in the crowd roared their approval. "He chose to publish stories about the Southern slaves as though they were like you and I. We know they are *not!* At best, they are wild beasts!"

The crowd became frenzied and pressed in tight around us. It was getting harder to breathe or move. Bodies glanced the flowers, pushed against the petals, and crushed the perfect curl of the scrolled poem in my pocket. "Please! Give us some room," I said. I noticed Hillard, the judge, and Channing standing motionless on the dais, seemingly in shock from Austin's words.

"I tell you," Austin paraded as he spoke. "Lovejoy was a criminal, and the men who killed him were no different than the orderly righteous mob that once threw tea into the bay in 1773! You know *that* story!"

Many laughed and applauded with great excitement. I was repulsed by the comparison and by the odors of some of those around us: a vile combination of stale tobacco, whiskey, and a need for a bath. My stomach twisted and the last thing I wanted was to get sick in such tight quarters, but this was worse than a rollicking sea.

Austin waved his arms. "Listen! LISTEN! A man has a right to do as he wishes with his own property, and slaves are the property of their owners. Those who murdered him did this nation a great service!"

The cheers sounded through the hall again.

"The principles that Channing and his associates wish to pass here this day are a travesty to justice! What do they mean by 'freedom of the press' or 'freedom of speech'? What about freedom to obey the laws? That's what I want to know! Did not Lovejoy break the laws of common sense? Was the British Crown tax the 'right' of England to use against us? Would we stand for that? NO! Dare we stand for any who demand the right to tell a man what to do with his own property? NEVER!"

I surveyed the jostling crowd. The tyranny of public opinion was having its way.

"I will not cast my vote in favor of the resolutions presented by Dr. Channing." Austin returned to the lectern and pummeled it with his fist. "I should sink into insignificance if I dared to agree with the principles of such ill-guided resolutions! Lovejoy was impudent to publish such provocations on an unwilling community and died as he should have known he might!"

If Sara had not fallen against me, I would not have known she'd fainted; such was the distraction as the unbridled denunciations of Lovejoy filled the hall. To my ears it sounded like thousands of thunderous hooves. But she did fall into my arms—and my flowers. She was difficult to hold up. I struggled, and we both might have toppled over had the crowd packed around us not been so dense. Happily she regained consciousness and partially assisted in her own recovery, and together, we resumed an upright position in the crowd. The flowers were flattened, however. I maneuvered us to a corner where there were fewer people and a source of outside air.

"It is lost," she said, close to my ear. "The resolutions will be voted down."

These tensions over slavery were forming fissures in the nation. It was dangerous, I knew, and it saddened me. Where might this lead, and why were men so adamantly opposed to the freedom of other men?

"I hope I shall be permitted to express my surprise at the sentiments of the last speaker—" A different voice, a strong and commanding voice, arose from the dais.

I looked up. "Who is that?"

"I don't know," Sara said. "I've never seen him before."

A young, smooth-complexioned man in his twenties stood beside the scoffing Austin who exited the dais. The new speaker faced the boisterous crowd. "I am surprised not only at such sentiments from such a man, but at the applause they have received."

"Sit down!" someone shouted.

"Let him speak," another called out.

The crowd quieted, and the young man continued. "Comparisons have been drawn between the events of the Revolution and the trage- dy at Alton; between Great Britain taxing the Colonies and Lovejoy's printing of papers denouncing the horrors of slavery; and between the drunken, murderous mob at Alton and those patriot fathers who threw a money-generating commodity of crumbled leaves overboard! Are these comparisons accurate? Appropriate?"

Great applause sounded.

"Is this Faneuil doctrine?" he asked.

Some yelled, "NO!"

"Indeed not!" The young man answered his own question. "The mob at Alton met to wrest from a citizen his just rights. We have been told that our forefathers did the same." He paused with the dramatic timing of a true orator. "But is this true? or is the glorious mantle of Revolutionary precedent being thrown over the shoulders of a murderous mob?"

"He's right!" someone shouted, and others joined in or jeered.

"Let us recall our history with some accuracy. Did the British Parliament have the right to tax these colonies? If they did, then we may draw such a parallel, but if they did not, then this parallel is false." He again paused for effect. "And false it is, since Lovejoy was stationed within constitutional bulwarks. He was not only defending the freedom of the press, but he was under his own roof, and sanc- tioned by proper local authorities. The mob that assailed him ignored the laws. The brave men who threw the tea overboard were resisting illegal exactions, not the law! The stamp act was not a law. Our state archives are loaded with the arguments of John Adams that proved the taxes laid by the British were unconstitutional and beyond its reach of power!"

The crowd roared with approval. The young man raised his hands for quiet.

"Not until all of this had been properly examined did the men of New England rush to arms. To now draw parallels between the conduct of our ancestors and those of a lawless mob is an insult to their memory!" With that statement part of the crowd became unruly, but he again quieted them with outstretched hands. "The patriots acted upon their rights as secured by the laws, whereas the murderers of Mr. Lovejoy and his friends disregarded the law and decided they *were* the law."

The impressive man stepped out from behind the lectern and moved to the front edge of the dais, his carriage tall and firm. I was impressed by his calm and considered it a chief reason why no one rushed to overpower him. Quiet tones can weaken storms.

"Gentlemen, when I heard the attorney general lay down principles which place the Lovejoy's murderers alongside patriots like Hancock, Quincy, and Adams, I thought the portraits you see lining these walls would have rebuked him as a slanderer of the dead! For the sentiments he uttered on soil consecrated by the Puritans and the blood of our patriots, the earth should have swallowed him up!"

The crowd broke into chaos. I was certain fisticuffs were near and wondered, not for the first time, if I should get Sara to safety.

"Let him speak!" Mrs. Chapman shouted as loud as any man. "Let Mr. Phillips speak!"

Phillips? I didn't recognize the name any more than the face.

"Wendell has the right to speak!" Mrs. Chapman shouted.

The battle of shouts and threats simmered, and Wendell Phillips continued.

I was impressed with both Mrs. Chapman's authority over the

crowd and Mr. Phillips's ability to make them listen and think. Such a reversal of tide seemed impossible but it happened before my eyes. Wendell Phillips detailed the troubles that had befallen Lovejoy who had seen three of his presses destroyed because of his support for the freedom of men who were enslaved. Finally, despite the protection of local authorities, and while standing his ground, an angry mob torched his shop and killed him and his helpers. While Phillips moved to his closing remarks, I finally remembered Sumner had mentioned this man's name. He was somehow associated with or featured in the *Liberator,* a publication put out by pro-abolitionists.

"Absorbed as we are in a thousand trifles, how has the nation all at once come to regard this issue? The answer ought to be clear. Men begin, as they did in 1776 and in 1640, to discuss principles, to weigh character, to find out what they believe in and who they are. Hopefully, we will awake before we are borne over the precipice."

The crowd seemed now mostly with him. I had seen powers demonstrated that day which were both disturbing and heartening. Humanity was capable of turning in opposite directions with an alacrity that was eye-opening. I determined there and then to convey these things to my students. We are capable of many things, not all of them good. It is horrible what we can commit, but it is transcendent what we can become. Phillip's oratory helped me realize more clearly than ever before that the fulcrum on which all things hinged, from which our very lives tipped one way or the other, might be as thin as a sheet of manuscript.

Dr. Channing, George Hillard, and Judge Hallett joined Wendell Phillips. "We must now decide who we are," Phillips said firmly to all of us. "The passage of the resolutions proposed by Dr. Channing, in spite of the opposition led by the attorney general of the Commonwealth, will show more clearly, more decisively, the deep indignation with which Bostonians regard the fate of Mr. Lovejoy and those who stood by his side. They are the true patriots, my friends, and Boston can now decide which manner of patriot *she* is. Should we pass these resolutions, as we must, then no such incident as happened to Lovejoy in one part of our Union can ever hope to tarnish the sacred soil of this part, our Boston. And may we become a beacon others may witness and imitate!"

The crowd cheered, the votes were taken, and the resolutions were passed. I bid farewell to Sara; congratulated Hillard and the others; and left sweaty, disheveled, and preoccupied. I had longed for new inspirations along my way to Beacon Street and they had come. A part of me felt that I should walk straight home and let these significant events sink in. Could anything be more important than what this day had brought? I was a poet, was I not? I was meant to weigh in. The question of slavery was more significant than any issues of the heart. I turned in the direction of home and made it an entire block before turning around and heading directly to Beacon Street. It would be good to let some time pass, to give myself a chance to let all I had witnessed settle in. I made no apologies in my honest belief that I would write tomorrow.

I walked up Beacon Hill with a plan. I would knock on the door and say that I had come to call on Fanny. There were likely endless reasons to fear such a bold move; but to entertain even one of them would surely lead to entertaining them all, and that would leave me grossly outnumbered, disheartened, and unwilling to act. No, I would not think further. *Knock and it will be opened unto you.* Who was I to disobey the scripture?

I rapped several times.

I heard a disturbance of some kind from within—a sort of frantic shuffling of feet—muffled voices—a giggle or two—then more shuffling and a slammed door. After several long moments I wondered if I should knock again, but before I could the front door opened. "Good day, Miss Mary," I said, bowing slightly.

"Why, it's you Henry." She sounded happy. "What a lovely bouquet!" Behind her stood her brother Tom, magnificently dressed in fine dinner clothes. I could see their father and stepmother seated on a couch in the center of the room similarly dressed.

"Henry!" Mr. Appleton rose to his feet and extended an arm to me. "Come. Come in. How nice to see you."

Mary gestured warmly, and I stepped inside, shook Tom's hand, and walked over to bow and kiss Mrs. Appleton's gloved hand. Mr. Appleton shook mine and pointed to a chair. "Please do sit for a moment. We are on our way to Ticknor's for dinner, but it is nice that we can enjoy a moment or two with you."

I needed to adjust my plan. "I am sorry for the unexpected intrusion. I had hoped to arrive earlier but you cannot imagine the happenings at Faneuil Hall, though I'm sure you'll read the stories in the papers tomorrow—"

"What happened?" Tom asked, crossing to stand beside the couch where his parents sat while Mary stood near a doorway, seeming unsure whether to stay or leave.

"Yes, what's happened?" Mr. Appleton sat back and folded his arms across his chest.

I was eager to tell them but also hoped to catch a glance of Fanny. Why hadn't she come to see who had arrived? "The papers will tell it better, I'm sure, but there was a near-riot between the abolitionists and anti-abolitionists. It was extremely thought-provoking."

"Oh my. Was Dr. Channing present?" Mrs. Appleton asked.

I nodded and wondered if Fanny would ever arrive. "Yes. I think he called the meeting."

"Actually, he's neither an abolitionist nor anti-abolitionist. Somewhere in between, I think, like many of us," Mr. Appleton said. "Isn't that what you recall, dear? If not for the petition Channing had written and the court order by Hallett, the mayor and the aldermen weren't even going to let the Abolitionists have use of the hall. I believe they were trying to pass a petition of some kind. Channing felt they should not be prevented the use of the public hall, so he lent his influence. So, you're saying it boiled over?"

"Austin made a real case for the anti-abolitionists. I thought there might be a fist fight, but some young man named Wendell Phillips stood and turned the crowd in the opposite direction with a most amazing, spontaneous oratory."

"Wendell Phillips? I have never heard of him." Mrs. Appleton turned to her husband. "Have you, dear?"

"I have not. Interesting though. Who is he, Henry?"

"I have no idea, sir." I craned my neck to see into the library.

"Hooray for Dr. Channing then," Tom said. "I'm more for the abolitionists than the pro-slavers, aren't you, father?"

"I detest slavery, of course," the elder Appleton replied, "but these things are disturbing. Who knows where they might lead. Slavery is an abominable institution, but I'm afraid no easy solution presents itself in short order. There are some economic realities to be considered. The South is a valuable market, and some things are not easily changed. Polarizing the nation can't be the answer."

Appleton was a wealthy merchant in the booming textiles industry. He needed the cotton from the South. I wasn't clear the entirety of his views but I figured him a moral man with notable compassion for others. "It did seem like violence was not far away," I mentioned, "but I am encouraged by what Phillips was able to do. He is someone to watch for, no doubt. Austin took it on the chin." I glanced toward the far hallway, uncaring how obvious I appeared. No one. I looked toward the stairs and then ran my gaze up the entire flight until it disappeared at a turn—nothing.

"Serves him right," Mrs. Appleton said, with a firm nod of her head. She looked at her daughter. "Mary dear, do see what is keeping Frances. We need to be going, soon." Mary rose quickly and seemed to float up the stairs before disappearing. Mrs. Appleton reached a hand toward me. "May I have someone get a vase for those flowers?"

I glanced down at the poor things, which could certainly use a drink, as could I, and then awkwardly cleared my throat. I had hoped to hand them to Fanny but I didn't want to be impolite and was about to surrender them when Tom rescued me.

"Mother, Henry probably has a mind as to how and to whom he wishes to present them."

"I was just being helpful," she replied, obviously annoyed.

"Of course, he does!" Mr. Appleton rose and crossed the room, his eyes lifting to the staircase where a lady was descending. "You look lovely, dear, and you've made all of us wait in the most fashionable style."

There she was. My Madonna. I watched her glide down the stairs with no sound or sign of footsteps, just deep blue taffeta brushing the marble steps.

"I am ready, Father," she said with what I interpreted as a slightly disapproving tone. "Oh?" she said, suddenly noticing me. "Why, Professor Longfellow, what a surprise." She walked over to me and stopped—a tower of grace.

"Fanny, these are for you," I croaked, holding out the flowers. They leaned a little to one side. Hopefully, she appreciated the idea of them more than their appearance.

As she looked at them, a small smile appeared on her lips and she accepted them with a slight dip of her chin. I wasn't sure if she was pleased or embarrassed.

"And this, too," I said, pulling the scroll from my coat pocket. "It's a poem." I looked around. Everyone smiled politely. Mary came down the stairs just then and hers was the warmest smile of all. I cleared my throat. "You don't have time, of course—I know you all need to get to the Ticknor's—so I won't recite it as I had planned, but may I just read the ending?" I looked around again and interpreted their smiles as permission.

"In all places, then, and in all seasons, flowers expand their light and soul-like wings, teaching us, by the most persuasive reasons, how akin they are to human things. And with childlike, credulous affection, we behold their tender buds expand, emblems of our own great resurrection, emblems of the bright and better land."

I stared at Fanny, the paper trembling slightly in my hands. I had imagined this moment, but how had I hoped it would end? She bent her head down and smelled the flowers in her hand. "It is an honor to hear such a verse recited by the one whose hand has given it form. I shall look forward to reading the whole of it soon." She turned and offered the flowers and the scroll to Mary. "Can you place these, Sister, please? I need to get my shawl." Fanny moved to the far end of the room.

I felt a hand on my shoulder. "Very nice, Henry," Mrs. Appleton said. "You must come again when we have time to visit. Perhaps you can recite more of your works then and in their entirety."

Mr. Appleton shook my hand firmly and patted my shoulder. "Nicely done, Henry. Do come again. Perhaps we can talk more of this meeting you witnessed. I didn't want to get into it today, but these things have no small effect on our interests, as you might know. The business of fabrics depend much upon the South and complexities abound."

"Well played, Henry!" Tom shook my hand. "I wish I had your talent."

Mary stood near me, the wilted flowers and wrinkled poem in her hands. "It was beautiful, Henry. I look forward to the full recital." She nearly curtsied before turning away with my offerings in the wrong pair of hands. The purple ribbon had fallen to the floor and I wondered if I should pick it up, but suddenly everyone was out the door and I rushed to catch up. As I walked down Beacon Street along the iron railing where I had once fallen, the Appleton clan ascended the hill in the opposite direction toward Ticknor's. I could hear their voices, but I couldn't make out their conversation. Nevertheless, I had been invited to return, and Fanny had used the word *honor*.

Persistence is a virtue, I told myself. Letters and poems and parlor visits could be employed in the right measure. If anyone knew about measures and tempo and timing and rhyme, a poet did, even if an emerging one.

By the time I had reached the midway point of the bridge across the Charles, I knew I had somewhat shown my hand, but hopefully not too foolishly.

Chapter 12

HOW MANY GENERATIONS HAVE fashioned an expression common to its own time bemoaning the absurdity of a man not listening to his own counsel? I remember during my early years as professor at Harvard that there were instances when I complained of my being continually subjected to schoolboys voicing their uninformed opinions about things beyond their grasp and of which they truly didn't care. What I do not recall is ever chastising myself for not personally applying what I hoped to teach them. I do here and now declare that the telling of one's history can sometimes reveal needed changes that come slow to a man despite his self-knowledge.

My lecture was in mid-session and proceeding fairly well. "Perhaps the greatest lesson, which the lives of literary men teach us, is told in a single word: *Wait!*" I stood in classroom number three in University Hall and was confident I had their rapt attention. Not only were students like Thoreau and Whitestone focused and alert, so were McCurdle and his kind. "Every man must patiently bide his time," I continued. "He must wait, especially in lands like our native land, where the pulse of life beats with such feverish and impatient throbs. Our national character wants the dignity of repose, yet we seem to live in the midst of a battle—there is such a din—such a hurrying to and fro." I stood in front of the window overlooking the college yard and motioned toward the not-too-distant parade of carriages and horses and people milling along the streets. "It is in these streets of a crowded city where it can be found difficult to walk slowly. You feel the rushing of the crowd and feel you must rush with it. In the press of your life, it is difficult to be calm."

"Unless one is bored!" McCurdle quipped.

"Ah, Mister McCurdle does us the dishonor of not raising his hand or standing, yet he does submit a theory that although I think it in error, is worthy of some consideration. Does boredom produce calm? I think not. Boredom produces anxiety and can lure one into reckless and rushed endeavors or impatient grabs for too easily gained pleasures or destructive excitement."

Red-faced, McCurdle cleared his throat and raised his hand.

"Yes, Mister McCurdle?"

"I did not mean boredom with this class, Professor," he said, standing.

"I didn't think you did."

"I only meant to be funny, I mean regarding life. I don't know how many times several of us gather in the dorms at night to inquire what we might find to do that's satisfying—other than homework. I sometimes feel too calm already."

"Valid, sir. In this stress of wind and tide to which I am referring, all professions can at times seem to drag their anchors, but, with calm and solemn footsteps a rising tide can bear against the rushing torrent, and push back the hurrying waters. With no less calm, a great mind ought to bear up against public opinion, the pressure of peers, the insatiable need for amusement, the quest for fame, and push back their hurrying streams. Therefore should every man wait—should bide his time."

Another student, Anderson, raised his hand and stood. "Do nothing, sir? Isn't that counter-productive?"

I had them. Baited and hooked again. I smiled. "Good! Good, Mister Anderson! So it is not enough to hear the words uttered by those professing instruction, is it? No! You must consider the spoken words uttered and decide their meaning, for context can alter the shades of intention."

Thoreau raised his hand and stood. "So when you urge us to wait, you do not mean to be without activity."

"Well done, Mister Thoreau! We do not wait in listless idleness—nor in useless pastime—nor in querulous dejection, but in constant, steady, cheerful endeavors, always willing and fulfilling, and accomplishing your task, that, when the occasion comes, you may be equal to it."

"And then our fame and riches multiply!" McCurdle blurted out.

I ignored the failed protocol; I was too excited to drive home the point. "And if they never come, Mister McCurdle, what matters it? What matters it to the world whether I, or you, or another man did such a deed, or wrote such a book, so be it the deed and book were well done!" I moved to another side of the room to let that sink in for a moment. "It is the part of an indiscreet and troublesome ambition, to care too much about fame—about what the world says of us. To be always looking into the faces of others for approval—to be always anxious for the effect of what we do and say, to be always shouting to hear the echo of our own voices!"

A young, shy lad, Howard James Butler, one who seldom spoke in class, although his written examinations proved sensible and well organized, lifted his hand.

"Mister Butler?"

He stood. "Thank you, sir. But isn't it the famous who are remembered? If we fail to attain notable reputations, do we not become lost in time? Do we not fade into insignificance?"

I didn't expect that question, not from him, but it moved me. Here he was, a gentle soul, a quiet lad, one in whose work was found notable merit and who seemingly possessed no need for public recognition and yet sounding fearful of anonymity. I wondered if his shyness were sadness. I paused longer than I had intended. I don't mean to over dramatize the point, but an image came to me then. I thought of the Christ when the mob threw the adulterous woman before him and demanded justice and the Master simply crouched and drew in the sand. I used to wonder what he wrote as though it might be some clue as to how he came up with that amazingly wise response about letting the one without sin be the one to throw the first stone. The mob silently steeled away, the Christ forgave the woman, and the story survived the ages. I stood there in that classroom thinking that the writing in the sand may have simply been the waiting upon inspiration for an answer at first unknown, for that is what Butler's question did to me—it made me think beyond my notes and to look to some deeper source.

After several moments of quiet on the part of everyone, including McCurdle, a thought came to me, and I was glad for the question and the reply it inspired. "A man may be famous for a moment or for an hour." I heard words inside my head and spoke them slowly, like molasses dripping from a spoon. "How—do we know—if it lasts? A man—may be unknown, unappreciated—or forgotten—but what— what if he is then remembered beyond his lifetime and for all time?"

I surveyed the class, certain we were all experiencing the muse, but their faces told me little, so I continued in a low tone. "If you look about you, you will see men who are wearing life away in a feverish anxiety of fame. The last we shall ever hear of them will be the funeral bell that tolls them to their early graves. Unhappy and unsuccessful men because their purpose was not to accomplish their task well, but to clutch money or fame; and they go to their graves with greater purposes unaccomplished and life-altering wishes unfulfilled. Better for them, and for the world, in their example, to have waited."

"Does anything matter, then?" Thoreau asked without raising his hand or waiting for a nod. "Is it all in vain?"

I don't recall another day of lectures in which I felt as strongly proud of those boys as on this particular day. I don't know, maybe it wasn't truly as I feel and hear and see it all these years later, but it doesn't matter whether my interpretation is true or not. It matters that it happened, and that I was there, and it is happening still in the reverberations of the silence uttering forth from that place and hour.

"Believe me," I said, "the talent of success is nothing more than doing what you can do well and doing well whatever you do—without a thought of fame. If it comes at all, it comes because it is deserved, not because it is sought after. And moreover, when arriving in this manner, there will be no misgivings—no disappointment—no hasty, feverish, exhausting excitement."

"But wouldn't that add up to a most boring life?" McCurdle had come full circle to ask the same question, but this time without any tone of mockery.

"No," I said without thinking. "No, because we are speaking of ideals. They are only ideals, and we will bump against our ideals often, because despite our heavenward aspirations we are also hell-bent on keeping it spicy." I dismissed the class with a wink and without another word. They left in a heavy shroud of silence.

———

After the lecture I felt a stroll was in order. I walked not so aimlessly as I told myself I was. Having arrived at the Boston Common, I now obtained a good view. The gray stone Grand Lodge of the Masons stood along the southeast edge; the formal gardens lay just beyond Charles Street to the west; and across the street from Ticknor's mansion on Beacon and Park, the Massachusetts State House rose at the northeast corner with its roof-crowning fountain. I tried to appear more intrigued by these structures than the crimson brick home directly north of where I stood at Frog Pond. The croaking of one of the little creatures hidden somewhere in the reeds playfully stoked my imagination. If this were spring and I were a frog I could stare at her house while safely seated upon a lily pad. The lady within those stately walls might venture outside for a stroll beside this pretty bog where perchance, she might see me, a devoted frog in need of a proverbial peck on his reptilian nose. *Poof!* I would rise, dressed smartly and cupping her gloved hand. I would bow and kiss her in return. But, alas, it was not spring and I was not a frog. Fortunately, I suppose, I was becoming something of the fool! More specifically, I was a Harvard professor trying to steal a peek at the target of his romantic interests on a mild February day.

I meandered along one of the many footpaths crisscrossing the park, and mastered the art of the indirect glance. I was careful to avoid missteps, determined as I was, to never again indulge in the buffoonery I had so laudably demonstrated in the past. But what I most enjoyed about this little game was that no one but God and I knew what I was doing.

"Longfellow! Fancy meeting you here!"

It was the effervescent Cornelius Felton in his hat and duster. "I say, what might you be doing other than trying to catch a glimpse of the Madonna you crave, eh?" He slapped my shoulder as he jogged close.

"Cornelius." I cleared my throat. "I see you, too, know a grand day for a constitutional when you encounter one. Just walking off a lecture, of course."

"Henry!" Cornelius, his wild hair escaping the borders of his broad brim, and his joyous face as round as the glasses he wore, reached up and squeezed my shoulders. "It's me, Cornelius! Your Greek god-friend who knows all things from my perch atop Olympus. I, of all people, have no doubts as to your motives. Fear not! I threaten no thunderclap of disapproval. Do as I have done, Henry, and go for the prized fleece!" His laugh bared every one of his small teeth.

I feigned ignorance and labored hard to believe my own deceit.

"You are a man possessed!" He slapped me on the back and

nudged me forward. "How goes Dante?"

"Dante lives on, although I'm mindful that I'm lecturing a room full of boys who don't have sufficient life experience to care more than they do, although a few show promise and maybe more than a few of late." I stole a glance to the side but saw no trace of movement in the Beacon Street windows, but Cornelius was staring at them as though watching for sunrise. "And where is your lovely betrothed?" I asked, looking at him, hoping the question would recapture his gaze.

"Ah, with the marriage vows not long away we must take some respite or else this sickness of love would keep us from all else." He winked, his tone jocular. He was not subtle in his examinations of the Beacon Street windows and I cringed. "She's at her mothers and we're here, that's all that matters now." Cornelius grabbed my sleeve and tugged hard. "What say we go rap on the door, old man?"

"Where? Whose door? Your fiance's?"

"No-oo," Cornelius exaggerated the word as if he were instructing his students in Greek. "*Your* fiance's home!"

I stopped in my tracks. "You know better than that, Cornelius. I need you to go away; I really do. I'm sorry, friend."

He laughed, not unkindly, and said, "Tell me something any of us in the Five of Clubs doesn't already know about you and this romantic quest of yours." I had turned and positioned myself so that at last he was looking at me and away from the house, but then I noticed a dark shape in the window beyond his shoulder. Cornelius spoke on, but I did not catch a single word because the front door of 39 Beacon Street had opened and two ladies stepped out in bright dresses, dark coats, and large hand warmers.

"Good God," I said, delighted, but somehow unable to move.

Cornelius's jumble of thoughts trailed off as he turned and watched the Appleton sisters walk down Beacon toward Charles Street. I hoped they would turn into the park but they did not.

"We must follow the beautiful young ladies!" Cornelius spoke louder than I thought prudent.

"Shh!" I wished I could rid myself of him.

"But we have to hurry, Henry, if we're to follow." He tugged me by the arm and led me to a path parallel with the street, so that one narrow lane of cobblestone separated the ladies from us. "She's not Medusa, Henry."

"Of course not!" I snapped. "Don't be a dolt."

"Then there's no reason to fear being turned to stone. Walk like you're made of flesh and blood, man."

I couldn't seem to find my center. My arms and legs suddenly felt out of sync and uncomfortably long. Not once had she looked my way. Mary glanced in our direction and then appeared to speak into Fanny's hood, but when they reached Charles Street they turned away from the garden and headed north. Cornelius tugged me into the street.

"Whoa!" I heard the carriage driver's shout of alarm. The horse reared, the wheels squeaked, and the two gentlemen passengers in the carriage yelled out in anger, but Cornelius simply tipped his hat and whirled me away. As I looked back, George Ticknor and Nathan Appleton were recovering and righting themselves, as Ticknor shouted, "Cornelius! Henry! Do be more careful!"

I tried to offer a sympathetic shrug and hoped the men understood that it was all Felton's fault. I turned my attention back to Fanny and Mary who looked over their shoulders briefly without slowing. It made me wonder whether they were enjoying a game of cat and mouse.

Suddenly, Cornelius waved and shouted, "MARY! FANNY! IT'S FELTON AND LONGFELLOW! WAIT FOR US!"

I swear I wished the carriage had struck him. "Felton!" I hissed. "What are you doing?"

The ladies stopped.

"See, Henry! Not so difficult." Cornelius tugged me to a stop and spoke firmly into my ear, "Do all the men of Boston a favor and just state your intentions to the woman and be done with it."

"What?"

"No poetry, Henry. Act!"

Cornelius walked ahead and the ladies radiated nothing but sweet surprise. "Henry! Corny!" Mary offered with a slight curtsy and a tip of her head.

"Professors," Fanny said with a polite smile. "We are heading to the shops at the end of Charles, at the corner of Pinckney. Would you care to escort us?"

"A fine suggestion." Cornelius offered his arm to Mary, who gladly took it and they moved on.

Fanny gazed at me, her face lovely but expressionless. "Professor?" She tilted her head to point the way and slipped her gloved hand around my arm and we followed Cornelius and Mary.

"Fanny—", I heard myself say but couldn't continue. There was so much to say and so little distance to Pinckney.

"You are near the Commons, often, aren't you?" she asked without looking at me.

"It's a picturesque park. I am drawn to it." I thought my tone resembled something mechanical, like a creaking pulley.

"The Ticknor's speak well of you." She glanced at me.

"He's responsible—"

"For your appointment at the college? Yes, I know," she said. "Have you enjoyed teaching there?"

"It's going well, I think. The lectures have been—I've sent you some—only excerpts, of course. The students seem to appreciate them, more than loathe them."

She laughed, and I felt elated.

"Yes, I recall receiving them. What were the topics?"

We walked slowly enough, but Felton and Mary were nearing the destination and I needed to speak. "Lives of literary men. Faust.

Dante. Goethe. And extemporaneous translations I do while walking about the class. I try to keep it engaging. Which portions did you read?"

"None."

"None?" I stopped, but she slipped her hand back into her muff and kept walking. I hurried after her.

"I'm sorry," she said. "My calendar has been overwhelming. We've twice left town since our return from Europe and haven't enjoyed many dinners at home. It seems our travels abroad have made our family desired house guests these days, at least until all the gossip is properly caught up." She stopped and extended her hand. "We're here. Thank you."

Cornelius and Mary had crossed the street to the store entrance but she was bidding me farewell on this side. "I can cross with you," I said.

"But isn't that the bridge you take home?" She pointed behind me.

"Yes, but—"

"Then this is fine." She took my hand and shook it firmly.

"Fanny!" I stepped closer and gently took hold of her arm.

She looked down at my hand and I released her. "Yes?"

"You have received my letters and gifts? Do you understand why I've thought to send them to you?"

She returned a quizzical expression. Her forehead furrowed and her mesmerizing eyes narrowed. "I'm afraid I don't, Professor Longfellow. What should I understand?"

"I have intentions—" I began.

Her forehead relaxed and her eyes widened and softened, thank the God of all creation, they softened and looked directly into mine. I tried to find a word to bridge the moment but wasn't sure what that word might be.

Her mouth opened slightly and her perfect teeth mesmerized me. In all of heaven, how does God make one so desirable? "Intentions?" she asked.

I cleared my throat and glanced at Mary and Felton happily chatting across the street.

Fanny nodded suddenly, clearly comprehending. "Professor, surely, you do not mean—"

"Henry!" Cornelius shouted.

It was now or never. "But I *do* mean," I said quickly. "I wonder if I may win your heart. Ever since Interlaken—"

She cocked her head, squeezed her eyes shut, and lifted her hands still tucked inside the warmer. "Dear Professor, please say no more." One hand slipped out and patted a stray lock of hair. She looked at me. "I am thankful for your words." Her eyes were large and dark and lovely. "But—"

"Please don't continue." The words escaped my mouth like a flood. "Please don't utter another word. Just stay where you are and say nothing—nothing that begins with that word. I can't bear it."

Her face transformed into a kind of smirk. "I assure you, dear Professor, I much enjoy your company—as a friend, of course—but a friend only. And though I am most flattered by your proposition, I must declare that such intentions are not mutual. It is important that you mistake nothing I am saying as encouragement toward your stated end. I must discourage any further advances of that kind though your friendship will always be valued. Good day." She twirled and swiftly stepped off the curb.

"Look out!" I yelled. Wheel brakes screeched and I lunged for her.

Fanny screamed.

"Whoa!" A great Chestnut horse reared, and the horse carriage veered dangerously close, the wheels scraping the street. "What the—?" the driver yelled.

I held Fanny in my arms only inches away from the dripping snout of the panicked horse. "Watch your feet!" I pulled her away.

"Please!" she said, waving her arms to free herself from my grasp. Her hand warmer flew into the gutter.

I bent to retrieve it but upon standing found she had left me.

"You again?"

I looked up at the irate driver for the second time today. "I–I'm sorry."

"Sorry? You want someone killed?"

I had no answer, but watched Fanny, across the street, inspecting her shoes and not looking my way. Mary and Cornelius attempted to assist her but she walked away from them. I held up the warmer and waved it in the air, but she ignored me and entered the store, never looking back. Mary and Cornelius crossed the street to arrive next to me.

"Are you all right, Henry?" Mary asked with tenderness.

Corny brushed my sleeves straighter.

"Here," Mary took the hand warmer. "I'll hold it. Come join us in the store across the street. Maybe it will be good to stand indoors for awhile."

I shook my head.

"Well?" the driver shouted. "Anyone willing to move out of the way?"

"Can you drive me to Brattle Street?" I asked, suddenly desperate to leave.

"You've got nerve!" the driver said, pulling the reins to steady the still anxious horse.

"And money," I said.

"Let's join the ladies in the store, Henry," Cornelius said, with a wheedling tone.

I shook my head and offered my best pleading look to the driver.

"Please, sir."

"Ah, get in. You'll be safer inside my cab than in front of it."

"Henry! You can catch another carriage. We're invited into the store. Think of it, man! Think!" Cornelius jabbed his forefinger against the side of his forehead but all I could think was how foolish he looked.

"I'm leaving, now. I have to. I'm sorry." I climbed into the carriage.

"Out of my way, you two," the driver shouted to my friends, wheeling the carriage straighter and shaking the reins.

"Good day, Professor!" Mary called as she moved aside. "I do hope you are unhurt. It was Fanny's haste, sir. You saved her from a terrible accident."

I wanted to look at the store window to see if Fanny was watching me but couldn't bear the possibility that she was not, so I didn't turn my head.

"Hold up! I say, hold up!'" It was Cornelius, jogging alongside.

"Whoa!" The carriage slowed. "Make up your mind!" the driver demanded.

Cornelius climbed in, breathing as heavily as ever; slid over; and bumped me hard. "Sorry. All right, carry on, driver." The ride resumed speed, and Cornelius elbowed me. "What are you thinking? We were invited into the store. You could have made your intentions known, man."

"I already did."

"You did? YOU DID? Tell me, what did she—" Cornelius froze and then patted my leg. "Oh."

I looked straight ahead as we wheeled down Charles Street.

"Maybe we can gather the Five of Clubs for some whist and wine."

I shook my head.

"We could visit the Eliots?"

I shook my head. Would he not cease speaking?

"Well then, what would you like to do, Henry?"

"I need to go home."

The carriage crossed the bridge to Cambridge. Halfway over, I looked down at the cold Charles River and wanted to jump in it.

Cornelius paid the fare and insisted on accompanying me into my rooms and pouring us each a glass of port. Eventually, he stopped talking about what may have gone wrong and fixed upon a discourse of ancient Greek mythology, which I found preferable, though difficult to focus on. After three glasses of wine, a cigar, and a brief exchange with Mrs. Craigie, he left but with a softly spoken word of caution placed deftly into my ear. "Don't let this business turn your heart cold, dear friend."

I was exhausted. Upstairs, I found a paper and pen and sat down at my desk. Obviously, face-to-face courtship wasn't in the stars, but I was not a knight without a sword. It was, after all, a man's gifts that made way for him. How could she have not seen the worth of a poet's heart laid bare?

Freshly dipped pen in hand, I knew I should write something, anything; perhaps the words would form themselves. I sat for a long time but nothing happened. What was it my heart ached to say? Maybe there existed words that could unlock her heart and cause her to cherish my interest. Perhaps, but it was not the desired destination that bottled me up, it was the question of where to begin that held me captive. Then it occurred to me. No matter where I hoped to go I could only begin from places I'd already been. Maybe that's why my thoughts of a certain medieval French author sprang up in my head. I moved my hand across the page and let my pen have its way.

Old Froissart tells us, in his Chronicles, *that when King Edward beheld the Countess of Salisbury at her castle gate, he thought he had never seen before so noble nor so fair a lady; he*

*was stricken therewith to the heart with a sparkle of fine love,
that endured long after; he thought no lady in the world so
worthy to be beloved, as she. And so likewise—*

I stopped. I crossed out everything and began again.

*I will not disguise the truth. She is my heroine; and I mean to
describe her with great truth and beauty, so that all shall be in
love with her, and I most of all.*

I crossed out everything again. What in God's name was I doing
besides scribbling? I leaned back in my chair and rubbed my face. I
recalled what Corny had whispered before he left and didn't like the
feeling it gave me. What did he know of my heart? I wrote into my
journal.

*Then come the gloomy hours, when the fire will neither burn
on our hearts nor in our hearts; and all without and within is
dismal, cold, and dark. Believe me, every heart has its secret
sorrows, which the world knows not, and oftentimes a man
may call a friend cold, when he is only sad.*

I looked out the window facing the Charles, and I wished I hadn't let
Corny nudge me into that fiasco. I wished I had waited.

Chapter 13

CONFLICTING EMOTIONS DAPPLED my soul like sunbeams flickering through dense trees to muddle the road with light and shade. Blending lectures and studies with social events I lived as part Harvard man, part social gadabout, and part lovelorn poet, but I did my best to keep that last part out of the public eye.

Socially, I rose to the top of the local ranks of whist players as I learned how to better play a weak hand. I attended the theater, the opera, and took the occasional long-distance carriage rides with friends like Felton. My journal and experimental verse kept my poetical aspirations and my mind sharp, but a great sadness hung over me. I wasn't depressed, I don't think, but whatever I felt was something less than joyous. Then something happened.

One gray morning I stood over the washbasin in my flannel gown with my hands at my side. It was February 27, my thirty-first birthday. When I splashed my face with the frigid water, I remembered a dream from the night before. It was a familiar one, though it wasn't exactly the same. I watched the water drip from my fingers into the basin and tried to replay the hazy images.

It was Mary, in the depths of the sea, her garments flowing in the currents, and gems glittering far below. One of her eyes was closed and the other open. I always disliked that part of the dream. Her face radiated, just like the other times I had dreamed this dream, and, as always, she sank farther into the deep, but that's when this dream turned different. This time the depths suddenly were brightened by something other than the distant jewels. The eye that was closed opened and, like the other, became bright and alive. She smiled at me and hope filled me. She spoke, but I couldn't hear her words. Amazingly, I could read her lips, which was something I had never before been able to do. I was certain she said, "Bless you." She smiled and closed her eyes and then disappeared into the dark waters.

I shook some of the water loose from my hands and dropped into a chair next to the basin table and hugged myself against the cold dampness. Words encircled me like clouds and echoed through my mind. I truly believed Mary was setting me free and as quickly as that revelation came to me, words arrived in whispers.

The being beauteous. Unto my youth was given.

I looked around the room, trying to locate the direction the whispering came from, but it was impossible. It came from everywhere at once. I closed my eyes.

Given to love me. Now a saint in heaven.

I thought I could hear her garments trailing across the floor.

With a slow and noiseless footstep. A messenger divine.

I opened my eyes and looked at the empty chair across from me.

She takes the chair beside me.

I turned my hand palm up on my knee.

Lays her gentle hand in mine.

I looked across the room to the chest of clothes I had yet to return to her family. Warmth tingled my shoulders as if a cloak had been placed upon them. I hurried to the table on the opposite side of the room, opened the drawer, and removed a sheet of paper. I dipped the pen in ink and wrote with speed. I scratched and tapped, looped and crossed, and then crumpled the paper up and started again. A familiar cycle but a fresh flow nonetheless. I don't know for how long I wrote, but I did not stop until I had finished.

What Longfellow Heard

When the hours of Day are numbered,
And the voices of the Night
Wake the better soul, that slumbered,
To a holy, calm delight;

Ere the evening lamps are lighted,
And, like phantoms grim and tall,
Shadows from the fitful firelight
Dance upon the parlor wall;

Then the form of the departed
Enters at the open door;
The beloved, the true-hearted,
Comes to visit me once more;

And she is the Being Beauteous,
Who unto my youth was given,
More than all things else to love me,
And is now a saint in heaven.

With a slow and noiseless footstep
Comes that messenger divine,
Takes the vacant chair beside me,
Lays her gentle hand in mine.

And she sits and gazes at me
With those deep and tender eyes,
Like the stars, so still and saint-like,

Looking downward from the skies.
Uttered not, yet comprehended,
Is the spirit's voiceless prayer,
Soft rebukes, in blessings ended,
Breathing from her lips of air.

Oh, though oft depressed and lonely,
All my fears are laid aside,
If I but remember only
Such as she has lived and died.

I looked at the poem for a long time and then slowly finished dressing. I dragged the trunk past the foot of the bed, out the door, and into the upstairs hallway. I would ship her things to her family tomorrow. I went back inside my room, examined what I had written, and picked up my pen again. I altered some of the passages into a rhythm that felt improved. I wondered if I should include other loved ones that had passed, so I drafted different versions. I wrote until my wrist hurt and a bell rang outside, and then clocks began to chime. It didn't matter. I was writing poetry that meant something.

In the morning, I wrote a brief letter to Mary's sister, allowing my pen to take its own course.

Cambridge, Sunday evening

My Dear Eliza,

By tomorrow's steamboat I shall send you this shipment, containing the clothes, which once belonged to your sister. What I have suffered in getting them ready to send you, I cannot describe. It is not necessary that I should. Cheerful as I may have seemed to you at times, there are other times when it seems to me that my heart would break. The world considers grief unmanly and is suspicious of that sorrow which is expressed by words and outward signs. Hence we strive to be gay and put a cheerful courage on, when our souls are very sad. But there are hours when the world is shut out and we can no longer hear the voices that cheer and encourage us. To me such hours come daily. I was so happy with my dear Mary that it is very hard to be alone. The sympathies of friendship are doubtless something—but after all how little, how unsatisfying they are to one who has been so loved as I have been! This is a selfish sorrow, I know: but neither reason nor reflections can still it. Affliction makes us childish. A grieved and wounded heart is hard to be persuaded. We do not wish to have our sorrow lessened. There are wounds, which are never entirely healed. A thousand associations call up the past, with all its gloom and shadow. Often a mere look or sound—a voice—the odor of a flower—the merest trifle is enough to awaken within me deep and unutterable emotions. Hardly a day passes that some face, or familiar object, or some passage in the book I am reading does not call up the image of my beloved wife so vividly that I pause and burst into tears, —and sometimes cannot rally again for hours.

And yet, my dear Eliza, in a few days, and we shall all be gone, and others sorrowing and rejoicing as we now do, will have taken our places: and we shall say, how childish it was for us to mourn for things so transitory. There may be some consolation in this; but we are nevertheless children. Our feelings overcome us. Yet, blessed are those who mourn, for they will be comforted. It comes in stages, because that is the only way we can endure it, but it does come, and we are comforted to an extant.

> *Your friend,*
> *Henry W. Longfellow*

The dream, the shipping of the trunk of clothing, and the sending of the letter to Mary's sister brought a scab to my wound, and I felt my capacities expand a little. I dressed in my finest clothes and purposed to find some good friend and enjoy the day while the sun yet shone.

Chapter 14

I INCREASINGLY TRAVELED TO town with Felton on foot as his remaining bachelor days were fast expiring. We dined, drank some fine wine, and attended concerts and lectures. One evening in March, we attended Emerson's lecture on *Being and Seeming*. On the way home, we stopped midway over the bridge and enjoyed the sight of the Charles River flowing beneath us.

"I sometimes imagine the tidewaters moving up the river from the sea, asking why not much tribute was paid this year."

Corny peered over the side and then at me. "What?"

"Then I imagine the brooks and rivers answering that there has been little harvest of snow and rain and that is why. Seasons return, they explain, but the details are different."

"Ah! I see," Corny chuckled, obviously game to go along with me. "But what of the seaweed and kelp? Surely they're worth something."

I liked his thoughts. "I agree. Maybe the river carries them to the flooded meadows like returning sailors carry oranges in handkerchiefs to friends in the country. Not pearls, but most satisfying in smaller ways."

"You amaze me, Longfellow, the way your mind works! Truly you are one of a kind."

For the next two months, we continued teaching, dining, carousing, and reflecting. We passed many evenings talking of matters that lay near our souls, like how to bear one's self doughtily in life's battle, and how to make the best of things. One evening, after he left joking and smoking, leaving behind an amusing trail of witticisms, quips, and spicy college gossip, I sat on the couch opposite Mrs. Craigie who was buried in Voltaire. I sank into a delicious canto of Dante's *Divine Comedy* and dreamed of romance and Italian sunsets. By bedtime, the Italian Poet had filled me once again with my own salient notions of love and desire.

———

It was a sunny day in May when I rode in the rear of a horse-drawn bus approaching the Common still musing over Dante's verses and in particular, his heart toward Beatrice. It was then I saw Fanny walking with her brother and sister. A moment more and I would have been around a corner and in a busy place where I could not quickly disembark. With no time to hesitate, I lurched and leapt and landed on the road—all without falling, though the pain in my shins felt like a hot iron branding my bones.

"Good God!" Tom Appleton exclaimed. "What manner of acrobatics is that? Are you all right, man?" He crossed the street and helped me straighten up.

Fanny looked concerned, but Mary beamed like her brother.

"Dear Henry," Mary said, "what a grand sight!" She was full of cheer as Tom and I joined them. "Next I expect you to throw a discus clear over the horizon!" She laughed and touched my shoulder.

I smiled and tried not to allow the heat of embarrassment to reach my face. I nodded to Fanny. "Miss Appleton."

"You might consider being a trapeze artist!" she said, her tone more joking than her gaze.

Tom patted me on the back. "Come, walk with us! That is, if you can!"

"*Please*," Mary added and jauntily looped her arm in mine.

"I can walk quite normally," I said with a strained chuckle, "though I grasp you have good reason to doubt me." My humor was much too forced, but it was all I had. I stared at Fanny while patting Mary's hand in the crux of my arm. Fanny's gait was like the rhythm of a perfect poem, exactly the same measure in swinging to the left as when swinging to the right. "And you might find great success, Miss Appleton, as a hypnotist," I said with a sudden air of confidence, "so mesmerizing are you when you move!"

Fanny twirled faster than I thought possible, and I was caught in what can only be considered an impolite direction of gaze. She offered me a disapproving look. Whatever embarrassment I had managed to diffuse was now upon me in full measure. Such an indiscretion had not been my conscious intention, and I hoped I could somehow project an innocent countenance that suggested it was an accidental occurrence, and not in the least consistent with how I typically conducted myself.

I tried shifting the focus. "I meant to communicate that the trapeze artist in me could then feel most at home in the company of another skilled artist, like a hypnotist, say, who would likely be a part of the same traveling troupe."

"Like a circus act?" she asked in a way that I could not read.

She had nodded her head, as she spoke, so I mirrored her action. "Yes, that's it," I said with too much eagerness, being cautious to look nowhere other than her eyes.

"I see," she said and began to turn away.

"I've an idea, sisters!" Tom said with great eagerness. I sensed he was rallying to my side. He strode over, withdrew Mary's hand from my arm, and placed it on his own. "Henry, my friend. Would you do me the honor of walking as protector to my most deliberate sister, Frances, in the event there may be bandits upon this road?"

Fanny frowned. "Bandits?" Even though her lips were a little pursed and her forehead slightly wrinkled she looked delicious in her layered clothing, her long locks catching the sun. I wanted to fall to my knees and beg forgiveness for all of the blunders I had made so far.

"Bandits, circus people, what does it matter?" Tom said with an infectious laugh. "Protect the maiden, Henry, for she's helpless to defend herself should any characters of questionable standing come her way. She's all bark and no bite and in need of a gentleman guard." He and Mary walked on, but Tom turned his head to finish. "An encircling regimen she'd prefer, no doubt, but a kind professor ought to do."

I offered her my arm.

"I fear no bandits," she said, glancing at my arm. "I do require a gentleman."

"Yes," I said, "that has always been my intention."

"Good." She took my arm and we followed Tom and Mary. After a few moments of trying to think of something to say, she surprised me by speaking first. "How are you doing regarding Mary?"

"Your sister?"

"No, your deceased wife."

Her casual tone did nothing to prevent the question from stunning me with more impact than the jump from the carriage.

"Is it difficult to move on?" she asked without looking at me.

I wondered if her brother and sister could hear us. This was a sacred topic. I struggled to produce a sound, an utterance of any kind, but none came.

"It must be difficult to lose the one you loved most and with whom you had dreamed of so many things. I am sorry for your pain, Professor. Truly." She looked at me then, but I could find no words. She kindly granted me the silence, and we walked on.

Two blocks later, I said, "She has released me."

"Pardon me?"

"Mary. She wants me to be happy among the living."

We reached the Appleton home then and stood at the base of the front steps. Fanny looked at me with what appeared to be bewilderment and unhooked her arm from mine.

Tom and Mary had already ascended the steps and stood peering down at us. "Would you like—" Tom began but Fanny intercepted his unfinished invitation.

"Thank you for the courteous stroll, Professor. It was pleasant." She whirled to face her brother and sister, hiked her skirts an inch, and waited only a second before ascending the steps. When she reached the top she looked up defiantly at her brother.

"Tom."

He dipped his chin and stepped aside, and she disappeared inside without another word or glance. Sadness appeared on Mary's face.

I offered my bravest smile.

"Sorry, old friend," Tom said, walking back down and holding out his hand. "I thought we might convene for some whist in the parlor or some such, but Fanny seems to have a different mind. I best not push it. She can be a hatful, you know."

I had never before thought of her that way, but maybe it was time to consider it. I shook his hand, tipped my hat to Mary, and headed for home.

By the time I reached Craigie House, I had replayed every moment of this encounter in my mind a dozen times. I sat and wrote down everything I remembered feeling that day, May 10, into my journal, holding nothing back. When I read it, I realized that I had never written anything quite so exposing before. Perhaps it was too revealing of things meant to be sacred. There was a place for romantic secrets but likely not in my daily journal. I wanted no one to discover those feelings except, perhaps, the one for whom they were intended and *only* then if they were welcomed. I tore out the pages and trimmed the remaining edges clean.

*Returned home miserable. It's raining now and the birds shriek-
ing. The storm will thresh all the blossoms off the trees. Where do
birds hide in such storms? Must they sit in wet clothes until the
great sun of tomorrow?*

In July, Corny married his true love. Not only was the Five of Clubs
more completely disbanded than before but gone was a kindred bachelor friend. Corny's wife was pleasant enough but tagging along only
made me more aware of my loneliness.

I drifted in and out of melancholy. I attended functions of many
kinds, but felt bored. I was never fortunate enough to encounter any
romantic or soul-satisfying friendship though I tried to appear eligible
at all the appropriate functions. Nothing came of it, nothing that
awakened me.

I felt little, heard only my own breath, and saw nothing. For
the next many weeks, life melted into a dreamy routine. I moved
in smooth and easy circles—no passion in sight. I was a falling leaf
that never touched down. I wasn't connected to any life-giving vine.
I was not crumbling, but the floating was in a descending pattern,
and I feared darkness ahead eventually should no one appear. Weeks
became months, which turned into a year. There were minor changes
(the college schedule was altered to exclude summer lectures and my
duties were further defined) and my life began feeling similar to those
days in Brunswick. My environment began to feel like a frock coat
that I had outgrown.

A new invention was introduced, a steel pen. I tried wielding it as
a newly fashioned sword that would lead me into literary battles with
new hopes of conquest or at least the promise of securing some larger
domain. But the invention, as lauded as it was, did not bring with it
any new breakthrough in my work. My muse was like a wine bottle
that swallowed its cork with little hope of salvaging anything drink-
able. I had never translated or lectured worse than I did that April.

Then a sunbeam came in the form of a letter written in German.

Baltisport, 28 April, 1839

Most Esteemed Friend,

A special chance gives me the opportunity by these lines to recall myself to your mind, and also to let you know into what corner of the earth you are to turn your thoughts, if for a moment you will favor me with your remembrance.

Some years already lie between the day when I so warmly took leave of you in never-to-be-forgotten Heidelberg and my lonely present. But the memory of that time of our friendly life together—of the winter evenings which we passed with each other in intimate talk and the glorious walks in spring-time through the country 'round Heidelberg—lives as fresh and warm in my soul as if we had parted only yesterday. Since then I have been again in Heidelberg, and for a longer time, and I continually thought with regret of you and our pleasant intercourse.

In the autumn of the same year in which you left Europe, after I had passed the summer with my sister at the baths in Bohemia, I went alone to Paris and spent a very enjoyable winter. In May I was some weeks in London, and the next winter I passed at Heidelberg. In the spring of last year I was obliged to take my long-postponed return home. It was hard for me to leave the beloved town, and I lived the last weeks entirely at the Castle, with the old Frenchman artist.

My native house stands upon a high shore, and from my window I look out far over the lovely blue sea and upon every ship that passes to the Bay of Finland. This is my only entertainment, for I live in the greatest solitude. I have ample leisure to think of the past and dear old friends even though I once encouraged you to not do the same. If you knew how much interested I should

*be in all that concerned you, you would not need that I should
entreat you to write me. Do take to heart my wish. Every year
ships sail from Boston to Petersburg and generally stop at my
port of Baltisport, should you ever have the mind to consider
which direction to sail next!*

*Farewell my companion of brighter days. Think with sympathy
of your heartily devoted—*

Baron J. Von Ramm

The Baron unwittingly awakened me. His words reminded me that
an entire universe encircled me, in time and space. Friends abound-
ed, even if occasionally forgotten they still remained. Rain falls, but
somewhere there is sunshine. It's so simple and easy to underrate or
dismiss as sentimental, but in times of distress, anything that keeps
your mouth above the waterline is appreciated. My muse began rising like bubbles in a glass of champagne. I felt like Lazarus walking
among the living, scraps of grave clothes dragging behind him, easy
to shake loose. And though this creative surge came on suddenly,
it did not slow quickly. The summer and fall of '39 proved to be a
wellspring for me. Out of my pain, out of the ashes, came beauty and
art. Pages of ink accumulated on my desk. In recounting my days
with the Baron I suddenly had come up with a literary context that
I could use to fashion my lectures, my translations, and most of my
experiences since then. I felt an uncanny confidence that I was about
to birth a book or a poem or maybe several that would be meaningful
and valued. I felt like Apollo or some other god, like the giant Sun
god in Greek mythology that Felton often mentioned, *Hyperion*!

The muse made me feel so powerful that I became insane or
foolish or both, but how else might one succeed if not willing to risk
failure? It is out of new and greater failures that the possibility of even
greater success might come!

I had often thought that life was full of mostly little disappointments and little pleasures, but now I could see that was only the half of it. Life, I suspected, was also filled with big disappointments and big pleasures. Life was hard and there was trouble in the world, but there was good reason to take heart. Troubles could be overcome, even if originally compounded by your own hand.

And so it was, in a crazed mix of passion and frenzied faith and diligent devotion, that I began crafting verse after verse, mixed with passages of prose. My pen left no feeling or experience unexplored. At some point, I ran my cushioned diligence off the road, so to speak, and into some errant verses of Dante. That experience birthed ever more romantic notions, and finding nothing to oppose them, I kept going, intoxicated by the possibilities. I knew little of where on the map of life and art I was headed, and I didn't care. By the middle of the year, I was near complete with a collection of poems, *Voices in the Night*, and had finished something that was more than a book, *Hyperion*. That book would be a shooting star for all the heavens to witness! And I had landed a publisher. I wrote letters, too—filled with all the flashing my liberated muse could muster.

July 23, 1839

My dear Greene,

There you are in Rome, with the world marching before you, and you have no more to say than if you were in East Greenwich. And when I want particulars, you laugh in my face, and then fill a whole page with broken columns, moonlight, and the Coliseum; as if I were a female cousin and kept an album. Now having disgorged this crude mass, let us pass to more important matters.

You will probably smile with an enthusiasm about this, and you may think to say, "Oh, he will get over it! He can get over it if he has a mind to!"

I have not got over it!

Depend upon it, my dear George, before this calendar expires I will have given up some fruit of my pen for all to digest and consider. More than this, soon I shall fire off a rocket, which I trust will make a commotion in a certain citadel on Beacon Street. Perhaps the garrison of one I have for some time admired will capitulate—or, perhaps the rocket may burst and kill me. Ha! We will know soon.

I mean to say that I have written a romance during the last year, into which I have put my feelings—my hopes and sufferings for the last three years. Things are shadowed forth with distinctness enough to be understood; and yet so mingled with fiction in the events set down as to raise doubt, and perplexity. The feelings of the book are true—the events of the story fictitious. Mostly. The heroine, of course, bears a resemblance to the lady without being an exact portrait; so that the reader will say "It is—no, it is not! And yet it must be!" Don't misunderstand me. There is no betrayal of confidence, no real scene described and the lady so painted (unless I deceive myself) as to make her fall in love with her own sweet image in the book.

And now, my dear George, look one moment at the circumstances under which I have been at work upon this book—or rather under which the book has been at work on me. My wife's death—my meeting with this lady—my return, and a whole year's delirium of hope, before she came, during which my imagination had time to forge fetters as strong as the threads of life—then her return and the catastrophes—multitudes of them—and an eighteen months' struggle—humiliation— wounded pride, wounded affection—derision—so many like you finding marital bliss yourselves—conflicting feelings enough to drive one mad. Well, during the last year, and under this pressure, the book has been produced. And if now and then there be a passage, which to a well man, in the light of sober reason may seem a little morbid—is it any wonder?

Now I think you will understand Hyperion (which I am calling it) and so far from it appearing extravagant to you, seen in this light, it will look absolutely tame. My heart has been put into the printing press and stamped on the pages.

Now I hardly need to tell you that I look forward with intense interest to next week. The publication of the book will probably call down upon my head tremendous censure; and I trust also equal applause. My friends here are very extravagant in their praises. If the public coincides with their judgment I shall be quite famous.

As for what it means to the dark lady? We shall soon see…

Very truly yours
Longfellow

When *Hyperion* came off the press, I knew I would yet live happily. No more the fear of becoming a fat mill-horse professor treading out grain with blinders around my eyes and a harness for a heart. My newly published work would change everything.

I sent a copy, along with a gift of a fine round Swiss cheese, to the Appleton home. With fall approaching, it was time to learn what the dark lady, my Madonna, my Beatrice, Fanny Appleton, thought of her relentless knight, the not-yet-too-old Professor Longfellow.

Chapter 15

I TOOK THE BUS TO Beacon Street donning not my blackest clothes but my brightest, with my new walking stick and shiniest vest. My gloves were tan and smooth, my fingers as warm as my heart, my hat as secure as my knowledge of how poetry can work on a noble woman with an intellectual air. I sat in the middle of the carriage, away from the seats positioned over the axles where the bumps were more pronounced and though jostled, arrived quite comfortably and in order. I stepped down, tipped generously, more than I could afford, and enjoyed the sound as my soles clapped the brick walk. I had timed the delivery of my package of love as perfectly as any verse I had ever penned. It had arrived one evening last week, probably before dinner, which would have worked well, considering the cheese included with it.

The world was now Fanny's and mine to share. I knocked on the oak door at 39 Beacon Street with the force and confidence of a man ready to storm heaven, my entrance secured by a work of selfless love captured in words.

A butler I did not recognize opened the door. "Yes?" the elderly gentleman asked.

"Professor!" Mary Appleton exclaimed, grinning as she approached from behind him. Her white dress, all lace and frills, glistened in the afternoon light. "What a dear, dear surprise! It has been too long since you've darkened our doorway. Do come in!"

She glided backwards and motioned inside with her elegant arm. The butler nodded and stood aside.

"Mary," I said with a broad smile and a tip of my hat. I wondered how many of the family members were at home and hoped I might be lucky enough to find Fanny seated alone in the parlor. By the time I stepped aside to permit the butler to receive my hat and cane and then moved farther aside to permit ample room for him to close the door, my heart had already skipped out of rhythm at the sight of the empty room beyond the foyer. "Have I missed your afternoon gathering?" I tried to remember the time of day they usually took company.

Mary took my arm and led me to the center of the room. "Only myself and Fanny are here. We haven't had afternoon gatherings in many weeks. Father has been consumed with business and mother left for New York only today. Tom is wandering somewhere in Boston, who can say where? Here, please be comfortable. Would you enjoy some refreshment?"

I sat, aching over the empty staircase that could lead me to my love, if only I had the courage to climb it. I returned my attention to my love's sister instead. "You look as lovely as a sunburst, Mary. As white and radiant as your reputation, and deservedly so."

"You are kind, Henry. May I get you some wine, or tea, or some other refreshment? And then you must tell me everything that is happening with you."

"A glass of wine would do me well."

"Horace, a glass of Rhine wine for Mr. Longfellow. I am fine."

The butler left. I took advantage of the moment to look in every direction, but there was still no sign of Fanny.

"Do tell me what's happening with you, Henry. Many good things, I'm sure."

"Your confidence is dear to me. You are correct; all is proceeding well these days. *Hyperion* is published, as you know."

"Yes. Thank you for the copy and the delicious cheese." She sat as one sat for a painter, lovely and joyous and still.

I waited but she said nothing more. "Have you had a chance to look at it?"

"Fanny has it."

A warm blanket enveloped me. I realized I was biting my lip and immediately ceased.

"None of us have had a chance to hold it," Mary continued. "Tell me, what is it about? This way I may acquire some great expectations to inspire me to steal it from her, if perchance it becomes possible to get near it."

Horace arrived and lowered the tray for my easy reach. I lifted the glass, sniffed it, and nodded. The butler withdrew. I sipped. Room temperature and wonderfully dry. "It is about many things really." I set the glass down.

"Such as?" She leaned forward and nodded without lessening her smile.

I inhaled, leaned back, and opened my mouth, but the motion of gliding green silk caught my peripheral vision and stopped me.

"There are exquisite things in the book" Fanny remarked as she cascaded down the staircase. It was an identical entrance to the one I had seen her make before. Did she do that on purpose?

"Fanny! I'm so glad you've come down. The professor is about to reveal some things about his book. I've explained that you've not let anyone even chance upon it, but that's about to end!" She clapped her hands together and grinned broadly.

Fanny smiled at her sister in a strange way, with a sideways tilt of her head, but she never broke her steady stride and stopped a few feet in front of me.

I leapt up, tugging my coat by the bottom corners and quickly smoothing my lapel. "Lady Fanny, it is good to see you."

Fanny turned. "Sister, I think it better you hear nothing of the book ahead of reading it. However, I strongly desire to speak with the professor about it. Might you be willing to remove yourself for a short time so that we do not spoil any of its surprises?"

Mary's glad face froze, her pretty mouth slightly open, but only for a moment. "Of course, Frances. Very sensible." Her attractive smile had returned, and she nodded at me. "Do not leave without my rejoining the conversation, Henry. As I said, it is always nice to receive your company in our home." She extended her hand, and curtsied slightly.

"Thank you, Mary. The occasion is no less delightful to me." I pecked her hand and then faced her most beautiful sister.

Fanny crossed to where Mary had been seated but waited until Mary was out of the room before she sat down, her posture rigid. I sat, too, but Fanny, seemingly lost in thought, stared toward a window. Uncomfortable, I sipped more wine. She at last turned and looked me straight in the eyes and was about to speak when Horace arrived. "May I bring anything for the lady?" he asked.

"Only some private time with the professor, Horace, thank you. I'll call for you if anything else is needed."

The butler bowed and left. I set my glass down and gazed into her eyes, finding them fixed upon me. They were as big and dark and lovely as I remembered, as I had written about them. I hoped my face made my feelings clear. "You have read my book, I take it?"

She took her time to answer, obviously being careful in the choosing of her words. It was as I had dreamed it would be—just the two of us. No mystery—a clear, up-front statement lauding the book—the one with large portions written just for her. Miracles did happen. God was alive. Only one thing didn't match perfectly, and that was her expression. She was not pursing her lips that were deep red and distracting, nor was she wrinkling her forehead, nor narrowing her eyes, thank God, but neither was she smiling. When she spoke, her words, though not prickly, lacked warmth. "You sent me a copy of your *Hyperion*, which was civil enough, and with it a Swiss cheese."

I laughed. Somehow the cheese seemed funny now. "Yes." I took up the wine glass, and then improved my posture. I lifted the glass higher. "To healthy appetites and good reads, if I may." I sipped but the good cheer died somewhere between the taste and the clinking of the glass as I set it on the table. It was her stare and solidly fixed jaw that were beginning to concern me. She hadn't blinked once that I could tell. I cleared my throat. "Do you really think it exquisite?"

"I mentioned there are exquisite things in it." She appeared about to say more but then didn't. She was battling something. It was possible my book had touched her even more deeply than I had hoped.

I thought to reach for the glass again, looking for a way to fill the void, but I was afraid of not being able to hold it steady. I clenched my fists in my lap, then forced them apart and folded my arms before pulling one of my sleeves longer. Blasted—what to do with my limbs! I sat back and placed my clasped hands in my lap. "And?"

"The style is infinitely polished and sparkling though many of the poetical passages rang familiar, I thought." She spoke, evenly toned, with barely a move of her form. Her full red lips did all the work. "In my opinion," she added, with the slightest nod.

Not a horrible thing to say. Perfection was difficult. She must know that also. "Sparkling?" I repeated. "That is a fine compliment. I know you are well read. That is no secret. If you say it sparkles then it must to some degree."

I took her next nod as agreement, but she remained unsmiling. "You ought to be praised for your scholastic lore and vivid imagination," she said. "You create infinite comparisons, very just and well carried out."

"Thank you so much." If only her expression matched her words, I would have been beside myself with joy.

"Some words tickle my bump of comparison vastly. For example, comparing a glacier's various branches to the fingers of a glove and the whole to a gauntlet that winter has thrown down and which the sun is trying vainly to raise on the point of a glittering lance. These I thought worthy of what the craft ought to do."

My hands were sweaty but my neck was cooling. "Thank you." I glanced anxiously.

"The hero is evidently you? Yes?"

My mouth became drier. I reached for the glass. My hand shook, as I feared it would, but I needed to do something, so uncertain was I of where this conversation was going. I gulped more than sipped and set the glass down, splashing a drop onto the table. "Pardon me." I removed the hankie from my front pocket and wiped the spill. She never once looked at it, only at me. I looked at the stain on my square of muslin, and carefully refolded it, not sure where to go next.

"Many of your old ideas and old lectures have been fused into graceful chapters, which is fair enough—a pity they should achieve their destiny solely by enlightening the dull brains of college boys or scornful maidens."

I looked up. Her eyes had narrowed. "Scornful?"

Her face was unreadable, her lips articulate. "The adventures have not the same zest of novelty for me as they may for other people, since I have had the misfortune—pardon me, the experience—of being behind the scenes. I've seen the sets without the advantages of footlights." A wrinkle formed at the very top of her forehead, directly below the soft curls of her hair.

"I'm afraid I'm not following. Can you be more clear?" I crossed my right leg over the left, cupped my knee with my hands, and then opened my hands, reversed my legs, and cupped my other knee. A stabbing pain lanced my lower back.

Fanny Appleton stood, her dress gathered tightly in her hands to prevent knocking into table items and stared down at me. "I have been hoisted into such a state of public notoriety by your impertinence that I am entirely disgusted by the honor."

Something like a trap door opened and I fell helplessly into the midst of Dante's inferno. God was dead, and Fanny's eyes were slits.

She walked with heavy steps to a credenza at the base of the stairway. She yanked open the top drawer and pulled out a book. I recognized it as a copy of *Hyperion*. She flipped it open, shuffled through the pages, traced the length of one or two and then whirled around. She spoke with the projection of a Shakespearian actress standing far upstage and read directly from the text. "But pray tell me," her tone clearly sarcastic, "who was that young lady, with the soft voice?" She glared at me. "Do you recall writing these words?"

"Of—of course. Y–yes." My voice was suddenly far shakier than my hands.

She continued from the text. "What young lady with the soft voice?" Her tone was not flattering. "The young lady in black, who sat by the window." She turned the page. "Oh, she is the daughter of an English officer, who died not long ago at Naples. She is passing the summer here with her mother, for her health." Fanny took a deep breath. "What is her name?" She looked up at me and recited the next line by memory. "Ashburton." Her fiery red lips chiseled the words. She stalked three steps closer and read the next line. "Is she beautiful?" She looked up and calmly stepped closer until arriving near enough that I thought she might step on my toe. "Would you do me the honor, dear Professor?"

"What? What honor? Anything, of course." My face was red hot.

"The honor of reciting the next line to the *engrossed* company before you." That strange smile with the sideways tilt of her head returned.

"I—I don't recall."

"Try. Here, I'll repeat the previous one. 'Is she beautiful?'"

I lowered my head.

"Very well," she said. "I'll do the honor. 'Not in the least, but very intellectual. A woman of genius, I should say.'" She snapped the book shut.

I lifted my hands with palms up and looked at her, hoping my eyes were as pleading as I felt. "Fanny, it's not meant to be as literal as you think."

"The heroine, 'Mary Ashburton' as you call her, is wooed—like some persons I know have been—by the reading of German ballads, is she not?"

It hurt my neck to crane so much. "Y–yes, of course, but–but you know that–that life, as in art or in art, as in life—well, what I mean is that you shouldn't—"

She bent closer, put her finger to my lips, and spoke inches from my face. "You were accurate when you implied within your *Hyperion* that her ears were *unwilling* ears." She literally spat this, and her spittle landed above my upper lip. She seemed taken aback and embarrassed, and something like a fuse was ignited or dynamite exploded. She bared her teeth in a way I had never imagined and actually grunted like some wild creature. In a moment she was twirling around in a circle so fast that her dress swung high around her calves and I saw more petticoat than she had ever before revealed. I wanted to cry out and rescue her, but from what? My own words? I had failed, and there was nothing for me to do other than to disappear—if I could—but she keened an unceasing torrent of words that continued to give my mind something to process. Otherwise, I am sure my heart might have instantly stopped and I would have fallen dead in her parlor.

With her hands on her hips and the book close to being dropped, she ceased her turning and said, "Yes, there were some instances of things exquisite and sparkling, but over all I thought it desultory, objectless, a thing of shreds and patches like someone's demented mind." Her voice and intensity rose like a crescendo of out of tune violins or something equally horrendous. "And one more thing, Professor Longfellow. The cheese you sent was rank when it arrived, which to me testifies of your admiration. Both it and you are equally strong and disagreeable!"

By now I was all the way back in my chair, my hands and legs spread wide, my mouth gaping open. Fanny tossed the book across the floor and ran to the stairway. I watched both the sliding book and her rapid departure. I got up clumsily and then moved swiftly to the center of the room. "Fanny, wait! Wait! Please! I don't understand. You misunderstood my intentions! Everything I did—everything I wrote—was for you! Fanny, please! The book also describes you—uh, *her*—as 'Raphael's beautiful Madonna,' and 'a striking figure,' and in other places 'there was not one discordant thing in her but a perfect harmony of figure, and face, and soul,' don't you remember? Fleming saw her as 'the revelation of the beauty and excellence of the female character and intellect.' Didn't you read all of it? Did you?"

She stopped halfway up the stairs. "Don't feel bound to flatter me, Mister Longfellow. It's no use, and I prefer to be entertained, not flattered. You think because you are writing to a woman she must be dosed with sugarplums. I *hate* sweet things!" She resumed her ascent but turned again. "That is, too many of them."

I stood at the bottom. "Fanny, please! Let us sit and talk about this calmly."

She stood at the top of the staircase and looked over the rail. "You've humiliated me in front of all society. I shall never forgive you." And then, with a rustle of fabric and a swirling of green, she was gone.

Winter followed.

Chapter 16

January 2, 1840

Dearissimo George,

It is now half-past nine at night. I have just been taking a solitary supper of sardines and wishing myself where they came from, namely in the Mediterranean.

Since my last letter I have published another book—a volume of poems, with the title Voices of the Night. *It contains "Psalms" and some of the earlier poems. Its success has been signal. It has not been out three weeks and the publisher has not more than fifty copies left.* Hyperion *they could not understand. No matter, I had the glorious satisfaction of writing it and thereby gained a great victory, not over the "dark lady" but over myself. I now once more rejoice in my freedom, and am no longer the thrall of anyone. I have great faith in one's writing himself clear from a passion—giving vent to the pent-up fire. But George, George! It was a horrible thing though at least and at last the newspapers that uttered such dispraise have grown quieter. How victorious silence would be.*

I have broken ground in a new field; namely, ballads, beginning with the "Wreck of the Schooner Hesperus," on the reef of Norman's Woe, in the great storm of a fortnight ago. I shall send it to some newspaper. I think I shall write more. I have great faith in not saying much about a thing until you can say, "I have done it," It is often with authors as with money-diggers; if a word is spoken, the treasure sinks.

Concerning that which you likely crave to know more of, I can only write in this way. The brazen lips of Fate have said, "Time is past!" The dark lady and I now move wholly in separate orbs, and hardly see each other's faces. The passion is dead; and can revive no more. Though on this account I lead a maimed life; yet it is better thus, than merely to gain her consent—her cold consent—even if it could have been done. So of this no more— no more—forevermore! For though I feel deeply what it is not to have gained the love of such a woman—I have long ceased to think of it—and remember it only when I see my elasticity is nigh gone, and my temples are as white as snow. The best of these recent years of my life were melted down in that fiery crucible. Yet I like to feel deep emotions. The next best thing to complete success is complete failure. Misery lies halfway be- tween—so better hot or cold rather than lukewarm. But I have thrown myself into a reverie, and I can write no more tonight. I shall smoke, and then to bed.

Affectionately yours
HWL

Indignities occupied me more than my letter admitted. Alligators of all kinds were upon me so I ventured forth little, except to conduct Dante lectures at the college, for a short while, but I even found a way out of those.

I rarely left Craigie House. Friends called but I refused their invi- tations. I took sick leave and rarely got out of my sleeping gown. I sat in the parlor across from Mrs. Craigie, my lone companion. It was not Voltaire in her hands that now hid her face but the *Boston Quarterly Review*, and on her reading table, waiting a turn, the *Mercantile Journal* and some others along with *Burton's Gentleman's Review*.

She folded the *Quarterly* with her forefingers and peered over the top. Her turban and eyes were all I saw until she lowered the crinkled paper. "It's not worth reading, Henry."

I sank into the davenport. Beads of sweat formed on my forehead. Something like a brick sat in my stomach. "That bad?"

"Authors are often misunderstood, Henry." Mrs. Craigie set down the paper and reached for another. "You know that."

"Read it to me, please."

"Henry." She looked at me in such a cockeyed way I thought her turban might tip over. "I will not," she said. I wondered if she might be bald. "Why torture yourself?" she added.

"It is a writer's lot to hear what his accusers say." I pointed to the paper on the floor. "Please."

Mrs. Craigie closed her eyes, shook her head, and picked it up. She opened her eyes, licked her thumb, peeled back some pages, and scanned the columns. She snapped the paper free of wrinkles and read: "I do not like the book. It is such a journal as a man who reads a great deal makes from the scraps in his table-drawer." She folded the top half over. "You want me to continue?"

"Yes, Mrs. Craigie." My irritation was due as much to her slowing the entire process as it was to the content of the criticisms.

She snapped the paper to shield her face. "It is overloaded with prettinesses, which would tell well in conversation, but being woven into narrative, deform where they should adorn. You cannot guess why the book was written. The direct personal relation we are brought to with the author is unpleasing. We wish he had but idealized his tale, or put on the veil of poetry! But as it is, we are embarrassed by his extreme communicativeness and wonder that a man, who seems in other respects to have a mind of delicate texture, could write a letter about his private life to a public on which he has yet no claim. Indeed, this book will not add to the reputation of its author, which stood so fair before its publication." Mrs. Craigie folded the paper into neat squares and set it down on the arm of her chair.

My head felt like an overworked anvil. It was an odd thought, I know, but that's exactly what came to my mind. I was an old anvil that had received so many blows that subsequent poundings made little impression. To be an anvil is to expect nothing except what anvils receive. "The next," I said, loosely waving my hand to the pile of papers on her reading table.

"None of them are positive this week, Henry. Why not wait for some that praise you and we can at least alternate the readings?"

"Please, Mrs. Craigie." I leaned my head into my sweaty palm and lifted my eyebrows.

She picked up the *Mercantile Journal* and read it to herself.

"Mrs. Craigie!"

"Oh, all right, Henry. If you wish to be a martyr for all of art and literature today, I'll not stop you."

"Thank you, though it is for neither of those things. Do read."

"For *romance* then." She lowered the paper and stuck out her tongue and then lifted it again to cover her face and resumed loud and clear. "*Hyperion* is a mongrel mixture of description and criticism, travels and bibliography, and common-places clad in purple. It is all folly without a rag to cover it."

I switched to rest my cheek on my other hand. "At least it was brief."

"I'm glad you're an optimist, Henry." Mrs. Craigie switched to the last paper. She opened it and began with no reservation. "Here's another one from the fellow named Edgar Allen Poe. I think he wrote the first one I read, too. Ever hear of him?"

I barely lifted my head. "I noticed his byline when you brought in the papers. I suppose I'm about to. I think he praised *Outré Mer* previously."

"Were it possible to throw into a bag the lofty thought and manner of the *Pilgrims of the Rhine*, together with the quirks and quibbles and true humor of *Tristram Shandy*, not forgetting a few of the heartier drolleries of *Rabelais*, and one or two of the phantasy pieces of the Lorrainean Callafot, the whole, when well shaken up, and thrown out, would be a very tolerable imitation of *Hyperion*."

I sat up and straightened my head. "That isn't so bad."

"I'm not finished, Henry."

I leaned forward. "Then read. Read!"

"Hate yourself, if you must." Mrs. Craigie snapped the paper and read devoid of emotion. "This may appear to be commendation, but we do not intend it as such. Works like this of Professor Longfellow are the triumphs of Tom O'Bedlam, and the grief of all true criticism. That such things succeed at all is attributable to the sad fact that there exist men of genius who, now and then, unmindful of duty, utter them. A man of true talent who would demur at the great labor requisite for the stern demands of high art, apparently makes no scruple of scattering at random a profusion of rich thoughts into pages of confusion. We dismiss his book in brief. We grant him high qualities, but deny him the future. Without design; without shape; without beginning, middle, or end, what earthly object has his book accomplished?" Mrs. Craigie began folding the paper but then suddenly tossed it to the floor, picked up her copy of Voltaire, and held it up. "This man wasn't much approved of either, yet I know he has things worthwhile to say."

I stood up. I saw the variety of papers and one magazine in various conditions of folded and unfolded, crumpled and not, and the slim leather-bound volume in her hand. I offered something that felt in the direction of a smile. "I was not after eminence in this instance, Mrs. Craigie." I walked toward the stairs.

"I know exactly what you intended, Henry. But eminence will be yours just the same. It'll come, and when it does it will be heaped upon you because there is nothing of guile in you. Though a little might help!"

I turned and she winked. I shrugged. "Please tell Margaret to send my food to my room. Do you mind?"

"Have I ever minded the ten thousand other times?"

"I don't mean to be unsocial, Mrs. Craigie—"

"Neither do I, young man. Do what you will. I've lived this long, I may yet live to see you at my table."

I lumbered up the steps. I reached the halfway landing when the doorknocker sounded. "Henry!" Cornelius Felton's booming voice penetrated the closed front door. "Henry Longfellow. Felton has arrived!"

"Henry!" Mrs. Craigie called from the parlor.

"I'm not taking visitors, Mrs. Craigie." I started up the second half of the stairs.

"Neither am I," she replied.

"Then the door shall go unanswered."

"Henry!" Felton continued barking. "Open the door. I hear your voice. Hillard is here. Don't be rude!"

"Henry!" Mrs. Craigie spoke quite loudly. "I will open the door and send them up if you do not have the courtesy to at least greet them."

"Mrs. Craigie." My voice sounded as tired as I intended.

"I've done enough of your bidding today, Henry. Now be a stalwart man of letters and show your face to the public, no matter how capricious they are."

I descended and lazily threw open the door.

"Henry! By God, the rumors are true. You do live here!" Cornelius was dressed as if calling on the most fashionable of Boston society, as was Hillard, but I disagreed with the choice of their carnations. Wrong colors. Cornelius eyed me head to toe. Hillard appeared carved in stone, so fixed was his gaping. I pushed open the screen. "Hello Corny. George."

Cornelius led the way, but Hillard spoke. "You appear something of Longfellow's ghost."

"I've never known you to answer in your gown. Are you truly ill?" Cornelius asked.

"Of most things," I said, and motioned them to follow me upstairs.

"Good afternoon, Mrs. Craigie!" Cornelius shouted to the parlor.

"Hello, Professor Felton. It's nice to see you again, and you also, Mr. Hillard. Do see that Henry gets dressed and fed. And take him outside for a long walk if you will."

"We'll do all we can," Hillard responded.

Upstairs in my chamber my two friends quickly found their favorite chairs. I walked over to the fireplace and stared at the charred log, wondering if I had the strength to build a fire for my guests.

"With Sumner still in Europe and you hiding out, the Five of Clubs is hurting for stimulating evenings," Cornelius said. "You must return."

"Perhaps you should rename it the Three of Clubs."

"You don't mean that, Longfellow," George said. "Come, let's be about today. It will do you good."

"Don't forget they enjoyed *Outré Mer*. You'll bounce back with something to their liking." Cornelius crossed to the fireplace. "Where's the Longfellow with the taste for fine food and good wine and literary repartee?"

"Gentlemen, I am not bothered by the harsh treatments of newspapers." I walked to the window, distancing myself and turning my back. The Charles River looked flat and still. "I care not a fig."

"Hardly!" George scoffed. "It's damn unimpressive to be so pitiful as this, Longfellow. Come on man, do something to break its spell. Join us in society. It's the best way to liven up."

I faced them. "I've fired a rocket and it has blown up in my face. I am in shreds and need more time."

Cornelius opened his arms wide and laughed. "Can there be a

better remedy than this group? Let's escape to the fruits of the vine and remembrances of great minds and the works that still speak. Doesn't it all spring from these? Will it not again? Come, Henry, get dressed and please do shave."

I felt the bristle of my chin and cheeks. I crossed out of the room and into the adjoining one where I walked to the far window overlooking the garden. I knew by their heavy footsteps they were in close pursuit. The plantings were mostly brown. I faced my friends. "The Lady Madonna has fired a full broadside into my heart and my soul is awash with my own blood. Can I be any more clear?" There, it was out. Now they knew it was not the newspaper reviews but the dark lady responsible for this state of mind—and dress. Now, hopefully, they might leave. Hillard looked at Felton and Felton at Hillard, but neither appeared surprised. Cornelius touched my shoulder.

"We know that," Cornelius said. "The remedy remains the same. Time and activities will heal the wound."

I lowered my shoulder to be free of Felton's touch. "You know that? How?" I stepped away. "See, I cannot risk going anywhere that she might be. She will humiliate me further, feeling well justified, no doubt." I placed my open palm over my chest. "She views me as having perpetrated a great injustice upon her and therefore, believing God on her side, will let me know it in plain words and in the presence of others, I fear."

Cornelius smiled but then wiped his mouth with his thumb. "Henry, Fanny is refined enough that she won't do that, and we will move in other circles; you'll see." He again approached me, but I returned to the window.

"I move nowhere but within these walls."

"LONGFELLOW!" Hillard roared from the center of the room. I couldn't help but look. "You are being damned unreasonable. Damned unreasonable! You cannot live within these walls. You are a Harvard professor, a charter member of our own Five of Clubs, an author, and a poet in fine standing in this community, despite your recent black eye." Hillard paraded the room. "How you respond now shall say volumes to those whom you fear are watching you with opera glasses. Deny them their fun!" Hillard's arms waved like flags, and his words quickened with his pace. "Go out and show yourself unafraid, undaunted, and living and breathing and laughing and writing on. That's the mark to aim for!" Hillard's movements about the room made me feel lightheaded, but his words made some sense.

"You are somewhat right," I said, looking back at the garden. There were small patches of barely noticeable color, but from my window it was impossible to say what exactly they were. Still, they might be somewhat alive.

"Ah, good, then you'll dress and join us?" Cornelius again touched my shoulder.

"No."

"What?" Whether incredulous or angry, Hillard clearly disapproved.

I did not care. "I will write."

"You ought to breathe and live a little more." Cornelius spoke softer than Hillard. "Before you take that up again."

I turned my back and faced the garden more completely. I spoke to the windowpane. "Thank you for calling, gentlemen. I am not so certain that I am a good author, and perhaps no writer of romance, but there is a thing I can do, and until and unless I do it, I cannot live, I cannot breathe, and I will not leave this place. Perhaps, if you wait a few days, you may see me again more resembling him whom you prefer. Until then, please excuse me."

"Good God, you are too sensitive, Longfellow. Come, Corny. We are not welcome here." Hillard's footsteps were swift and heavy and ceased somewhere in the hallway. "Felton, are you coming?"

"I look forward to your return." Felton's voice was kind and inches from my shoulder. "Meanwhile, don't forget Dante or the many other things sown in you." Felton's touch on my arm was gentle, and then it was gone. His footsteps were slower and lighter than Hillard's but soon both were heard descending the stairs. I could hear their muffled voices exchanging pleasantries with Mrs. Craigie. The opening and closing of the front door sealed the affair closed, and I breathed a sigh of relief.

I recalled hearing that Sumner was excelling in Europe. Letters had informed the club that he was nearly lionized as a strong voice from the American shores. And why not? He was versed in law and literature and possessed many admirable qualities appreciated there. He had met notable people including that most prolific of English authors, Charles Dickens, and mentioned the possibility that Mr. Dickens might come to America in the future and, if so, he planned to visit our little group when he did. I hoped so, but even more I hoped for dear Sumner's return. I missed his levelheadedness. I missed his bold conversational style. I missed his love of literature and his passion for discussing it. Most of all, his was a kindred bachelor soul. I reasoned that I was like Dante and must live apart from the one I most desired. The first woman I loved was dead, and the second wanted nothing to do with me. So far as I was concerned, Sumner was a friend in spirit and truth—a passionate soul whose sense of mission and purpose mirrored my own. It helped that he was also single and had no qualms about it.

Chapter 17

"LONGFELLOW!" SUMNER HAD been marvelously improved by his foreign travel. He appeared more at ease, more self-assured, and with little sign of his earlier affectations. The five of us enjoyed a reunion dinner at Pine Bank at four o'clock on a Saturday in May. Cleveland looked pale—at home his wife doted over him more than a little—but he remained as engaged as possible given Sumner's domination with a nearly continuous discourse from dinner until eleven o'clock. He was full of anecdotes about many famous people on the European stage. Hillard smiled enviably and obviously was relieved to have his law partner returned. Felton seemed equally pleased with the new Charles.

"You would adore Dickens," Charles said, mostly to me. "His eyes flash as blue as your own, and he has a zest for life unrivaled except for mine! Oh! And we might as well consider the streets of Spain paved with gold if charm and lovely women are afforded their due. I never once forgot your reports of the Basque region, Henry, but I could not find my way out of Madrid for long before winding up in some other country! There was as much to do as ever and no way to do it all. So, I'll take your word for it if you take mine on all else, for I have returned with a vengeance. Despite our national ills I am certain this country is destined for great things! It is from a rich and noble blood we descend, and with a new slate and a new land we will proceed and improve the course of history!"

"I feel as though I've been sitting under the great falls of Niagara," Cleveland said in a rare moment of levity.

"May it be naught but inspiration you are drenched in," said Charles without missing a beat.

"We must call you Don Carlos from hereafter," was all I could think to add, although I didn't mean it to fit so perfectly at the time. The historical Carlos had been passionate and noble in many respects but also an inflexible reactionary. It was more the former than the latter I intended.

"This country is our oyster!" Charles raised his glass.

"To oysters and roisters!" Corny cleverly followed, straight on his heels.

"Hear, hear!" George chimed. His occasional melancholy over his domestic realities was nowhere in sight.

I laughed and drank. Sumner's joy became our joy, and Corny's resounding laughter helped enlarge it to the exclusion of all else for now. I did notice Cleveland not quite up to the humor of the others. We all had our little defeats, no doubt, but Cleveland seemed a bit preoccupied by whatever his might be. His eyes were alert but his countenance something less than brimming.

After that evening, I felt a new hope for happiness in my life. I resumed my lectures, improving my hold on Dante, or rather his hold on me, and was often joined by Charles as I once more began my walks about town. I avoided the Common and dined in strategic places where uncomfortable run-ins were not likely to occur. Strange it was, to be avoiding the one whom I had ached for instead of endeavoring to effect chance meetings. However, whatever the measure of remaining pain it was mitigated by the wonderfully distracting conversations I had regularly with Charles. It felt like we were stepping back into happier times when dreams were unassailed and the fruits of the future appeared still attainable. A kind of giddiness entered my soul and experimentation seemed worthwhile again. It paid off handsomely as I attempted a new structure in my poems, namely ballads, and I enjoyed some far kinder reviews to displace the old. It all seemed to be flowing smoothly until Charles and my social navigating began drifting into some older, more familiar places.

Charles Sumner's fine reputation of late resulted in more and more members of the well-established Bostonian set wanting to hear of his European exploits and discover how much the tall and now broad-shouldered, barrel-chested, and thoughtful man had matured. I recall how Nathan Appleton, and his brother Sam, having since become even more successful textile magnates, had invited Charles into their circle, and by default, brought near my world to Fanny's. At first, this filled me with trepidation, but it soon appeared possibly providential. After all, though I now can easily recognize it as only a matter of some months since my previous encounters with her, it felt then like a long passage of time and induced me to believe that things might have improved with our possibilities as much as they had for Sumner's prospects in Boston society. I further reasoned that I had long ago learned that a map viewed on paper was far different than one traveled by foot, and, so—well, we might misjudge some things from time to time.

I remember I had sat by my window the night before. The air was crisp with the new fragrance of the coming fall and the moon blazed red. My lonesomeness entered a current I had previously avoided but which I now felt to be exhilarating, and I allowed myself to dream of the dark lady. I knew she was far away and not dreaming of me, but surprisingly, this realization did not cause me pain. A thrilling self-deception entered my soul, egging me to believe I was now re-covered and able to withstand encounters of any kind with Fanny. Since Charles was leading me deeper and deeper into her circles, I determined God must also somehow be involved, coaxing me ever closer to the one I still greatly admired, now that I was again honest about it.

———

The party at the Ticknor's was the occasion to prove my sentiments right or wrong. Everyone was there. I was at total peace with myself and confident that I had within me all that was required to operate with a pleasant demeanor that would be generously distributed, without prejudice, to all present. Unfortunately, no sooner had I arrived that I saw, of all people, Hillard paying court to Fanny in a darkened corner. My blood boiled. I knew I had no right, no claim, but he was my friend; knew of my former struggles; and he, though suffering (according to him) with an unequal yoke in marriage, was nevertheless, married! And it did not make me feel too highly of her either. I was more than a little ruffled.

"Have you been out in the sun, Longfellow?" It was Corny.

I shook my head and redirected my gaze.

"You are redder than a fox!" he said, laughing so hard I feared others would be drawn to us.

"Henry! Corny!" Charles Sumner's voice boomed across the room. "Do come join us!"

Nathan and Sam Appleton; Judge Story, who also headed the law department at Harvard; and old Professor Ticknor surrounded Charles. Their side-by-side smiles shone like lights strung along the rail of a ship leading to one point at the bow. We could do nothing but head their way.

"Gentlemen!" Nathan Appleton stretched out his hand and vigorously shook mine. The others did likewise.

"Henry," Professor Ticknor's voice was still strong, despite how much he had aged. "It is so good to see you again."

"You have been strangely absent these days," Nathan added. "Your gentle ways and kind spirit have been missed around the Appleton home."

"That's because he not only commits to lecturing our young men in the great halls of Harvard, but he offers no less devotion to that perpetually flowing pen of his." Charles patted my shoulder robustly but his words gave me footing.

"I am so very proud of how you've filled my chair, son," Ticknor said, suddenly overcome with emotion and pulling out his handkerchief to dab his eyes.

"As are we all!" Corny added. "New England is the better for it!"

"Not only New England but the nation!" Charles added.

"If we can manage to keep the nation together," Sam Appleton threw in.

"But we must! There can be no room for Southern impudence when the laws of right and wrong are clear in the minds of every thinking man." Charles's voice deepened with resolve.

"Things are not always black and white." Nathan motioned to a waiter and a tray of fresh drinks was brought to us. "Abolition as an ideology is not fully practical, I'm afraid."

"Can morality be only a half-way proposition?" Charles asked. "Do we denounce thievery but permit rape? We do not!"

"No need for crude comparisons, Charles." Judge Story patted his shoulder like a father would his own son. "I've taught you better than that."

"You think it crude? I thought it obvious." Charles appeared hurt.

Professor Ticknor exchanged glances with Judge Story, though Charles failed to notice. Corny and I did, and the Appletons, too.

The waiter offered me the tray, but I shook my head. I needed my faculties. I was losing my sense of comfort and my appetite for food and drink had abated when I saw Fanny with Hillard.

"Gentlemen!" It was Hillard himself. "Allow me to introduce Samuel Howe, head of the Perkins Institute for the Blind." He was unknown to me but apparently an old friend of Sumner's.

"Samuel!" Charles offered him a bear hug. "Gentlemen, I present you a mind with no fear and a chivalrous man with refined taste to boot!"

"We are one fine mutual admiration society!" Corny added, I think in an attempt to change the subject from politics and race. I feigned my delight and felt sorry for my lack of integrity, but I now loathed Hillard. I looked past him and searched the room, but no one occupied the corner Fanny had been in. Then I heard her laugh and turned all the way around to find her enjoying the flatteries of three other men, none of whom I knew. I understood in an instant that I was being a jealous ass. I turned to George and nodded, trying to wordlessly apologize for something he likely did not suspect, and then I looked at Fanny once more. She moved gracefully, nodding everywhere but in my direction. At last, she turned toward me, but only for a moment and seemingly without recognition. When my attention returned to the group it was no longer in assembly. The Appleton's had begun a conversation with some other men, and Judge Story and Professor Ticknor had moved to chairs on the other side of the room. I had no idea where Corny and the other two men had gone, likely a different room. Only Charles remained.

"Why would he say that to me?" my friend asked.

"Who?"

"Judge Story. I thought you heard what he said to me." His usual glow of late was gone.

"I'm afraid I did not." I deliberately turned my attention to him. "What did he say?"

"He urged me to avoid radicalism."

"What do you think he meant?" I suspected I knew, but I wanted to steer clear of conflict while remaining engrossed in conversation. I did not want to be discovered staring again at the Madonna.

"I have no idea. What's worse is that he never brings up the subject of my chairing his department anymore or even of a simple professorship. He has aged in confusing ways. He's proving to be as impossible to please as my own father was, rest his soul."

Charles never felt much sympathy for his deceased father, and we all knew why. He had kept his father's insensitive sternness no secret to the club, but with Story he had enjoyed a bond and, apparently, there had been some career promises made. "I doubt you're seeing it clearly, Charles. He adores you as a son. We all know that."

"I am not sure." He shook his shoulders like he was ridding himself of some bothersome cloak. "Oh well."

I opened my mouth, wanting to pour out my pitiful laments about Fanny, but I knew from experience it would be better to keep quiet. I sighed.

"What is it, Longo?"

I smiled at his nickname for me that I didn't like. He had been calling me that of late and I never told him it was not a favorite. I opened my mouth then but sighed again. "I need to retire from society, I'm afraid."

"I'll join you." His words surprised me.

I waited for him outside of the Ticknor's home while he said proper goodbyes.

As we walked down Beacon Hill, past the Appleton home and toward the bridge, Charles said, "I'll walk you as far as the river." His home with his mother and sisters was only a block away on Hancock Street, so his willingness to walk several blocks out of his way felt more than kind. "You are troubled, Longo, and I want to know why."

"I have been unfit for too many exertions of late," I mumbled.

"There is a certain melancholy about you that I do not understand. Your success with *Voices of the Night* has been signal, and I expect your upcoming ballads to be no less so. The praises we give you when reviewing them during club sessions are not merely flatteries, I assure you. Mark my words, "The Wreck of the Hesperus" and the poem about the smithy will bring you fame, if not also fortune. You are a voice, my friend. Do not doubt it."

"I have been home four years since my return from Europe. I had imagined better things by now." We turned down Charles Street.

"Ha! I know. When my foot touched shore last spring, I felt sure my path would be ablaze with renown, but obviously the Judge doesn't agree. Not everyone receives me as I expected."

We both seemed to be thinking more, but we spoke nothing else until we arrived at the entrance to the bridge. "Thank you, Charles."

"Let's cross halfway. We can part there."

We made small talk about the river and finally stopped to gaze over the railing at its winding flow to the sea. "Charles Street, Charles River, and Charles Sumner," I said. "A grand combination. I'm not able to count how many times I've stopped here. Sometimes with Corny or someone else, but many times alone."

"It is a peaceful location."

"It has been a balm for me. I often relate rivers with the stream of life."

"Perhaps you may write of this one some day, in song I mean, in that Longfellow verse of yours."

Oft in sadness and in illness, I have watched thy current glide.

There it was, the rise of verse. I wanted to tell Charles, but the verses continued and I dared not interrupt them.

Till the beauty of your stillness, overflowed me like a tide.

"Where did you go, Longo?"

I held his question in the docket of my mind while the verses flowed through me.

And in better hours and brighter, When I saw thy waters gleam,
I have felt my heart beat lighter, and leap onward with thy stream.

"Longo?"

I smiled. "Still here. Just thinking."

"We shall take up arms again and face this tyrant called life." He stretched his arms and yawned like some great bear. "But not this night."

"Have you any other plans tonight?"

"No! My pillow is all that beckons me. Tomorrow requires me refreshed." He took hold of my hand. He did not know his strength. I tried not to wince. "It is good to be friends in this age and in this hour, is it not? Good night, Longo."

"Goodnight, Don Carlos!"

He laughed. I watched him walk in and out of lamplights until he disappeared into the night. I looked back at the river and a new thought arose.

More than this, thy name reminds me, of my friend, true and tried,
And that name, like magic binds me, closer, closer to thy side.

I realized I had a new poem. If I could find a way to build it and finish it, I might be able to include it in my next volume. This gave me some comfort, but poems were fickle. Already I was thinking of two other friends named Charles and wondering if it were best to include allusions to all three or just this one. I didn't know. So many questions needed answering before this unlikely midwife birthed a poem.

As I stood on the bridge, I recalled the Greek hero of mythology, Ajax. He had been battling his foe Hector when Zeus covered their battlefield in fog so that Ajax could not see the one whom he battled. In the Iliad, Ajax's prayer was for light. If he was to die in battle, he wanted to be able to see, to die in the light. A new meaning from the myth arose in me. Ajax did not call for his foe to be removed or his fate to be altered—but only for light so that he could see what he was up against. That's when I uttered my own prayer and it came forth like a song.

I would have to figure out something to do with all of this, but not now. The night was chilly, and a considerable walk remained.

Chapter 18

I WAS THIRTY-FIVE IN 1842 when Mrs. Craigie died, and only the canker worms and her library remained. I inherited those from her, though I much preferred her quiet company if I had the choice.

I was still a wounded man and feared a life alone knowing I was a soul who needed a female companion to cherish and be cherished by. I was enjoying a little success with my two published books of poems, and the Harvard lectures had been going well.

I was invited to develop an anthology of poems by European poets. It was a prestigious project. I felt honored. Thoreau and other students were blossoming under my eyes. Nate Hawthorne was enjoying some success with his moral pen, and we chatted from time to time, praising one another and imagining works we might attempt together, though I doubted we ever would. My social enterprises improved. Though Sumner's return to the club was no small joy to me, Cleveland left for Cuba on account of his health, and I missed him greatly. Little did I know his departure would be the last time I would ever see him. He would die on that tiny island within two years.

I was still dying of a broken heart, yet lived on determined to wear nothing but dignity on my sleeve. Distractions came and worked their temporary balms, some more spectacularly than others. One of the more delightful experiences was when Dickens arrived in Boston to commence his tour of America.

The "Incomparable Boz" received me a few days after his wildly celebrated arrival. He had a bright face with arresting blue eyes and long black hair. All of Boston was astir. I met him in his rooms at Tremont House as did Corny and Charles who already knew him and made my visit possible. He had innumerable invitations and barely a moment's rest, but he seemed to relish our company and expressed "a glorious delight" when he heard our Five of Clubs was inspired by his own *Pickwick Papers* and the hilarious Pickwick Club.

There are, of course, many things I could tell you about those days with Dickens, then only twenty-nine years old and already so brilliant and celebrated. We went for a long walk, about ten miles it seemed, just the two of us, and I showed him some key sites where our two nations had faced off during the Revolution. I took him to the Bunker Hill Monument and showed him the Old North Church where the lanterns had been hung to warn of the arriving British and thought of a poem I might write about it. We attended a ridiculously large celebratory dinner in his honor at Papanti's Hall with ten courses that included oysters prepared three different ways and four delicious veal dishes. I counted over thirty guests rising with toasts. His replying toast is worthy of recall. "To America and England, may they never have any division but the Atlantic between them!"

I recall the breakfast at my house, which he and a few close friends attended. My home felt very warm and welcoming that morning, and I knew Mrs. Craigie would be beside herself with joy if she were alive to see this. Corny reminded me very much of a beaming child when he arrived with both hands full of flowers. He had become a devoted companion to our esteemed friend and went so far as to board a train with him for the next leg of his American trip—a tour of New York City. Upon returning, Corny regaled us with uproarious stories of their nights out and even produced a letter addressed to me, inviting me to the author's home should I ever venture again to England.

Despite these pleasantries, I began thinking I must get away from the convolutions of my life in America. Even the Five of Clubs was departing from the delights of things literary and historical and turning to things contemporary and confused. The South was threatening to bite the proverbial hand that fed it, speaking of secession and impressing their vile institution of slavery northward and westward in seditious ways that would only grow like a blight upon the land. More and more, in college and out, in the street and at the table, the conversations turned to the troubles of our times without consensus about how to mend the troubles of the hour. Opinions were strong and fissures appeared, and yet, as always, I was more obsessed with the cracks and crevices in my own soul. I feared more for my life than for the lives of others, though I never saw it that way. I saw myself as worthy but wounded. I considered myself good intentioned but deprived of opportunity. My writing offered sugarplums when only a tourniquet would do. My eyes and head ached, various burning sensations riddled my every joint and movement, and deep and restful sleep eluded me.

Dickens's invitation prompted me to remember my time in England and on the continent. When I had first set foot in those faraway places and looked in the direction of my own future, I recalled having been *certain* then what now would bring, but I had misjudged.

Eminence had definitely not come. With its absence was also a lack of legacy, a barrenness of progeny, in all ways imaginable. Mary was dead, our child unborn; Frances was unapproachable and true fame—the kind that lives into the next century and the one after— unlikely. My poems were trifles and the things I most deeply felt had yet to find place on paper. They flowed in my blood but not from my pen. Fear had become my master. Life felt pointless. So, I made a decision.

"The waters at Marienberg!" Cornelius was aghast. "But your lectures! The corporation will never permit it."

"Certainly not," Sumner agreed. "I, more than anyone else here, lose the most if you depart for Europe. I am desolate without your company. Your sympathies and kind words have been too abundant to easily surrender. Why must you go?"

"To try the effect of the cold baths at the old convent on the Rhine," I explained. "The water cure!"

"But why, Henry? What ails you?"

"Corny, I cannot continue. I am caved in. I have no zest for anything. My highest dreams are vanquished, my life halfway done. I fear—I fear I might do…"

"Henry." Cornelius suddenly understood what I had almost said. His voice softened. "I did not realize how troubled you are within. I've known of your sadness, of course, but to think it is so great that you would risk your position at Harvard and allude to a tragic fate causes me great alarm. I know for certain they cannot afford to pay you for long while hiring another in your absence."

"I understand the possibility of the outcome, but I have no choice. I am broken. The old must be removed and something fresh must take its place or—or—"

"Don't say it!" Sumner boomed. "And don't ever do it!" He placed his hands upon my shoulders and gripped hard. "If you feel this deeply, there must be a way, though at the expense of my own happiness in this American backwater. How will I survive without Longfellow in my corner, speaking truth to my heart, like an oracle of God? Hm? How? But, if you insist, and I hear that you do, we will find a way."

I didn't want it to happen, but a tear rolled down my left cheek and then another. I tried to turn away but Sumner's grip had me.

Cornelius stepped forward. "I could offer to cover your supervisory capacity and charge them nothing for it. That way, they'll experience no increased costs. But for how long, Henry? It cannot be indefinite."

I nudged Sumner's hands away and sat down on the foot of my bed. "Six months?" It was more plea than question.

"If the corporation concurs, we will fully support you, and we will be with you in spirit." Cornelius's eyes were round and troubled.

Sumner sat beside me, and the whole bed leaned hard to the left. "We will hold you up in our prayers, dear friend. You shall see! You will return with heart and spirit soaring!"

Chapter 19

IT WAS THE FIRST WEEK in June when I arrived at Marienberg. I spoke German well enough to understand what everyone said but the treatment process remained unclear. I decided to write once and once only and then to retire my pen until the treatments were completed. I looked through my windows to the housetops below, and then sat at the writing table and penned a letter to my friends.

Marienberg at Boppard, April 23, 1842

To Cornelius Conway Felton, George Stillman Hillard
and Charles Sumner

My dear Children

I have arrived today. You may know the entire route but I include it here. Arrived in Havre after twenty-two days across the sea, but there was no steamer for Antwerp; and the boat for Rotterdam sailed the day before, so I went to Paris in a Diligence. After four days in the Hotel de Paris I took the train to Antwerp, Ghent, Bruges; back to Bruxelles, through Aix-la-Chapelle, and Cologne, and finally up the Rhine to this ancient cloister, embosomed in high hills overlooking the German town of Boppard. Initial consultations with doctor said much, revealed little. I take the first plunge tomorrow.

My windows look down into the garden, and a wooded valley, with glimpses of the Rhine. It makes a most spectacular sweeping curve around the whole location. It is all exceedingly pleasant, though I am impatient to commence my baths. At present there are only about thirty patients here.

As for me, I will write nothing save this letter while I am here. I am here for my health; and am in retirement among these hills of the Rhine. I shall have little time for study or observation. The elasticity of my mind is gone. Until I get well I shall do nothing.

Much love to all of you; and kind remembrances to the Ticknor's, Norton's, Howe, the Guilds &c &c &c

H.W.L.

Four o'clock in the morning came well before sun-up and my mind was as dark as the pitch around me. It took several moments before I realized I had been hearing this infernal knocking, like church bells declaring a late hour, for some time. But this was no late hour, and the banging and beckoning did not cease.

"Mister Longfellow, it is time!" The voice was polite but persistent.

I had no energy to exit my bed. "Come back later, please!" I moaned.

The door unlatched and a solitary figure stood in the doorway with a candlestick and a key. "That will not do, sir. We must not violate the protocol." The shadowy figure became taller and clearer as it approached. It was a thin man with a long mustache and thick eyebrows. He held a large bundle under one arm. "You are in your sleeping gown?"

"Of course I'm in my sleeping gown. I am sleeping!" I shielded my eyes from the flickering candle as the man lowered it within inches of my face.

"That is well enough. You may remain in your gown, but please remove your covers. It is time to begin."

"Can we not wait for the sun?"

The man set the bundle down. It was a pile of thick blankets. "No, we cannot." The man drew my covers all the way down past the bottoms of my feet.

"What are you doing?" I felt to make sure all modesty was in place and propped up on an elbow.

"No, please stay reclined, fully on your back, please."

"Why? What is to happen? Are you certain you're in the correct room?"

The man returned the candle to flicker near my face. "Professor Longfellow, yes?"

"As best I know. It is early enough that I might be mistaken."

"Amusing, sir," he said without a hint of humor. "I am not mistaken. This is the beginning of your treatment. We are to sweat out impurities in the same way a fever breaks the hold of illness. These blankets will properly prepare your physiology for the morning bath." The man set the candle down on the bed stand and lifted a blanket. "These are wool and will be properly effective." He snapped it to flutter over and worked it to float a soft landing along the length of my form. Next, the man swiftly knifed the edges of the blanket under the entire perimeter of my body.

"That's quite tight. I assure you, I've no intention of escaping."

"It must be that way so you sweat profusely, sir." The man snapped another blanket and floated it into perfect position, followed by another series of sharp jabs under the bottom sides of my shoulders, arms, legs and feet.

"I feel like a human corset."

"No, sir, you are a man encased in woolen blankets." The man unveiled a third and then a fourth and fifth to bundle me in a fivefold wrap.

"You have set me on fire!" I couldn't wiggle a finger. "This is quite peculiar."

"You must lie still for an hour."

"An hour? Impossible!" I tried to create some space between my arms and sides.

"You must not wriggle free." The man made another round of stabbing tucks. "It is critical you perspire to a great degree." He then drew up my original set of covers, including the quilt. "I will return in an hour. Please do not free yourself or the day and the treatment will be wasted." The man retrieved his candle, and closed the door to abandon me to heat and darkness.

I wished I had shaved. My cheeks and chin prickled. My face grew warm. Droplets formed on my forehead as if I'd been splattered. Creases in my neck and places around my eyes grew hot and moist while the inside of my mouth became dry and sticky. Uncomfortable heat arose in various places, drawing my attention to specific spots—between my toes, behind my knees, inside my legs, across my palms, and under my arms. My head tingled. Each thread of hair became a needle and my scalp a pincushion. The droplets on my forehead grew larger and rolled down into my eyes; others streamed down my cheeks racing to the creases in my neck. This was madness. There was no way I could last the hour.

I came here for baths, not lava treatments. Who can endure this? Certainly not I! My mind grew as hot as my body, and my thoughts ran like the perspiration tracing my limbs: wild thoughts, reckless thoughts, crazed.

I drifted into a dream without realizing it. Sumner was lying in bed next to me covered in tar up to his neck. I cried out, "Fanny is lost!" and fell on his neck and wept. But Sumner was not in my arms. It was Felton pointing with his floppy hat to a place in the midst of the Charles River. We were atop the bridge connecting Cambridge to Boston, and Corny said, "Don't do it, Longfellow." But I, dressed in medieval robes and hood, teetered upon the rail. "I must!" I opened my arms and fell forward. I landed in a gurgling flow of flaming lava, pouring over the ruins of Rome and smothering fields of screaming children. I was on fire but I was not consumed. I saw a giant chestnut tree with cradle enough between its two enormous branches that I knew shelter could be found. I grasped for it, swung out of the fiery river, and landed on my knees in the crotch of the tree, but it was not a tree. I was kneeling before a horribly perspiring Mary in the throes of childbirth, her knees bent and legs wide, and into my hands gushed something warm. I looked down, and from between the branches of the tree flowed a mass of bloody flesh and autumn leaves. It burned my hands. "MY CHILD!" I screamed, looking skyward and yelling as though I could rattle heaven from its place. I startled awake and saw nothing but shades of darkness, curved arches, and a whisper of light from the window that must have been the moon. I craned my neck but my movement was limited. I turned the other way and remembered where I was and why I was in my chamber wrapped like a carpet being shipped to far away shores. "I CANNOT DO THIS!" I cried out.

My body felt soaked in fire. Something like steam or wafts of heat emanated from me with seeming deadly intent. The air about my face felt like a fog.

"Mister Longfellow, it is time." The man with the mustache and candle was back. He unwrapped me for what felt like an eternity of time. Each blanket peeled was like a layer of thick skin being removed until I at last could move and breathe. This brought with it a sensation of coolness. I sat up, and dizziness sent me flopping back down. "Not too fast, sir. When you are ready step into this robe."

I looked at the man. He stood unblinking with robe open. Another older man, with a long white beard held the candle. I had never seen him before but I really didn't care who was there. I slowly sat up and cautiously arose. "I don't want this useless rag upon me," I said, tugging on the wet fabric clinging to me.

"You needn't keep it. It will be washed for you."

I had trouble removing my sopped sleeping gown, and the older man assisted me, but it did not matter that I was naked before strangers. Modesty was abandoned. I could not tolerate sweaty material against my skin. The robe felt smooth and cool.

"Please, Mister Longfellow," a female voice spoke. "Sit here." A woman? I saw her move into the glow of the candlelight pushing a wheelchair. She was old, but her face was strong and her cheeks hollow. She had a large mole on her square chin, and for the first time I wondered if I would ever really recover. "Byron will assist you," she said quietly.

The man with the mustache helped me ease into the seat. The woman then pushed me out of my room, while the men followed. The corridor was long and creepy. The shadows, cast by the lanterns upon the walls, moved over us like cables. We passed under a giant arch into another long hallway and arrived at a massive door with steel rings and great hinges. The two men worked together to push it open. It groaned like a ship rising on a tide, and soon we were rolling down a great long ramp, passing from one pool of torchlight to the next. After we had descended three or four of these ramps we came to an open space. It was well lit by torches and lanterns, and round pools glistened between ancient columns of granite. At the far end was a giant pipe that dropped gushing water into a main pool where it flowed into several others pools through narrow canals. I followed the course of the currents and saw a great drain at the opposite end where the water disappeared somewhere beneath the old convent.

"As you are ready, sir," Byron said, "plunge into one of these smaller baths of running water. Bathe yourself as much as you can, soaking your entire body. Massage the water into your joints and muscles as well as you can." The three practitioners waited on me, standing silent, their eyes cast downward. I cleared my throat and stood slowly, not wanting any dizziness. At the edge of a small pool I looked back, but all eyes remained downcast. I slowly pulled one arm out of my robe, but no one paid me the least attention. I draped the robe onto the chair and slipped my right foot in. It was wonderfully cool. I stepped in and felt a most welcoming relief. I moved about and squatted to immerse my body to chest level. The current flowed briskly on all sides. I sat down with my legs extended. The current was brisk enough to require me to steady myself; else I'd be pushed backwards. The water brought me coolness and comfort, and the current nearly washed me by itself, but I splashed and rubbed and dunked and soaked. I could easily have done this for hours.

"It is time, sir," Byron said suddenly.

"Time for what?" The water dripped down my face and my hair was matted, but I didn't care.

"To get dressed and enjoy a morning walk."

———

The walk passed through the gardens and by several fountains, all of which I had been instructed to drink from. The waters were from the surroundings hills and were rich with nutrients and minerals to restore the health. For about an hour, I walked up and down the rolling hills and saw the housetops and chimneys below the monastery's perch, but not too far away. The Rhine surrounded this place on three sides in a massive curve, almost a u-shape. It was pleasant, quiet, and warm. Creative thoughts came as I ladled from the next fountain. Poetic thoughts. Proverbs and insights, pithy statements and worldly maxims—all wandered about in my head as my body wandered the hills. These thoughts flowed as easily as the baths had. I felt more relaxed than I had been in years. My eyes still pained me and my joints were not as flexible as they had once been but my mind felt rested.

I had not planned to write yet thoughts came. They opened in my head as blossoms did in spring, seemingly without effort. They arose from the difficulties I had known, from the thwarting of efforts I had made and the botching of plans I had intended. It was as if the calculations required to put it all together again began operating on their own, because I felt unqualified to solve the least of them. I didn't really know if "peace and goodwill" was answer enough, but it was all that came and it comforted me, so I embraced it.

I returned to the cloister. They fed me milk and bread with butter and strawberries for breakfast. There were six or seven others dining with me on the terrace, so I enjoyed some pleasant conversation. I looked for someone with whom to have a more stimulating exchange but found no one. After I was poured another glass of water, making my daily total so far seven, I was encouraged to walk again in the gardens but to return at eleven o'clock for something called a douche.

This second water treatment of the day was an inside shower behind the modesty of a curtain and timber partition in a cavernous room of enormous size. The waters came through pipes from various places among the hills. My first douche was under a spout that dropped water from thirty to thirty-five feet overhead. It fell upon me with such force that the cold water felt warm if only from the weight of impact. However, to my dismay, the shower was only permitted to last three minutes, and I was once again sent on my way to meander about the grounds and left alone to my musings for another whole hour. This was followed by another flowing bath for thirty minutes, a light dinner without wine, another walk, some billiards and then free time until five, another flowing bath, another long walk—this one into the neighboring town of Boppard—supper from seven-thirty until nine with the exact menu as breakfast, and finally, bed at ten. I was again awakened at four o'clock to be wrapped like so much bacon and repeated the daily schedule day after day.

I found ways to modify the regimen, though I was careful not to disclose my embellishments to any of the staff nor even my fellow patients. In nearby St. Goar, I met a local poet named Ferdinand Freiligrath and bought a copy of one of his collections. Some of his verses were striking. Several times I walked to town in the late afternoon to meet with him; drink some of the local Rhine wine, especially the Johannisberger; dip into the Rhine for a swim; and occasionally discuss literature and art with him and his friends. The young poet wrote with a voice about social injustice and called for reforms of tyrants and monarchs. I enjoyed listening to him read aloud:

> *He who swings the mighty hammer,*
> *He who reaps the fields of corn,*
> *He who breaks the marshy meadow*
> *To provide for wife, for children,*
> *He who rows against the current,*
> *He who weary at the loom*
> *Weaves with wool and tow and flax*
> *That his fair-haired young may flourish.*
>
> *Honor that man! Praise the worker!*
> *Honor every callous hand!*
> *Honor every drop of sweat*
> *That is shed in mill and foundry.*
> *Honor every dripping forehead*
> *At the plow. And let that man*
> *Who with mind and spirit's labor*
> *Hungering plows be not forgotten.*

His poems made me want to move away from obsessing over my wants and needs and self-preservation. I was reminded of the scripture about perfect love casting out fear and wondered about it differently than before. It might mean that perfect love—in its selflessness—was clearer and more courageous, less afraid of what some might say or seek to censure – because it was more concerned about the fate and sufferings of others.

Here I had been nearly bleeding to death in my soul over wounds made by selfish desire. The madness over the dark lady had blinded me. I admired Ferdinand's willingness to write truth no matter how dangerous and threatening it might be to him, no matter what it might do to the security of his life, which was relevant in his case.

I also considered the concept of some souls being more ferocious than others and knew myself to be something other than fierce. What kind of man and artist was I then? Where might I stand and to what extent might I craft art to speak to the needs of others, needs that were greater than my want of affection or dreams of domestic tranquility? Had not this several-year diversion been fashioned largely by the rejection of a woman whom I imagined to be the answer to my tragic loss of Mary, another compliment to my soul?

I returned to the convent with my head full of questions and a renewed commitment to sweating out whatever toxins remained. I was not faithful to the prohibition on letter writing, however. I wrote countless letters each night and sometimes in place of my lunch hour. I wrote Sumner and Greene, Felton and Hillard, my mother and father, my sister and others. The urge to write grew, and my need to express myself became great again. I had mined the deepest shafts of mountainous caves for I had labored and endured, and my soul now burst with a need for connection. I desired to give a gift without thought of recompense.

The letters were not enough. It seemed that despite all the impurities my body released daily, there were other poisons needing extraction. I remembered something from the first line of Dante's *Divine Comedy*.

> *Midway upon the journey of our life,*
> *I found myself within a forest dark,*
> *for the straightforward pathway had been lost.*

What Longfellow Heard

The Latin phrase for "midway" was *Mezzo Cammin* and I imagined it as the title of what pulsed from my mind to my hand in want of ink. From within my bedchamber at Marienberg, after twenty days of hot and cold treatments and stimulating conversations with Ferdinand, I dipped my pen for a sonnet whose time had come.

> *Half of my life is gone, and I have let*
> *The years slip from me and have not fulfilled*
> *The aspiration of my youth, to build*
> *Some tower of song with lofty parapet.*
> *Not indolence, nor pleasure, nor the fret*
> *Of restless passions that would not be stilled,*
> *But sorrow, and a care that almost killed,*
> *Kept me from what I may accomplish yet;*
> *Though, half-way up the hill, I see the Past*
> *Lying beneath me with its sounds and sights,—*
> *A city in the twilight dim and vast,*
> *With smoking roofs, soft bells, and gleaming lights,—*
> *And hear above me on the autumnal blast*
> *The cataract of Death far thundering from the heights.*

Once released, I left Marienberg for London. I stayed at Dickens's house on Devonshire Terrace near Regent's Park on the outskirts of the great city and admired the novelist's wife and four children and the surrounding gardens and the nightly visits by preeminent artists and statesmen. At first, our activities were of a social and friendly kind. Dickens introduced me to some of the popular fashion trends. The English clothing hung looser than the French style I had worn until now, and I took great advantage of each fashion minister typically in service to Dickens but now provided to me at the bequest of my famous friend. They waited on me hand and foot at very early hours each day. There was McDowall the boot-maker, Beale the haberdasher, Laffin the trousers-maker, and Blackmore the coat-cutter. Dickens laughed at the unholy hours I subjected the men to, but I relished seeking them out and fitting myself into an entirely new wardrobe. If this were to be a new life then a new look should accompany it.

But all of this aside, what truly surprised me was the information Charles shared with me concerning his American tour experience, particularly the people he encountered in the South, but not only the South. My true initiation to his piercing insights came when Charles gave me a copy of his just completed book, *American Notes*, with an alert that he hoped to soon discuss it with me.

Over the next few days, he didn't bring it up, though I devoured his text. Meanwhile, we feasted at well-attended dinners, drank a vast variety of wine, and attended the Royal Shakespeare Company's magnificent theatrical production of *As You Like It*.

"How stands your visit, hey Longfellow?" His head never ceased moving, and his loose-hanging hair might as well have been caught in a perpetual breeze.

"A fast-moving train, if nothing else," I replied with the first image that came to mind. "And I do love a good train ride!"

Charles was impeccably dressed in polished leather shoes and a loose-fitting black suit that allowed him ample room for his every animation. One block into our walk he slapped his top hat against his thigh, surveyed the street corner, and made a proposition. "I think I have an idea you'll find delicious!"

"I don't think I've room for another bite, no matter how tasty the fare," I replied, rubbing my stomach between the buttons of my overcoat.

"Indeed, nor can I, but I speak of a different kind of delight." Charles replaced his top hat and squared off before me. His eyes, which I had sworn were blue in Boston, looked browner now than the light green they appeared when he was earlier seated by the window light at teatime. "I want to take you to a castle! How does that idea settle?"

"I've been known to enjoy such excursions."

"This, by far is the best plan for the moment. We'll hail a carriage and take a delightful jaunt to the countryside to a magnificent ruin by the name of Rochester."

It took nearly an hour to reach it, but it was nothing less than Dickens had promised—a magnificent, dominant sight upon a hillside. An immense structure of pale stone towers several stories high and surrounded by decayed walls and wooden supports. There were posted notices barring entrance by order of the local constable.

Charles waited for the carriage to be well out of hearing when he looked at me with mischief in his eyes. "You are not opposed to a slight usurpation, I trust?"

"What?"

"The only way in is by climbing over a fence or two and scaling a stone wall here and there." Charles winked, grinned, and lunged ahead.

I looked in every direction before pursuing him. "Are you certain we will not be arrested?"

Charles laughed without halting. "Not certain at all, old chap."

I was none too comfortable, but I didn't want to disappoint my literary friend. As I ran after him, holding tight to my hat, I wondered how much like the great Englishman I might really be. Maybe somewhere deep inside of me was the same stuff that produced grandiose works that led to significance, fame, and renown. But I had recently felt certain that this aim would no longer obsess me. Yet, here I was, rushing about with Charles Dickens as those exhilarating thoughts came to me.

I tore my new trousers in one of the climbs. I looked over my shoulder for angry policemen, but Dickens journeyed on, darting in and out of dungeons and stairwells unconcerned with anything but the moment. I struggled to keep up and realized I didn't know myself very well at all. Not any more. Was I inquisitive or was I not? Was I adventurous or not? Was my imagination or my drive anything at all compared to the English luminary before me?

We breached the inner walls, exhausted the lower levels, and now traversed the narrow walkways of stone with crumbling arches on both sides. We trekked higher until the height became worrisome. I dared a peek through an arch overlooking the courtyard now scores of feet below. It was a great distance higher than the bridge over the Charles and more dizzying. I moved back to the center of the meager walkway. Charles was farther ahead but had slowed to inspect something. I cautiously moved closer.

He cheerfully sat on a stone ledge with his back facing what risked being a great fall and tugged off one shoe to rub his foot. When his hat toppled off onto the ledge, he reached for it but it was too late. It blew off the ledge and floated a long way down. He looked at me and laughed. "No matter."

I pulled my hat tighter and placed my hands on my lower back as I stretched my lungs with a deep inhale. "Do they patrol these grounds much?"

"Henry, about my *American Notes* —" Dickens replaced his shoe, leapt to his feet, and darted back onto another walkway. "In it I have spoken honestly and fairly, but it will not please everyone. You and your friends will like me better for it, but others will think me the devil. I have several copies I would like you to take back with you as gifts for the Five of Clubs and a few others. It will be published, of course, but I wanted to send these in advance of the American publication. Please tell me what you think."

I nodded, while catching my breath. I recalled my time with the Baron when we had found the French artist sketching deep within the old castle in the snow. The memory made me feel younger and may have inspired my daring. I looked at Charles who appeared surprisingly emotional. Uncertain. Anxious. I wondered if he might be more like me in some ways, and felt sympathetic. I responded to his request. "It is jovial and good-natured, and at times very severe. The chapter on slavery is vital. It might prove helpful for America to hear the objective views of those who visit our land and see some of the horrors of it in ways too many Americans, in their frenzy of self-interests, have become blind to. I, for one, am also guilty. I am repulsed by the institution but can't say that I grasp what is best to do about it. It is ripping our nation apart, no doubt. Meanwhile, African men, women, and children suffer the most outrageous indignities at the hands of slavery."

Charles had paused to hear me, but now proceeded to move higher into an even more questionable area of the castle where the stones seemed capable of crumbling under our feet.

"I attribute to three classes those who uphold slavery in America." Charles stopped when he realized I was not following his footsteps. "Come, Henry, just a little farther. The view changes slightly, but enough to make it more interesting and worth a few extra steps." He resumed his walking, talking tour. I took a deep breath and followed behind.

"The first," Charles went on, "are the owners who act as though they are in possession of human cattle. This type admits the frightful nature of the Institution, but only in the abstract. They recognize the dangers to society with which it is fraught, but like users of opium, are unable to stop. Do not doubt, however tardy the inevitable outcomes of slavery may be, they are as certain to arrive as the Day of Judgment."

"I do not consider the human soul, despite differences in color, to be like cattle."

"Nor do I, but I am referring to those who uphold slavery, not those who are against it. The second class who keeps the ungodly system alive are the overseers and breeders, the buyers and sellers of slaves, who doggedly deny the horrors of the system in the teeth of a mass of evidence. This kind will not stop their pitiless profiteering until the bloody chapter has a bloody end. They would gladly involve America in a war, civil or foreign, provided its sole objective is to assert their right to perpetuate slavery, to whip and work and torture slaves, and to always be unquestioned by any human authority. When these people speak of freedom, they really mean the freedom to oppress their fellow man and to be savage, merciless, and cruel."

I forgot about the heights of the castle and recalled that evening at Faneuil Hall. "And they justify it," I said with new vigor, "with the most reprehensible doggerel."

"Yes, and they play dumb when confronted with obvious truth."

"Do they play dumb or have they deceived themselves into becoming dumb?"

Charles stopped and thought, shook his head, and shrugged his shoulders. "Good question. The third kind are not the least numerous or influential, and is composed of all that delicate gentility which cannot bear a superior and cannot brook an equal; of that class whose Republicanism means, 'I will not tolerate a man above me: and of those below, none must approach too near;' whose pride, in a land where voluntary servitude is shunned as a disgrace, must be ministered to by slaves; and whose inalienable rights can only have their growth in wrongs to the negro."

I considered his words. I thought of Fanny's father, whom I admired as an astute businessman and respected as a decent man. But, like other good men I knew, he was subject to blinders, no doubt due to not wanting to upset the cart of his success that was doing well for so many. "These types you speak of are not always easily identified. Many of them are otherwise gentle and kind—"

"Kind?" Dickens sounded indignant. "Kind to their own!"

I thought harder, not interested in defending or condemning, but hoping to grasp the truth, whatever it was. "They often have lifestyles that have done a great deal of good for themselves and their progeny. I think it becomes a hazard of their station to become unable to step back and risk diminishing returns."

Charles Dickens stopped close to the edge under a sprawling arch, the ground nearly one hundred feet below. "Unwilling, not unable! Some advocates of slavery, say, 'It is a bad system; and for myself I would willingly get rid of it, if I could. But it is not so bad, as you in England take it to be. You are deceived by the representations of the emancipationists. My slaves are attached to me. I care for them; I do not allow them to be severely treated.' That is their justification? Of course they don't always treat them badly! Would it not impair their value and be against the profitable interests of such men? They don't treat them badly because it is in their profitable interests not to."

I reached for his arm and tugged him away from the precipice. "There are vicious ways within all of mankind, Charles. It is our fallen nature."

He moved away from the edge, but continued to climb higher. "Yes. I agree the abuse of irresponsible power is a temptation. It is the most difficult of earthly temptations to be resisted. But there are other temptations we know to be wrong, are there not? Consider murder, violence, or rape. Are these not wrong and known to be wrong among all of mankind? Of course they are! Though some men still commit such things because of inclinations within them, most of us understand it remains our duty and obligation to resist them, despite the temptation. Therefore, before you consider whether or not a basically good man beats or mistreats his slaves or takes unfair advantage of them, realize the crucial question remains unasked, and this is by design. Such men like to cloud the question as if there is no real correlation between slavery and other grossly obvious immoralities. The question is not, as some would have us believe, whether a master has a right to lash out and maim a slave whose life and limb he rules! The question is when will we at last blot out the abuse of one man having unaccountable power over another?" Charles stopped at the highest point of the crumbling castle where protective walls lay in ruin and the late afternoon breeze was noticeably colder and stronger.

"You raise difficult questions," I replied without moving as high. I placed one hand against the interior wall that appeared most solid. "It is a complexity that grieves the spirit. If only the masses would not tolerate it."

Charles's appeared ready to say more, but then his chest heaved, he sounded a great sigh, and his heels once more nearly touched the edge. I wanted to reach for him and tug him away, but was afraid any touch not perfectly made might send him to his death.

"Please," I offered my hands in surrender. "Please step away from the edge, Charles. I'm afraid your zeal has left your feet uninformed about your surroundings."

Charles glanced around, as if aware of the edge for the first time, and stepped to safer footing.

"What you say is true," I continued. "Your *American Notes* recites it as well, if not better than you do now. It will be hard received by many Americans, but truth hurts when one is on the wrong side of it. Hopefully, it will pierce hearts and provoke true justice to awaken."

Charles seemed unsatisfied and headed downward. "I have little reason to believe that the American people will tenderly receive these views. I have no desire to court, by any adventitious means, the popular applause. It is enough for me to know that what I have spoken cannot cost me a single friend on the other side of the Atlantic, who is, in anything, deserving of the name. For the rest, I put my trust, implicitly, in the spirit in which they have been conceived and penned; and I can bide my time." Charles stopped and turned and looked straight at me. His eyes appeared green. I decided his eyes must be hazel and apparently changed with his moods. "So, dear Henry, what say you?"

"I am your friend, as Felton, Sumner, Hillard, and the rest of our enclave, I think you know."

"Yes. I do." Charles suddenly appeared delighted and broadly opened his arms. "What do you think of Rochester Castle? A worthwhile climb?"

I was relieved we were descending and chuckled as I replied, "Fascinating places, these ruins. Many passions no doubt rose and fell within these very walls, and now nothing remains of the battles but the silent stones about them."

"The stones would cry out if they could," Charles said, cheerfully.

I liked that comment and, as we descended several flights, replayed it in my head, recognizing it from the scriptures and wondering if it properly applied.

"Did you tear your trousers?" Charles asked, as we walked under the main arch.

My pleasant feeling evaporated. I had almost forgotten. My new trousers, so comfortable and fashionable, damaged enough to be retired after one day. "I shall have to visit Laffin again."

"He will certainly grieve after you've gone—or find much needed rest!" Dickens laughed and skipped down the entryway steps.

I tried to smile as I nimbly tucked the tear inside itself in hopes of preventing further damage and followed the eminent author home. All the way I couldn't stop thinking how very deeply his passions ran and felt shame that my concerns vacillated between the full import of his words and the condition of my pants.

———

I lay in bed in the Dickens guest chamber the night before my departure home holding in my hand a letter from Sumner that I had just read, and finding myself agitated—the very sort of agitation I had come to Europe to be rid of. It was not a fire whose fuel consisted of the torturous rejections of the dark lady, but more accurately, a cord of flaming wood comprised of big questions that I could not answer.

Here I was, halfway through life and having rounded a bend expecting to see a path leading to a golden horizon but instead blinded by hedges. I was in a thicket—a dickens of a thicket—with a bonfire at my feet. I was lost. Again.

Dickens was a master storyteller because he was a masterful man with masterful ideas, moved by the injustice around him and motivated to speak truth in ways that penetrated the minds of men and made them think about how they and society might change. There was also my new friend, Freiligrath, whose courageous voice was unafraid to denounce the monarchies of his land. And there were those of whom I could predict greatness. Felton, a professor of Greek and a brilliant mind that grasped lessons of lore and applied history to modern dilemma; Hillard who handled the duties of lawyering with admirable skill; and of course Sumner who was transforming into something powerful and strong. But who was I?

I looked again at the letter in my hand. Sumner had sent it to me here in England, and his words burned like a branding iron.

Henry,

What red-hot staves has your mind thrown up? What ideas have been started by this trip soon ending? A poem or two? A poem on the sea? Oh! I long for those verses on slavery. Write some stirring words that shall move the whole land. Send them home and we'll publish them. Occupy yourself for the benefit of all with that heavenly gift of invention.

Cordially your friend forever,
Charles Sumner

Chapter 20

I BADE MY FAREWELL to Dickens and his family and then rode a melancholy rail to Bristol to embark for home. It was late October and the winds were strong.

With copies of *American Notes* and two volumes of Freiligrath in hand, and a line of stewards behind me carrying three trunks of new clothes and one case of Schloss Johannisberger, I boarded the Great Western Steamer for New York.

The great steam-powered paddle wheel beat a rough passage into violence and storm. Forced to remain berthed below by a captain fearful of passengers washing over the rails, pounding waves and leaking portholes surrounded me with frigid saltwater spray, sloshing floors and echoing waves. I tossed in my cabin like a clapper in a bell. I had no desire to go above board, though I wished I could vomit in places other than my sleeping quarters. I tossed and turned, groaned, and pitied myself for eight days, wedged into a corner and staring out the round window into a mix of swirling gray mist laced with veins of froth and foam. I was awash in misery and gloom.

On the ninth day, still required to remain below, new thoughts scolded me. Men with a calling ought to cease feeling self-pity and begin instead to see the world as it is and speak out for those who have no voice.

I felt in my pockets. I had only a pencil, but I sharpened it as best I could and opened my leather-bound notebook whose paper was miraculously dry. I wanted to write with a hope of healing others. The illnesses of my own land—the greatest ill of the land—the ill of the oppressed, the purchased, and the abused. I felt unsure about my abilities to do so, but I pressed the lead to the paper and moved my hand.

> *Paul and Silas, in their prison,*
> *Sang of Christ, the Lord arisen,*
> *And an earthquake's arm of might*
> *Broke their dungeon-gates at night.*
> *But, alas! what holy angel*
> *Brings the Slave this glad evangel?*
> *And what earthquake's arm of might*
> *Breaks his dungeon-gates at night?*

What was the hope of the slave? Did he not dream of his freedom? Night after night, I pondered the questions stirred by the conversations with Freiligrath and Dickens and the letter from Sumner. The experiences and images of my own comfortable life clashed with the distress of those I'd seen from afar and had known of since the days of my youth. What could I do? What could I contribute to help bring an end to this most wicked institution? I rocked and reeled in the cabin and hardly slept for a dozen days. I created a copious amount and pieced together verses, mixing and matching as I thought and wrote. I looked through the porthole into the deep and I imagined shapes and forms; and I knew I could not feign innocence of tragedies that must have occurred a thousand times over or maybe more—a million times—and continued still.

> *In Ocean's wide domains,*
> *Half buried in the sands,*
> *Lie skeletons in chains,*
> *With shackled feet and hands.*

Beyond the fall of dews,
Deeper than plummet lies,
Float ships, with all their crews,
No more to sink nor rise.
There the black Slave-ship swims,
Freighted with human forms,
Whose fettered, fleshless limbs
Are not the sport of storms.
These are the bones of Slaves;
They gleam from the abyss;
They cry, from yawning waves,
"We are the Witnesses!"

The more I rocked along in the dim light, the more I could see. If a man did not do what a good man must do, what further evil might occur? Was not God, though infinitely patient, ultimately just? Would not truth rise up to defend the Africans? If not in the form of good white men doing what they should, what form might requisite justice take, and which was more ominous to behold?

There is a poor, blind Samson in this land,
Shorn of his strength and bound in bonds of steel,
Who may, in some grim revel, raise his hand,
And shake the pillars of this Commonweal,
Till the vast Temple of our liberties.
A shapeless mass of wreck and rubbish lies.

Another five days of banishment to my iron crib under the sea and I realized there was only more to say. This indecency was not just of a massive kind but also a specific one where individual life was mistreated and scorned. It was too horrid to imagine, but imagine it I did. There were slavers whose blood ran in the veins of their slave's offspring, but whom the slaver considered not his own. Corruption and greed were ruinous to the soul. It made monsters of men.

"The soil is barren,—the farm is old";
The thoughtful planter said;
Then looked upon the Slaver's gold,
And then upon the maid.
His heart within him was at strife
With such accursed gains:
For he knew whose passions gave her life,
Whose blood ran in her veins.
But the voice of nature was too weak;
He took the glittering gold!
Then pale as death grew the maiden's cheek,
Her hands as icy cold.
The Slaver led her from the door,
He led her by the hand,
To be his slave and paramour
In a strange and distant land!

After fifteen days of rolling berth and churning stomach, pounding head and thrashing sea, I finished several poems and was permitted above board where I saw the coast of America, the opening to New York Harbor. My heart soared. I knew somewhere in the throng was Corny and Charles and the rest of what I hoped would at last be a fresh start to a new life.

Chapter 21

TOM APPLETON WAS decked out in his finest silk shirt, a supremely tailored vest and waistcoat, puffy cravat, and neatly creased trousers. Trimming his noticeable presence were his sharpest witticisms, sowed here and there in the ears of Boston's upper crust. Happy and gay, he milled about the party at the Nortons's regaling the groups of huddled gentility with his humor, zest, and unmitigated joy. He was leaving in a few days to enjoy adventures in the lands from which I had returned almost a year ago. In his pocket was a letter of introduction to Dickens that I had handed him this very night. Tom was easily proving to be the envied personality of the hour.

"I cannot thank you enough, dear Longfellow! You are the kindest of souls, the gentlest of lambs among wolves, and the only real poet America can boast of. I am the richer for knowing you!" Tom raised his glass of Johannisberger, another contribution of mine, and then leaned in to whisper. "As are others and, may I suggest, one in particular who of late pays some notice to your luminosity from under her youthful canopy. I think her reluctance is at last falling away like leaves in autumn. Eh?"

I was shocked by his suggestion. "There must be another poet, very near to where I'm standing, who is rising to eminence among those of our little society. In fact, he wears your shoes!" I clinked his glass and sipped, peeking over the rim to spy Fanny across the room. As had been the case for so long now, interested parties surrounded her with more on their minds than Tom's *bon voyage*. It hadn't bothered me—not too much—for I knew well the impassable highlands that divided my north from her south. I was over it now, and the tinges of pain here and there were nothing more than the pangs of having failed an objective, and not the rumblings of a heart still aching.

"None can compete with you!" Tom winked.

My deeds of late had been satisfying. My *Poems on Slavery* received gratifying recognition. Those who had read an advanced copy were lifting my upcoming *Spanish Student* on a wave of optimistic predictions of its "inevitable" success. My valuation and close friendships with men like Dickens outshone the harsh views of my few critics like Margaret Fuller and Edgar Allen Poe. I had returned home with renewed focus on writing and lecturing, and I was coming into my own. I would be thirty-six in a few months, and I knew I was a better man.

"Henry, there you are!" Corny spoke from several steps away. "We're putting together a game of whist in the parlor. Will you join us?" He patted Tom on the shoulder as he stepped close. "You shall be missed, Tom, but we'll expect letters each week."

"You will not be disappointed if you don't mind imagining what they say. I assure you my intent will be weekly, though my execution something less." They clinked glasses and grinned merrily.

"What do you say, Henry? Whist?"

I heard every word Corny said and was well aware of the humor and affections at hand, but the lavender gown had traced the floor across the center of the room and gracefully headed toward a window in the corner, and without a swarm of pests following. Too many times I had interpreted such a circumstance as a providential doorway requiring action, but every time it had ended badly. I needed to choose anew whether to whist away the evening or waste another effort.

"Henry?" Felton repeated, nodding toward a room beyond, where jovial voices could be heard.

If not for that moment, that measure of time so small that anyone else might have missed it, that instant when her large, dark eyes peered at me from across the room, before she turned away to gaze at a painting on the wall, I might have said, "Whist." But I had noticed.

I heard Corny repeat my name but I walked away thinking, sadly, about how she paid me no notice as I approached. Then again, it might be a good omen as easily as a bad one. I stopped beside her. "Good evening, Miss Appleton."

She turned and I remembered falling out of a tree when I was eight. It had knocked the air out of me, and I could do nothing, move nothing, think nothing except struggle to remember how to inhale and exhale in ways not too dramatic.

Fanny dipped her chin and partially curtsied. "It is very nice to see you here, Professor. I'm certain it means much to Tom as it does to all of us."

My right thigh tingled and I had no idea why. I shifted my weight and tilted my head back. "He's at his wittiest." I smiled large and looked out the window. "He will thoroughly delight our friends overseas, I am certain."

"You must know I will be quite lonely after he leaves." Her words were like gentle doves that beat their wings against my temples. I turned my gaze from the darkness outdoors to the glow of her countenance. Her dark curls, her pale skin, her ruby lips, her large eyes were the most beautiful I had ever seen. I went back and forth, memorizing every feature; drinking her as a cup of wine; delicately, patiently, sipping only as permitted, as proper decorum allowed. "You must come and comfort me, Mister Longfellow."

"What?" I awoke from my trance, found myself adrift. "I'm sorry, what?"

She laughed and turned aside as if dancing and then smiled and touched my sleeve. "After Tom leaves, you must come and comfort me. It will be terribly lonely without him, but I am certain your presence will do much to ease my tensions."

Was I dreaming?

"And I hope it will prove to ease yours as well." She squeezed my arm, and I remained silent. "Henry?"

"Miss Appleton," I replied. "I am most happy to receive your invitation. You will pardon me if I am overtaken with brevity. I am simply endeavoring to discern whether I am awake or dreaming."

Fanny Appleton laughed in a most natural way, making no effort to maintain poise or form. Her face wrinkled, her mouth opened wide, and her eyes sparkled like stars. "You tickle me, Henry. I promise you, you are wide-awake. How else could one speak so well with his presence and his pen unless he is fully awake? And speak well, you do."

I set down my wine glass and clasped my hands behind my back. "Your kindness is of greater affect than any cure I've ever known, Marienberg baths included!"

"Then you'll come and visit?"

"Most assuredly."

"Often?"

I knew I must step away. It was all too perfect and nothing should blot out the enchantment. I felt the wells of tears in my eyes and knew my time short. "And soon, if that be your wish."

"It is, sir." She performed the most graceful and fullest curtsy ever afforded me and finished with an unexpected touch on my wrist. "Please excuse me, for my father has been motioning to me for several minutes, and if I do not depart, I fear he will approach us and spoil this lovely encounter."

I turned and saw her father, waving her approach. I watched the full length of her journey and the full length of her form. She was lavender and lace, and my chest felt warm. After she joined her father and his friends, the small group wandered into another room, exactly the one where Felton had indicated the game of whist was to be played. I could go there, needing no other reason but to inspect the game and query an invite, but why bother? Perfection was too rare to risk spoiling by overuse. There was nothing more needed, nothing remaining to be gained. I looked at my wine glass but didn't lift it. I left it filled and slipped silently away to Craigie House, exchanged my suit for my favorite sleeping gown, slept as deeply as the silent floor of the ocean, and felt as warm as the glowing hearth at the foot of my bed.

Chapter 22

IT WAS ON THE WALK along the edge of Frog Pond, in plain
view of all who traversed the Common, but not in plain hearing,
when Fanny spoke for the first time in the soft, intimate tones I had
previously only imagined. Her words were filled with intentions I had
ached to hear until I ached no more and had made peace. But now,
her words floated on the wings of her breath, caressing my wounds.

Her summer dress that had appeared yellow in the lamplight
of her home when I came for her that morning was different now.
In the brightness of the late morning sun, the flowing garment was
luminous and white. It was her face and eyes that transfixed me. Her
skin was without blemish; her cheek bones distinct but softly sloped
and tinged with blush; her mouth an ebbing and flowing promise of
buried treasures within; and her large, dark eyes glowed like black
pearls. She carried me off of my feet. I knew we could cross Frog
Pond on lily pads if only she had led me there, but her kind words of
appreciation stopped us and her eyes glistened as if she had just risen
from the sea.

"Henry?" It was clearly a question; her tone was asking permission to be candid, but I could not speak. I simply nodded, unable
to open my mouth for fear of what my soul might release. "I chose
this place because I used to see you walk here. I watched you from
a narrow space between curtains and counted how many times your
gaze came the way of my house."

My face tightened and it must have displayed something amusing because she stopped and raised the side of her hand to her mouth, but she could not repress the giggle. "Twenty-five times on one occasion." She laughed so hard she drew up both hands to mask her face, and though she mostly covered it, I saw the one tear gliding down her cheek like a tiny raindrop on a window. I didn't think about it but found my hands on her shoulders. My only means of saying anything was the forced widening of my eyes. Finally, my throat and heart and mouth found a sympathetic cadence and sensible sounds came forth without removing the lynch pin of my emotions.

"You were watching me?" My tone was fairly well-managed.

"I was afraid." She lifted her arms to press my hands away from her shoulders but looped my right arm in the crook of her left and resumed our walk along the pond.

My feelings spread across my chest like a peacock's tail. I felt many things but couldn't articulate even one of them. There were too many things aglow. Wondrous things. Powerful things. Deep things. "Afraid? Of me?"

"Of the truth."

"The truth of what?"

She unhooked my arm and turned away. Even from behind I could see she was wiping away tears. I heard her sobs and stepped next to her. How had her laughter turned to these tortured tears? I gently touched her arm, but she turned away again. "I don't know how to tell you," she said.

"Tell me what? I long to hear the overflow of your heart." I noticed a fashionable couple looking our way as they strolled on the other side of Beacon Street, but it did not matter. "Whatever it is, tell me."

Fanny Appleton turned around and lifted her eyes to my own. Her cheeks were wet with tears, and her lips trembled. "You have already been married."

I opened my mouth to protest but could not. I could not betray Mary Potter's honor or the genuine love we shared in those days, yet I urgently longed to proclaim my most sincere passion for Fanny. My admiration and love for her were no less powerful, no less real.

"I know it is selfish of me. But I know I can never be first in your heart, and for this reason I have been unable to permit you to gain ground in your advances toward me."

I felt as if a black pit had opened before me. What could I say?

"I felt the need to spurn you to protect myself, I am ashamed to say. I am very fond of you, Professor Longfellow, and it was necessary for me to acknowledge this to you. But as you can see, I am quite selfish, and the kind and quality of love and marriage that such a woman as me, or any woman so far as I know, can accept, is one that is true and genuine and—" Her voice trailed off and her head lowered. I could barely hear her for a moment, but her last word was clear: "—exclusive." Fanny raised her chin and lifted the hem of her dress and began a swift walk toward her house.

Everything in me wanted to run after her but I was locked in place. Here was a rhyme scheme I did not know. The harmony and reconciliation escaped me. The meter was undiscovered. I watched her stop as she was rounding the pond though she did not turn toward me. Whatever she was contemplating apparently held her in check.

"Let the dead past bury its dead," I said in a powerful voice. The words just fell out of my mouth, but they seemed to comfort her. Fanny released her hem, turned, and wiped her face with a lace handkerchief. Her bosom lifted as she breathed deeply, and then like an angel come to share impossible truth, she said, "Despite these feelings, dear Henry, despite the hub-bub of my words, I do love you, sir. I think I have always loved you though the heart does not always know itself, but if you ever have a mind to restate your intentions to me, I will never again bring up the subject of your first marriage. I felt I needed to explain what had held me back, but you need not explain yourself." She looked so desirable. Her hair combs had loosened and strands of hair framed her face in uneven lengths of curls and waves. I felt as if I were seeing her in a state she had never allowed a man to see before. Yet, she stood bravely and spoke clearly, with no remnant of the tremble from moments before. "I only ask that should you again ever declare your love, that you promise your faithful exclusivity from that day forward, and I shall vow to return it to you in ways uncommon and genuine. Good day, Henry. I'm glad we had this walk by the pond."

I watched her every step, her every movement, until she reached the front door at 39 Beacon Street. After she entered, I checked every curtain for movement and saw a narrow parting from the curtains of her upstairs chamber. I lifted my head and stared until the curtains parted an inch or two wider, and then I tipped my hat, lifted my cane, and bowed—before the pond, the lily pads, the passers-by, and the dark lady. I walked home while I pondered the romantic use of sonnets and ballads and poems until, at last, upon reaching Craigie House, I chose a simple note instead. I wrote things I did not want heard or read by anyone but her. I instructed her to burn the note after reading it, that if she never did anything else for me, it must be this one thing, to burn it straight away. I wrote all of the things I longed to say, but I stopped short of comparing or measuring quantities of love. I heavily emphasized the here and now, the present and the future, the professed and the proclaimed. I told her the things I truly felt and dreamed and believed and hoped about her, trusting those words to be what she most needed to know. Without inhibition or reservation, I wrote the most naked truth concerning the things my heart longed to give and to receive from her. I peered at my note for a long time after I was essentially done, and wondered how to finish it. I knew how I wanted to end it, but I suddenly wondered whether or not I should. I had no choice, it was now or never, so I ended the letter with the only question my heart truly desired an answer to. I sent it to her house and waited as one waits in a dream—no anxiety, no fear, no hope, and no fluctuating emotions—only stillness. I had laid bare my heart, and it would be or it wouldn't. I didn't dare hope, but I didn't allow fear. I lived only to hear a reply. There was nothing more to be done.

One week passed. I decided I could accept life without her and continue to be the Harvard professor and an accomplished poet with friends aplenty and a heart that would never love again, or I could be a resurrected man full of power and joy and love. Either was possible, and it was up to whatever providence might permit. I had not the strength or foolishness to dare insist upon anything other. The request was made known to all powers and principalities in heaven and on earth, and God's will be done.

On May 10, 1843, her note arrived.

Dearest Henry,

Your note has comforted me greatly. I trust with all my heart that it is—and will be as you say—that a better dawn has exorcised the phantoms and healthy beams will rest as in a perpetual home within those once-haunted walls you speak of.

I believe the dead past has buried its dead, and that we might safely walk over their graves, thanking God that at last we could live to give each other only happy thoughts. I put aside all anxiety and fear, trusting upon your promise, and I accept your proposal this day and forever. And no one shall know your words but heaven, and myself, for though the note is but ash in the fireplace, your words burn eternally upon my breast and in my heart.

Godspeed, Henry. You shall find me waiting…

With utmost affection,
Fanny

I leapt from my chair, grabbed my hat and cane, and left Craigie House with the speed of an arrow. I was too restless to sit in a carriage and did not want to meet anyone along the way. I ran in places, then walked fast, then faster, and then ran again all the way to the bridge spanning the Charles. I stopped only a moment to rejoice that it was no longer a bridge of sadness but of joy. I rushed on. There were blossoms and birds and sunshine and eyes full of tears. This was what Dante had called his Vita Nuova of happiness in the prelude to the Divine Comedy. A new life!

I married Fanny in her Brattle Street home on July 13 in 1843. The dark lady appeared in her muslin gown and lace veil with orange blossoms in her hair. Later, she also handed me her sketchbook from Europe with an inscription: *To Paul Fleming from Mary Ashburton.* We could only laugh.

We spent the next many days and nights locked up in the eastern half of Craigie House. Mrs. Craigie's passing had permitted me to rent not only the rooms that had been mine but also move into those that had been hers. We transformed each of them into our sacred nest. As we lay in our bed and Fanny slept snugly in my arms, I reflected that whether or not I became eminent was of no consequence. My greatest desire was the life we would build together, sharing our interests in love, family, and each other. I desired only happiness, and I was determined to never let it slip from me.

About two weeks later, we traveled by carriage to visit my family in Portland and then caught up with her vacationing clan in Nahant. Joined by Charles Sumner, we boarded a train to the Catskill Mountains. We welcomed him because we knew he was suffering from a sense of abandonment, from being the last bachelor among the Five of Clubs. However, we never expected his wedding gift to be what he brought and recited from: Bossuet's *Funeral Orations.* Charles was a man of surprises. We listened, bored but amused that he might think our love of literature would somehow accommodate a preference for verses about the inevitability of death, despite this being our honeymoon.

I held my darling's hand, gazed out the train window, and allowed Sumner's readings to merge with the monotonous rumbling of the train. I still cared about social injustice, I still despised slavery and adored literature and poetry, but nothing was more meaningful to me than my wife.

"Well, all that is well and good, dear friend. But while you two stand happily united our nation moves in a contrary direction!" Charles was red in the face and in no posture for ceasing his tirade. It evidently made no difference that he was our temporary guest and not the other way around.

"It's called a honeymoon, Charles, not a permanent withdrawal from life," I said more than once and always with a smile. Fanny and I were too happy to enter into his current indignations over the growing rifts between the North and the South.

He turned to the attendant standing nearby and added, "Do you know how many books could have been purchased if such vast sums had not been expended on such an ignoble purpose as war? An entire library could have been supplied, perhaps several."

The train journey to the mountains included a stop in Springfield. On impulse, we visited the Armory where we now stood. In one section, artillery gun barrels lined the wall from floor to ceiling, resembling a massive stockade fence in my view. Fanny's comparison was better.

"They look like a pipe organ," she said. "Imagine what mournful music death plays on them."

"That's a magnificent thought, Fanny!" I beamed at my brilliant wife.

"There can be no excuse for wars; we know that," Charles ranted.

"But to arrange and display their implements like sculpture or fine art is a shock to any man's system. It should not be!"

Fanny and I agreed with the heart of Sumner's observations if not the manner in which they were expressed. He stirred emotions, despite my truly not wanting to be affected by his words just then. All I wanted was Fanny in my arms. She filled my mind and soul with consuming desire. She was not only beautiful but also brilliant. Her mind was a treasure trove, and her form was something I endlessly wanted to enjoy.

"Let us then grow warlike in our opposition to war!" Fanny chided him.

This seemed to subdue him into momentary retrospection. Whether to examine his assumptions or due to feminine intimidation, I wasn't sure. But Fanny was clearly no one to mirror men's ideas. She thought independently and wasn't timid about challenging a premise. Her smiling face and bright eyes stared at Charles, waiting for a reply, but then quickly changed to a look of soft concern. "I meant no insult, Charles." Evidently, she concluded that his silence was due to her wit. "I indeed share your stance against war, though too fierce a denouncement might not yield an outcome altogether different from the one denounced." She turned to me, I thought, looking for an agreeing nod, but before I could respond, she continued. "I think you should write a peace poem, Henry. One that transforms this Arsenal of Springfield into something more beneficial to the world."

Charles's face lit up like a schoolboy's. "Do it, Henry. She's right."

Other than the *Poems on Slavery*, I hadn't written much since I had left Dickens and Freiligrath in Europe. I had translated a dozen or more of Dante's cantos but not much else. Translations didn't originate from the richest deposits of creativity I possessed; they were more like running a plow through one's mind. In that process a thousand things get tossed up which otherwise might lay in rot, but in the end, that sort of harvesting of creative ideas might be little more than an excuse for being lazy, as if leaning on another man's shoulder to support oneself rather than standing on your own legs. It added up to my feeling delinquent, but my new marriage held everything hostage—and, I have to admit, it didn't much bother me that it did. Sometimes my writing unction felt like a spark looking to ignite a forest of inspiration, but other times it was an object of scorn because it pestered me. Right now, it felt like a bug in my eye.

"—political office, too!" Charles had continued speaking but only his last few words got through.

"To be sought by who, you?" I tried to sound as though I had followed his arguments as we headed to the train.

"The both of us!"

I looked at my wife, hoping Fanny might contribute, but she only listened.

"Not I." I shrugged.

"Yes, you!" Charles stepped ahead and turned to face us, walking backwards. "Think of it. We could change the course of the river politic!"

"Ha! Be careful, or you'll fall." He turned forward to my relief, and I continued. "I rejoice in liberty and freedom from slavery for all people, but don't think for a moment I will enter into a political arena. Never!"

"Why not, Henry? Think of it. Your pen. My oratory. Your clear-mindedness, my bold, legal-mindedness. Who would Webster and Clay be in the luminosity of Longfellow and Sumner?"

"All aboard!" the conductor yelled.

"Partisan politics is too violent and vindictive for my taste. I would be an unworthy champion in public debate." We boarded the train and squeezed along the aisle.

"I will assume that part of it. But your presence, your wisdom, and your pen would be a great supply line to my front lines." Charles was so excited his breathing was in fits and gasps.

Fanny remained silent with no decipherable countenance. She was intentionally being neutral, although neutrality was not her stance. It intrigued me and now pleased me how she deployed her own strategies and intents. I knew that at the end of it all, she would stand by me. I remember thinking, as we took our seats, how difficult it was to imagine any greater love and admiration than what I felt for her.

"Well?" Charles was not settling for an absent reply.

I hadn't meant to ignore him; I had been relishing thoughts of Fanny. "I'm sorry, Charles. The answer will always be in the negative. A man must not veer from who and what he is."

Frustrated, Charles uttered something indistinguishable, but with a tone of surrender, as best I could tell. I looked at Fanny, wondering if she might speak now.

"Write a peace poem," she said with a quick wink and smoothed her dress.

The sound of steel wheels over iron rails and wooden beams resumed and continued for quite some time as words came forth from somewhere deep inside.

I hear even now the infinite fierce chorus,
The cries of agony, the endless groan,
Which, through the ages that have gone before us,
In long reverberations reach our own.

Is it, O man, with such discordant noises,
With such accursed instruments as these,
Thou drownest Nature's sweet and kindly voices,
And jarrest the celestial harmonies?

Were half the power that fills the world with terror,
Were half the wealth bestowed on camps and courts,
Given to redeem the human mind from error,
There would be no need of arsenals or forts:

What Longfellow Heard

The warrior's name would be a name abhorred!
And every nation, that should lift again
Its hand against a brother, on its forehead
Would wear forevermore the curse of Cain!

Chapter 23

As a wedding gift, Nathan Appleton had purchased Craigie House and all the land in front stretching to the river. It was a season where the sunbeams reached down through the trees with promises of warmth and the river of life flowed swiftly with motion and grace. Our son Charles, a stout fellow with a large mouth and dark complexion, was born almost a year later on June 9, 1844. He arrived with all of his fingers and all of his toes and our happy life was filled with newborn joys.

"What in heaven's name is that?" Fanny asked.

"Nothing less than a remnant of your wedding cake!" Her brother Tom reentered the room holding a platter high with both hands as if presenting a prized turkey. The contents resembled an imbalanced, pasty-looking tower. "Happy Anniversary!"

"You've kept it a year?" I was seated at the head of the table where we had just finished our first dinner in our newly furnished dining room on the western side of the house. Charles, Corny, and George Hillard turned their faces away from little Charley in the basket and toward the cake.

"Is it edible?" Charles asked.

"Tom." Fanny took the platter and examined the dessert more closely. "What a sweet thought!" She lowered it to my eye level. "A slice of cake from our wedding day, Henry. Isn't that darling?"

"Miracle of the icehouse," Tom added just before he made faces at my son. "Fuddle cup boo!"

Corny examined the dessert, "Darling yes, but delectable? Who can guess?"

George was about to add some observation of his own, but baby Charley seized all of our attention with a howling complaint. Nurse Blake hurried over to lift him and tap between his shoulder blades. "He's training, that's all he's doing," she said.

Tom held up his hands, declaring his innocence in the matter.

It was impossible at that moment to imagine what my son's shoulder blades would come to symbolize for me. Fanny and I were in the earliest days of blissful matrimony and nothing could nudge us from our extreme joy.

"Training!" Fanny laughed as she had been so often doing of late, setting the cake in front of me. "That's nurse-talk for 'screaming.' Charley seems to have his mother's iron will." She crossed to the nurse with outstretched arms and received Charley who instantly stopped crying once in his mother's embrace.

"If we must attempt such consumption let us do ourselves the help of hitching it to a proper toast!" Corny crossed to the hutch and held up the iced Claret.

"A proper thought," Hillard said. "Shall I do the honor of pouring for the king and queen?" He retrieved the bottle from Corny and filled our wine glasses. "Not only an ascending career and a marriage made in heaven, but a year of happy matrimony and a baby to boot!"

We stood and waited for each of us to raise a full glass and for Fanny to hand Charley to the nurse. "No one boots this baby!" she said with a laugh.

"Less than one week old and already I wonder what manner of man he will become," I said aloud, but intended the comment mostly for myself.

"In his father's steps, no question!" Corny said.

"Hear! Hear!" Charles boomed.

"Tell us, Lady Ashburton," Corny said with a wink. "How fares married life with the poet-professor, husband, and pop?"

We all chuckled. I watched Fanny daintily sip her wine. She was radiant in her beige dress and tilted her head and gazed at me. "These days have been nothing less than a golden chain! And our little Charley is the diamond clasp!" She looked to Corny and the others. "I doubt these walls have ever witnessed happier times."

"Or a lovelier presence!" I added.

"Hear! Hear!" Charles boomed again.

After unanimous agreement that the cake was as stale as yesterday's bread we moved to the parlor with enough cushioned seating for all. The breeze from the window was slight but ruffled Fanny's dress enough to make her appear she was floating across the room.

"Father will not approve these curtains!" Tom said, holding one in his fingers. "These are not American." He studied Fanny with a quizzical look.

"Shh, brother! You mustn't boast of them. Father will know soon enough."

"He'll complain that you didn't get them from our mill."

"Henry and I love European fabrics. They work much more harmoniously with the antiquities and furnishings we've gathered so far. We'll buy from Father soon enough."

"Buy?" Tom playfully scoffed. "Father will permit you to do no such thing; you know that."

"You know what I mean." She playfully tapped his cheek and sat beside me.

Nurse Blake stood in the doorway with baby Charley cuddled in her arms. "I'll be putting him down now, Mrs. Longfellow. Do you wish anything more?"

"Yes, dear. Bring him close for a kiss and then you can take him up."

As Fanny kissed and coddled our son, I saw the elder Charles setting his attention on Tom and I hoped it wasn't to be what I had seen him do too many times in recent weeks. I didn't have to wait long to find out. As soon as Nurse Blake and Charley left the room, he started in.

"I didn't notice your father at the school committee meeting," he said matter-of-factly.

Fanny exchanged a quick glance with me. I noticed Hillard and Corny doing the same.

"I know nothing of that," Tom said. "Am I mistaken, Henry, or is this the room where the cankerworms pay tribute? Do they still make the pilgrimage you once told me of?"

I laughed. "They're close enough at hand but have been forbidden entrance since the hour Mrs. Craigie departed."

"Henry's tarred the trunks, but I'm afraid the Elms are doomed."

"It's time to plant anew, I think."

Unfortunately, this diversion had not diverted Charles, but only delayed him. He crossed to the window, feigning interest in the topic. He squinted as he peered out, apparently trying to find one of the little creatures. "We give so much support to the private schools. Imagine what could be accomplished if we introduced some of the reforms I learned of in Europe."

"A noble intention," Tom said.

"Unfortunately," Charles stepped away from the window and moved very close to my reclining brother-in-law. "There's a sort of elitism in our blessed Whig party. In the name of being adverse to upsetting the apple cart, they, intentionally or not, seem insensitive to the hindrance such inaction becomes to those less fortunate or less well positioned, you might say."

Tom stood and offered a friendly smile. "A rational thought, my good friend." He crossed to the cold hearth and examined the wall around it. He seemed to admire the new wallpaper we had installed only weeks before. "But it may be wise to consider associations when moving within the party. I understand Horace Mann to be an effective secretary of the Massachusetts board of education, but by reputation he is more prone to challenge the establishment in ways considered insubordinate." He looked at Fanny. "The wallpaper, too? Father will not think warmly of this." He winked at her and then faced Charles. "Beware of which company you keep is all I can say, Charles."

I saw Corny shake his head over that remark. Hillard sat almost motionless, as if waiting for the inevitable.

"Bad company?" Charles already sounded indignant. "He has only addressed the unsanitary conditions of our public schools and the underpayment of teachers and things clearly in need of support."

"To those ends I cheer you on, but be careful how you get there, that's all. Destinations are only half the equation. How you travel there is the other." Tom spoke with a slight tone of indifference.

"Humph." Thankfully, that's all Charles added. He may have spoken more if the awkward silence had been longer, but Corny saw an opening and seized it.

"Henry!" he said with the enthusiasm of a child. "We must gain entrance to your new study. Show us what you intend to do with that sacred space, so we can imagine what more you might birth in the days ahead!" He crossed all the way through the doorway to stand in the foyer. "Come! Will this not be where the Five of Clubs meet next?"

We all moved toward the room. Fanny touched my arm and kissed my cheek.

"Gentlemen, as much as I adore that place of uncommon creativity, I will depart your company, for there are many things a happy wife desires to do on a beautiful summer day!"

Not one failed to kiss her hand, except for Corny who had already wandered into my study. I kissed Fanny last and fully before following the men into my new writing quarters.

My pen became a cornucopia of songs. *The Belfry of Bruges and Other Poems* rang out from my soul and into the hearts of appreciative readers. It included "The Arsenal at Springfield," the one inspired by Fanny's urging for a peace poem. I included "The Bridge," which was inspired by my many walks over the bridge between Cambridge and Boston. Not long after, my first long-form poem, "Evangeline," experienced massive success, like no other work I had yet written.

This is the forest primeval. The murmuring pines and the hemlocks,
Bearded with moss, in garments green, indistinct in the twilight.

It was about two lovers, Evangeline and Gabriel, separated on their wedding day by foreign invaders. The heroine searched twenty years for her true love, getting so close to him one night without realizing it: they were each aboard a ship moving in the opposite direction of the other. She ultimately found him on his deathbed only to watch him die, and then she died shortly after, to be at last united in death. "Hiawatha" followed, which I infused with a delightful beat and cadence inspired by a Finnish epic I discovered during my European travels. That poem was my attempt to preserve some of the beauties of our vanishing race of native Indians.

In the wake of these and other creations, appreciation and fame rode in with the tide to fill my heart and my home, but so did criticisms and difficulties. Edgar Allen Poe and a new critic, Margaret Fuller, gave me little quarter, but I held my peace, though some of my friends replied in print.

It was other more serious developments that began appearing that promised the terrors to come. We just didn't know how bad it would be. My friend Charles became narrower in his focus as his obsession with the immorality of slavery became greater. His early attempts at educational reform led to a brief phase of penal reforms, but it was the antislavery movement that possessed him to the exclusion of all else. His unfolding style of bombastic oratory did not shy from personal attacks against those he thought the most incorrect of all and his growing circle of reform-minded friends altered his social standing. Even Corny stopped talking to him. So did Nathan Appleton, George Ticknor, and Judge Story. When the Judge died later the following year, Charles began work to split the Whig Party into two sections— the Cotton Whigs, as the more conservative wing of the party came to be called, and the Conscience Whigs, led by Charles and his fellow radicals. Wendell Phillips was among his number, and in many ways admirable, but the rhetoric, especially when uttered by Charles, was inflammatory. Pro- and antislavery groups grew in their antagonizing of each other, but none were the firebrand Charles was.

Fanny and I loved him, and though we agreed with and admired his basic moral compass, we could not adopt his extreme rhetoric or his combative style. Instead, we offered him the quiet solitude of our home and family in hopes we might help and encourage his better ways while privately praying for his stubborn ones. The Five of Clubs had already stopped meeting, but Sumner came to our home on Sundays, being careful to avoid any run-ins with Fanny's father.

"I do not like conflict, Charles. Neither does Fanny." Though it was late in the day it was hot enough that we sat on the porch with chilled tall glasses of lemonade. Charles, on the other hand, seemed hell bent on making it as hot as Dante's inferno with his unceasing demands.

"Longo, you already wrote the *Poems on Slavery*, you can do more!"

"Charles," Fanny said in a tone as soft as the cotton over which Charles was often provoked, "beware strife and division, and keep your arguments relegated to courtrooms and legislative houses, but not domestic ones."

Charles opened his mouth in protest but then closed it.

"Do you ever dream of being safe at a fireside of your own where you can work on that book you have often dreamt of?" I asked.

He considered this for a long moment until a pestering fly provoked a most persistent backlash from his giant hands and rolled up *Boston Quarterly*. Succeeding in that, he slapped his palms on his knees. "The children of the earth are all of one blood."

We sat quietly and watched the sun turn the sky blazing red, while the much-hoped-for cool of the evening never came.

Chapter 24

There is no flock, however watched and tended,
But one dead lamb is there!
There is no fireside, howsoe'er defended,
But has one vacant chair.

And though at times impetuous with emotion
And anguish long suppressed,
The swelling heart heaves moaning like the ocean,
That cannot be at rest.

We will be patient, and assuage the feeling
We may not wholly stay;
By silence sanctifying, not concealing,
The grief that must have way.

Along the way of those ten years, our little girl, Frances, lived only one year before dying in our arms. An inappeasable longing came to Fanny and I that we could hardly bear, but even that was not the great deluge to which I have hinted, or to be more accurate—the great baptism of fire. For in those days, it was not uncommon to lose loved ones young and not so old. I had already lost a wife and an unknown child, but so did I lose a sister and so did another sister of mine lose her husband. So did Fanny lose her mother, Sumner his father and sister, and so did many other friends and foes die. Losses of other kinds occurred.

Greene divorced his lovely Italian wife and our correspondence fell off during these years. I attributed the fault to him and it hurt our friendship. I lost my own father in 1849 and my mother in 1851.

Each of these occasions added lines to my face and exacted tolls from my peace, but they were the expected, unavoidable possibilities we were all resigned to accept. Though inevitable, such experiences were not absent of painful emotion, but they were grasped as part of life. Still, there were variations of meter and nuances of verse that escaped everyone's imagination. Some things were too unbearable to imagine, and our minds and hearts refused to go there in advance. You don't prepare for what you never suspect. Those places come only if life forces them upon you.

No one escapes the banging, clanging, ear-drum breaking clatter and clap of silence that blows into every life and every era, wanted or not, believed in or not. Even in a poem, there are deeper things between the verses than within them. And, in life, not so much the lines we speak but those we wear are where the real story is told. It matters as much what you didn't write as what you didn't believe and as what you didn't expect. Everything is vital because it's all carried by the wind.

And, the wind blows as it wants, diffuses as it must, forms and reforms, appears and disappears, travels from one direction to another or from three thousand places to ten thousand more, but always it is one. And it does not conceal. It separates everything until all and each may be held and understood and no new thing is found that wasn't discovered before though it may have been forgotten for a little while. Dante understood this, and that is why he named his opus a comedy, which it has taken me a lifetime to understand.

Do not abandon the journey of life, even when feeling as one who wanders lost.

It is necessary to feel that way if any good is to come of it.

By 1856, I was forty-nine years old. Fanny was almost forty, and we had five healthy children. Charley was twelve, Ernest eleven, Alice six, Edith three, and Anne one. Many of my works had been published; some in subsequent editions, and thousands upon thousands of copies were selling here and abroad. I resigned from my position at Harvard and moved forward as a full-time poet and author. Had I told you then what was going on I would have told it differently than I must tell it now, for as wrapped up in happiness and domestic bliss as Fanny and I and the children were, and as important as those things truly were to us, and as fulfilling as my fruitful occupations had become, there were other soundings in the river of life that should have been reckoned with because none of us were to be spared. I did not hear the roars of the impending falls or respect enough the foes of all things.

It's an old saying that death comes in threes. The numbers are actually larger because when an Olympian storm approaches the surrounding air pressure drops, the leaves turn, and the hard rain spares no ground.

Despite my loathing of guns, twelve-year-old Charley managed to win my approval, over Fanny's objection, to let him have one—on the condition he fired only caps with it. "What harm can come of it?" I asked stupidly.

The answer was that he and a friend went off one day only to return with Charley's left hand mangled. His thumb was gone and his fingers lacerated. They had walked a mile to return home, Charley's hand bandaged with a tourniquet fashioned with a piece of shirt and a strap from the powder flask. He didn't cry, but I hurt for him and felt ashamed of myself for having allowed the gift.

"The temptation was too great for him." Fanny's voice was full of distress, and though no words of accusation followed, the glare in her eyes said much to me.

I punished myself for detesting guns while allowing my son to play with one. The consequences seemed to underscore the scripture about reaping what you sow or the one about those who live by the sword being destined to die by it. One might call it an omen, or a lesson to be learned. I call it the chill in the air, the force of the wind heralding the coming storm. Feelings—and charges of innocence and guilt—formed like a fog into a mass of blue and gray.

———

Charles Sumner had been in office since December 1, 1851, having been sworn in the same day Henry Clay had stepped down. Recalling his political trajectory to date, he had begun as a faction within the Whigs known as the Young Whigs. They came to be known as the Conscience Whigs and then the Free Soil men. As of late, they fashioned themselves Republicans, and though a minority party in Congress they had made great strides. Their power was growing, and Charles was their champion. His oratory had swelled to notorious proportions and was as much hated by some as venerated by others. Fueled by his antislavery convictions and enraged by various iterations of the Fugitive Slave Act, which required the turning in to authorities of any runaway slaves and seizing the westward expansion issues about whether new states were permitted slavery or not, comprised the volatile mix leading to his speech in May, barely a month after young Charley's accident. His speech lasted two days and happened on the Senate floor with most senators present and the gallery filled with spectators and newsmen. Both enemies and friends paid rapt attention.

"I call this, 'The Crime Against Kansas'," Charles began, "and will expose the opposition as having conspired with one idea and only one idea. The previously passed Missouri Compromise and the swindle known as the Kansas-Nebraska act served that same idea. The idea? Slavery! To make Kansas, whatever the cost, a slave state and to make every new state a slave state."

The senator from Illinois, Stephen Douglas; Senator Toucey of Connecticut; and Toombs of Georgia noisily shuffled papers and spoke to each other in loud whispers. They rudely moved about trying to get Sumner off his rhythm, but he was like a dog on a scent. They soon wearied of their shenanigans and listened quietly.

Charles had been fighting an inward battle his entire adult life about whether to charge after literary pursuits or political ones. He did his best to merge the two by alluding to Dante, Milton, Virgil, and others while he spoke. It was as impressive as a locomotive rushing past with thundering cars, screeching wheels, and flying sparks. The metal of his message was white hot. He spoke about the four apologies and four remedies associated with the slavery-antislavery confrontation, and both sides heard what they wanted to hear, fueling their already adopted perspectives and reinforcing the polarization already at hand. But Charles didn't stop there. He went where I never could have gone, where most of us would never go, but all of us would be forced to follow. It was the most chilling part of the blowing wind. Once felt, you knew the storm had come so close that there was nowhere to hide. You had to choose your shelter and pick the place where you would place your feet.

Though Senator Butler of South Carolina was absent, Charles personally attacked him. "He is the Don Quixote of slavery! He chooses his mistress to be slavery and has spoken his vows to her who is always lovely in his eyes, though ugly to others; polluted in the sight of the world, though chaste to him. And we must not spare Senator Douglas his rightful place as the squire of slavery, its very Sancho Panza, ready to perform whatever humiliating offices are required."

Senator Douglas angrily rose to pace along the rear of the chamber. "That damn fool will get himself killed by another damn fool."

Back and forth, Charles attacked the strongest pro-slavery voices in personal ways. "Senator Butler discharges the loose expectoration of his speech with incoherent phrases. There is no deviation from truth that he does not make, nothing sacred he does not disfigure, and he is unable to open his mouth but out flies a blunder."

He attacked James Mason of Virginia: "Our forefathers must these days avert their faces from that once glorious state because Mason represents a new kind of Virginia, one that breeds human beings as cattle."

Michigan senator Lewis Cass rose as soon as Charles took his seat to a silenced and stunned audience. "You, sir, have uttered the most un-American and unpatriotic speech ever grated on the ears of the members of this high body."

Douglas rose and added, "The dishonorable senator of Massachusetts offers us nothing but the same old hash, badly seasoned with a series of classic allusions, each one distinguished for its lasciviousness and obscenity. Per chance it is his object to provoke us to kick him as we would a dog in the street that he may get sympathy."

Senator Mason chimed in. "I hear depravity and vice from the Massachusetts senator in a most odious form uncoiled in our respectable presence. He attacks the quarter of the country from which I come. Due to my standing in a common government, I must recognize him as a political equal, but all others will, from this day forward, acknowledge him as one to shun and despise."

Charles rose, looking more confident. "The senator from Illinois speaks of the bowie-knife and bludgeon as though they are the proper emblems of senatorial debate. He should know better. No person with the upright form of a man can be—." Charles stopped, but whether for dramatic effect or reconsideration was unclear.

"SAY IT." Douglas insisted.

"I will say it. No person with the upright form of a man can be allowed, without violation of all decency, to waft perpetual stench or be permitted to model a noisome, squat, animal-like behavior and be thought to be a proper model of an American senator. Will the senator from Illinois take notice?"

"I will!" Douglas scoffed. "And therefore will not imitate you, sir."

"Again you fill this chamber with your offensive odor." Charles appeared completely unruffled.

"You are not of sound mind," Senator Mason said without rising.

———

Although the press had a hay day with the momentous speech, they only fueled the national polarization. It blazed like a wildfire, suddenly jumping forward in all directions, leaving nothing untouched.

On May 22 the whirlwind appeared in the form of Congressman Preston Brooks, cousin to Senator Butler of South Carolina, whom Charles had buffeted with insult despite the Southerner being absent the day of the speech. Brooks came upon Charles working at his senate floor desk, which was bolted to the floor. Charles was a large man and fit snugly into the confined space.

"Mr. Sumner?"

Charles ceased writing. "Yes?" The man before him was of sleight build, well dressed, and held a gold-headed walking stick.

"I have read your speech twice carefully and consider it a libel on South Carolina."

Charles surveyed the man and then shifted to prepare to rise, but Brooks suddenly lifted his cane and struck a blow upon my friend's head. He did this several times in rapid succession with blows so heavy the cane broke.

"Every strike goes where I intend it, sir," the little man said.

Charles's head coursed with blood that flowed into his eyes. He was so confused by the concussions that he rose in such a way that he uprooted the desk from the floor. He staggered like a drunken man into the aisle. He twirled and fell into other desks, struggled to rise, and bumped incoherently into chairs as Brooks repeatedly beat upon him with the golden head of the broken cane until Representative Ambrose Murray rushed in and grabbed his arm. Brooks rushed out while others slowly arrived to give my friend aid.

———

"I cannot believe this happened," Charles said days later. He was so wounded he had to go to Europe to recover and did not return to the Senate for over three years, but his empty chair became a rallying point. While Brooks became the hero of the South, Charles's speech and the suffering he endured became the unifying cry of the North and the wounds of the nation congealed into separate bruises like the blood of the senator's own wounds. It was clear we had fallen over the precipice. Nothing resembled what it had been before. One southern state seceded and the threats of others followed, and all at once the nation was ripped asunder.

Sumner's new Republican party won the 1860 presidential election and Abraham Lincoln became president. By then, seven slave states had seceded from the union and hate reigned in most quarters. I became a Republican and voted as one. I felt there existed an injustice needing to be withstood. I had never believed in war and hated everything about it. I had always been stifled and paralyzed by conflict but found that there were now only two places to pick for your footing. Given the choice there was no question that Fanny and I stood on the side of humanity and freedom, the ending of slavery, and the preserving of the union. Wondering if it were possible to resolve this in a different manner was no longer practical. In April of '61, Fort Sumter was fired upon, and four more Southern states seceded. The war had begun.

When it rains, it pours; and when fires burn out of control the air fills with the putrid scent of wafting death. Tragically, even smoke eventually ignites and all things beautiful are turned to ashes.

Chapter 25

I RETURNED FROM THE CELLAR with a bottle of red
Falernian, entered my study, and noticed the tray where my cigar
eked out its last trail of smoke. I snuffed it out to be safe.

"It is so hot and sticky." Fanny ran her fingers through Edith's
curls seated in front of the cold hearth. "Typical July," she said. "Too
muggy, I think, for such curls, beautiful as they are."

"You're not going to cut them, are you?" I found my pen,
scratched my clean-shaven chin with the dull end, and crossed to my
writing desk. I wanted to note the scene in my journal, sweet as it was.
I pulled it off my shelf and set it atop the manuscript pages already
on my desk.

"They are too beautiful!" Fanny looked up from the armchair
beside the dormant fireplace. Her muslin dress fanned out from her
small waist to form a near-half circle in front of the chair, the hem
embroidered with stylized wreaths and foliage. Her enormous sleeves
ballooned from the shoulders as she dangled loose curls from both
sides of Edith's face. Fanny looked at me. "Aren't they?"

"Please, Mama!" Edith's voice was pitched high. "They make my
neck itch."

"Darling, women swoon for such curls." Fanny pulled the curls
back to hide them behind Edith's head. "What do you think, Henry?"

I thought Fanny dream-like in plain muslin, her feminine face
and delicate wrists the only accessories needed, but that's not what
she was asking. "Ah," I said with intentional awe in my voice as I

moved closer. "I do see something lovelier than curls." I touched my daughter's nose with mine. "A face!"

"Papa, can I? Can I have a haircut?" Edith pleaded.

I drew back and knelt on the hearth rug in front of her and mocked a quizzical expression. I lifted the curls on one side of her face with my pen, as if I were a doctor with a medical instrument. "These are valuable commodities to simply do away with so soon."

"But they bother me." Edith's pout betrayed her fear of losing the argument.

I glanced up. "Mercy?"

Fanny's large eyes glowed with willingness.

I looked at Edith. "A patient's cries ought not to be disregarded." I allowed the curls to drop from my pen. I stood and gently patted her head. "I fear an operation is in order." Edith lit up and hugged my leg. For a child almost eight, her grip was powerful. "Darling, we can cut off your curls," I playfully protested, "but not my circulation!"

"We'll do the deed in the library where the light is better." Fanny rose and kissed my cheek and guided a jubilant Edith toward the door behind the chair where the hoop in her skirt nearly toppled a lamp, but I caught it.

"What's a deed?" Annie asked as she arrived with a skip from the hallway into my study.

I caught her just as she leapt. "Whoa! I must appear the pure plaything today." At five-years-old, she was still small enough to be lifted. I kissed her nose and cheek. "Edith's getting her hair cut."

"Can I help?" Annie squirmed out of my grasp and dropped to the floor with both feet running. She chased after her mother and sister. I leaned into the doorway and called across the library. "Fanny, save a keepsake or there may be no evidence the curls ever lived."

"Exactly what I have in mind to do," Fanny said. She directed the girls to the window seat overlooking the garden. "I'll seal a few in an envelope."

"Good idea." I returned to my desk but not before overhearing Annie's excited voice. "What's a keepsake?" Fanny answered something, but by that time I had replaced my journal on the shelf and attended to my latest manuscript. With the two older boys and Alice out visiting, and with Fanny and the two younger girls now amused, I could get in some writing. I stared at my efforts and gnawed the end of my pen. Where to resume? Then I remembered the wine I had brought up. I noticed it on the table by the vanquished cigar. I crossed the room again, closed the door to the library, and sat down, intending to pour myself a glass. I lowered my arms onto the rests and stared into the lifeless hearth. The charred log appeared as black alabaster, petrified in time. The gouges and split crevices could be black mountains and ravines on another scale, a place of desolation and loneliness like somewhere in Dante's inferno. But it could also be the calm that follows a storm. In time it might silently decay into dust to be scattered by the wind. It might return in some other form like green pastures or verdant plains or tall hedges with succulent fruit. I smiled. These were good thoughts. Who knew where they might lead? The chair was comfortable. I felt the pen drop from my fingers, but it remained atop the armrest. No need to move. My eyes felt heavy and I rested my chin on my collar. I thought a snooze a better choice than the wine. As I drifted, I remember hearing a bird chirp outside the house. I recognized the song. It was the cardinal—the tiny bird with its plumage ablaze.

————

"Henry!" Fanny's voice was shrill. "HENRY!" she screamed as if in violent pain.

I opened my eyes. I was slumped deep in the chair, my legs extended and my feet crossed at the ankles. The hearth was as black as night but I smelled fire.

"HENRY!" Fanny's terrified voice sent ice through my every

limb. I jumped up. What was happening? "Fanny!" I yelled and spun around.

Standing in the doorway between my study and the library was an apparition of hell's flames with Fanny suffering in the midst. But it was not an apparition.

"Oh my God, HENRY!" She stood holding two torches but they were not torches. Her balloon sleeves were plumes of fire, held upright but away from her face. Her face was yet untouched by flame but was beaded with large globs of sweat, her mouth contorted in exaggerated anguish like a grotesque theatre mask. Her billowing skirt crackled with fire, the muslin disintegrating into black webs of stringy, tar-like substance, branding her with singeing sounds, its' flames licking her waist.

I lunged to the floor, grabbed the hearth rug, and jumped up, knocking over the lamp I had earlier saved from her hoop. I wrapped her in the rug and, remembering the hoop, groped downwards with my left hand and took hold. My hand boiled with pain as I groped for the hoop and yanked it hard. It snapped easily along with shreds of flaming skirt and I threw it to the floor, but it wouldn't go free from my hand. It clung to me like hot grease. I used my right hand to snuff the flames around her midsection and legs with the rug.

"It's not working!" Fanny ran from me into the library.

I lunged after her. "Fanny! Roll on the floor!" I peeled the hoop fragment from my left hand and it took layers of skin with it. I reached her.

"HENRY!" She collapsed into my chest, her flaming arms glancing my nose and face. I looped my left arm under her legs and my right behind her lower back and cradled her.

White-faced, Annie and Edith gaped in horror, but I took no time to comprehend their fate. I rushed Fanny out of the library, up the hallway, and into the vestibule intending to round the corner into the parlor and eventually the dining room where I knew a pitcher of water would be found, but I slipped on the foyer carpet and we crashed to the floor. I rolled on top of her and pulled up the corners of the rug and rolled her inside it though I failed to cover her completely. I smothered every flame I could find, some of them appearing like tiny cloves here and there and in places I thought I'd already extinguished. I jumped up and rushed through the parlor into the dining room. Where the hell was the pitcher? There! In the corner I lifted it from the basin and rushed back to Fanny lying motionless on the floor. I poured the water over her shoulders and face though no flames appeared. There was smoke and flakes of fabric crusted to her form, resembling the charred black remains in the fireplace. I knelt beside her and lifted her head in my hands. My tears rained on her face, which was not burnt, and her large eyes were narrowly open and her face relaxed. "Fanny?"

"Papa?" I looked up and quivering Edith stood at the foot of the stairs, Annie clinging to her waist in wide-eyed fear. "Momma caught fire."

"Run upstairs!" I shouted. "Get Hannah. Tell her to find a doctor. HURRY!"

Edith looked up the stairs but didn't move. She looked back and burst into tears.

"Please, honey." I softened my voice. "It's going to be all right. But I need you to go to the attic and get Hannah."

Edith pointed up the stairs and I followed her arm with my eyes. Our au pair, Hannah Davie, stood at the top as white as any ghost, as still as a statue. She was half-dressed and her hair was piled high, but her gaze was fixed on Fanny.

"Hannah! I need you to find a doctor."

Her eyes flooded her face, but she didn't otherwise stir.

"HANNAH! MOVE!"

Hannah wiped her face and slowly moved down the stairs as if growing more afraid with each descending step.

"HANNAH! QUICKLY!" I pointed to the hall tree. "Throw that on and go find a doctor. You must hurry."

Hannah grabbed the housecoat from the hall tree and rushed outside, leaving the door wide open. My girls quaked at the foot of the stairs. My face and hand stung as if they had been lopped off, and Fanny whimpered. Her chest was mangled and almost mummified with curled-up tatters of peeling black ashes. It rose and fell with each struggling breath. I caressed her cheek with my right hand. "Don't leave me, Fanny. Don't leave me, my love. I am here."

She mumbled something.

"Don't speak, my love. It will be all right. We will wait here for help." The heat from outside arrived through the open door but a slight breeze momentarily cooled us.

She mumbled again and I leaned closer. "Shh."

She spoke again, and this time I heard. "I'm sorry."

———

The grim expression on the face of the doctor whom Hannah brought back, confirmed what I feared. The burns to Fanny were so extreme there was little chance of recovery—and if she did, the practical aspects seemed impossible.

The three of us carefully lifted her upstairs, and she was now in our bed under a heavy dose of ether. I knelt shaking beside her. I couldn't stop my muscles from flexing and convulsing. I could feel every one of them doing as they pleased. I couldn't stop anything. I controlled nothing. I could not imagine how she could live. I had witnessed her form, now under layers of blankets, to be as gnarled as the root of a fallen tree, as black as the walls of a chimney. Only her face, though ashen, had some kind of serenity and was free of mutilation, but it appeared more absent of life than comforted in peace. Her hair remained, badly tangled, and instead of curls was singed at the edges.

"Tell me this is a dream." I looked at the doctor. He was an older man with white muttonchops and baggy eyes, a frail frame, and height equal to mine. "Please tell me this is a dream."

Hannah arrived. "They're all set," she said to the doctor. The two of them then guided me out of the room and down the hall into Charley and Ernest's room. They helped me sit on the edge of Charley's bed.

"I want to give you some of the same," the doctor said. "It will help you sleep and give me a chance to address your wounds, too."

I had forgotten my wounds, but my nose and neck and cheek began to pulse with a dull pain that grew sharper with every breath, every moment, and every recollection. I reached to touch my nose but the doctor seized my hand by the wrist.

"You mustn't." The doctor gently lowered my hand and then as gently lifted the other one, but this time taking hold of my left forearm. As he lifted it, I saw what I had not seen until then—a badly blistered and intensely red hand. My skin was all wrinkled in places and missing in others.

"Miss Hannah," the doctor said. "Please take hold of his arm here, as I have. Keep it upright, please."

Hannah smiled at me as she took my arm.

"Where are the girls?" I suddenly remembered them. I tried to sit up but the doctor pressed, forcing me back.

"Please stay prostrate, Mister Longfellow."

"I have taken them to the neighbors," Hannah said. She caressed my shoulder.

"It is good you were here," I said.

The doctor placed a hand on each side of my head and gently turned it, first to the left and then to the right. "We must lance the blister and I will apply salve and dressings to these wounds, but you will feel none of it for now." He lowered my head onto the pillow and stepped away.

My nose and cheek felt raw and hot, and every time I thought about it, it hurt more, but there were so many other things to think about. What will become of our children? How will they hold their mother again, and what sort of life can she live? This couldn't have happened. It just couldn't be true.

"Tell me what this smells like," the doctor said as he patted my face with a damp towel. He held it so tight upon my face I thought I might suffocate. It smelled like mint.

———

I awoke in, a darkened room. "Fanny?" I could not wait to see her walk in and then I would know that it had all been a bad dream. But it was frightening to be in that room—this was the boys' room, and if I had been dreaming, why was I in here? I tried to sit up, but when I pressed my hands on the bed to rise I felt a large mit on my left hand, like a round ball of clothing. I lifted it and saw the bandages. I quickly reached for my face with my right hand and felt more bandages around my head, across my cheek and covering most of my nose except for two holes for my nostrils. "FANNY!" I yelled.

"Mister Longfellow!" Hannah sprang up from a chair by the door. "You are awake?" She rose, stumbled with her own fatigue, rubbing her eyes. "Can I get you anything?"

"What day is this? Where's Fanny?" I demanded, trying to swing my feet over the side of the bed. A deep pain shot through my face, across my neck, and ran like a thick cable down my left leg, and I collapsed onto my back. "Where's Fanny? FANNY? Where are the children? Annie! Edith! Alice!" I glared at Hannah. "Where are they? Hannah!"

Hannah trembled. "Please, Mister Longfellow, do not upset yourself. I will help you. I can get something for you. What do you need?"

I saw Fanny full of flames in my mind's eye and raised my

bandaged hand again to make sure it was what I feared. It had not been a dream? This madness was real. "NOOOOOOOO! GOD, NOOOO!" I gripped my thickened head with my good hand and violently kicked the bed with my heels and shouted to all of heaven. "I cannot bear this."

Hannah struggled with something at my bedside, but before I could process what it was she placed another mint-smelling towel upon my face. "God's peace is with you, Mister Longfellow. God's peace, sir."

I sucked hard for breath. I needed to shout louder but the power to yell drained from me. I lay staring at the ceiling. Hannah's face hovered over mine.

"Mister Longfellow?" She held something in her hand. It was a spoon—a tablespoon. She placed a hand behind my head, slightly lifted it, and pushed the spoon into my mouth. She disappeared for a moment and then repeated the action. It tasted like oil.

Fanny died the next day, and the viewing was downstairs on what would have been our eighteenth wedding anniversary. I could not attend, but I heard the murmur of voices and the incessant sobbing from friends and family. But I was too weak and inconsolable to function in any way or to see anyone.

Outside the wind howled and the Civil War continued uncivil, tallying dead boys, maimed men, heartbroken women, and inconsolable children wondering why.

Chapter 26

Nahant, August 18, 1861

Dearest Mary,

How I am alive after what my eyes have seen, I know not. I am resigned. I thank God hourly for the beautiful life your sister and I lived together. I feel that only you and I knew her thoroughly. You can understand what an inexpressible delight she was to me, always and in all things. I never looked at her without a thrill of pleasure. She never came into a room where I was without my heart beating quicker, nor went out without my feeling that something of the light went with her. I loved her so entirely, and I know she was very happy.

Truly, you are right when you say there was no one like her. And now that she is gone, I can only utter a cry from the depth of despair. If I could be with you for a while, I should be greatly comforted; only to you and I can I speak out all that is in my heart about her.

I am afraid I am very selfish in my sorrow; but not an hour passes without my thinking of you, and of how you will bear the double woe, of a father's and sister's death at once. Dear, affectionate old man! The last day of his life, all day long, he sat holding a lily in his hand, a flower from Fanny's funeral.

For the future I have no plans. I cannot yet lift my eyes in that direction. I only look backward, not forward. The only question is, what will be best for the children?

My heart aches and bleeds sorely for our poor children.

Full of affection, ever most truly,
H. W. L.

I did my best with the children over the next two years. I did little else. Ernest was prone to whining but tried to be brave, and the girls seemed able to carry on with sunny dispositions. They were my greatest joy at a time when our fractured nation continued warring and hundreds of thousands had died. Charles Sumner had returned as a Washington-based senator in a slightly tempered form. Corny had died unexpectedly, and I had grown much older in appearance. My face was covered with a thick white beard that mixed with the hair that flowed down from my head. Our eldest son, Charley, restless and angry, had run away to fight in the war.

Exhausted on this particular evening near Christmas, I stood behind my upright desk, staring at a small statue of Goethe. I fondly remembered how fanciful Fanny had thought me to be to surround myself with inspirational furnishings and knick-knacks of assorted kinds. I had since acquired others and situated them all around my study. A crayon portrait of Sumner graced one wall. Another wall donned a portrait of Nat Hawthorne when he was much younger. On a table opposite stood a bust of my old friend, George Greene, who had recently gotten back in touch. On another wall hung a portrait of Corny. I missed them all. On a highly placed bracket stood a statuette of Dante.

I stared at the curled, blank sheet on my desk. This morning had been difficult. It was always difficult going on without Fanny, even now. Raising the children, celebrating the holidays, trembling over my son and his unknown whereabouts at war. Writing something worth writing in the midst of all of these things was unnerving.

And then something pleasant happened. Outside the bells rang and the gonging decibels washed over my soul like a warm blanket. There it was. I knew the feeling—a rush of words from afar. I knew I must make sense of these feelings, make them do my bidding. I peered out across my front yard, beyond the picket fence, and over the field to the distant Charles River. The church bells echoed, and my muse arrived for the first time in a long time. I yanked the drawer of my desk and then grabbed my inkwell and pen. I smoothed the thick paper, impatient with its insistence to curl back. The words burst forth, brought on by the clanging steel bells. The windows rattled, but whether by the wind or the resonance of bells, I was not sure, and I didn't care.

I heard the bells near Christmas Day...

It felt as if steam blasted through me as it might through a hairline fracture in a massive pipefitting. Energy pumped through my chest. My fingers squeezed the pen. I scratched out one word and wrote in another.

I heard the bells on Christmas Day...

True enough.

Their old...familiar...sounds...

I shook my head.

Carols...play. And wild and sweet...the chimes...

I traced my bottom lip with my tongue.

And wild and sweet the...words...repeat...

I refreshed my pen.

Of peace on earth, goodwill to men...

I closed my eyes.

A great snap sounded. I jerked and looked. Out of the corner of my eye I saw a spark jump from the fire to the fire screen. Ink splattered my paper. The logs popped with tiny explosions of timber gases. The wind rattled the windows, and a cold draft touched me through puffed curtains.

The bells had ceased and the muse was gone.

I felt completely rattled and sought rest in one of my chairs by the fire. It was the same chair I had been dozing in when I had first heard Fanny scream for help, and the memories flooded back as they had been doing again and again since that horrible night two years ago. Fortunately, I heard something else.

Above me, in the girls' room, I heard the patter of their feet. Their door opened, more shuffling, and their door closed. I heard them tiptoeing onto the stairway and saw the shadows of their young forms dance upon the wall as they attempted to sneak downstairs. Alice led the way and looked as grave as ever, so serious and mindful of being proper and pleasing. Edith with her golden hair followed next, as cautious and stealth as the others hoped to be. Annie followed last and alone gave them away with her not-so-suppressed laughter. They gathered along the edge of the doorway to my study, hiding though their shadows were in plain sight. I sat up and turned my back to them, helping them to succeed. I knew what they had in mind for they had been doing it for some time now since their mother had gone away. It was their heaven-led spirit of kindness that prompted them every night before bedtime. They rushed from the doorway, hoping to take me by surprise.

"Papa!" Annie shouted as she leapt into my lap.

"Boo!" Alice seized my shoulders from behind the chair.

"Look at me!" Edith twirled like a ballerina at my feet.

I raised my hands in mock surprise. "Oh my! Is it the children's hour so soon!"

Hannah arrived and waited by the entry to my study, as happily familiar with the routine as the rest of us. Meanwhile, my daughters climbed about me, shifting endlessly to sit with me in the chair in a tangle of arms and legs. "Say it, Papa! Say it!" Annie shouted with glee.

"Come on, Papa, you know what we want to hear," Alice said in an even tone.

"Tell us about the mouse tower," Edith insisted, pecking me on the cheek.

I recited the poem I wrote for them, and it blessed my heart that they never seemed to tire of it. "They climb into my turret!" I said.

"Where's your turret, Papa? I want to sit there!" Annie insisted.

"You already are!"

"It's his chair," Alice explained.

"Don't interrupt, him. Go on, Papa!" Edith begged.

"If I try to escape they surround me. They seem to be everywhere!"

"You don't try to escape!" Annie rightly says. "You like us here, don't you?"

"Hush, Annie. Go on, Papa!"

"They almost devour me with kisses, their arms about me entwine. Till I think of the Bishop of Bingen in his mouse tower on the Rhine!"

"What's the Rhine?" Annie asked.

"A river in Germany," I happily replied.

"Like the Charles River?" Edith asked.

"I thought you weren't going to interrupt him," Alice protested.

I pulled Alice closer and kissed her head. "Do you think, o' blue-eyed banditti, because you have scaled the wall, such an old mustache as I am, is not a match for you all?"

Annie tried to get me laughing as she forced her little hands under my vest to tickle me. Edith did the same, and Alice kissed me on the nose. I kissed and tickled each of them successively. "I have you fast in my fortress and will not let you depart. I put you down in the dungeon in the round tower of my heart!"

The tickling turned serious and everyone was tickling everyone until I saw that it had almost gone too far. At least one was about to turn from laughing to crying. "Now, now, hold on!" The girls settled and looked up, their faces flush, their hair messed and their eyes sparkling—just like their mother's. "And there I will keep you forever. Yes, forever and a day!"

They hugged my neck, we spoke our prayers, and off to bed they went. I watched them leave my room and ascend the stairs with Hannah.

Ernest arrived next, looking glum. "I miss Charley."

My momentary joy disappeared. "I know."

Ernest lumbered in and sat down in the other chair.

"Do you think he's safe?"

"I don't know." I had sought Charles Sumner's influence in Washington, but there was little that could be done. "Don't work yourself into a fit, Ernest. And don't be as headstrong as your brother, please. It is all too much to bear." I tapped him on the shoulder. "Let's find something interesting to read in the library. It will help us sleep." Ernest nodded and we walked into the adjoining room.

To my surprise, someone banged on the front door, and I heard Hannah trotting down the stairs to answer it. A moment later she was in the library. "Mister Longfellow. A telegram." She handed it to me and waited in silence.

I stared. It could only mean one thing. My hand shook, and I handed it back to her. Ernest stood behind me. "Open it, Hanna," I said.

Hanna was slow but did as requested. She tore the envelope, slid out the folded telegram, and opened it. Her eyes widened and she gasped. "Oh Lord."

"Father?" Ernest stepped beside me. "What is it?"

I could not speak, nor could I bear to look at the telegram. I could only tremble. I mumbled something, not even knowing what I would have said had my tongue worked. I wandered into my study and placed my right hand on my writing desk but could not hold back my sob. I knew what the telegram must contain. It could only be sorrow. I thought to motion Ernest to read it for himself but was distracted by Hanna who sank into one of the fireside chairs and cried into her apron. When I looked at Ernest, I saw he was already holding the telegram. His eyes flooded; his cheeks trailed with tears; and his small, round mouth muttered the beloved name in a mournful tone, "Charley."

Sleep was impossible that evening. In the morning, at daybreak, I dressed and forced myself outside. I needed to move and breathe. I gripped my long white locks and strode with aching joints. It was so early I had little fear of running into anyone. My desperate voice collided with the moaning wind. "Charley!"

I reached the highest point of the bridge over the Charles River, and my tears flowed like a current. I crossed from Cambridge to Boston and headed toward the Common. I traversed the snow-pocked trail along the icy edge. The flurries, the motion of the river, not one gliding square sail, none of it escaped me, but all of it was a confluence of deep feelings and flooding words. The words were rudderless, I knew. They shed their textual moorings and severed their anchors to my published volumes and taunted me. I began to wonder whether I had ever said what I intended to say or if I was a fake and a liar more interested in comfort and security than conviction. What did any of it matter? Everyone was dead or soon would be. The nation warred, my soul was in tatters, and my wife and son were dead. What use was I to anyone? Nothing I had ever written could shield anyone from death and heartbreak.

Disgrace has many tongues. My fears are windows.

Those were my words. Tattered ones. Words I had captured in ink and herded between velum covers. They raged now, no longer slaves to the galley. Works of my hands were now traitors. They poured from the tunnels of my heart and streamed like rivers through my head to bubble and foam. My ears became pools of mocking songs.

I quickened my pace, ahead of the rising sun, ahead of the dairy deliveries but fearful to be in no way ahead of my time. I searched the river as I ran, wanting to conjure her feminine form to rise from the waters. Fanny!

Like a lily on a river, she floats upon my thoughts.

Reckless questions reverberated in my brain like a bell in a tower. Was I losing my mind? Fanny had loved me and I had loved her and we had loved Charley, but that love was in ashes.

You chase some form of loveliness—not knowing friend from foe.

I stopped. I had written those words. But I had not intended them to describe my future or my present. The terrible pounding ceased. At first, I heard only my struggling breathing, but then I listened to the streaming of the Charles. I knelt and finally spread face-first onto the cold, hard ground, wanting to sleep. I felt the gravel in my whiskers and in the wrinkles of my eyes. The haunting voices of manuscripts returned.

My brightest hopes make fears as light does shadow.

I dragged myself to peer into the cold waters. Even my reflection replied with corrupted lyrics. *Not so stately is the man of many winters, an oak covered with snowflakes. The face of a clock with hands removed. Behold our maker, Longfellow!*

I knelt in the snow. There was no peace to be had. I curled and sobbed along the edge of the Charles River. I wanted to stop time; I wanted Fanny and Charley back.

After a long time, I hoisted myself to my feet. I lifted my hard French hat, glossy and brushed up at the sides; tilted it backwards; and tucked it over my gray hair. I reached inside the collar of my overcoat and pulled my scarf smooth. Words clamored along the edges of my brain, threatening to breach the levees. I brushed off the earth and rock and snow, adjusted my coat, and smoothed my gloves. I picked up my cane and faced the distant Common. What was the use to go there? She lived there no more. So much was gone. I started home but words burst upon me.

I have no friends. My thoughts are my sole companions.

I hadn't published those yet. Those were bedside words. Words without a home.

Her cold, white hand. Her dead, dumb lips.

More unpublished words forced themselves in. They ruled my brain as Greek Gods, doing as they pleased, redefining, as they desired. They spoke as they saw fit to speak. In context or out, it did not matter. They rang in my head like cracking church bells. Not every hour or half-hour, but every moment. Never ceasing.

I am aware how many days have been idly spent.

The words were mine; I birthed them, but like unruly children they spoke when not summoned. I gazed downward, studied the river's current, hoping to silence my ears by feasting my eyes. The frothy veins of the river danced, as they coursed over rocks, polishing them smooth, and then tumbling into narrow channels to foam before tall, trembling reeds. I watched the flakes of reed escape toward the sea when a different verse sounded in me.

Defeat may be victory in disguise; the lowest ebb is the turn of the tide.

I remembered. My words could be more a medicine than a knife, more winepress than rack. I poked my walking stick in the swift-moving waters and grieved the loss of Charley. He had received a mortal wound the telegram said.

The water spat a gleaming droplet onto my leather boot and rolled beneath my sole. I stepped away from the water's edge and walked on. The hand I had inured in the fire that stole Fanny away hung weakly at my side. The wet flakes chilled my nose while the air resounded with the vibrations of echoing church bells. It was morning and the village was awakening. I enjoyed the percussions until bells of a lesser kind drew near.

A horse-drawn sleigh pulled by a handsome steed with a harness of sparkling bells swished to a halt. It was laden with poinsettias and brown packages, commandeered by a fur-coated driver with a puffy Russian hat and large red mittens. The steel runners that had glided effortlessly over the snow sparkled. "Good day, Longfellow!"

I waved my walking stick. "And a good day to you!" I hoped I appeared nothing similar to how I felt. Perhaps sensing my mood, he tipped his hat and drove on. The muffled hoof beats and the tinkling bells faded away. As I walked I saw windows I had earlier passed, but not noticed. They were decorated with wreaths and pine boughs, all fastened with ribbons. Some glowed with firelight. Other panes framed pines decorated with cutouts and flickering candles. I crossed the field to Brattle Street and strode toward Craigie House—our castle—passed the dormant lilac bushes, and reached the front walk. I opened the picket gate. The house stood silent in snow-covered repose. I proceeded up the straight walk, tapped my boots on the front porch, and reached for the grand white door that suddenly, almost magically, opened.

"Papa!" Annie shouted. "We were frightened!" She pushed the door wider. I opened my arms.

"Annie!" Miss Hanna scolded. "You'll catch your death of cold."

I lifted my daughter with a grunt, clutching her with my better hand and then moving her so my weaker hand was safe. "No matter," I said. "All is well."

Hanna fussed with a shawl over her. "Annie Allegra, you've nothing proper on your feet," she said. "I'm sorry, Mister Longfellow."

"Why were you frightened, dear?" I asked.

She replied with a snug embrace.

Alice stood on the center landing, her face still and gentle, and her blue eyes large and wet. Edith came from the center hall, her long, blonde locks trailing. "Papa!"

"Father," Ernest said. "Where have you been?" He stood near Alice, his brows taut.

"Come, come, children." Miss Hanna pulled her own shawl tighter. "Let your father gain entrance so we may shut the door. It's frightful cold out."

"Yes," I said. "Move away." I held Annie with one arm, handed my walking stick to Ernest, and then touched Edith's shoulder. She lifted my better hand and brushed her face with it. I nodded a warm smile to Alice, watching pensively from steps away.

"You are fine, Father?" Alice asked, her voice as small and chilled as snow.

"Come," I said. "Follow me. Why is it you are all ripe with angst? Am I not in your midst; can you not feel my bones?" I led them into the study, suddenly aware how loathe they were to experience any more loss.

The fire crackled, and I crossed to where there was ample space around the window seat beside my writing desk. I lowered Annie, and she raced to sit down first while Edith clung to one leg, demanding to be raked across the floor. Ernest strode silent and took a knee beside us. I peeled off my coat and hat and handed them to Miss Hanna.

"You look tired," Ernest said.

I pried Edith loose, and noted Alice's delicate hands tightly clasped.

"Some tea?" Miss Hanna asked.

"Yes, and some hot cider for the children."

"May I have tea, Father?" Alice asked.

I nodded and tapped the remaining space on the seat cushion. Alice huddled close.

"Father, where were you?" Ernest asked. "We awoke to find you gone."

"I thought Santa took you." Annie twirled her ringlets.

"Truly." Alice played her somber tone. "Where did you go, so early? We sat for breakfast and you were nowhere to be found."

"I am sorry for the fright. I had no idea I'd not return well before any of you awoke."

"But it's almost Christmas," Edith said. "We can't sleep."

I smiled. "It's not Christmas yet, but it shall not escape us."

"But what did you do?" Ernest asked. "Where were you?"

"We were so worried for you, Father," Alice gripped my forearm.

"For heaven's sake, here I am," I said gently. "I went for a quiet walk this morning, and, as I said, I had hoped to return before one of my blue-eyed banditti stirred." I winked being sure my youngest saw it clear. I then told them all I had seen from the river reeds to the sleigh of gifts driven by a man who looked more than a bit like Santa. They smiled and laughed and hung on my every word.

"I've brought some ginger snaps." Miss Hanna arrived with a tray of steaming mugs, just as I finished. Annie and Edith jumped with excitement while Ernest moved stacks of books to make room for the tray. "Careful, children. The mugs are hot."

I stood and nudged Alice. "Darling, give Miss Hanna some room."

Alice rose on her tiptoes, and I bent down. "Is it anything having to do with Charley?" she whispered.

Ice formed in the back of my throat and ran to the pit of my stomach, but I tightened my jaw and kept it hidden. I stood straight, slowly tugged the fingers of my powder blue glove and folding it neatly, I placed it in Alice's soft hands and closed them over the fabric. I stared into her sparkling blue eyes. My jaw loosened. "Let us speak of cookies and warm drinks right now."

Ernest handed me a steaming mug. "To your health, Father."

I watched Alice accept her mug of tea. "Thank you," I said to Ernest, warming my hands with it.

Ernest leaned close to my ear as the girls chattered away, choosing mugs and cookies. "I haven't said anything to anyone about Charley."

"That is good," I whispered. "I needed a walk this morning. It was near impossible to lie in bed. You can imagine why." I turned to face the others. "Does anyone here sled?"

"Sled?" Cookie crumbs lined Annie's mouth.

"I do!" Edith said. "I love to sled."

"And you?" I turned to Alice. "Are you too grown up to race through snow?"

"Not if my father sleds." Alice almost smiled.

"Well." I picked up a cookie. "If you will allow me to spend a little time in my study this morning, we may all reconnoiter at noon for some adventure. Agreeable?"

"Yes! Yes!" Annie shouted.

"We're going sledding with Papa!" Edith spilled her cider and went silent.

I studied the puddle on the rug. "Now you've done it."

"I'm sorry." Edith's bottom lip trembled.

"You've officially christened the carpet for the holiday season!" I grinned.

Edith smiled, her tongue peeking through her gapped front teeth.

"Okay, children," Miss Hanna said, beginning to coral them. "Let us clear the study and proceed as planned. We've got some gingerbread in the kitchen that needs decorating."

It took several minutes, but the energy slowed and all but Ernest left my study. The voices of the others trailed down the center hall. Ernest knelt and placed another log in the fire. He stoked the flames. "Stay warm, Father."

Chapter 27

WITH CHRISTMAS NOT FAR AWAY, Ernest and I took the Fall River Boat to Washington to recover Charley. "A mortal wound to the face" was the only explanation the telegram provided, and I began to wonder if there were any chance he might still be alive if only for a few hours, so that I could tell him how much I love him. In truth, I had no idea the exact nature of his wound and didn't want to suggest any such hopeless possibilities to Ernest. We had suffered enough.

With no available berths, we remained in the saloon amidships. We ventured to the outside rails and I thought of earlier travels when I had been a wide-eyed youth crossing the great sea, but no such romance remained. Life was now a series of deaths and with too many too close. The familiar queasiness returned to my stomach and I hurried inside before it became too late to avoid vomiting.

Seated around a table, I wanted to encourage Ernest but could not muster the energy. My head bustled with as much traffic as the locks we had passed through, and fatigue hung upon me as thick as the smoke rising from the giant pipe in the center of the ship. It wasn't fair to Ernie, but I was powerless.

"What are you thinking, Father?"

I lifted my eyes to meet his anxious gaze. Instantly, he reminded me of Fanny.

"Father?" Ernest sounded alarmed.

I heard him from somewhere far above me as if I were at the bottom of a deep well. His voice seemed to bounce off walls of stone. I wanted to assure him but the depths summoned me into silence. His echoes melted until they sounded like birds—*No!*—cannons.

It was Charley and Ernie lying side by side atop Munjoy's Hill. They appeared as dead as Burroughs and Blythe, when their faces had burst into flames. I tried to snuff out the flames with my hands, with my overcoat, with a rug from under my feet, but I could not. They suddenly cried and screamed but I could not douse the flames.

"Father! FATHER! COME OUT OF IT!" Ernest shouted and shook me.

I opened my eyes. I saw my son and onlookers gathered around the table in the saloon of the Fall River boat. Ernest was flushed and shaking. "Father, please!"

I wanted to speak but only swallowed and discovered myself to be lying on the floor beside the table. "Help me," I said. Ernest and the others lifted me up into a chair.

"Mister Longfellow," a finely dressed man said, "Are you well, sir? Should we make land for you, sir? Tell us how we can help."

"Yes," said another man in a dark suit as he gazed intently. "Whatever we can do for you, sir."

I was ashamed. "Ernest?"

"I am here, Father." My son smiled. He didn't look like Burroughs. He looked like his mother and I gripped him.

"Ernest!"

"Move away, everyone," the first man said. "Give the poet room. Give him space, I say." He placed a hand on my shoulder. "May I assist you outside? The fresh air might do you well, or may I escort you to your stateroom?"

"We have no room, sir. The berths are all taken," Ernest said.

"I see." He cast a sympathetic glance at me. "If you like, Mr. Longfellow, you may rest in my room until you recover."

I shook my head. "No, sir, but I thank you for your kindness."

"You had some kind of episode," the man said. "You fainted. Your boy here explained the purpose of your travels. I offer my sincere condolences, Mister Longfellow. Truly."

My legs weakened. I nodded but the motion aggravated more dizziness. "Ernest, please help me outside."

"I can assist you. I am—" the man offered.

"No, please," I waved him off. "You have already been too kind. A young man doesn't need this kind of assistance and an old man doesn't want it."

"Yes, sir. God bless you." The man stood back.

Ernest and I made slow progress to the starboard rail, but I felt no strength return. "Call the man, Ernie, and ask him for his berth. I have no choice."

"It is my honor," the man said, only a few feet away. "Come, I can help. I am a doctor."

It was a journey of many steps, but I was soon on the man's bed inside a modest stateroom. Ernest spoke something but I was too exhausted to focus. I held up my hand to plead for silence, but the voices continued. I could not distinguish who was talking to whom. I wanted to sleep but the room rolled and my stomach twisted. I didn't know what year it was. I couldn't remember if I was married or not and, if I had a wife, was she named Mary or Frances or Fanny? I suspected I was some kind of writer, but did I write poetry or prose? It didn't matter. The best was far behind and something smelled like mint.

———

"Mister Longfellow?"

I woke up but didn't know where I was.

"I'd like to wheel you around deck if I may." It was a doctor. He had a wheelchair alongside my bed. "The captain was kind enough to give us use of this. I would have suggested this sooner if I had known one existed aboard. Would you like to give it a try?"

"I think it an excellent idea, don't you, Father?" Ernest asked.

It was a wicker chair on wooden wheels. "What ship is this?"

"The Fall River boat, Father. Do you remember now? You have been resting. There was a heavy gale all night on the Sound. I'm glad you missed it."

"With a little help from some medicine," the doctor added with a kind smile.

"Ether?" I asked.

"And a little laudanum."

I remembered where I was. I tried to stand. The room tilted, but not from the sea. "Whoa."

"I've got you," the doctor said. "Take your father by the other arm, lad."

Ernest braced me from the opposite side and helped the doctor lower me into the chair. It was hard and very straight-backed, not particularly comfortable.

"Would you like a pillow?" The kindly doctor held one in his hand.

I nodded and leaned forward while he gently nudged it between my lower back and the wicker. "Thank you," I managed.

The chair began to roll and Ernest moved to the doorway and opened it. Then the doctor tipped the chair backwards, and Ernest reached under it to pull it through the narrow passage. I jostled and rocked and felt relieved when I was again level and wheeling along the rail.

"I prefer not to give you any more medication. You've slept well enough through the entire voyage but it is time to go ashore. It will be best for you to try and regain your strength. But if you can't manage the strain—"

"I can manage!" I snapped and then quickly apologized. I didn't mean to sound gruff but I didn't want any more sleep. I wanted to recover my eldest son. We'd call on Sumner, and he would help.

"Mister Longfellow," the doctor said, interrupting my thoughts. "I would otherwise be most honored to accompany you on the rest of your trip but other business will demand my attention once we are ashore. Shall I help you find another medical man to assist you?"

I held up my hand and the chair stopped. I twisted around. "What do I owe you for your kindness to us?"

"Owe? Why nothing, of course. It was simply a matter of helping a friend in need. Besides, I was only returning the comfort your poems have given me and my family over the years."

I smiled and made an effort to stand. My son was quick to help.

"You needn't stand, Mister Longfellow. I'll wheel you ashore down the gangway."

"No," I said, finally rising to my full stature. I was dizzy but my thoughts were clear. "I appreciate your assistance, sir. If you ever make it to Cambridge, I insist you visit us at Craigie House. But now, I must move under my own strength. How much of it is left, though, I do not know."

"I think you are physically quite strong, sir. It is the mental strain that has slowed you. You are recovering and more rest will be needed, but you are correct. It is time to add physical activity, although not too much." He secured the chair against the rail and stood close. "Perhaps we can walk down the gangway together."

"Thank you." I felt relief to be out of the chair and to find that my legs actually worked, more or less. We disembarked. A porter hurried to catch up with our bags, and it wasn't long before Ernest and I were aboard a train to Washington. My mortally wounded son was waiting somewhere, maybe barely alive or likely dead, with a musket ball in his head.

The train ride was quiet and I felt calm, but I could not sleep. I turned to Ernest. "My thoughts are traitors."

"What?" Ernie looked at me with a blank expression, as if he had also been somewhere else. Behind him the countryside quickly flashed by. "What did you say?"

"My thoughts," I tried to understand what I had intended before sputtering. "They are confusing me. I don't know how to arrange them. I don't really know what to think."

My son placed a comforting touch on my wrist. "I know, Father. But you do look much better than you did aboard ship."

I studied my beautiful boy. He looked very much like Fanny and so much of her peaceful temperament was inside of him and in his eyes. He deserved at least one safe harbor in life. "I promise to stay as long as I am able, son."

"We will find Charley, Father. You will see."

"You're a good son, Ernest." I rested my head on his shoulder and thought of Sumner. It had been a long time. We had written letters, of course, but it had been a long time since we were in the same room. I was sorry I was reuniting with him under the circumstances; the matter of Charley's whereabouts wouldn't make the reunion joyous. Like the rushing countryside outside the train window, my world had changed in rapid order, covering great distance with unexpected and tragic stops along the way.

Sumner met us at the station in Washington. From there we ventured to three places where we were told Charley would be found. Three times we came up empty. Wearied and saddened, we walked to Sumner's office, when our presence drew some attention.

"Look! The poet and the politician!"

I was in no mood for well-meaning strangers.

"Hey!" The man shouted again. "Senator! It's Alex!"

Charles stopped in his tracks, nearly causing Ernest and me to collide with him. He caught the approaching stranger by the shoulders, ready to scold, I thought, but instead, he squeezed the man with affection. "Alexander!" Charles looked to me. "Henry! This is Alexander Gardner, a good friend of mine and a fine photographer, by the way."

I nodded, but fixed my gaze in the direction of Sumner's quarters.

"Do my eyes deceive me or have I chanced upon two of New England's most famous? It is an honor, Mr. Longfellow." The photographer extended his hand.

I shook it meekly, cleared my throat, and looked at Charles. "I don't—"

The photographer interrupted me. "You gentlemen must allow me to photograph the two of you. How long are you in town for?"

"I'm sorry, Alex, but we are on urgent business this day. Perhaps another time."

"Nonsense! The politics and poetry of New England in my very presence and you want me to walk on. I cannot!"

"Maybe so," I said softly, "but I must go." I needed to get inside and rest. Sumner said something, but Ernest's hurried shuffling alongside of me prevented any real hearing. I strode straight to Sumner's front door. By the time I turned, Charles had caught up and ascended the small stoop.

"I'm sorry, Henry. He didn't realize the nature of your visit." Charles unlocked the door and held it open.

I guided Ernest inside with a gentle nudge on the back and followed after. "I hope you made apologies for me."

"Of course." Charles closed the door.

The brownstone was comfortable and quiet, free of the bustle of the city and the noise of the train station but as desolate of Charley's whereabouts as everywhere else had been. "Somebody ought to know something," I complained. "Such inefficiency."

"The clerk at the war office seemed to think—" Ernest began.

"The clerk at the war office was an ass," I said. "Charles, do you have any port?"

Charles crossed to a cabinet. "I have better." He opened the small mahogany door and withdrew a bottle. "Schloss-Johannisberger, which you sent me."

I flipped my coat and sat down in the wingback. It wasn't comfortable. I crossed to the couch. "Do you mind?"

"Put your feet up if you like, Henry." Charles peeled the neck of the bottle and twisted the corkscrew inside. "Ernest, can you get me some glasses from the hutch?"

I watched Ernest cross the room and rethought my attitude. "I'm sorry, both of you. It's confounding to be told so many conflicting things. Either Charley is dead or he is alive. Either he is wounded or he is not. Either he is here or he is still on the battlefield. Which is it?" I looked at my feet and then watched Ernest deliver two glasses to Charles. "Ernest? Can you do me the favor?" I held up my boot but only inches.

He rushed over, knelt, and tugged off the boot.

I could feel the relief at once. "Thank you, Son. You may have a small glass of wine, if you wish, especially under these circumstances." I held up the other boot, and Ernest tugged it off.

"No, thank you, Father."

Charles handed me a glass of wine. I lifted it to my nose and smelled it deeply. "Do you have a cellar here?"

Charles sat in the wingback, the chair straining under his large frame. "Yes, but it's not to be compared to the famous cellar of Craigie." He offered a wry smile.

"Would you like anything to drink, Ernest?"

"No, sir. Thank you." He sat on the opposite end of the couch.

I eyed my son and felt proud. He was courteous despite what I knew to be jumbled emotions going on inside of him. I suspected they were similar to my own. I looked at Sumner and wondered how much he could admit about the war and the possibilities for Charley.

"I know a Colonel Devereaux in Alexandria. I can telegraph him for more precise and current information," Charles said.

"Ernest?" I smiled at my son.

"Yes, Father?" His wide eyes and kind smile almost brought me to tears.

I breathed deeply and spoke slowly. "Would you mind stepping outside and hailing a carriage?"

"Where are we going?"

I turned to Charles. "There is a steamboat to Alexandria?"

"Yes, but that's not necessary. I can send word."

I looked at Ernest. "To catch a steamer, Son. Please! Find us a carriage."

"Yes, Father." Ernest tipped his head to Charles, "Sir," and headed outside.

Charles placed both of his meaty hands atop his knees. "Henry?"

I returned his gaze but only after a very slow sip of his wine. "I'm so glad you had the Johannesberger. It soothes me."

Charles frowned back. "Henry. Would you like me to accompany you? This may not turn out well at all."

"Little has." I flexed my toes several times.

"These are the worst of times."

"The best seems far behind. I have lost two wives, a darling daughter, and now Charley. Even Felton is gone, so no somber mirth to cheer us with some diversionary balm—not that it would prove effective now." I stared at my friend whose eyes were heavy and sad. "I am a dead man, Charles. There is such little spark left within me. I live only for my children." It was already time to put my boots back on.

"Battle is wearisome, no matter how just." Charles ran his large hand through his tangled locks. "If it is just at all."

"There were days when everyone was so certain and so willing to fight." I picked up a boot. "I wonder what they say now with the blood of our sons on our hands." I pushed my foot in. "Life is strife, Charles." I plopped the other boot in place and pushed in my other foot. "It seems impossible to believe we ever saw it any differently." I settled my feet into the heels.

"It is difficult for me to consider us like this, Henry. And think of it, Gardner wanted to take our picture as some beacon of hope."

I looked up at my friend.

"If he only knew," Charles continued, "how weary we've become." I thought about what the photographer intended as I watched Charles cross to the window to part the curtains. "The whole country is weary, Henry. It is hard to know what to hope for." Charles rapped on the window and turned around. "Ernest has the carriage."

"You're still one who inspires me, Charles."

Charles momentarily brightened. "As are you, Henry." His resignation immediately returned. "It is not enough, apparently."

"Maybe Gardner is right." I crossed to the door.

"About what?" Charles opened it.

"Poetry and politics. We can only do what we can do. That's all. Maybe it inspires others to do what each can do. Maybe that's the only answer."

Charles placed his heavy hand upon my shoulder. "At least that sounds like the old Henry I remember. If there be anything praiseworthy, you're certainly one to express it."

"When I return from Alexandria, I will sit for that photograph, but only if you sit with me. For now, I must find Colonel Devereaux. If you can, let him know I am coming."

Charles's face twisted. I had seen that expression before. I had again puzzled my friend, but, in truth, my friend had again opened my mind. I descended the stoop and turned around. "No one man can do it all by himself, Charles. We each have a task, I think."

"And what task is that, old friend?" Charles stood in his doorway, slightly hunched over to keep from hitting his head.

"As always, you have a nose for the question of the hour."

Charles's expression suggested he did not understand me but neither was I certain of my thoughts, although understanding felt close at hand.

———

Aboard the steamboat, I gazed at my son and thought about how I had run aground in self-pity and despair for the past two years. My zest for life had failed me. The desolation of the nation and of my life felt connected in a downward spiral. I had been hoping for something outside of myself to manifest but now wondered if it was as simple as the light that opened the blossoms in the spring. One doesn't peel open the petals to see the beauty of the flower; that only kills it. Light needs to shine and something beautiful emerges. Right now I could offer no answers. I had no power, no magical verses to make everything right. I couldn't force flowers into bloom, but I could do what I could do in the presence of my sweet and beautiful son. "Ernest." I spoke softly. "I want to tell you all of the things I loved about your mother."

"What?"

"She loved you and each of your siblings without measure, but I am afraid that in my pain I have somehow kept her priceless wisdom and goodness from you. Forgive me, Son."

"Forgive? You have done nothing wrong."

"Two years have gone by and I have done everything wrong. I have felt no relief. So little has interested me, and my efforts have been poor. I fear I have robbed you."

"Robbed? No, sir, you have not."

"I've been trying to rally, little by little, but I have gained hardly an inch. I had stretches of time where I seemed to gain, but the recoil—especially when alone at night—was terrible. Lately, it has been hard to restrict it to my chambers when you all are fast asleep.

And now, with Charley likely dead, I yielded to a complete and utter breakdown. This is unfair to you."

"You have done well, Father. No more is needed."

"I have not been able to make record of anything. My thoughts seemed better wrapped in silence. What I have felt and suffered I have not been able to record or to repeat. With me, all deep feelings are silent and sacred. To recount them is to magnify them, and they are powerful enough in single file. I thought nothing remained but trivial, everyday nothings, but I see it was not true. It was not true for you and it mustn't be true for me, for we have our days and times to move through and we each need what the other can give and nothing is without value. We must each do our part, and I am so sorry to have robbed you. But I promise you, Son, I promise not to rob you again. I will magnify the things that matter most—the things my eyes have been permitted to see and my pen has been called to write."

"I am happy that you feel strongly about this Father but I am not sure I understand."

"You know how Charles Sumner can state so powerfully the black and white truths of right and wrong and how so forcefully he batters down castle gates?"

"Yes, I think so."

"He is worthy of admiration, and I am happy to encourage him not to fail, but not so I. I am not a battering ram."

"Thankfully, no, Father. You are kind and thoughtful. You are also wise."

"Perhaps. But I am something else."

"What?"

"I am a church bell, Ernest. Isn't that wonderful?"

My son did not reply. Instead, his face froze and then slowly darkened. He was clearly uncertain about the comparison and concerned about my mental state, but I knew there was no need to fear. I hoped my kind smile provided him with some assurance. I was as sane as ever I had been. I would have to be. Charley was likely dead. I squeezed my son's knee. "It is time to stop being afraid."

———

Train car after train car proved empty of soldiers in Alexandria and Colonel Devereaux's information proved repeatedly to be in error. Twice Ernest and I took the steamboat back to Washington only to return to Alexandria to be met with disappointment. Then on a cold December day, we stood in the rain and waited for one last train to arrive but it had no passenger cars, only one baggage car. I turned to Ernest. "Back to Washington, son. It has become a series of false hopes and the constant begging of unanswerable questions. We will—"

"Longfellow!" Colonel Devereaux shouted from the side of the now opened baggage car. "Soldiers!"

I moved so quickly I reached the car before Ernest. I stopped in front of the partially slid open doors and peered closely into Devereaux's eyes for any trace of hope, but the Colonel's stare promised nothing and his shrug did not help. I placed my right hand along the edge of one door and looked in. There were at least a dozen soldiers, maybe more, lying scattered about the car. It smelled of sweat and urine, and a few men groaned. I quickly scanned for anyone whose face was bandaged, ignoring the lone soldier who stood bare-chested except for the gauze wrapped about his shoulders and who steadied himself with the sidewall as he approached the doors. I noticed he was missing a thumb on his left hand. "Charley!" I reached up with both arms, and my lost son stepped into the light and climbed down. "Charley, Charley, Charley," I sobbed, reaching for him.

"Careful, Father. My back. Don't squeeze me!"

I stepped back and studied his face. It was as I remembered, young and strong and without wound or scar. "You were not shot in the face?"

"No, sir. Through my back from one shoulder blade to the other."

"Charley!" Ernest cried with arms open wide.

"Please, no hug. Hug my leg! Hug my leg!"

Ernest dropped to the ground and squeezed one of his brother's legs. Charley looked down and grinned, and I felt stronger than I had in years.

"You are blessed," Colonel Devereaux said.

I nodded and glanced into the car where others remained in pain, and some began to exit. The colonel moved to assist them after he waved others to come and help. Bandaged arms, heads, and waists moved in and out of the light. One man had half a leg. Another was missing both arms, and some were wrapped so completely in blankets and gauze it was hard to tell what remained. I looked at Ernest who wept at his brother's feet. "It is good to see you two," Charley said. "Thank you for being here, Father. I hope you are not too angry."

I knelt beside Ernest and hugged Charley's other leg.

Once back at Sumner's, many surgeons arrived at the senator's request, and Charley was treated to the best the capital had to offer.

Hours later, I sat in my finest dark clothes in the small wooden chair on the right of the table. Charles sat in the larger chair to the left in his gray suit and black topcoat, his left arm resting atop the table in front of two books, one full of laws, the other of songs. I looked straight at my friend, eye level to his chest.

"No, straight ahead," Gardner said, "directly into the camera."

I complied.

The man ducked his head under the drape behind the camera and then peeked out. "Charles, look toward the wall. No too much, more toward the lamp against the wall. Yes. Now hold still, both of you. No smiles, but some expression you can hold for a time. Good."

I sat with my hands on my lap and peace in my soul. Understanding one's times and one's place within them was empowering and soothing. I could not wait to hug my children and sit by my own fireside. I thought of my writing desk and tried not to smile but smile I did.

"No, no, no!" Gardner caught himself and adjusted his tone. "I'm sorry, Mr. Longfellow, but we'll have to do it again."

This time, I managed to remain somber on the outside, but inside happiness was flowing like the rushing of many waters, like the blooming of myriad flowers and the echoing of bells without number. I could hardly wait to get back to Craigie House.

"Yes!" Gardner nearly jumped an inch from the floor. "It is finished!"

Chapter 28

ON THE EVENING OF my return to Craigie; and after much
celebration with tears, laughter, and hugs among our family; and with
my entire brood asleep in their beds upstairs, I settled into my most
comfortable fireside chair in my study with an unread letter in my
hand. A friend I hadn't seen in awhile joined me to sit in the opposite
chair. He had written me the letter, but I had been unable to get to
it during all of the recent activities. We agreed I would read it aloud
tonight so that we both might hear it. He waited patiently while I first
mouthed another prayer of gratitude for the safe return of my son,
and then we spoke of olden days.

My soul was full of a new understanding. I no longer put my
trust in the past or the future, nor did I require or expect eventual
outcomes despite whatever quality of life I had or had not lived. Life
was hard, and it tested each of us in ways we were bound to fail
ever and anon. I simply felt thankful for whatever measure of joy
already experienced, for any happiness I might have managed to give
away, and for the healing that came through grieving, as well as the
certainty of knowing I would always find within the heart of another,
a longing for a touch from mine.

My old friend and I gazed at each other; I think we were studying
our respective faces. My, we had aged! He motioned to the letter in
my hand, and I knew it was time to read it aloud:

My dear Longfellow,

So many years ago, you and I were together at Naples, wandering up and down amid the wonders of that historical city, and, consciously in some things and unconsciously in others, laying up those precious associations that are youth's best preparation for age. We were young then, with life all before us; and, in the midst of the records of a great past, our thoughts would still turn to our own future. Yet, even in looking forward, they caught the coloring of that past, making things bright to our eyes, which, from a purely American point of view, would have worn a different aspect. From then till now the spell of those days has been upon us. One day, I shall never forget it, we returned at sunset from a long afternoon amid the statues and relics of the Museo Borbonico. Evening was coming on with a sweet promise of the stars; and our minds and hearts were so full that we could not think of shutting ourselves up in our rooms, or of mingling with the crowd on the Toledo. We wanted to be alone, and yet to feel that there was life all around us. We went up to the flat roof of the house, where, as we walked, we could look down into the crowded street, and out upon the wonderful bay, and across the bay to Ischia and Capri and Sorrento, and over the housetops and villas and vineyards to Vesuvius. The ominous pillar of smoke hung suspended above the fatal mountain, reminding us of Pliny, its first and noblest victim. A golden vapor crowned the bold promontory of Sorrento, and we thought of Tasso. Capri was calmly sleeping, like a sea-bird upon the waters; and we seemed to hear the voice of Tacitus from across the gulf of eighteen centuries, telling us that the pen is still powerful to absolve or to condemn long after the imperial scepter has fallen from the withered hand. There, too, lay the native island of him whose daring mind conceived the fearful vengeance of the Sicilian Vespers. We did not yet know Niccolini; but his grand verses had already begun their work of regeneration in the Italian heart. Virgil's tomb was not far off. The spot consecrated by Sannazzaro's ashes was near us. And over all, with a thrill like that of solemn music, fell the splendor of the Italian sunset. We talked and mused by turns, till the twilight deepened and the stars came forth to mingle their mysterious influences with the overmastering magic of the scene. It was then that you unfolded to me your plans of life, and showed me from what "deep cisterns" you had already learned to draw. From that day the office of literature took a new place in my thoughts. I felt its forming power as I had never felt it before, and began to look with a calm resignation upon its trials, and with true appreciation upon its rewards. Thenceforth, little as I have done with what I wished to do, literature has been the inspiration, the guide, and the comfort of my life. As the memory of those days comes back to comfort me, I hope they comfort you along with the deep gratitude I send forthwith, for to you whose work ceases to fail in its authenticity, I believe you have remained faithful to your pen and we are the better for it.

> *Ever, my dear Longfellow,*
> *Faithfully and affectionately yours,*
> *George Washington Greene*

I wiped away tears. "No," I said to Greene, "thank you for your kind words." We conversed and he drifted into a melancholy comparison of his life with mine. He grieved over his lack and my abundance of publication. "No, George." I tapped his knee. "Comparisons between men are worthless. If you must compare make your comparison between humankind and the rest of nature. That has value." I looked to my desk and in a moment felt there was nothing I could not write, nothing I could not find words enough to express. I crossed to my writing desk happy to find the sheet remaining where I had left it. I read to George and myself what I had written only days ago.

I heard the bells on Christmas Day
Their old, familiar carols play,
And wild and sweet
The words repeat
Of peace on earth, goodwill to men!

I picked up my pen. "Forgive me, George, I must write."

"Of course, my friend. You are Henry Wadsworth Longfellow. Take all the time you need. " He leaned back and relit his cigar.

My pen moved across the page, forming words with ink as easily as pulling a loose thread from the knitting of my heart.

And thought how, as the day had come,
The belfries of all Christendom
Had rolled along
The unbroken song
Of peace on earth, good-will to men!

I looked out the window, across the field, to the distant Charles River. Words flowed as smoothly as the currents.

Till, ringing, singing on its way,
The world revolved from night to day,
A voice, a chime,
A chant sublime
Of peace on earth, good-will to men!

I looked across my desk to Charley's Union saber mounted above the fireplace. The fire snapped just then, but it did not disrupt my muse as it had been prone to do since Fanny's death. I wrote more.

Then from each black, accursed mouth
The cannon thundered in the South,
And with the sound
The carols drowned
Of peace on earth, goodwill to men!

It was as if an earthquake rent
The heart-stones of a continent,
And made forlorn
The households born
Of peace on earth, goodwill to men!

And in despair I bowed my head;
"There is no peace on earth" I said;
"For hate is strong,
And mocks the song
Of peace on earth, goodwill to men!"

I stopped. I could end it right there. But, clarity had come. It was so simple it could be missed. If I mistakenly believed that somehow the highest things constantly escaped me and that I must maintain an endless quest for more, I could have spent an eternity missing the point. But I felt, heard, and saw clearly. There were no new poems or laws that hadn't already been written or obeyed or broken or sung in cadence or dissonance already—in some form. There was nothing new under the sun, yet there remained infinite, endless ways to experience it fresh, relevant, and anew.

I noticed the signed copy of *Nicholas Nickleby* on my shelf and remembered my friend whom I admired, but whose gifts were not mine. I knew I wasn't Dickens. I wasn't Sumner, Felton, or Poe. I wasn't Hawthorne or Emerson, Dr. Channing or Lincoln. I was Henry. I was not a lion nor a critic, not a statesman nor a clergyman; I was a poet of a simple kind.

The church bells of Cambridge rang outside and their reverberations touched my study. I closed my eyes and listened to them as I had always done. I wondered what others heard in the resonance. A call to duty or to worship? The time of day or a day in time?

Here I was, not so old and scarred as I was deepened and changed. Not changed from whom I was or had always been but changed from what I expected of myself. I knew who I was. I changed from questioning who I am to being who I am. I am a friend to those in need of comfort, to those who long to rejoice, and to those who pray for hope.

I wrote the final stanza of my poem, "Christmas Bells," and was satisfied.

Chapter 29

COME SIT BY MY FIRESIDE as George and I had that night and let us recall those days long ago on the rooftop in Naples watching the smoke of Vesuvius fade away. At the base of that once mighty volcano, buried under the rock, exist two petrified cities, Herculaneum and Pompeii. They lay there now as they had when George and I gazed in their direction. The souls who had dwelt in those cities had known the best of heaven and the worst of hell. They had known the joys and sorrows of mingling together upon the boulevards; gesticulating with their hands while expounding their personal stories and remembrances; breaking bread together and kissing their loved ones in the sunlight, the moonlight, the starlight, and the invisible light until the tragic day when all were expunged. Since then their earth-absorbed remains have laid beneath the rubble like treasures in a City of Gold.

Their time had its poets and philosophers, its statesmen and merchants, and every other type of trade and vocation and passionate pursuit—as do all eras. To none has been kept unreachable the joys and sorrows that each must discover anew.

There is nothing new under the sun or the lava rock, but neither are any of the endless treasures absent or exhausted. Each generation must excavate them anew with whatever tools they are given, else the treasure is forgotten and trampled underfoot. The greatest sadness— the only one true sadness—is the recognition that there are always some who deny it, refuse to embrace it, and say it is not so. The sadness is not theirs, for their anger consumes them and is their meal, but the sadness belongs to us who witness their bitterness and feel the consequences of their hate. We do not hate in return; we only grieve. Yet, we who mourn are comforted, and the sadness does not overtake our simple, selfless generosity. So, dear friend who has journeyed with me thus far:

Tell me not in mournful numbers
Life is but an empty dream,
For the soul is dead that slumbers
And things are not what they seem.

Life is real! Life Is earnest!
And the grave is not its goal;
Dust thou art, to dust returnest,
Was not spoken of the soul.

Not enjoyment, and not sorrow,
Is our destined end or way;
But to act, that each tomorrow
Find us farther than today.

Art is long, and Time is fleeting,
And our hearts, though stout and brave,
Still, like muffled drums, are beating
Funeral marches to the grave.

In the world's broad field of battle,
In the bivouac of life,
Be not like dumb, driven cattle!
Be a hero in the strife!

Trust no Future, however pleasant!
Let the dead Past bury its dead!

Act, act in the living Present!
Heart within, and God overhead!

Lives of great men all remind us
We can make our lives sublime,
And, departing, leave behind us
Footprints on the sands of time;

Footprints, that perhaps another,
Sailing over life's solemn main,
A forlorn and shipwrecked brother,
Seeing, shall take heart again.

Let us, then, be up and doing,
With a heart for any fate;
Still achieving, still pursuing,
Learn to labor and to wait.

We now reach the end of our journey together. You have inclined your ear and have discerned well. My words have been expressed, but there remain yours. Do not hesitate to teach or inspire with your pen or your words of those things you have felt and heard and seen. Ignore those who dismiss them as mere sentiment.

There will be those who listen.

Bonus Features Include:

- Deleted Scene with Author's Note
- Epilogue
- Longfellow Museums and Links
- Photographs and Descriptions
- Bibliography and Related Sources
- The Creative Process

AUTHOR'S NOTE: Originally, this novel was written in the third person point of view and featured a prologue detailing Charley Longfellow's battlefield experience in the Civil War. This chapter was much enjoyed by early readers of the manuscript; however, it did not survive the final edit. It remains a compelling scene so I've shared it with you here for your additional enjoyment.

—Author Jon Nappa

Prologue

"FORM A PICKET," Brigadier General David Gregg shouted from atop his mount. "Not one nasty Reb will get behind us."

Charley Longfellow watched through the light mist of cool rain. Like so many of the officers, General Gregg was several years older, probably around thirty, with a frizzled beard that contrasted sharply with his finely combed locks. His double-breasted Union coat displayed gold buttons arranged in brackets of four, except for below the end of his beard where one was missing. He was soft around the middle, but his face was lean and his eyes unfriendly. Beads of water hung along the edge of his wide-brimmed hat.

Like the other mounted commanders under Gregg's charge, Charley listened closely. "We will operate as a rear guard until we reach Fairfax." Charley felt tall in his saddle. His father the poet should see him now. He was second lieutenant in the First Massachusetts Cavalry recently attached to Gregg's division. It was quite true his father forbade him to join the war, but he wouldn't be able to deny him this achievement. "We'll maneuver at Wolf Run Shoals before moving along the rail from Fairfax station to Warrenton. We'll form our picket from there to Bealton. Off to it!" The commanders broke asunder and rode to their regiments. Charley kicked his heels into his horse's sides and headed for his. Running away to war wasn't his first choice, but his father's resistance had made it impossible to do otherwise.

Charley nearly arrived at Company "G" when his horse slipped in the slick grass. He didn't fall, but he was embarrassed. This is exactly the sort of thing he didn't want his father to see. His horse was a four-year-old sorrel and not much more than green broke. He could have had a fine horse if his father had supported his decision to enlist. His father could have bought him an impressive steed, worthy of battle. Charley yanked hard on the reins. Running away to enlist may have forfeited some benefits that came with his family name, but not his honor. He could do this on his own. He side-pulled the reins and kicked. The horse snorted and jerked. Charley kicked harder, snapped leather against the right flank, and cantered the remaining distance to where his regiment was breaking camp.

"Any news?" Johnny Baker asked. He peered up from his kneeling position on the damp ground, while he tied his bedroll. "Where we off to?" His baby face glistened from the light rain. Another one without a hat.

"Fairfax, while the army moves north." Charley dismounted and tugged his front-billed cap down tight. His horse nuzzled his pocket. Charley grabbed the bridle and yanked the horse's head away.

Johnny fastened his bedroll to the back of his saddle when Charley heard galloping hooves. He saw Springer charge up. His was a decent horse with a smooth gait, but that didn't make Springer any better of a rider. His elbows, feet, shoulders, and head jerked and bobbed like a marionette with tangled strings. Charley was sure he'd fall off any minute.

"Mount up!" Springer pulled hard on his reins and stopped fast. He jolted so far forward his groin crushed against the saddle horn. His upper body bent over, and he grabbed the horse's neck with one arm but didn't fall. He straightened up and quickly slid back. His face was twisted. He stood in his stirrups, gasped, and then settled into his saddle. "Baker, put on your riding boots. This ain't no pow wow." He smacked his lips, kicked his horse, and bounced away toward the next huddle of rain-soaked soldiers.

Charley saw the moccasins on Johnny's feet. He hadn't noticed the lad had again switched his footwear. "Johnny, you've got to keep your boots on. If one of the officers sees that, he'll tan your hide."

"They're too big." Johnny wiped the rain from his eyes.

"No matter. Hurry, we're wasting time."

Johnny Baker pulled out his boots from his saddlebags and tossed them on the ground. He shucked off his moccasins, pulled something out from the bottom of one, and quickly jammed it into one of his boots.

"What are you doing?" Charley asked.

"Nothin'." Johnny stashed the moccasins into his bags and pushed his foot into the boot he had hidden something in.

Charley held out his right hand.

"Forget it," Johnny said. "It's personal."

"I'm ordering you. Let me see what you jammed in your boot."

Johnny's eyes pleaded.

"Hand it over," Charley said.

Johnny's shoulders dropped. He pulled out his foot and retrieved a small piece of paper from inside the boot and gave it up.

Charley unfolded it and saw what he had expected. The number eighteen was scrawled on it. He looked Johnny Baker in the eyes. "How old are you, boy?"

"I told you before," Johnny said, a trace of defiance in his voice. "I'm over eighteen."

"I understand the ruse," Charley said. "I've seen it before. Standing on the numbered paper makes your claim sort of truthful. I get it, but it isn't so." He took a deep breath. It was like he was his father and Johnny was him. He sighed louder than he intended. "I appreciate your desire for some truth in your words but I want to know. How old are you?"

Johnny lowered his head. "Fifteen."

"Longfellow!" Captain Jenkins bellowed.

Charley whirled around and saw his superior officer striding toward them, holding the reins of a magnificent steed behind him. The captain's long-handled mustache perfectly framed the downward corners of his mouth. His red hair matched the fire in his eyes. "What in blue blazes are you doing? Mount up and get in line!" He stopped inches away from Charley and glanced at the paper. "What's that?"

"It's Baker's, sir." Charley folded the paper in half.

"Don't tell me," Captain Jenkins said. "Not another—"

"No, sir," Charley said. "Just a letter from home."

"We're not picnicking here soldiers. We're in war! Now mount up and get in line." The captain climbed his horse and galloped away.

Mud, courtesy of the rapid departure, splattered Charley's face. "Yes, sir." He wiped it off, handed the paper to Johnny Baker, and then mounted his horse.

"Thank you, Charley," Johnny Baker said.

Charley looked down from atop his horse. "That's 'Lieutenant.'"

"Yes, Lieutenant Longfellow." Johnny Baker grinned like the lad he was. "Thanks."

"I'm eighteen," Charley said. "But if I were fifteen, I'd still be here." He rode away and took his place in line.

"Giddy yap!" Springer clumsily rode from over the ridge.

Charley watched Springer position into line and recalled the first time he had seen General Stonewall Jackson. It had been at Chancellorsville. The famous Confederate was also awkward on a horse. It was just a glimpse on a scouting patrol, but it was the famous Rebel. He was frumpy and sucked some kind of fruit, like a lemon, and then disappeared into the brush. Charley never saw him again. He never saw much of anything that day. The artillery brigades put so much smoke in the air that nobody could see anything.

It was his friend, First Lieutenant Alton Phillips, who assured him it was Stonewall Jackson. He said the old coot always rode poorly and sucked on lemons.

Charley's mood soured. Alton had died during the Chancellorsville campaign. Damn Rebels. Alton was from Chicopee and had a girl. She was pretty in the photograph. Charley made sure it was in Alton's hand when they shipped his body home on a train. After he watched the train chug away it was only minutes later that they departed to form a picket near Bealton, exactly like they were planning to do now. Only this time, Charley was healthy and would go all the way. The last time, he came down with typhoid and malaria so he missed Gettysburg. His father couldn't have planned it any better if he had the chance, but Charley had different plans. He wasn't a poet, but he would make a name for himself. He had seen lots of action since returning to the battlefield in August.

"Advance!"

Other shouts echoed through the ranks, and the slow procession began. Horses whinnied, wagon wheels groaned, men hacked and sneezed, and the rain floated like a mist. It took several minutes, but Charley's section finally plodded forward. The ground was turned over pretty good and the mud smacked loud.

As his horse trudged along, Charley remembered others he had served with, like Quartermaster Sergeant Read. He had liked him. They might have become best friends. Read had been standing right next to him in the fight at Culpepper, only weeks ago, when the artillery boomed so loud Charley thought it came from a nearby hill. Turned out it was nearly a mile away, but it sounded much closer.

He remembered wondering where the shell was going to hit when suddenly he was thrown to the ground, his ears rang, and something warm flowed down his face. When his head and the smoke cleared, he saw Read squirming and screaming with one of his legs shorn off, and Charley was covered with the sergeant's blood. He could smell it again, like burnt coffee. Comparing it to coffee helped him manage the memory.

A lot of men had died—a lot of young men. Charley would rather die than lose a leg, but then he thought about Alton Phillip's pretty girlfriend and wondered if she'd rather have Alton alive with one leg or not have him at all. He remembered his father and changed his mind. Maybe it would be better to lose a leg than a life. It'd be too tough for his old man to lose someone else. Charley started to remember his mother but the pain was too great. He shifted in his saddle. These slow marches always led him to drifting thoughts. If he ever saw the sergeant again he would ask him what he'd choose.

"What's the date?"

"Huh?" Charley saw a soldier he didn't know riding beside him. The rain was lighter but had become colder. He thought about pulling out his cloak. He was one of the few who had one.

"The date? Do you know it?" the freckle-faced soldier asked. His horse was white and stepped high through the thickening mud.

"The thirteenth," Charley said. He could feel his clothes clinging to his limbs. "November thirteenth." He tilted his hat and water streamed down.

"Thanks," the soldier said. "I keep losing track."

"Fine horse," Charley said.

"Tennessee Walker. They're fine steppers. What's your name?"

"Charley."

"Charley what?"

Charley looked at the young, red-haired soldier. He didn't feel like having the same conversation he always had whenever someone learned his family name. "Just Charley, but you can call me Lieutenant."

"Ok, Lieutenant," the soldier said. "I'm Preston Jenkins."

"Like Captain Jenkins?"

"That's my brother," Preston said. "He was mighty surprised when our regiment attached to yours."

Charley reached toward his saddlebag, wanting to retrieve his cloak.

"Have you killed any Rebs?" Preston asked.

Charley straightened. The lad's freckles were bunched up on his cheeks, framing a comical smile.

"Have you?" Preston asked again.

A sound like cracking timber pierced the air. A red blotch soaked the center of Preston's shirt and quickly grew large. The red-haired boy soldier looked at it and then at Charley. "Cheesh," he said. His eyes rolled back and he fell out of his saddle into the mud. Loud snaps and pops blasted everywhere. Horses reared up. Men cursed. Bodies fell.

"You there! Swing a line all the way left into that brush!" a captain yelled.

"Muskets front and center!" another shouted.

"Longfellow!" Jenkins raced his horse and halted five feet away. "Take some men and circle back to the right. See what you can kick up over there." He pointed to a windbreak fifty yards off.

Charley stared at his commanding officer and then looked down at the younger Jenkins sprawled dead on the ground. He looked back at the captain who had already galloped farther up the line. There was no time to wonder. Charley craned his horse, waved his arm, and called out, "Baker, Chesney, Anderson, this way!"

The four of them raced across the field, mud flying and gunpowder exploding. Charley's horse slipped, its front legs buckling, sending Charley to land in wet grass. He rolled and broke the brunt of his fall, but upon standing saw the others riding away. He rushed to his horse but the horse was badly lame. He pulled out his musket and swept his gaze across the field. The rain was lessening, but all was glistening with wet and the mud was thick.

Brigadier General Gregg and the entire federal cavalry were in disarray. Major General Warren's infantry was disjointed as everyone had broken for cover, most of them lying down in mud or wet grass and firing blind into thickets. A shell burst yards away. Rock and mud flew high. Charley saw Preston Jenkins's white horse. He ran toward the animal, slinging his rifle over his shoulder and checking to make sure his sidearm pistol was secure. He slowed as he neared the horse, not wanting to spook it. He gingerly took hold of the saddle horn with both hands. He slipped his left foot into the stirrup and carefully swung his right leg over. The horse sidestepped but remained calm as Charley took the reins. He kicked with both heels and the Tennessee Walker charged ahead. The gait was so smooth it hardly seemed like a gallop but Charley gained on the soldiers under his command. He caught them near the windbreak. "Hurry!" He raced past them. "Follow me!"

The white horse leapt the windbreak with amazing ease and turned south to run alongside it. Not bad for a Tennessee Walker. Charley saw the others not ten yards behind. He saw a large oak tree about fifty yards ahead and pointed. He heard yells and explosions along the other side and wondered where it came from. The artillery might be a mile away but the musket fire had to be closer. Musket balls could fly a half-mile before striking, but they had to be much closer if you can hear them and see soldiers drop on the spot.

"REB!" Johnny Baker yelled. He raced to catch up with Charley near the oak. The lad jumped off his horse and flew through the air like a sack of potatoes. He thumped into the brush at the base of the tree.

Charley reared up as the other two soldiers arrived. He stared into the pine brush where Johnny had disappeared and heard yells and grunts and snapping branches, but saw nothing except swaying sticks and pine needles. He jumped down, pulled out his musket, and fixed the bayonet. A Confederate soldier burst from the cover and stared right into Charley's eyes. The rebel looked scared, about ten year's old, and held a bloody knife in his hand. A sudden pop numbed Charley's ear. Instinctively, he grabbed it but quickly returned his eyes to the young rebel with the knife. The boy's face was mangled, and he fell backwards.

Chesney walked forward slowly, the barrel of his breech-loading rifle still smoking. "Damn. He's just a runt. Sorry 'bout the ear but he would've cut you."

Charley raced into the brush holding his right ear with one hand and his musket with the other. "Johnny?" He saw Baker's boots.

"I'm still here," the lad said. He was on his back with a deep knife wound just below his left shoulder. "Just torn some."

Charley knelt and set his rifle down. His right ear pounded but he could hear with his left. He reached into a pouch on his belt and pulled out a rolled up bandage. Chesney and Anderson arrived and kept sharp eyes in all directions. "What kind of shenanigans was that?" Charley asked Johnny Baker. "You want to join the circus?"

Johnny motioned with his head to the Confederate rifle on the ground. "I saw that muzzle loader pointing right at you, through the sticks. Didn't figure there was time to tie up the horse and stretch some."

Charley wrapped the bandage tight. Johnny grimaced. "I never saw it. Thanks, soldier."

"Over there," Chesney said. "Three of them. See?"

"I see 'em," Anderson said. "Let's pick 'em off at the same time so they can't turn and fire."

"Good idea," Chesney said. "Lieutenant? We need you to take aim."

Charley looked up. "What?"

"Three of them, three of us," Chesney said. "Understand?"

Charley looked at his musket lying in the grass.

"Hurry, sir," Anderson said. "They're sniping away at our regiment. Now's our chance."

Charley handed the remaining bandage to Johnny and took up his rifle. He knelt next to Anderson. "Ready," Charley said. He wondered why it didn't feel so easy as he had imagined. They were Rebs. Killers. The enemy.

"I've got the one to the left," Chesney said.

"I've got the middle," Anderson said.

Charley tried to stop thinking and just do what they were trained to do. "Aim," he said.

The three rifles protruded from the brush. Several seconds passed.

"Come on," Chesney urged in a loud whisper.

Charley waited another two seconds.

"Sir?" Anderson asked.

"Fire."

The three rifles popped and jerked. Smoke rose from each barrel.

The three Confederate soldiers instantly dropped.

"Glory!" Chesney said. "Did you see that?"

"We did it!" Anderson said. "My first kill that I can be sure of."

"Wow," Johnny Baker said, crawling near. "Like dominoes."

"My second," Chesney said. "Counting the runt."

"What about you?" Anderson asked. "How many for you, Lieutenant? Is that your first?"

Charley stood and gripped his rifle tight, attempting to stop the shaking in his hands. "Let's remount and report. I'm betting those were scouts. Someone's closer than anticipated." Distant artillery booms echoed and the muddy field on the other side of the windbreak quickly ripped into a series of craters, but Charley's regiment was in new cover and nothing but the rain-soaked earth was torn.

Charley remounted and was sure it would all be easier now that he had done it. He had killed up close and was a Union soldier. Nothing would ever take this story away from him. He thought it would have felt better but it was what it was.

After two more hours of unproductive shelling and a sudden downpour of pelting rain, the skirmishing ceased and the chilly afternoon degraded into a soaking, freezing night. Several officers sat around a trio of lanterns within a large tent listening to Major General George G. Meade. As the general droned on, Charley sat outside the tent with a handful of junior officers, under protection of an awning bulging in the middle from the pooling rain. He had the benefit of his rain cloak though he shivered considerably. He leaned his left ear toward the tent flaps and heard well enough despite the soreness of his right ear and the ceaseless rain.

"From what our scouts have reported, I estimate Lee has no more than fifty thousand men situated on the opposite bank of the Rapidian," General Meade said with his trademark monotone timber. "We outnumber him by more than thirty thousand and will use that to our advantage."

"How do you propose we cross the river without disadvantage?" an officer asked. Charley couldn't distinguish his voice. Suddenly, someone bumped into him, nearly causing him to sprawl into the tent. It was Springer. "Ssh!" Charley regained his balance and carefully, almost surgically, pulled the tent flaps closer together.

"What's going on?" Springer asked in too loud a whisper.

Charley placed his forefinger over his lips and leaned forward.

"There are three fords he's left unguarded," Major General Meade replied. "If we are quick to make use of them we can reach Orange Plank Road well ahead of any action and gain the upper hand."

"We'll need to be prompt to preserve the surprise." Major General Warren's husky voice sounded faint as though the damp weather had afflicted his throat, perhaps in tandem with having barked multiple commands all day long.

"We've always been able to count on your second corps for that," Brigadier General Gregg said, biting off the end of a cigar and licking the wrapping.

Major General Warren smiled slightly. "Appreciate it, but the weather's a factor."

"Indeed," Major General Meade said. "We must perform this action first thing in the morning. Everything rides on rapid compliance from each of you." He pulled out his own cigar, bit off an end and spat it out, ran the length of the cigar under his large nose, and shoved one quarter of it into his mouth. He struck a match from off his belt. "Warren, you'll head past Robertson's tavern needing to get beyond it before any Reb knows you're here." He puffed until the end flared. "And you, Gregg, need to get beyond New Hope Church with the cavalry before wily Jeb Stuart and his horsemen know what struck them." He blew a large puff of smoke.

Charley whispered. "Our company is slated to battle Jeb Stuart's riders tomorrow."

"STUART?" Springer nearly choked.

"Shut up!" Charley replied in his own loud whisper. He peeked through the flaps and noticed several more officers lighting cigars. The tent filled with scent and smoke. Captain Jenkins sat in the rear, his arms wrapped around his drawn-up knees and his head down. Someone nudged him and offered a cigar. Jenkins looked up. His face remained pale and still, his eyes narrow but dry. He took the cigar, placed it in his mouth, and lowered his head. Charley knew for certain the captain was aware of his brother's death. It was a shame. He had seemed like a funny kid. Charley momentarily shook his head as if a shiver had come and gone. Can't get soft. Sentiment ruins a soldier.

Major General Meade stood before Major General George Sykes. "And you, sir, I propose you to come up behind Gregg's cavalry with your fifth corps to hold the high ground west of the church."

"Sounds right." Major General Sykes deeply inhaled his cigar. He jutted out his bottom jaw and exhaled smoke straight up to the roof of the tent.

Charley thought the atmosphere ironic as it filled with as much smoke as a battlefield under an artillery barrage, only this smoke wasn't black and acrid but wispy and more blue and gray with a somewhat appealing scent.

Major General Warren approached Sykes and Meade. "I could use a secondary unit to help us hold the grounds beyond the tavern once we secure it."

"Precisely," Major General Meade said. He pointed to Major General William French. "And that will be you, Frenchy. Bring up the entire third corps past the widow Morris farm and do just as Warren suggests."

"You can count on the Union Third Corps, gentlemen." Major General French coughed, his eyes red and rapidly blinking. He was one of a few without a cigar between his teeth.

Major General Meade laughed at the sight of French. He patted him and nearly knocked the smaller man off balance. "And that, gentlemen, is how we will gain Lee's flank!" Meade held his cigar with only his teeth and shook hands with every officer around him.

Charley leaned back. "Early maneuvers tomorrow, boys." He stood and adjusted his cloak. "I suggest we get what sleep we can. Note the date. November 24, 1863 may be the finest action we have seen." He strode out from under the protection of the awning and into the pelting rain. His boots sloshed while he glanced to his left and saw a string of horses. His new horse was among them, as soaked and still as the surrounding trees. Captain Jenkins had said little else at the time but had approved of Charley keeping it. Only thing was, Charley desperately wished he hadn't been told the horse was named Evangeline. His father's influence was everywhere, even the battlefield.

When morning came, there was no march. Neither did they break camp the next day. The rains didn't stop until November 26th. Major General Meade's Army of the Potomac finally crossed the Rapidian but the roads were muddy and the advance was mightily hindered.

On the morning of November 27, Second Lieutenant Charley Longfellow, and the rest of his company moved to confront the Confederate horsemen on the Plank Road before New Hope Church. "The rain delay may be our Achilles. They are not so surprised as we had hoped," Charley said.

"They are not surprised at all." Springer pointed to the hill behind the church. A regiment was entrenched atop the western slope. It was not Major General George Sykes' Union Fifth Corps as had been planned, but it was Major General Henry Heth's Confederate Division, and they were aiming muskets.

Charley reined Evangeline to a halt and spotted the white-gloved Jeb Stuart in his redlined cape with one arm raised. The commander of the Confederate cavalry cantered his horse behind a row of rebel horsemen, rallying them to hold their position in front of the church. The flowing cape made it certain it was the Rebel commander himself, although the ostrich feather jutting up from his hat and the gold spurs glistening from the heels of his boots were as much a giveaway as any.

"Fire!" Major General Jeb Stuart yanked his arm downward.

The muskets sounded like firecrackers, triggering the First Massachusetts Cavalry to rear back and frantically race for cover. Charley's horse ran smoothly toward the trees along the northern edge of the road. There was a ditch and space enough between two trees to leap into the thin grove of slender pines. Charley kicked with his heels and leaned forward, anticipating the jump. The horse extended its front legs and lifted high over the trench. Charley rose slightly off the saddle when a searing pain pierced his left shoulder. It felt like a rod of fire spearing his upper body, jolting his spine, and bursting through his right shoulder. A massive tingling like a million sizzling sparklers branched throughout his extremities. He dumped over the right side of his steed and landed face down in the ditch while his horse raced on.

Charley could scarcely move, unable to feel anything but the fire inside. He opened his eyes and saw Evangeline standing safely between the trees beyond the ditch, white and calm. This is not what he wanted his father to see. A dull ache pulsed from his back and spread up his neck and into his head. A pressure formed behind his eyes. He strained to look again but his horse now appeared ghostly. It looked like it was dressed in flowing muslin. Then he realized it wasn't his horse but his mother beckoning him. She was as lovely as he remembered, but then her muslin dress burst into flames and she screamed in agony. Charley stretched out his hand. He could still hear and think and feel but blackness closed in from all sides, and then all became nothing.

Epilogue

Henry Wadsworth Longfellow died peaceably in his home on March 24, 1882. He was the first American poet memorialized in Westminster Abbey's Poets' Corner in 1884.

LONGFELLOW MUSEUMS AND LINKS

A monument to Longfellow stands in Washington, D.C. and another in Longfellow Square in Portland, Maine. Craigie House, in Cambridge, Massachusetts, has been maintained by the National Park Service and is open to the public (visit https://www.nps.gov/long/index.htm). Maine's first house museum is Longfellow's boyhood home located on Congress Street in Portland, Maine, and is also open to the public (visit http://www.mainehistory.org/).

There are many other links to the works, life, and memory of Henry Wadsworth Longfellow. An Internet search using the poet's name is a good start for further exploration. One site recommended by the author is http://www.bartleby.com/270/. Longfellow's entire thirty-one-volume *Poems of Places* can be found there.

PHOTOGRAPHS AND DESCRIPTIONS

Above is Henry's home during his entire adult lifetime. It was here where he lived and loved and wrote many of his famous works. It was within these walls where Fanny's tragic accident occurred. Photo courtesy of National Park Service, Longfellow House-Washington's Headquarters National Historic Site, by Garrett Cloer.

This is the poet's study. Note the stand-up writing desk beside the window, the Goethe statuette, and the surroundings that inspired him. Photo courtesy of National Park Service,

Longfellow House-Washington's Headquarters National Historic Site, by David Bohl.

This is where Henry was napping in his chair when, through the door behind him, Fanny burst into the room engulfed in flames. Courtesy of National Park Service, Longfellow House-Washington's Headquarters National Historic Site.

Henry and Frances with sons, Charley and Ernest. Photo courtesy of National Park Service, Longfellow House-Washington's Headquarters National Historic Site.

This is the only known representation of Mary Storer Potter, Henry's first wife. Artist Unknown. Created December 31, 1832. From Collections of Maine Historical Society.

This is the photograph taken by Alexander Gardner in Washington, D.C. that became known as "The Politics and Poetry of New England." Courtesy of the Library of Congress.

BIBLIOGRAPHY AND RELATED SOURCES

In addition to the repository of Henry Wadsworth Longfellow's manuscripts and journal entries archived at the Houghton Library at Harvard, the author pored over many unpublished and previously published sources, most of which are listed here.

Calhoun, Charles. *Longfellow: A Rediscovered Life*. Boston: Beacon, 2004.

Hilen, Andrew, Ed. *The Letters of Henry Wadsworth Longfellow. Volumes I, II, III and IV*. Cambridge, Mass.: The Belknap Press of Harvard University Press, 1972.

Hilen, Andrew, Ed. *The Diary of Clara Crowninshield: A European Tour with Longfellow 1835–1836*. Seattle: University of Washington Press, 1956.

Donald, David Herbert. *Charles Sumner and the Coming of the Civil War*. New York: Fawcett Columbine, 1960.

Gorman, Herbert S. *A Victorian American: Henry Wadsworth Longfellow*. George H. Duran Publisher, 1926.

Irmscher, Christopher. *Longfellow Redux*. Urbana and Chicago: University of Illinois Press, 2006.

Irmscher, Christopher. *Public Poet, Private Man: Henry Wadswoth Longfellow at 200*. Amherst and Boston: University of Massachusetts Press, 2009. Published in cooperation with the Houghton Library, Harvard University.

Kennedy, W. Sloane. *Henry W. Longfellow*. Cambridge: Moses King, 1882.

Longfellow, Henry Wadsworth. *Hyperion*. Wildside Press, Pennsylvania, 2002.

Longfellow, Henry Wadsworth. *Outre-Mer: A Pilgrimage Beyond the Sea*. Pennsylvania: Wildside Press, Pennsylvania, 2008. Reprint of volume I and volume II first published in 1833 and 1834 by Lily, Wait, and Company.

Longfellow, Samuel. Ed. *The Works of Henry Wadsworth Longfellow with Biographical and Critical Notes and His Life with Extracts from his Journals and Correspondence, Volumes XII, XIII and XIV*. Boston: Ticknor & Co., 1886 and 1887.

Wagenknecht, Edward. *Henry Wadsworth Longfellow: His Poetry and Prose*. New York: Ungar, 1986.

Wagenknecht, Edward. Ed. *Mrs. Longfellow: Selected Letters and Journals of Fanny Appleton Longfellow (1817–1861)*. New York, London, and Toronto: Longmans, Green and Co. 1956.

Wagenknecht, Edward. *Longfellow: A Full-Length Portrait*. New York, London, and Toronto: Longmans, Green and Co. 1955.

THE CREATIVE PROCESS
Author's Notes

In any work of historical fiction, it is often wondered by readers so intrigued, which parts are true and which are imagined. By necessity, this work is classified as a novel of fiction since many of the intimate moments of conversation, actions, and events are dramatized in detail. Where there have been holes in the historical record they are herein fleshed out and dramatically represented. Additionally, Longfellow was careful to erase, blacken, or cut out passages of his letters, notes, and journals, considering some too sacred to share. Many accounts were burnt, though a majority have survived and are faithfully preserved in various places both here and abroad in museums, universities, libraries, and private collections. This novel's imagined aspects are fully informed by known and recorded facts. Many of the letters included herein are actual, in partial or full form, with only minor updating, revision, addition, or deletion, if any at all. Also, as many historians have attested, Longfellow's *Outre-Mer* was considered largely autobiographical of his first European journey, and as revealed by Henry's own admission and Fanny's initial chagrin, *Hyperion* was known to include too thinly veiled coverage of Henry and Fanny's first encounters. Many scenes are herein depicted as first presented in those works by Longfellow himself. Finally, in many of the passages dramatizing the voice inside of Longfellow's head are found the poet's actual words, as found in his poetry, his prose, his journals, and his notes. This novel endeavors to be as true to the spirit of Longfellow as such intimate familiarity with his known life and works do inspire, and in the judgment of this author, permit.

You can visit Longfellow's lifelong home, a national historic site in Cambridge, Massachusetts, and his historically preserved boyhood home in Portland, Maine.